'An intelligent psychological drama
with a gasp-making twist.'
– *Good Housekeeping Magazine* Thriller of the Month

'A sinister, deliciously wicked foray into the dark
recesses of our personality. Lynes is a promising
addition to the prolific list of stellar writers of
psychological thrillers.'
– *Nudge Book Magazine*

'A slam dunk of a debut up there with the big hitters.
Move over *Gone Girl* you've got company on
the top shelf.'
– *Read & Rated*

'S. E. Lynes has raised the bar when it comes to
phenomenal story telling.'
– *Between Dreams I Read*

'Breathlessly exciting.'
– *Linda's Book Bag*

'Oozes with atmospheric tones, vivid descriptions and
pure, haunting emotions.'
– *Reviewed The Book*

'Sent chills down my spine ... completely enticing.'
– *Damn Pebbles*

D1322397

VALENTINA

S. E. Lynes

blackbird

First published in 2016 by Blackbird Digital Books

Blackbird Digital Books
2/25 Earls Terrace
London W8 6LP

www.blackbird-books.com

Copyright © S. E. Lynes 2016

The moral right of the author has been asserted.

A CIP catalogue record for this book is available from the British Library
ISBN-978-0-9933070-8-9
[eBook ISBN 978-0-9933070-9-6]

Cover design by Robert Ball
www.robertmball.com

Printed and bound in Great Britain by Clays Ltd., St. Ives PLC

For Jean

***

She always loved fairy stories: Hansel and Gretel, Little Red Riding Hood – tales of misadventure and revenge and cottages hidden in the deep dark wood. At night, when she wanted to lull herself to sleep, she would close her eyes and conjure up one of those imaginary cottages. It was white, in her mind's eye, with a low roof and wisps of blue smoke curling up from a pink brick chimney. It was in a clearing, covered in vines and lit by a million blinking stars. So when she saw this place, she knew it was hers.

And here she is. Can you see her at the clearing edge, in the dark and the silence that are so absolute? Impossible not to be seduced by a silence like that, she's thinking, watching from the shadows, waiting. Here, no one bothers you. Here, all that happens between one day and the next is the slow stretch of black sky over fields. No stars tonight. Tonight, the sky is lagged with cloud, insulation so thick it would guarantee anyone the deepest of sleeps. They're sleeping now, inside, tucked up in their warm bed, while outside her teeth chatter, her toes freeze.

And it is freezing. It is bone-penetrating, lip-chapping, bollock-tightening freezing. Look at the ice, hanging in frosted pendants from the low window ledges, the short white walls hunkering down against the cold. Feel the cold, pushing its wet, frozen fingers down the back of your neck. Enough to make you tremble in your boots – so why? Why is this woman standing out here alone, shivering away at this God-forsaken hour on a Scottish winter's night? You probably think it's all a bit strange, probably think she's not quite herself. And you'd be right.

Forty-eight hours ago, she would have said the same.

Now, the air has changed. From under the lazy arm of the sycamore she smells bitterness. If she looks closely, she can see the glimmer on the roof giving way to patches of matt lead grey. That's the ice melting. Heat pushing through slate. Any time now, the living room curtains will recoil: crisp cotton transformed to gothic lace. At a certain temperature, the flames will break the windows. They will pull at the sky, beg for escape with their long ragged wings only to give up, recede, reach out again.

Fire is a fascinating spectacle. It's hypnotic. She should get away now, really, before she becomes too transfixed to move.

***

PART I

ONE

I remember the day we moved here, back when the two of us thought only happiness lay ahead, how the tyres crunched on the gravel, how the tree branches knocked against the roof of the jeep. The pair of us were leaning so far forward we practically had our noses squished against the windscreen. I remember running into the hall, clambering upstairs and back down again, dashing into the garden and out onto the vast lawn. Honestly, I was so excited about our new home, about our new life straight from a magazine, I even laid a fire for us that first day. We didn't need one – it was late May – but I laid one anyway.

We didn't light the fire that first night. It was the second night, I think, and the funny thing was, instead of going up the chimney, the smoke billowed back the way, right into the lounge. Next thing, the smoke alarm goes off. What a laugh. See us, all aren't-we-brilliant one minute, the next, we're running around like turkeys at Christmas trying to find the damn thing. We found it, of course. It was on the ceiling by the living room door.

"Push the button," I shout up at Mikey. "It'll wake the baby."

Mikey's standing on a chair by this point, jabbing with a kitchen knife at this white plastic saucer thing with its flashing red light and all the while the screaming racket's setting our teeth on edge.

"I am pushing it," he shouts back. "I keep pushing it but it doesn't do anything!"

"Mikey! Let me try!"

He steps down, hands me the knife. "Listen, you're more practical. You try."

But I couldn't reach it – I'm too short. In the end we had to bring the stepladder from the barn and I had to go round taking the batteries out of every single smoke alarm in the house. It was only supposed to be a short-term measure, until I changed them for something less sensitive. But I suppose I never got around to it.

And then, on the Saturday, Mikey had to go. He'd got a job offshore, you see, that's why we moved up to Aberdeenshire. It meant that he'd be away to the rig two weeks out of every four. I knew it was going to happen, don't get me wrong. I'd psyched myself up for it, knowing the first week or two would be the trickiest. And so that morning, I had to wave him off from the front step, Isla's head hiding my tears. I had to watch the taxi disappear down the lane, clouds of exhaust lingering in the air, like things we meant to say but never did.

That afternoon I couldn't settle. I tidied up, sorted through some of the packing boxes, even made soup, for God's sake. When I coaxed Isla to eat her mushed up greens, my voice trembled with a kind of simmering hysteria. That's what comes from trying too hard to pretend everything's OK. Your real feelings do nothing but knock at the surface of you. You know you can't let them out. You know that if you do, you might never get them back in.

And then I was up half the night – pacing, shushing, pleading with Isla to go to sleep. Then, when she finally did sleep, I was scared, way more scared than I'd thought I'd be. The black of night out in the countryside has this way of chasing reason into the darkest corners of the rooms, bringing its shifting shapes and throwing them against the walls. I hadn't figured on how frightening the nights would be without Mikey, out here, so far away from the city, and now I lay awake and alone, primed for every noise. What was that scratch at the door? Was that a figure I could see at the window? Was that creak a foot on the stairs?

At 4am I heard a car outside and opened my eyes to see an amber beam slide across the bedroom ceiling. I shot out of bed and ran to the front window. A little way into the lane, a car had parked. The headlights died for a moment then relit. The car pulled out of the mouth of the lane and crawled past the front of the cottage, away up towards the big house at the end of the track. I waited, straining to see through the trees, but saw nothing. I opened the window a crack. The freezing air shot down the front of my nightie, sending me swearing through chattering teeth as I dashed to get my dressing gown. As I returned, the car passed by the cottage in the opposite direction and headed back up the lane. Slowly, the red tail-lights receded to nothing.

Someone must have taken a wrong turn. And at this hour of the night. Maybe someone had had too much to drink and lost his way home. That was the logical conclusion, the one I used to talk myself down from the crazy ledge as I crawled back under the covers, dressing gown still wrapped tight for comfort, to stop me from shaking.

The next morning at 6am, I staggered down to the kitchen, made tea and sat cradling Isla in the half-light. And from there I saw it: an entire fortnight without him stretching ahead of me. The day was too long. There were too many hours in it. And there were thirteen more days like this until he came back. As I said, I'd known it would be tough, of course I had. I'm not stupid. But in all the excitement, all the novelty, I hadn't reckoned on this: my own intolerance for solitude. Stands to reason. I grew up in a flat with three brothers. I worked in news. I lived for other people.

So that was the problem, you see. Loneliness. If I hadn't got so lonely, I would never have met her. I know that now. I'm fucking well *blessed* with knowledge now. But it'd be easy to start beating myself up, blaming myself for everything, so I hold on to that loneliness and how it felt, otherwise I'd go mad. And as with most outcomes, there's a chain of events, isn't there? This happened and because of it, that happened: simple cause and effect.

I must have left the cottage a little after 7:45am. Ridiculous o'clock, for crying out loud; the dawn chorus were barely getting around to clearing their throats. I was pretty sure I'd seen a supermarket on my side of town, over the River Dee, so I thought I may as well drive there, pick up a few messages while I was at it. And so, two hours out of my bed, there's me, a grey-faced zombie woman pushing her baby girl up and down fluorescent aisles. I must have looked like a poster girl for postnatal depression but I wasn't depressed, at least I don't think I was. I was just plain done in.

Still keyed up from the spooked out night I'd had, I popped into the hardware store next door and bought some locks for the cottage windows and two thick bolts for the front and back doors. After that, I headed for the beach. Fresh air was always my mother's cure-all so I thought it might blow away my heebie-jeebies.

I found my way to the coast. It was blowing a hoolie there, right enough, a real hold onto your eyebrows job. Let me make a wee point about the weather here: it has these mood swings like you wouldn't believe – but, as the saying goes, if you don't like it, wait five minutes. So, with the wind howling round my ears, I put Isla in her sling, put on her wee gloves and hat and, after grabbing a coffee and croissant from a café, made my way down to the wet sands.

The shoreline was deserted, save for a couple of windsurf nuts scooting over the grey spikes of a frigid North Sea. Oh, and the seagulls of course, screeching and scrapping overhead, bunching and swooping. On the groyne post, a fat gull perched, a bloated coastal overlord, eyeing me up, twitching, blinking: *I'm watching you, incomer.* Along the shoreline, about a mile away, were what looked like cooling towers or something, to the right, the harbour wall, and a white lighthouse perspective had shrunk to no bigger than my thumb. Far out, flat against the horizon: tankers, trawlers maybe, out for the day's catch.

I turned a slow circle, took in the parade of cafés, the rickety-looking rollercoaster and beyond, about half a mile away, the impregnable blocks and turrets of the granite city. This city was like any other, I thought: full of people. Except, unlike Glasgow, here I didn't know any of those people and they didn't know me. So far conversation had been no more than transaction: a coffee, a paper, a bag of groceries. *Here's your change. Will that be all? Goodbye now.* It was as if everyone I'd seen or spoken to was behind a screen. I felt that if I reached out, my fingertips would only press against glass.

A sharp snatch at my hand. The rustle and tear of a paper bag. I cried out, covered Isla's head with my arm, staggered back and fell. My coffee dropped to the ground, pooled, and was sucked away by the sand. Immediately above me, like shears sharpening against a blade, came the jealous scream of the gulls. Still trying to figure out what the hell had happened, I looked up and saw my breakfast in the greedy beak of one as it flew away, hanging and limp as dead prey.

"I can never go back to Govan now, Isla," I said, chafing my hands together to clear off the wet, gritty sand. "I've just been mugged by a seagull."

The first few days run together in my memory, to be honest. I know I found the pool pretty quickly, being a bit of a water-baby myself, and took Isla there. I know I tried to make eye contact with the other mothers, all as sleep deprived and bedraggled as me, that I tried to communicate through a roll of the eyes that here we all were, getting through the day. We were colleagues, weren't we, floating and distant in the world's biggest office? Surely we could talk to one another? But as their cubicle doors closed behind them with a bang I realised that, no, we couldn't.

I drove up to Beechgrove Terrace. I wanted to find the BBC, thinking I might look for work there. I found it, made a mental note of where it was and resolved to drop off my CV in a couple of months' time. I found a park nearby and, thinking I might find a friendly face, went in. A woman about my age was pushing her boy on the swing so I carried Isla over on my hip. Bear in mind, won't you, that at this point I'm still smiling away like I'm on Prozac or something. Looking back I must've looked like an axe murderer but I was only trying my best.

"How old is he?" I said, nodding at her wee one.

"Eighteen months." She did not take her eyes from her child.

"This is Isla," I said, swinging her forward a little. "She's four months now."

She glanced at Isla but said nothing so I added, "We've just moved here actually. From Glasgow."

It appeared to be killing her to turn her head in my direction. Maybe she had a stiff neck. She almost smiled before she moved away, before she strapped her son into his buggy and made for home. I felt like shouting after her: *don't flatter yourself, Doll. I only wanted a wee blether, for fuck's sake, not lifelong fucking friendship.*

But that's not exactly the way to meet people either, is it?

I fed Isla on the bench, my face by now set in a rictus grin. I burped her and stood her on my lap, felt her push against my thighs with her tiny feet. I made faces, asked her who was a lovely girl and all the daft things you say to a baby until I realised my hands were growing numb. My nose, too, felt almost damp with a wintery cold and, when I looked up, I saw the sun had gone. Wait – the sky had gone. In its place a thick white mist had descended all around me like dry ice.

So this was the Aberdeen haar, I thought, the famous sea fret that lowered its dank weight onto the city without appointment, without warning. And here I was, right in the middle.

By the time I got Isla to the car, I was shivering, the fog even thicker than before. I set the GPS for home, turned the heater on full blast to take off the chill. Even once I'd put on my sweater, I was still trembling, my hands spread against the fan. Outside, the haar pushed against the car windows, swallowed whole the end of the car bonnet. Headlights on full beam, I hooked myself over the steering wheel and set off.

On the road, I could see no more than the tail-lights of the car in front. On the other side, the other cars bloomed from the fog, headlamps like police searchlights. In the rear view mirror, Isla's baby blue eyes stared out, as if she'd been alarmed by a sudden psychic event which, to be honest, is what it felt like. I crept in second gear back towards the river. At the Brig O'Dee roundabout, I took a right towards Banchory. I drove on, tight-shouldered, vigilant. The haar seemed to dissolve a little. Two cars ahead had formed now as if born from the ghostly mass, now the houses at the side of the road stepped from the dissipating white, clumps of woodland, fences, gateposts.

And then the air cleared. Completely. Just like that.

I sat back from the steering wheel, turned off the headlights and eased my foot down on the accelerator. But when I checked my rear view, I saw the cloud had not, in fact, gone. It had simply not followed me. It had waited at the edge of the city and had shaped itself into what looked to me like a monstrous paw, the thick swollen hand of an ogre, grasping but not moving forward, as if thwarted not by any physical boundary but by fear of what lay ahead.

More than a wee bit creeped out, I pushed on. Before me, the landscape spread and to my relief I recognised where I was. The road narrowed and I knew I had to take a left. No houses now, only the lone horse in the field – the signpost that I was not far from home. I slowed the car and took in the tender dip of the horse's long back, the slide of its neck as it tore at the grass in a chaos of quivering lips. I thought of *Gulliver's Travels*, which I'd read when I was about thirteen, of how the Houyhnhnms had blown my teenage mind. I'd always wished I'd known how to pronounce the damn word, even to myself. Whiminims? Hooeyhunhums? Whatever, what I remember most is that those magical horses had to say *the thing which is not* because, in their world, there was no word for lie.

After tea, I put extra locks on three of the downstairs windows with the battery-powered screwdriver my dad had bought me for my twenty-first birthday. While Isla kicked about under her mobile, I even managed to screw the bolt onto the front door and still have time to stand back and admire my handiwork.

"No one," I said to Isla, "not even the Big Bad Wolf could get through that."

I never did put the bolt on the back door. Which is a blessing, now I think about it.

The hour came for Mikey to return home from work, to kiss my neck and reach into the fridge for a beer. *Hey Shone, what's for dinner?*

"Three jumps at the cupboard door for you, pal," I answered aloud, watched him laugh in my mind's eye.

I switched on the radio, twiddled the tuner until Adele came crackling through like some spooky chanteuse from the afterlife. I sang along at the top of my lungs but when the song finished, I felt even more bereft. I wanted so badly to call my mum or Jeanie but I didn't want to sound sorry for myself. This was the life I'd chosen. This was the dream.

At 7:30pm I was about to try Isla in her cot when the landline rang.

I lunged for it. "Hello?"

"That was quick." It was Mikey. "How's it going?"

"Ach, we're fine." I jiggled Isla about to stop her from whining. "I've got my wee pal, haven't I? How's the rig?"

There was a pause. I listened for the sea.

"So," he said. "Seen anyone today?"

"I spoke to the cashier in the supermarket. She was nice."

He never asked if I was lonely. Probably afraid of what I'd say. Maybe I was afraid. If he'd asked, I might have said, maybe should have said *yes, I am lonely. I'm going off my head here.* But I kept it in when I spoke to him and saved the tears for when I was on my own. Nothing major, just eyes filling here and there, the odd shoe thrown across the room.

There was one time I really went for it though – shaking, snotters, the works. It was that very first trip. I was washing up the breakfast things, staring through the low, square back window out over the lawn to the leylandii at the far end. Hands in the suds, I was giving myself another sink-side pep talk: *It'll get easier, Shone. Early days are always tough. If anyone can make this work, it's you.* But no sooner had I said the words when I burst into tears. Funny, how one minute you've got your colleagues in hysterics with some joke you're telling by the coffee machine and the next you're in a cottage in the middle of nowhere talking rubbish to yourself.

And then I remembered 'dry your eyes'. It's something my mum always used to say. I'm not sure if it's Scottish or what, but it's for when someone's feeling sorry for themselves when they've got nothing really to be sorry about. I had a loving partner, a beautiful baby daughter and a fairy tale cottage – more, much more, than I'd ever dreamed of. Self-pity, that's what this crying at the sink business was all about and I knew it. What was going on here was not death, not divorce, not anything I'd even bother writing about for the paper, it was no more than *nae pals, pal.*

So I walked into the hall where I'd hung the mirror and I looked at my silly, red, swollen face.

"Dry your eyes, Shona," I said. "Get a life."

I had to act. If I was going to find work once the dust settled, I needed childcare. I'd have to get Isla used to someone other than me sooner rather than later and, besides, at this rate I was going to end up in a special ambulance. I needed friends too. And I certainly couldn't make any of those by sitting at home waiting for a neighbour to come and borrow a cup of sugar, could I?

We had no neighbours. And I didn't have any sugar.

***

There's still not enough light to make out the trees at the back of the cottage. But she doesn't need to see them to know they are there: the leylandii and the pines, the beeches and the oaks, bunched like criminals at the limit of the land. There was a time when she didn't know their names – they were simply trees. What she can see from here is the grey front door, the dense leaves and frilled velvet petals of the briar rose, the thorns that prick and draw blood. See how the tendrils reach around the windows. See how they grip on, claim ownership. Maybe the rose knows, as she does, that possession is nine-tenths of the law.

***

TWO

By the time Mikey called from the rig that evening, I was brightness itself.

"Guess what?" I said. "I'm going to see a nursery on Monday. The Blue Moon, it's called."

"Doesn't sound like a nursery." How lovely he sounded. I could have eaten that Scouse accent, that voice. "The Blue Moon, did you say? Sounds like a nightclub. Do they have strippers?"

"I'll let you know," I said, laughing.

"What time do you have to be there?"

"Two o'clock."

"Two o'clock, right. And that's this Monday coming? Sure you'll find it OK?"

"Cheeky sod. Of course I will."

"Shouldn't cost too much, should it?" he asked.

"Not too much. I mean, I don't know. I didn't ask. But it's OK, isn't it?"

I heard him hesitate. Not heard, sensed, and wished he could come home right away so I could chat to him in person. I pressed my fingertips to the mirror. Around my nails, the skin whitened. Mikey couldn't come home. He was in the middle of the North Sea.

"Mikey, listen," I said. "You're not here. You don't know what it's like. If you expect me to carry on like this with no one to talk to day after day ..."

"I wasn't saying that ..."

"I was only thinking a few hours," I rushed in. "Give me a chance to meet people. And once Isla's settled I could maybe think about picking up some freelance stuff, set up some meetings."

"Shona, stop. It's fine. Honestly."

12

I didn't say anything for a moment. All I could think of was that I'd never before had to ask permission to spend money, not since I was a kid. I'd always worked, since I was fourteen – a paper round, Saturday jobs, waitressing, babysitting. So I'd always had my own cash, always spent it how the hell I liked. But now, the work I did was important, yes, but it was not paid. I supposed I'd have to ask or at least discuss things like this in future.

Maybe I'd been oversensitive. Mikey had never mentioned a budget in all the time we'd been together. He was the extravagant one, not least of all because his parents always seemed to have lump sums to give to their precious only child, cheques that took my breath away flung out over restaurant dinners whenever they were back from the villa. Always on my best behaviour on these occasions, I would eat carefully while slowly his mother's mouth slackened, the Mersey swelling her vowels, hissing against her consonants, her tanned eyelids thickening, drooping. She got so very drunk, drunker than any of the neds I knew from back home. So I sat and smiled and ate my strawberry parfait, his mother slurring wetly at my shoulder: *of course Michael's twice the man his father ever was. Opportunist, he calls himself! * Her spit wet in my ear. *Cheating bastard, I call it.*

Special Brew or vintage Malbec, drunk is drunk.

"Shona?" Mikey broke the silence. "Come on, I didn't mean anything by it. Besides, if they do have strippers, I'll drop her off for you myself."

Once we'd said our goodbyes, I stood for a moment staring at the five misty oval rings my fingertips had made on the mirror. Slowly, they vanished, a fading imprint of where I had been.

I got to The Blue Moon at five to two on the Monday. The sunny promise of the morning had given way to cold sky, heavy, graphite clouds. I'd caught the forecast in the car on the way in: rain, they'd said, possible thundery showers.

13

And there on the step, baby clinging koala-like to her hip, was Valentina.

She struck me the way women can strike other women – because she was pretty, I suppose, and dressed in a pink cheesecloth maxi skirt. At her waist, she'd knotted a plain white t-shirt, thrown a green woollen shawl over the top. I remember thinking she was one of those women who get away with throwing on any old thing and, running in luscious waves down her back, she had this magnificent auburn hair. Titian, I think it's called, not the classic redhead you see more commonly up here.

"Hey, I like your haircut," she said – before either of us had even said hello. She seemed to have an accent: Australian, possibly New Zealand. "It's cute, what is it, a pixie cut?"

"Thanks," I said, rubbing my head in embarrassment.

"Suits you. Very gamine. This is Zac by the way." She swung the baby closer to me. I noticed, couldn't help but notice, her wedding band, the glint of diamond in her engagement ring. Incongruous somehow, given her hippy style.

"Hello, Zac," I said, smiling at the baby who said "ahwa" before burying his face in his mother's arm.

She rolled her eyes and stuck out her hand. "Ignore him, he talks bollocks. I'm Valentina by the way. We're here for a trial if anyone ever answers the frickin' door."

I managed to introduce Isla and myself but I was still laughing at her saying bollocks, especially in front of a child.

"Don't laugh," she said, laughing herself now. "I'm afraid of what his first word's gonna be. His seat belt doesn't work and every time I try to fasten the bloody thing I end up dropping the F-bomb right in his face. My ma's coming to stay in a few months for Christ's sakes and I know the moment he sees her he's gonna come out and say it: f-u-c-k." She sighed, a little theatrically, and fixed me with an emerald green stare. "I need to clean up my act."

We laughed. After so long cooped up alone, the release of it felt good.

As no one had yet come to the door, I reached up and pressed the bell. The first *ding dong* repeated itself three times and when it finished we looked at one another and smiled, expecting perhaps to continue our conversation. But the melody, such as it was, repeated itself and, while we stood there waiting for the interminable *ding dongs* to end, unsure of where to look, I examined her red shoes, which were flat and looked hand-stitched. I thought the bells had ended and opened my mouth to speak, but they hit yet another repetition. Our eyes met again and we raised our eyebrows at each other and smirked. At last the chimes stopped, but not before rounding off with two prolonged *dongs*.

Valentina was rolling her eyes.

"For whom the bell tolls," she drawled. "Christ, I thought it would never end."

"Doorbell with delusions of grandeur," I said. "I like your shoes by the way."

"These things?" She stuck out her foot, pointed her toe. "They're really old actually. But thanks."

"Did you buy them here?"

"God, no, you're joking. Got them in ... back home, actually."

"Back home?"

"Australia." A shark smile, two great white rows of teeth, a jagged canine snagged on her bottom lip. Her skin was pale, but creamy pale not pasty like mine, creamy and uniform, apart from a spray of tiny freckles across the bridge of her nose.

"Australia," I said, "whereabouts?"

The nursery door opened and I felt a twinge of disappointment that our chat had been interrupted. A spotty lass of no more than sixteen gave us a dreary hello and led us up the dark stairs. Inside, babies sat around on the floor and the whole place held the whiff of off milk, biscuits and,

I have to say it, deodorised poo. A stick-thin woman of about fifty with a millipede of grey at the roots of her dull brown hair introduced herself as the manager and ticked off Isla's name in the diary. There was a fuss then over Zac – they had no record of him ever being booked to come in.

Valentina leant over the countertop and ran her finger down the diary. "I spoke to a girl last week. She must've forgotten to write it down." She straightened up, stood quite still and said nothing more, simply continued to look in the most incredibly direct way at the manager, as if performing some ancient Eastern mind trick.

"I suppose we can fit him in," the manager said, shrinking, turning her attention back to me and prising Isla from my grasp as you'd remove scissors from a small child. "It's good to leave them early while they barely notice."

I didn't want Isla to barely notice. I couldn't have said how I wanted her to react, to be honest. But as the manager carried her away, my wee girl didn't cry at all and I was troubled by the sight of her in a stranger's arms – so placid, so trusting.

We were shooed out then, Valentina and I, as if the two of us were already friends. The heavy wooden door closed behind us. The sound of children that had lingered in the hallway died.

"It'll get easier, don't worry," Valentina said, her bouncing voice summery and light. "It's hard for you, not her. Zac's always had childcare and I've heard really good things about this place."

"How old's Zac?"

"Four months."

"Same as Isla."

"Cool!" Her eyes really were a peculiar shade of green. Like wet parsley – verdant but dark.

"I just want to go back and get her." Heat rose in my face. I looked away, blinking hard. "I've never left her before and it's … I don't have family here and my partner goes away with his work, you know, and we live out in the country, I mean, I'm not saying ... the cottage is beautiful and everything but it's ... it's remote, you know, and if I'm honest I'm finding it harder than I thought I would and I thought Isla might ... but now I'm not so sure ..."

Valentina laid her hand on my arm. "Listen, do you want to grab a coffee?"

I met her gaze. "I would love that."

Meeting Valentina that day reminded me a lot of the first time I met Mikey. There was the same flirtatious energy spreading like peacock feathers at our backs, the same good humoured testing each other out. Since the night before last, when my life ended, I've been doing a lot of thinking. I've done nothing but think, to be honest, about all sorts of things and meeting Mikey is one of them.

I'd gone to a panto with my pal, Jean, whom I was renting a room off at the time. Jeanie's about ten years older than me. A senior journalist, she'd been my mentor when I'd first joined *The Tribune*. She's funny and kind and has the sharpest nose for a story I've ever known. She's the type of person people cross the room for, just so they can tell her their craic, or a new joke, and have the pleasure of making her laugh. That's how much everyone loves Jeanie.

She had come over to my desk earlier that day and said her big brother, Robbie, was in an amateur production of *Peter Pan* at St. Matthew's Church in Bishopriggs, did I want to go along. At the time I was newly single after a six-month relationship that was never going to be anything had deflated like a tyre with a slow puncture.

"Ach, no thanks Jeanie," I said. "I'm all right."

"Don't be a fanny," she said, picking up my pen and drawing a silly face on my notepad. "We can grab a drink after."

"Who's Robbie playing?"

"Mr. Smee. The fat bastard, you know? Come on, Shona. It might be a load of shite but it's better than moping at home on your own."

Typical Jeanie. She always did look out for me.

"Go on then," I said.

So off we went to see Mr. Smee. But it was Captain Hook I was watching – tall, thick black hair, ridiculous fake beard right enough and the poshest English accent you ever heard. In Scotland a posh English accent's all you need to be the baddie but he had the strong features too, the longish nose and chin, the booming singing voice, the swagger. I could not take my eyes off him. And that's not merely a figure of speech.

"Who's that?" I whispered to Jeanie, leaning against her on the dark pew.

"Mark or Mike ... something like that. Have a look in the programme."

I lit the programme with my phone and read through the cast list. I didn't have to read far.

Captain Hook ...... Michael Quinn.

Jeanie nudged me in the ribs. "Will I ask him to come on for a drink with our Robbie after, aye, I will."

"Not on my account."

"'Course not."

When the panto finished, before I could stop her, Jeanie texted her brother to say she and I were going ahead to The Crow, did he fancy coming along and did he want to bring his pal, Hookie? About ten minutes later Robbie arrived at the pub saying Mikey was on his way, that he'd stopped to get some cash. I wondered how much longer he'd be, what he'd look like up close.

The bar was five deep. It was so hot in there, with that hanging, too-much-information smell of bodies there always is now that you can't smoke inside. While I tried not to watch the door, Jeanie fussed Robbie, told him he was great.

"Ah, get to fuck," he said, waving her away. "Make yourselves useful will you and find somewhere to stand. I'll get these."

We were about to do that when in walks Mikey, all teeth, elbowing through the crowd. He was wearing a black leather motor racing style jacket with what looked like a falcon logo on the chest and I was surprised to see he still had the silly beard on. And there were wisps of black acrylic in his eyebrows too, making fuzzy muppet eyebrows which he wiggled as he made his way over. I laughed. He joined us in the stramash, still grinning. Close up, turned out he had a rim of orange foundation at his hairline where he hadn't washed his stage make-up off properly. Normally that would have put me off. But this wasn't normally.

Robbie by this point was three back from the bar but still managed to introduce us over the heads, pointing, shouting. "Jeanie, Shona, this is Michael Quinn. Mikey, this is my sister, Jeanie and her pal Shona McGilvery from *The Tribune*."

Subtle as a breeze block, Jeanie said, "I'd better help our Robbie with the swallies. What's yours Mikey, pint?"

"Callie Eighty." He gave her the thumbs up. "Cheers."

Off she went, leaving us to it. I didn't know where to look, what to say. But I guess I must've been wanting to make an impression because in the end I closed one eye, pulled on his beard and said in a silly pirate voice, "Can't be bothered to take your beard off, then, Cap'ain? A-hargh."

"Ow," he shouted – and grabbed both my hands.

"I – I –" I slipped my hands from his, mortified. "I ... sorry ... thought it was fake."

"No." He held onto his chin. To contain the pain, I imagined. "No, it's real."

19

"Oh God, I'm so sorry," I said. "I've never met a pirate before. Need to dust up my pirate etiquette ... Jim lad, pieces of eight, shiver me timbers ... what are timbers anyway, did you even wonder that? Oh God, seriously, are you all right?"

"I'll live." He was laughing, thank God. "You're all right."

All right. The hissing T of a Liverpool accent. The River Mersey ran in his veins like the Clyde ran in mine. Shipyards. Docklands haunted by ghosts. I'd always had this notion that Glasgow and Liverpool were linked because of that heritage, in their souls or something. Twinned like they do with French towns. I don't know, I'd always thought of Scousers as being like us Weegies – blowing their wages on a Friday night, looking a million dollars on a pittance, generous, sensitive, sometimes to the point of chippy. Murderous when crossed.

"Which bit of you is real then?" I said. "That your real voice for a start? Here's me thinking you were ever so posh."

"Well now, you shouldn't always believe what you hear." He looked down his nose at me in the cocky way he has. "I am ever so posh, I'll have you know. My parents've got a bay window."

"A *bay* window? Didn't realise you came from aristocracy."

In the dense heat of the pub my cheeks burned. We had to shout to talk, push ourselves into an alcove by the door and it was wrong of me, I know, especially as Robbie hadn't even got back from the bar yet, but I kind of wanted him and Jeanie to clear off. Terrible, but I felt that straight away and you can't help how you feel can you? Valentina was always saying that. She was a great one for that.

So we chatted away and that's when I found out he was over at Heriot-Watt University studying for a Master's in petroleum engineering.

20

"What's an engineer doing in a panto?" I asked. "And if you stay in Edinburgh, how come you're through in Glasgow? Don't they have theatre groups where you stay?" My fifth question, I counted, and told myself to shut up.

"My girlfriend has a place here so I stay over and get the train back in the morning."

Girlfriend, I thought.

Shit, I thought.

Served me right.

"What are you anyway," he was saying, "some sort of journalist?"

"Lucky guess, Sherlock. I'm here with Jeanie aren't I, so ..." For the second time I was floundering, this time on account of the girlfriend grenade. But – good thing about being Scottish in these moments? You can pass off any flirting you might have engaged in by mistake as pure Gallic friendliness. And I guess he could do the same: that famous cheeky Scouse charm.

"So you're a hack then, eh," he said.

"What's that supposed to mean?"

He grinned – water off a duck's back. "What d'you do then, go round digging in people's bins? Doorstep the rich and famous?"

I shook my head, as if he were a sad, sad man, which made him grin all the more. "I'm interested in the truth, if that's what you mean."

"Truth and justice and all that?"

"Aye. Truth and justice. You cannae keep a good journo from the truth."

"And what's your drink?" he asked.

"I'll give you three guesses."

"Let's see. Heavy? Stella? Guinness?"

"Wrong." It was my turn to put on the posh voice. "You'll have to give me your first-born child now. Mine's a white wine spritzer. You see, I'm considerably more sophisticated than you think."

21

There we were, then, being friendly. I found out he played keyboards, had become a Munro bagger since he moved north. I found out he'd met his girlfriend at uni, that she was reading Geology and came from Hampshire. She sounded clever, at home in the place her education had brought her to, since she'd always expected to get there. She sounded like she played a classical instrument, I thought, a cello or a harp or something like that. These things I imagined about her, along with flawless skin, killer body, cordon bleu cooking skills and wished her, only momentarily mind, involved in a fatal music-related accident – strangled by a cello string, maybe, or crushed to death by a massive harp.

THREE

Jeanie called me at my desk the day after the panto, having thoughtfully prepared a profile I never asked her for.

"OK, so he's twenty-six."

"Hmm, toy boy." I turned to look at her – she was only across the office, on the features desk.

She pulled her glasses to the end of her nose, gave me a big wink, her voice still close in my ear. "Shut up, you're only a few years older." She pushed her glasses back up her nose and ran her pen down her notes. "Let's see, he went travelling for a year after his first degree, which was at Sheffield where, get this, he was the lead singer in a band called The Electric Cavemen."

"That's absolutely atrocious." Cradling the phone in my neck, I turned back to my screen, pretended to carry on with my article.

"This is all from Robbie. Let's see, he's mad into plays and cinema, apparently, so that's right up your street."

"What about that girl he lives with?"

"Only at weekends. She was Wendy, do you remember her? The blonde. She didn't come to the pub. Had a 'late supper' apparently. At ten o'clock at night? Who has their tea at that time? All a bit la-di-da if you ask me."

Wendy. I closed my eyes and tried to bring her to mind but no – couldn't picture her at all. I cursed myself. Why hadn't I taken any notice of her? Because I was all eyes on Mikey, that's why. And he never said anything about her being in the panto, the chancer, even though I'd asked about her.

"They're going through a bad patch," Jeanie was saying.

"Are they now?"

"Uh-huh. He's going to end it soon, according to our Robbie."

"That's terrible."

"Isn't it?"

He waited a month. It was January by then. I was at work when out of the blue he rang as if he'd seen me the day before and was calling to say how d'you do.

"So, Shona McGilvery," he said. "How do you fancy coming out and getting really pissed one night?"

"That's what aristocrats do, is it?" I kept my voice low and steady, tried to act like this was normal, him ringing to ask me out. Meanwhile, I'd stood up and was making crazy faces over at Jeanie, one hand pulled up into my sleeve, one eye shut, one leg bent. I was hopping up and down in front of my desk by the time her mouth dropped into the emphatic O of understanding.

"We drink gin, mostly," he was saying. "The quinine in the tonic keeps us warm in the draughty old houses, don't you know."

God, I loved that accent.

"Of course it does," I said, too excited to think of a comeback.

"How does Friday sound?"

We arranged to meet in the Pot Still in town at 7pm. I shimmied around the block a couple of times so as not to be early. On the third lap, quarter past, I saw him standing outside the door, face set in anxious anticipation. I felt voyeuristic, to be honest, like I'd caught an illicit glimpse of a vulnerable core, something I knew he'd keep hidden as soon as our eyes met.

He spotted me and his face relaxed into its default confident grin. "You're late, Miss McGilvery."

Cocky bastard, I thought. You don't fool me.

"And you," I said, "have shaved your beard off."

He looked about five years younger than when I'd last seen him, his face smooth against mine when he bent to kiss me on the cheek.

"Health and safety," he said, rubbing his chin. "Don't want any mad women making a grab for it." He stood up straight, pulled his hand into the sleeve of his jacket and closed one eye. "I've kept the hook, though."

"I'll bet you have."

I met his eye but immediately had to look at the floor. This was new: the two of us, here together on purpose. And there's only so much you can pass off as Gallic friendliness.

The bar was pretty full, the Friday after-work crowd having one or five for the road.

"Have a whisky," he said. "They do great whiskies here."

I said yes, sure, as it was Friday. I knew fine the place did whiskies – it was what the bar was known for. To be honest, I would've preferred a white wine spritzer but I didn't want to wreck his big line.

What did we talk about? Mostly literature that first time, I think, which surprised me. I don't know what I'd thought a journalist and an engineer would find to say to each other, but I couldn't believe he'd read so much. The crowd thinned. With our third drink we got settled at a small round table near the bar.

"Most people discover the world when they go travelling," he said, elbows on the table top. I noticed his eyes were deep brown, that they sloped a wee bit at the edges, which made him look kind. I noticed too that he could be earnest when he wanted to be – after a few drinks anyway. "I discovered books," he went on, shifting in his seat. "Everyone swaps so you read whatever you get. Sometimes I feel like I need to go to the cinema every night, or the theatre, whatever, and then spend the rest of the night reading. Every night, do you know what I mean? There are all these people out there who've read so much and know so much and I feel like I'll be playing catch up for the rest of my life."

"That's exactly how I feel," I said. And, oh God, did I. "At uni there were all these folk who seemed to already know it – Latin, history, you name it – like they'd been born knowing it, you know?"

"I do know. I really do."

We smiled at each other. After a moment, he made a silly face, to save us both. "Want to know something embarrassing?"

"Go on."

"When I got back from travelling, I wrote to Martin Amis and told him I was his number one fan."

"Oh, now, that is embarrassing."

"And that was before I read *Misery*."

"Don't worry," I said, laughing. "I won't tell anyone."

When they called time, he said it had come too soon, that he wasn't ready for the evening to end.

"There'll be other evenings," I said. "If you play your cards right."

He leant forward and kissed me on the cheek, sat back and grinned, as if he'd done something naughty. "Will you come for a walk with me?"

"I will walk to the end of the earth with you," I said.

No I didn't, don't be silly. I just thought it. What I actually said was, "OK."

We were heading down Hope Street, towards the corner with West Regent Lane when a bunch of lads came hurtling towards us along the pavement. All limbs and scuffle, they could have been no more than five or six in number. The noise they were making, the speed they were travelling, this was the kind of drunk trouble you got in town at midnight on a Friday. Curses flew, fists rose and landed. My body registered the deep jolt that comes with impromptu violence. I pushed Mikey to the wall, into the shadows. We stayed still, stayed silent. I hoped they would rumble on by. But they stopped, dispersed a moment, catching their breath. In the middle, a young lad of about seventeen staggered into the road and fell into the gutter.

"Kick him," one of the others shouted. "Come on."

"It's four against one," I whispered to Mikey. "That's no' fair."

"Shona, you're ..." he hissed but I was already striding forward, into the light.

"Oi," I shouted. "Don't you dare. You'll do no such thing."

I was in amongst them. Maybe my woman's voice was a shock to them – the wrong pitch, the wrong time of night, because they paused, still breathing heavily, caught in an ugly game of musical statues. Maybe they were trying to figure out who'd shouted. I'm barely five foot two.

"He's only a lad," I said. "Go on with you, go on. You don't want to do be doing this."

"What's it to you?" It was the one who'd suggested they kick the poor kid to certain brain damage. He was big, looked like he played rugby or did weights.

"What's it to you, yourself, Big Man?" I looked up into his face, one step shy of wagging my finger. All I had was my diminutive height, the fact I could have been someone's older sister. "Come on. He's nae more than a wee scrap. Go home now, on you go." I took a step closer, saw in the flicker of the big fella's eyes that it was over. But still I worried he might hear my heart knocking against my ribs. "I'll make sure he's OK. OK, pal? Trust me, you'll feel better in the morning."

I reached up and put my hand on his shoulder. It was a risk, it was all a risk, but I wasn't thinking, hadn't been thinking for the past few minutes. "Listen, there's two for one on pints in The Corinthian tonight. They're open till two. You want to get over there, pick yourselves up a nice girl instead of hanging out here on the street all night, eh? What d'you think?"

He shrugged me off, then turned to his crew.

"What's she say?" said one.

27

"Says there's two for one down The Corinthian." He then turned back to me. "Is that true?"

"'Course." I put my hand to my chest. "Guide's honour. Ask for Craigie. Tell him Shona sent you." I stuck out my hand. "I'm Shona by the way."

"Davie."

"Davie? My wee brother's called Davie."

We shook hands. I waved to his pals, said hello – all of it bullshit, all of it saving face.

"And that's Mikey by the wall," I said, thumbing over my shoulder to a shadow with a pair of feet. I nearly said he was English but thought better of it and anyway they were off, on to the next scrape.

Once they'd gone, Mikey came over and helped me pull the lad up. He was OK. Drunk, shaken and bruised, but OK.

"Let's get him home," I said.

I hailed a cab and we took him back to his digs. Over on Kyle Street, I think it was. To be honest, I was relieved we made it there without him puking all over us. We watched him shamble across the pavement, watched him scribble around the door with his key before finally sinking it into the lock. Once the door shut behind him, I gave my address to the driver – I was still staying with Jeanie in town then – and threw myself back in my seat.

Mikey, who had apparently lost the power of speech up to that point, sat forward and looked into my eyes.

"What?" I said.

His face came close. His edges blurred. "Was that true about the two for one?"

"What do you think?"

"I think you're amazing."

I closed my eyes for his kiss. Beneath us, the wheels gargled on the Glasgow street. He came home with me and stayed, stayed again and never quite left. We never stopped talking, except when we were eating supper in front of a movie or all over one another in bed. There were nights he

28

had to sleep in Edinburgh – he had to sit his finals and of course the train fares were expensive – but then in the summer he got a bar job in Glasgow. He told me he wanted to chill for a bit, didn't want rush into a career. But I know he got that job for me. No one can take that away from me, not even now. And when he told me his parents had bought a flat for him, did I want to move in, I said yes please, which is up there with telling Martin Amis you're his number one fan. But I didn't care.

Joy made me careless.

Valentina suggested we go for coffee in my car as hers was at the garage for repairs. Sure, I said. No problem. Before we moved north, Mikey had traded in the Golf for a second-hand Cherokee Jeep. For practical reasons, he'd said, though I suspected he secretly fancied himself in it – as a country squire or some such nonsense.

"Aberdeen is quite grey isn't it," I said as we walked down to the car. It was true. The houses, offices, shops, all the buildings looked like they'd been sculpted from rock, not built brick by brick.

"It is on a day like today," she said. "But, I tell you what, when the sun comes out, it's like there's diamonds in the walls." She linked my arm, leaned into me. The gesture felt too intimate for the few minutes we'd known one another but I brushed it off as a cultural difference and told myself to relax.

"All that glitters isn't gold though, eh?" I said. "It's your basic igneous rock. Granite's volcanic. That's why it glitters like that." I smiled, felt my cheeks flush. "Sorry, that's Mikey talking. He's my other half, you know? Works in oil so I must've learnt something along the way."

"Impressive," she said, eyes wide. "I wouldn't know a rock from a lump of wood."

We'd reached the jeep. I unhooked my arm from hers and clicked on the key. The lights flashed, the doors unlocked with a thunk.

"No way," she said. "Is this yours?"

"I hope so, otherwise we'll be in big trouble with the police."

She laughed, the way you do when you don't know a person well, and climbed in alongside me. "I tell you what," she said, buckling herself in. "Nah, forget it. It's a crazy idea."

"What is?"

"Nothing, forget it."

"You want to go clubbing, is that it? Twenty-four hour whisky binge? Go on, out with it." I was wiping my side of the windscreen with my sleeve pulled over my hand. Now that we were together in the car, I found it hard to look straight at her – she was too close range, the space too cramped for the both of us.

"I so love this jeep." She bounced on the seat. Like a kangaroo, I thought, but didn't say. "Reminds me of back home. I feel like we could roll over all the little cars like a tank. Get out of my way! No? Crush!"

"Aye right, it's great for traffic jams that way."

She laughed again while I concentrated on getting the key into the ignition. "What's this crazy idea you've had anyway?"

She rubbed her hands together. "I was thinking, what if we get a couple of takeaways and you can show me that lovely cottage of yours?"

"Really? You want to go to my place?" I'd only just got out of there and didn't exactly have going straight back in mind. But I'd never had anyone take an interest in where I lived before. *Wow, you live in a flat, I'd love to see it*, isn't exactly a phrase you hear every day but maybe *wow, you live in a cottage in the country* was. "Are you sure?"

"Listen, I'd invite you to my place but it's three floors up, no lift, and the pavements are full of litter. Union Grove, you know? Bloody seagulls are terrible, tearing through the trash, waking you up with their squawking. I'd love a place in the country."

30

"OK," I said. "You're on."

On the way to the cottage, we spoke mostly about our babies. Valentina seemed to find everything I said amusing and I guess I was flattered by that. Being with her wasn't like being at the mother and baby group back in Glasgow. I guess, if I'm honest, no matter how friendly everyone had been there, a lot of what they said was really all about what clever parents they were. *Daisy walked her first steps yesterday; Hamish has twenty words now* – that kind of thing. When Valentina talked about Zac, she admitted to a more flawed, a more real experience.

"He's like his dad," she said. "Whines on and on and on until I'm banging my head against the wall and it's all I can do not to throw him out of the goddamn window. The baby, I mean." She gave a sad laugh.

"I totally know what you mean," I replied. It was true, I found such relief in what Valentina was saying I could have rolled down the car window and shouted the words to the wind.

We'd reached the South Deeside Road. To the left, a grand, leafy driveway, all that was visible of Ardoe House Hotel; to the right, the River Dee, flowing down from the Cairngorms out to the North Sea, to the rigs, to Mikey.

Valentina tucked one leg up under the other, turned to me as I drove. "What do you do to get Isla to shut up, you know, when she won't stop crying?"

I thought for a second. "I mostly use duct tape."

She giggled.

"Masking tape, forget it," I continued, "not strong enough, they rip it off. Anything wider and they fucking suffocate on you."

"You're terrible," she said. "I won't ask how you get her to eat her vegetables."

I raised my eyebrows, leant back a little from the steering wheel. "Let me just say we live in a very remote spot."

We exchanged a glance and chuckled. The jeep bumped over the potholes of the lane, the overhanging branches trailed over the windscreen and there it was: the cottage.

Valentina gasped. She actually caught her breath, audibly, and said, "My God, Shona, it's even lovelier than I imagined."

For a second I thought she was taking the mickey, or play-acting. Then I thought she was going to jump out before I'd even stopped the car. As it was, she opened the door just as I pulled up and got out the moment I cranked the handbrake. I locked the car and made my way to where she was standing, open-mouthed, like she was admiring the Taj Mahal or something.

"Come on," I said. "It's only a house."

Valentina followed me up the drive and into the porch. When we stopped at the front door, she stood so close behind me that I could feel her breath warm on my ear. I became flustered, I couldn't get the key to work.

"Here," she said, "let me." She took the key and opened the door in a second.

"Go on in," I said.

But she already had.

You've not forgotten about her, have you? Out here alone in the cold and the dark? It's been a tricky business out here tonight, she'd tell you that herself. There were moments when she couldn't see the hand in front of her face and, of course, the lane is potholed to hell. The moon helped. Drifted out from behind those clouds long enough to light her way to the picket fence, to the gate. It was easy to sneak across the front of the cottage then. The back was more difficult – those flower pots no more than shadowy trolls on the mossy paving stones and the lawn reaching away into the blackness of an abyss. That got to her all right, but she didn't make a sound. She knew when she planned this that everything would have to be done in total silence. She is an impostor, you see. This is not her home. These are not her flickering walls. This is not her life.

FOUR

In my cottage, the kitchen continues around to what I've always called the secret back door, making a kind of horseshoe. By the time I'd hung my coat up and stepped further inside, the secret back door was clattering against the outside wall. I stepped out and made my way to the patio at the back.

Valentina was a couple of metres away, twirling around in the vast grassy space like Julie Andrews at the beginning of *The Sound of Music*.

"Wooh," she cried out. "Wooh! Wooh! This is awesome."

"Glad you like it." I kept my voice low, thinking she might lower hers to match. I figured this was what Australians must be like; they came from a hot climate, wide spaces. The truth was, though, with her twirling and her shouting, she was expressing so exactly what I had felt the first time I saw the place. Except that I lived here. This cottage was mine.

Back in the kitchen, I made coffee and cut some of the gingerbread I'd made, out of a desperate need to find something to do, at the weekend. It was my mum's recipe – she'd read it out to me down the phone, ran through the instructions as if I were a perfect idiot. I'd done everything she'd said but it had still sunk in the middle.

Valentina took a big bite and closed her eyes, her eyelashes long, spider-leg thick with black mascara.

"God, this is awesome," she said. "Did you make it?"

"It's not awesome, it's as heavy as a brick." I took another bite all the same. "Playing with dollies does my head in, so I thought I'd pop my cake making cherry, you know? I gave Isla the wooden spoon to lick – that kept her quiet for a few minutes. I let her take the tape off her mouth, obviously."

She smiled and shook her head, unwrapped her hippy scarf from her neck and placed it on the chair next to her. "Aren't you worried about salmonella?"

"I wasn't. Until now, of course. Thanks. Thanks a lot."

She clapped her hand over her mouth. "God, I'm such a moron."

"No, you're all right. If only I'd thought of raw eggs before. Maybe I'll try them on Mikey when he gets back from offshore, that'll teach him to leave me here on my own in the middle of nowhere." I pulled a mad face. "I've already threatened to put peanuts in his coffee if he's a minute late getting home."

"Of course." She laughed, then frowned. "You mean so he chokes, right?"

"No actually," I replied. "He's allergic."

"Really? Poor guy. That sucks."

Looking back, I can see that all this joking was no more than the novelty of one another, but it felt good too to reconnect with another old friend: me, my old self, Shona, the same and there all along, laughing darkly in her bright new life. There with Valentina that first time, I can remember it dawning on me that, yes, I had a child, but I could still joke around if I wanted and nothing terrible would happen.

"So, you gonna give me a tour or what?" she asked when we'd finished our coffee.

"Sure."

The stairwell was 'ripper', the bathroom 'darling', the bedrooms 'cute'. She was 'in love', she said, with every room. I thought about how, in Glasgow, they'd tell her to get to fuck. But being Australian, she got away with it. At least, I let her get away with it.

"We call these two rooms the kids' rooms," I said, "even though we've only got Isla so far."

"That's so sweet, to have plans for another already. You guys must love each other like crazy." She ran ahead – to mine and Mikey's room. She went straight in, ran her fingers along the built in wardrobes, picked up the photo from the chest of drawers.

"Is this Michael?"

"Mikey, yes. That was us at my parents' silver wedding."

She put the photo back without a word. "I like your bed." She sat on the edge, bounced up and down as she had in the car. "Oh, it's perfect. Not too hard, not too soft. Just right." She grinned. "I sound like Goldilocks, don't I?"

"You'll be after my porridge next. I have to warn you – I take it salty." I smiled and held my hand out to her. "We should probably be getting back. We said four, didn't we?"

"Sod that." She threw herself back and spread her arms. Her hair fell over the pillow, bright as coral on white rock. "I want to stay here." After a moment, she sprang up, eyes ablaze, that mischievous expression I was already getting to know making her mouth pucker. "Hey! I could move in! We could change the locks and when Michael gets back from the rig we could jeer at him from the bedroom window and tell him he can't come in."

"So, hold on, what?" I shook my head at her. "I thought we were with Goldilocks, that sounds more like The Three Little Pigs, and anyway we have to let him in, don't we? How else are we going to poison his coffee?" I reached for her hand. And this time she took it.

It all seems like such a long time ago now but it wasn't. Months, that's all. Less than a pregnancy and, God knows, a pregnancy can change your life overnight. I'll never forget discovering I was expecting that summer, how I journeyed through the slow accumulation of facts as if I were wading upriver, arriving eventually at the source: the metallic taste in my mouth, the breathlessness if I so much as quickened my pace, oh, and the sick feeling if I even went near a glass of wine. It was that last thing that made me think something was up. I love a drink. But I've never been one for recording the dates of my cycle with a discreet letter P on the calendar or anything like that. So by the time I put two and two together, I was twelve weeks gone.

By this time we were living in Mikey's flat in Hyndland but I actually grew up in Govan. In Govan you could hear your neighbours' televisions through the walls, whereas in leafy Hyndland the flats were what I'd call apartments – high ceilings and original coving that Mikey told me was called Lincrusta, oak skirting three foot high. Mikey being from Liverpool, Hyndland wasn't home to him either but we were settled enough, as settled as you can be, making a home after only three months together. We were each other's home, you could say. Wherever he was, I wanted to be and he always said he felt the same. *Thing about you, Shone,* he used to say, *is you get me.*

I'd bought the tester kit in my lunch hour and took it into the loo when I got home from work. I was supposed to wait and use the morning's first pee but I couldn't, I was too anxious to know. I sat watching the stick, my jeans around my ankles. The blue lines got darker: one, then two. My chest expanded like an accordion. I'd thought those things took ages but no, they're quick. I checked the instructions. One line, the test had worked but the result was negative. Two lines, the test had worked and ... no mistaking, I was having Mikey's baby.

I went to phone my mum but stopped myself. Jeanie had already texted:

Have you done it yet?

But I didn't answer. Mikey had to be the first to know, and I had to tell him face to face.

Waiting for him to come home was torture. He was still working in a pub, still putting off the inevitable and now I was going to present him with that very thing: the inevitable. I worried it would weigh him down, that faced with the responsibility he would panic. And leave. I cleaned the flat from top to bottom, kept looking out the window for him coming up the road. Seeing no sign, I made spaghetti Bolognese, for something to do.

Mikey got in about eight o'clock – a lot later than usual – complaining that he'd had to cover for *some dickhead philosophy student* who hadn't turned up for his shift. He came into the kitchen, kissed the back of my neck with a loud smack and reached for a couple of beers from the fridge. I said hi and carried on stirring the sauce like my life depended on it.

"Sorry I'm so late." He leant against the countertop, crossed his feet and held out one of the beer bottles to me.

"No thanks," I said, unable to keep my face straight.

"Why are you smiling like that?"

I turned down the gas and faced him full on. "You know how you said you wanted to have kids?"

"One day, yeah." He tipped the bottle to his lips.

"One day in about, oh, I don't know, six months?"

He took the bottle away so fast it foamed at the neck. His eyes widened. Face the colour of stone, he stepped backwards. "What?"

"I'm pregnant."

He backed into the kitchen table, hard, as if I'd punched him in the stomach. Felt around the edge as if he were needing to grip onto something to steady himself. The beer froth slid like saliva down the length of the green bottle.

"Are you no' pleased?" I helped him into the chair.

He began to pant, low and shallow. I took the bottle from his hand, helped him put his head between his knees.

"Mikey?" I started to laugh. I couldn't help it. "Mikey, darlin', are you all right?"

"I'm fine, I'm ..." His voice was thin, as if he were talking through a long tube.

"Are you no' pleased? Mikey? Talk to me."

He reached up, took my hand and squeezed it. "It's just. It's just a shock, that's all."

"Wait there," I said. "I'll get you a wee nip."

I ran over to the shelf where we kept the only spirits we had: a bottle of Glenmorangie Mikey's dad had brought us as a flat-warming present and one of Smirnoff. I poured a big dram of the whisky and took it to him. He'd managed to sit upright again, his brow damp, his face still greyish. He took the glass from me and knocked back the whisky.

"Are you OK?" I asked him.

"Yeah." He gave me a half-smile. "I'll have to get a proper job now, won't I?"

I threw my arms around him and sobbed into his neck. You might think that sounds daft, or soppy, but I was so relieved. I'd thought for a minute he'd ... well, never mind what I thought. What I thought barely matters, not any more.

The next day Mikey came home with a beautiful gift: a stork made from driftwood.

"To say sorry for needing a whisky," he said, holding my hand on the kitchen table, stroking my knuckles with his thumb. "To say I'm happy. To say, bring it on."

We kissed. What do you want me to say about that? It was lovely.

It was love.

He began to look for serious work. All the oil jobs were in Aberdeen, but he knew someone who worked for a consultancy here in Glasgow and said he could pick up some work there. It was contract work and meant him being away quite a bit – sometimes three days out of a week. I missed him, obviously, but at the end of a long day in the office nibbling on ginger snaps to stave off morning sickness, trying not to puke over my keyboard or worse, over someone I was interviewing, I didn't mind too much that he wasn't at home some nights to keep me up late talking – or the other. I was happy to crash out.

The only time I got really lonely was towards the end when I got signed off work with oedema. A risk of pre-eclampsia, the midwife said, so I had to stay at home all day with my feet in the air. That was when I realised that the main thing I liked about my job was the simple fact of going in, having a laugh and a blether, a coffee break, sometimes a cheeky cigarette out on Renfield Street. At *The Tribune*, everyone was so clever and funny, the craic was brilliant, how could I not miss it? They were more than colleagues; they were friends.

So while Mikey was away I spent most of the time on the phone to Jeanie at work, catching up on stories they were chasing, getting the gossip, or watching television with the sound on high: late morning panel shows, old movies, the lunchtime news. And it turned out I'd have to get used to Mikey being away because after Isla was born, that's when he came home with the big announcement.

"I've been offered a job," he said. "A permanent one. Drilling Supervisor. On a platform, you know." Coat still on, briefcase still in his hand, standing there like a tax inspector in the middle of the lounge. He wasn't smiling, even though he'd got a proper job, which had been his aim.

"I'd be at home less," he went on, dropping his bag on the floor, pulling off his coat. "But it'd be good, you know, from a career perspective."

Isla started crying. I picked her up, shushed her, put her to my breast. "Sounds like you've already made up your mind." I couldn't look at him, made out like Isla was having a job latching on. "What do you mean, less time at home?"

"It's two on, two off."

"What's that?" I knew fine what it was.

"On the platform, you know, two weeks at sea, two weeks at home."

"I thought you wanted to hang onto your youth," I said. "Now you want to jump onto a floating prison once a month?"

"But that was before the baby, Shone. Things have changed."

"I know they've changed. No one knows that more than me but that's awful drastic, isn't it? Offshore? I thought you wanted a work-life balance."

"I'll be working towards that – for our future. I might have to put the hours in, you know, get something going before I ease up a bit. I don't know why you're being so hard on me."

I huffed, shook my head. "I thought you said anyone who let their job take over their life lacked imagination. Your words, darlin', not mine."

"Shona, come on. You don't need to be like that. Let's talk about it like grownups."

"Two weeks in four is half your life."

"That's a very emotional way to put it."

"I am emotional, Mikey. I've just had a baby."

"OK, look." He raised the flat of his palms to me. "Let's stop this. I won't take it if you don't want me to. It's a great opportunity, that's all." I was still looking at Isla, her wee head, her perfect sucking lips: kiss kiss kiss. When I eventually looked up, his eyebrows were up in his forehead somewhere, his Scouse grin showing all his teeth. I wouldn't call him classically good-looking, more charismatic, with large features, a nineteen-fifties black and white movie face. So I always thought anyway.

"Come on, Shone," he said. "This is for all of us, you know it is. We'll have more money. Well, eventually."

"I don't care about money. Not like I shop in Dolce & Gabbana, is it?"

"I know but it's not about buying stuff, is it? It means choice."

I remembered when Isla was born, how he had sworn all sorts of tearful allegiances to her and to me, moved to near madness by it all. These pledges included a desire to provide for us and I did see that. But I was stuck against the wall of my own stubbornness and I hadn't figured how to get back into the room.

"Choice for you," I muttered, half-hearted, embarrassed.

"Come on." He sat down, put his arm around me, kissed my head. "I meant for you too. It'd be nice to have choices, wouldn't it, not have to scrape a living?"

"My parents didn't scrape."

"I wasn't talking about your parents. Christ, you're so bloody chippy. Stop reacting and think for a second. We could be ... comfortable. Not have to worry all the time. We could make a family. We could have three kids, four, as many as you like."

"OK, OK." I was smiling by now despite myself. I'd had no sleep for a month, I was daft as a brush with no sleep.

"What do you think, Shone?"

"It won't stop me going back to *The Tribune* will it?"

"Of course not. We'll organise childcare when the time comes. And you've got your mum and dad to help out."

"It's only for a year or two, I suppose."

"That's right."

"I guess you've got to start your career sometime."

He pushed his lips into my hair. "I do."

I knew, had known the moment he'd started talking, that it was the right thing to do. I wanted us to be independent, couldn't stand the thought that his parents had bought the flat and certainly didn't want any more of their help. The sooner we stood on our own two feet, the better.

I turned to kiss him, briefly, on the lips. "Maybe I'll see what they've got in Dolce & Gabbana."

Mikey accepted the job. From the off, he travelled up to Aberdeen a lot. There were training courses on helicopter emergency, first aid, health and safety. He had a lot to set up. And then, in the March I think it was, when Isla was five weeks old, the rotation began.

I was used to him being away on business by then but a full two weeks was a long haul. I'd joined a mother and baby group to add to the NCT group I saw every week for coffee, met up regularly with Jeanie and the guys from work for lunch and a catch up on the craic. I was determined to enjoy my maternity leave, not let it be overshadowed by Mikey's absences. And of course my mum came through three or four times that first trip and sat with me or walked with me or rocked the baby while I grabbed forty winks. She was delighted.

"You know I'll take her when you go back to work," she said – not to me, by the way, oh no. She hadn't talked to me directly for weeks. Instead, she'd developed this habit of saying everything she had to say through Isla, as if Isla were some kind of walkie-talkie.

"Your mummy knows I'll have you anytime," she cooed into her face. "Yes I will, I'll have you, yes I will, yes. Who's a lovely babba for their granny?"

She went to pieces all right, did my ma. So did I, I guess. I was skunk-drunk on a cocktail of hormones, sleeplessness and mad, blind, limitless love. Although I was looking forward to being in the office again, I began to wonder how I would ever leave Isla for one day, let alone five.

So the hours were whiled, the days were killed. It wasn't perfect, it wasn't exciting, but it was good, better than a lot of people have, and I was happy. But Mikey returned from his first trip with another announcement, or whatever it's called when your partner comes home, picks up your baby girl and says, "We should move to Aberdeen."

Actually, I'm not being fair here. I'd known a move north was on the cards when I moved in with him – before that, even. Aberdeen is the oil capital, so it wasn't as big a shock as I'm making it out to be, especially in view of the offshore job. But I was shocked all the same.

"Up North?" I said. "What do you want to live there for all of a sudden?"

"I've been thinking. It's where the heliport is, obviously. I'll get more time at home. But mostly I thought we could get ourselves a nice little place in the countryside somewhere. It's beautiful up there, you should see it." He moved Isla to his shoulder. She curled into it, in her pink Babygro, like a brooch made of blancmange. "With what we could get for this place, we could buy a converted steading or an old church or a gamekeeper's cottage, whatever, as long as it's not too big. But something special, a dream place for a family. Think of all that fresh air."

"Sounds like you've got it all worked out."

"I have." He knelt down on the floor in front of me. "I want this for us, Shone. It'll be an adventure. We can buy a jeep, find somewhere incredible, a real fairy tale place in the woods." He took my hand, eyes full of excitement, and kissed my knuckles.

"There's countryside outside Glasgow, you know." But even as I said it, I knew it was a non-starter. Once he came off the rotation, and he would eventually, his job would always be Aberdeen-based. What would we do then? Not like he could commute from Ayrshire, was it? Fly from Loch Lomond, catch the red-eye from Bute or Argyll. No, I was the journalist, I was the one whose job was flexible. And the sooner we moved, the sooner I could take steps to set up something for myself, professionally and personally.

"We can have big parties," he said, squeezing my fingers till they hurt. "Hell, we'll have ceilidhs! 'Where?' I hear you cry. 'In the barn, silly. The barn next to the farmhouse.'"

"Aye, right." I giggled, caught up in his dream for us all.

"It'll be brilliant." He kissed me hard on the mouth. "Swear to God. It'll be amazing."

Mikey could probably sell soup to Baxter's, ice cream to old Farmer Mackie, teacakes to Tunnock's. And I guessed he was playing the big man, the big *pater familias*, and that the role was still new to him. I suppose, looking back, I was playing the little woman. If I'm guilty of something, maybe it's that.

FIVE

If he'd told me before I got pregnant that we were moving away from my family, my job and all my friends, I'd have told him to get lost and I'd have used stronger language than that. I'd never have left Glasgow. No way. I'd heard Aberdonians turned off the grill while they flipped the bacon over, dried out their teabags on the washing line so they could use them again.

But as pregnancy had changed Mikey, something had grown in me too, right there in the bump, alongside Isla. A new set of priorities had been incubated, all previous imperatives cut off and tossed away with the umbilical cord. I'd wanted him, us, home at night – every night – once the baby was born. But you can't always have what you want, can you? And here he was, offering me something different, OK, but the best he had. Where we lived was, if not immaterial, then a hell of a lot less important than love. Mikey and Isla, they were my home now.

"We won't do this if you don't want to, Shone," he said, when we were clearing up the kitchen that evening. "The two on, two off, everything. I can go in there tomorrow and say no."

I flapped the dishcloth at him, put my face in his and treated him to my thickest Govan. "Dinna haver, Big Man," I said. "Takes more than a move up the road to worry me, pal."

He laughed and kissed me on the nose.

"You're amazing," he said, and I remembered he'd said that on our first proper date. I liked that he was worried for me. I'd interviewed enough people by then to know that there were some, many even, whose sense of entitlement

45

flowed in their veins. Hard work and gratitude flowed in mine, I think. So you might think I fell without a fight but I was … being practical. It wasn't a question of man vs. woman, more of an arrangement to suit the larger thing, the more important thing: the family. You had to be a team in marriage, my mum always said. You've got to jump in with both feet or not at all. If you both dig in, where does that get you? I don't know, thinking about it, maybe I wanted in that moment to be always and at all times the girl he'd chosen, the one he thought was amazing.

A few nights after the Aberdeen announcement, Mikey went out for a few beers with some of his colleagues. I was barely back to my bed from feeding Isla and still awake when he came staggering into the bedroom, fell to his knees and sank his face in the duvet.

I turned on the bedside light. "Mikey?"

The clock said 3am. He rolled his head to the side and said, "Does it bother you we're not married?" His voice was slurred.

"What? What are you asking me that for?" I stared at the back of his head, black against the white bedding. "Mikey, you've had too much to drink, that's all. We can get married any old time. Hey. Mikey?" He didn't move. "Come on, don't be like that now, all floppy and maudlin. We're going to make a life together, that's all that matters, isn't it?" I tried singing to him – Joni Mitchell – all about not needing an official piece of paper to keep us together. But it didn't work. He groaned.

I budged across the bed to him and took his head in my hands. "Hey, stupid." His lovely brown eyes were as sad as a street urchin's. "You're my old man, aren't you?"

I can't say it worked.

"You're my kindred spirit, Shone," he droned, tears filling his eyes. "My soulmate. You get it, you really get it, do you know what I mean? You get me."

Typical pished-up conversation, except it was one-sided because all I'd had was one can of stout at teatime and a hot chocolate before bed to help with milk production. Sacred cow, me.

It had rained while Valentina and I had been indoors. In the front garden, the grass shone, giving off that fresh, cleansed smell you get after a good downpour. We climbed back into the jeep.

"So, how did you meet your fella?" I asked once we were on the road.

"I met him in a club in London," she said, drawing finger pictures in the steam on the car window.

"London? How come you were there?"

"I was travelling and one of my backpack buddies had this friend who was in a band. They were playing in some pub so I went along. Red was lead guitar and yes, I let him pluck my strings."

I smiled. "Red?"

"Because of his red hair. I guess that's one thing we have in common."

"Wow," I said. "I met Mikey in a smelly pub in Glasgow. He was wearing old lady foundation and had a very dodgy beard."

"Oh, don't be fooled," she replied, still drawing on the car window. "I thought he was so cool. It was only after he'd knocked me up and put a ring on my finger that I found out his real name was Graham."

"Would you still have married him if you'd known?" I joked.

"Never." Her laugh, when it came, was hollow.

I didn't say any more but after a moment she stopped with the window art and went on. "I thought he was so genuine, you know?" Her voice had become louder, too loud for the car, the anger in it palpable. "I thought he was this free spirit, but he's not free, he's lazy. Smokes his dope, talks about ... oh, he talks and talks and smokes and smokes and talks about all the things he's going to do. All of it future tense. He's a man with plans." She turned to me and rolled her eyes.

"Does he work?"

"I suppose you could call it that. In a vintage record store, you know, while he waits for a record deal to drop out of the sky?"

"I love music," I said, trying to sound positive. "I'll have to check out his store. Whereabouts is it? What's it called?"

But she'd gone back to her finger painting, as if she hadn't heard me.

"Michael has a proper job," she said after a moment. "He has a career."

"Mikey, you mean? Aye. But the whole offshore thing is far from ideal, especially with a little one."

"I know what you mean." She turned to me, her face soft with sympathy.

I felt a stab of irritation. No, not a stab, that's too strong, a needle. I wanted to ask her what the hell she thought she knew about living half your life without your other half – which, thinking about it, would've been a bit of a mouthful.

"I get lonely," I said instead. "Especially out at the cottage. I'm used to noise. That's why I booked Isla into the nursery. I'm going to get some work once she's settled."

"Absolutely. Never give up your independence, Shona. Any woman who gives up work is an idiot."

I gave her a sideways glance, saw her mouth drop open.

"I didn't mean you! You've had the move and everything. I just mean you can't put your feet up and rely on it all working out, that's all. That's a fool's paradise."

"I wouldn't call it paradise and I hardly ever put my feet up," I said, with more irritation that I would've liked. "And I would've said all those things before I had Isla. I would've said them right up until the moment Mikey said he was going offshore. And I tell you what, I'm much more tired after a day with Isla than I ever was after a day at the paper." I could feel my belly heating with anger. "And I'll tell you something else, Mikey's as dependent on me as I am on him. There's no way he could do what he does and still have everything he has if it wasn't for me."

"Truth, Sister. But no one pays you, do they?"

"I know and that's not ideal, but we need to respect each other's choices, don't we? Women, I mean? The world would be a much better place if we did." I was on my soapbox now, right enough. "No one criticises a man for staying at home. No one criticises a man for having a demanding career. They get lauded, whatever they do. Whichever choice they make is a noble act. When it's a man."

I wanted to add, well, so much more, but she was looking at me with the kind of concerned expression you give someone who's about to jump off a bridge, so I simply said, "I reckon, if you're going to be with someone, at some point you've got to trust each other, haven't you? Trust. That's really what it's about."

We made our way down to the main road, past the horse in the field, grazing away. My lonely little houyhnhnm.

"So, talking of work," I said. "What do you do?"

She knitted her hands, pushed them out in front of her then raised them up in a stretch.

"I'm a yoga teacher," she said, "and a trainee reflexologist. Do you know every part of the sole of your foot corresponds to a part of your body?"

I nodded. I thought everyone knew that, but I let her tell me all about it anyway. She was thinking about learning crystals too, she told me. I tried not to snigger. Things like that crack me up.

"I'll do your feet next time," she said as we neared town.

"You're on. Get my chakras in order, they're a bloody mess."

But again, she didn't seem to be listening. She twisted in her seat and looked through the back window of the car, as if we were being chased by the police or something.

She turned back, looked intently ahead. "We should go faster," she said, patting the dashboard with both hands.

"Ach, I think the limit's forty along here."

Her green eyes flashed, wild gems in glancing torchlight. "No one's looking. Go on, Shona. Put your frickin' foot down, girl. It'll be fun."

"I'm fine like this, to be honest. The road's bendy and we're almost in town."

"I know but we could go a little bit faster, don't you think? Come on. Let's be crazy. We'll be mums again in five minutes."

I put my foot down, took the car up to forty-five, forty-seven, forty-nine.

"Faster," she said, laughing.

My chest tightened. I didn't want to let her down. I was too lonely, too glad of her friendship. But I'm not a total idiot.

"No," I said, slowing into the last bend. "It's not safe."

"Suit yourself." She pushed out her bottom lip, like a child. But she wasn't a child.

Moving up this way took longer to organise than we'd originally thought, on account of Mikey being away so much and of course having the baby. He was constantly online looking at properties, even going up to Aberdeen at weekends to look at anything promising. He took on that responsibility because I was still breastfeeding Isla, still dozy with the sleepless nights. But all throughout that time, we plotted constantly together: what we would do, where we would live. Cuddled up in front of the fake coal fire at the flat, we decided to stick to that pie in the sky idea of buying something in the country. We made our life the thing of fairy stories.

"Two city slickers heading straight for the wilds of Aberdeenshire," Mikey said.

"We must be mad."

We laughed at ourselves, threw a belated welcome to the world party for Isla and told our pals the news. *You'll never hack it,* they said. *You two, up there? Are you for real? I'll gie yer one hard winter – you'll be running back here, begging them to let you back in.* Mikey took it on the chin – that kind of banter is in his blood too – it doesn't mean anything, it's just the way we talk. But they were right enough about the countryside – it was a screwball idea. I don't know what possessed us.

I blame the house.

If I hadn't seen the cottage, we'd probably have moved into a nice enough flat in town, one of those sturdy granite places that glittered in the sunshine. I would never've had to dig through half a mile of snow in a morning to reach the post box at the end of my own drive. But I can remember so clearly when Mikey told me he'd found this great place. He'd been up in Aberdeen for three days, frantically trying to find something, and he called me in the morning to tell me to get myself and Isla on a train as soon as I could. He met us at the station, practically bursting with excitement, drove us through town and out into the countryside. What I remember most about the drive was the slow birthing of the car from the granite body of the city, out into a world of limitless green. Land as far as the eye could see, the sweep of fields to the left, short, thick boundary posts making my eyes flick flick flick as we passed; to the right, the river, wide and muscular, flashing from between clumps of woodland. I remember that, and how hyper Mikey was.

"This is an unbelievable stroke of luck," he said. "The buyers have pulled out and it goes back on the market tomorrow. Right place right time, Shone. I told the estate agent four o'clock. Wait till you see it." We twisted and turned and eventually came up this potholed track. "Mum and Dad'll tide us over until we sell the Glasgow place so if you like it we can move fast."

I was about to argue that I didn't think we should accept any more money from his parents when I saw it. It kind of peeped out from beneath the boughs as if it'd been expecting us and, actually, we were a wee bit late. When we got to the clearing my first thought was: this is it, this is my home. My second thought was: where are all the neighbours? My third: what's the catch?

We got out of the car. The estate agent was standing outside waiting, dressed in a red skirt suit and looking more than a bit like an air hostess.

"Good afternoon." She glanced at her notes. "Mr. and Mrs. Quinn, was it?"

We nodded and said hello – no point correcting her.

"And this is your second viewing?"

Mikey grinned at me, made a silly face, then looked back to her. "My second. Shona's first."

The woman checked her clipboard, a crimson circle appearing on each of her cheeks.

"Where is everybody anyway?" Mikey was looking all around him, hands on his hips. "I meant to ask last time – where exactly is the nearest house?"

"The nearest dwelling is away half a mile up the road," the estate agent said, waving her hand over to where the lane continued into murky tree shadow. "There's a new development being built a few miles south and there's a chapel up over the other side of the fields."

I thought about electricity, heating. I thought about plumbing, telephone lines. What did it all connect to? But I didn't ask. I didn't want to appear stupid.

I'd seen the countryside before, of course I had, I'm not saying I hadn't. I'd even asked for walking boots for my twenty-first birthday. OK, they were still in the box but I was always determined to embrace things that hadn't necessarily been part of my own childhood: long walks, Sunday lunch out, country living. Not in a snobbish way, I'm proud of where I'm from. Just to be open, you know? Not let myself be limited. So no, the countryside wasn't new to me, it was more that I hadn't thought in any depth about the practicalities. But here it was, this house, standing there like it was already mine.

I linked my arm through Mikey's and we followed her up the driveway.

"This is the one," I said.

"You've not seen inside yet."

"I don't need to."

"Don't you now?" He stole a quick kiss and we followed the estate agent through the gate. The front garden has this white picket fence around the perimeter of the lawn. What a silly little boundary line, I thought, in such a vast space. What on earth would we need a fence for, out here?

"So this is Burns Cottage," said the estate agent, unlocking the front door. She stopped on the front step. "As in the poet. And this area, everything you can see, is all Royal Deeside." She had this air of importance, with her *as in the poet* and her three-sixty swooping hand gestures. "Not too far from Balmoral, where the Queen has her holiday residence and of course you have Lochnagar about an hour away, if you like hill walking."

Mikey raised his eyebrows at me. I made a silly face at him. Were we egging each other on? I don't know. Maybe after twenty-eight years surrounded by nothing but noise I thought the peace and quiet would be good. Maybe, deep down, I thought this was better.

***

Fire will send them flying from their bed. They will cover their mouths, choking on the noxious fumes of burning upholstery, wood, carpet. But why, frankly, should either of them sleep soundly when she will never again be at peace? Why should they be allowed to dream when her dreams are dead in the ground? Who gave them the right to the life that should be hers?

***

SIX

In Scotland, there's no better time of year than May. If you don't count the mood swings and the spooky haar up here, the weather can be warm, even hot sometimes and the midges aren't yet out in full force. That's when we finally moved. The last month was tough because Mikey was pretty much up in Aberdeen all the time, except for weekends, finishing his training, starting on the work he would have to do. He had to show commitment, he said, in those all-important first six months. It was tough but I was proud of him and at least I knew we were doing the right thing by moving.

The cottage looked different again in the sunshine; the walls whiter than ever, the dormer windows in the roof expressive as inquisitive eyebrows. We parked a little away from the removal van and I threw open the jeep door.

"No problem parking," I shouted, running ahead, in through the wee front porch, leaving Mikey to bring Isla.

Under our new low ceilings, the furniture looked as if it had been inflated in the van. In Glasgow we'd had two bedrooms not four, but the proportions of the cottage were so much smaller than the flat. I ran out into the garden, back in through the house and out front to see Mikey sitting on the blue sofa outside on the driveway.

"Mikey, we should have measured up. Everything's too big."

But he was talking to someone on the phone. "Only room for one bloody couch," he was saying, chuckling. "We'll have to put it into storage." He turned to me and waved but continued his conversation. "We've kept the leather one and the two armchairs but they'll have to knock a wall down to get the blue one in as well." He laid his hand over the phone and mouthed that it was his mum.

I was sure she'd be telling him that it was all the cottage's fault, not his. Judging by what I'd seen of her doting ways in the few times I'd met her, I was surprised she hadn't arrived already to make tea and hand it to her golden boy on a tray with biscuits, maybe get down on all fours so she could be the coffee table for him to rest his feet on. I was surprised she hadn't come flying in, knocked the wall down, built an extension, hired a forklift and driven the damn sofa in herself. That might sound harsh. But love for humankind is not my strong suit just now.

"No, it's all right, Mum," I heard him say. "No, no, tell Dad not to do that, we're fine, I can sort it. Honestly."

See? What did I tell you?

I went back into the cottage, thinking it was a miracle Mikey could do anything for himself. Inside, the desk – barely noticeable in the corner of the living room in our Glasgow place – now filled half the kitchen. I got one of the movers to dismantle it for me and we carried it out to the stable. There was plenty of room there for anything that wouldn't fit into the house, at least for now.

"Takeaway, Madam?" Mikey asked when the removal men had gone, when we'd popped the cork on our bottle of champagne and I'd bathed Isla and put her to bed. It was after nine by then but still, I noticed, perfectly light.

"Good idea."

There was no WiFi at all and the 3G was patchy to say the least, so we looked in the dog-eared Yellow Pages the previous occupants had left. The Hong Kong Palace didn't deliver this far out. Neither did the Taj Mahal.

"That's it," I cried. "Put this heap o' shite back on the market."

"Don't worry," he replied, spreading his hands. "I will go in search."

I threw my arms around his neck and kissed him. "My big man. My hunter-gatherer."

Mikey jumped in the car, wound down the window and gave me that grin. He was all gee'd up, wanting everything to be great. We both wanted everything to be great. We wanted, I thought, not to be wrong.

"Put a couple of chairs in the garden, do," he said, in his treacly posh Captain Hook voice. "We shall dine out on our land, don't you know." He honked the horn three times.

"Sure you'll find me all right?" I called after him in an equally fake cut-glass accent. "Get the butler to show you through."

My God, we were high as kites. And you laugh at anything, don't you, when you're happy? You'd laugh at a joke you'd heard a hundred times. I wandered into the gigantic garden and, with a blanket round my shoulders, sat alone, trying not to drink the rest of the champagne. I sat alone and stared at the flat green grass, at the trees whose names I did not yet know. There's a wee patio at the back of the house, with a pond. Between the lily pads and the beady eyeball clusters of frogspawn, the carp darted about, their scales flashing at times under the surface.

I poured myself another cheeky glass, saw that I was halfway down the bottle. I checked my phone to see if there was a text from Mikey. There wasn't, only one from Jeanie:

Hope you're settling in. Good luck. J.

I replied:

It's amazing. Can't wait for you to visit. xxx

I texted Mikey then, too:

Get ketchup. And make sure they put on loads of salt and vinegar! Love you xxxxxxx

Four, five, six, seven kisses.

It grew cold, too cold to sit out so I went inside. I figured he must be trailing round town, trying to find food, poor devil. I hunted about for the emergency candles. They were nowhere to be found so I dug about in the bedroom boxes and found a bedside light instead. I rigged that up by the front window in the lounge – a homecoming beacon in the darkness – and grabbed cutlery and plates from another box in the kitchen. Two of the bigger boxes became a makeshift table in the lounge, an old sheet we'd used to cover the dresser a tablecloth. I sat on the leather sofa, clapped my hands and blew out a long satisfied breath. But I couldn't settle so that's when I laid the fire. They'd left sticks and logs and there was loads of newspaper from the unpacking – easy peasy. I was about to light it when I heard the front door bang.

A second later, Mikey was in the doorway, holding up two white paper bags. "Cod and chips deluxe for her ladyship. Might be a bit cold ..."

"I was away to send a search party. Did you have to go catch the fish yourself?"

He plonked the bags on a packing box and took off his jacket. He looked like he'd been running round all over town. His face shone with sweat, poor thing. "You've laid a fire, I see."

"Lady Firebird at your service. I don't have to light it though. You look a bit hot."

"I'm boiling actually. Maybe light it later?"

"Ach, we can light it tomorrow, it's no biggie." I folded out the white wrappers, the smell of fat and salt and fish and – oh, there's nothing like a fish supper when you're starving. I poured him a glass, poured myself one for the road. The bottle emptied its last drop.

"What happened to the blue sofa by the way?" I asked him.

"The men took it. It's in storage but I might sell it on eBay, because, trust me, we will not be moving any time soon." He drank his glass down in one and gasped.

"I've been thinking," he said after a few mouthfuls. "We should make that pond into a sandpit."

"Right you are."

"I'll do it tomorrow morning."

"Steady on. We've got ages."

"No, we'll be busy, we'll get sidetracked." His words were muffled by chips. "I should do it."

"But she's not even walking yet."

"She will be soon. And when you're too busy looking the other way, that's when bad things happen."

"I suppose." The thought made me feel suddenly low.

"Cheers anyway," he said, perhaps sensing he'd killed the mood. "This is great, isn't it?"

"It is. It's magic." My throat tightened. "I can't believe it's ours."

"Are you crying?"

"No." I said. "I can't quite take it in."

"God, you're sweet." He leant over, pushed away my tears with his thumbs and kissed me on the mouth. His lips were oily, seasoned with salt and vinegar. He leant back, then in again for another, longer, deeper kiss. We hadn't kissed that way since Isla was born.

"We should test the bed after," he said. "See if the springs still work after the move."

"Aye," I said. "See if we still work."

Shame the seagulls don't make it that far inland. They would have had a rare treat that night, feasting on the cold chips we threw – like the idiot city folk we were – into the garden, not wanting to stink the house out. Something must have eaten them because, in the morning, they were gone.

We tried to make the few days we had before he went offshore a bit of a holiday by going on a few trips. There was no rush to unpack, after all – we had the rest of our lives together. Mikey took me to Dunnottar Castle on the coast – stunning as it was to walk around the ruins out there on the clifftop, it was too cold for our picnic so we ate it in the jeep.

"Look at us," I said, laughing. "Eating our dinner in the car like old folk."

He was laughing too. "You should see your face. It's bright red."

"Aye, with cold. In May!"

Another day he took me to Balmedie Beach, where he told me he'd been on one of his training exercises. He was desperate to show me, full of it. It was like a film set – not a soul in sight, acres of virgin sand, dunes twenty feet high. We took turns holding Isla while the other rolled down the dunes, ending up in a bruised, hysterical heap at the bottom. Mikey produced a kite from his rucksack – he'd bought it as a surprise – a jumble of primary colours that once airborne became a rainbow.

"Isn't this beautiful?" he shouted, the wind carrying his words out to sea. "Isn't this great?"

Everything was new, everything was exciting. We were playing house, it seemed, playing at being grownups. When you're in love, I suppose everything feels like a game.

By the Thursday before his Saturday departure, we'd arranged all the furniture, organised most of the crockery, pans and all of that. We'd set up the little table in the open hallway and decided to use that space as part of the kitchen. At around five, Mikey came in through the back door.

"I've organised the stable a bit better," he said, pulling off his jacket. "The travel cot's at the front so you can grab it when you need it for Isla."

"OK. Upstairs we're still up to our eyes in boxes but I can go through that when ... I'll do that."

"Great." He picked Isla up off the furry rug where she'd been having a kick, looking up at her mirror mobile. He brought her close and nuzzled her face with his. "Now then, who's Daddy's little girl then, eh?"

It was a lovely sight – him so big and dark and rough against her, so small and blonde and soft, his voice deep and near against her high, distant-sounding gabble.

"She'll be saying Daddy soon."

"Because she's Daddy's girl," he said to her (no one was talking to me any more), rubbing his nose against hers. "Say Daddy. Say Da. Dee. Da. Dee ..."

I watched them, the countertop at my back, not wanting to move nearer, afraid to break the spell.

"I thought I'd hang the silk screen print by the front door," I said, half to myself. "And I was thinking maybe the dresser could go in the hallway to extend the kitchen, you know?"

He didn't respond. He put Isla back on her rug and pulled out a bottle of red from the kitchen cupboard. Isla squealed, stuck out her arms, started to twirl her hands.

"You can't leave her like that," I said. "She doesn't know what's going on." I picked her up, held her facing outwards and swayed from side to side. She quietened immediately.

Mikey swigged at his wine and came over to hand me mine. Apology wrote itself into the lines on his brow. "So. Saturday's the day after tomorrow."

"Aye, I know." I kissed Isla's head.

"You won't be able to call me once I'm on the rig."

"You've told me that."

He looked around the room before settling his gaze on me. "You could go and stay at your mum and dad's."

"Ach, I'm not going to run to my mammy's every time you go offshore. Sooner I get used to it the better." I turned away, concentrated hard on making up the formula with the boiled water I'd kept from the kettle. I'd started substituting the five o'clock feed to try to get her to sleep better. I simply had to get more sleep. I was becoming tearful, incoherent sometimes. Like now.

He laid his hand on my neck, his soft, thick, warm fingers dipping beneath the rim of my t-shirt.

"I've got you a present."

As I turned to him he took a step back. He was holding a box-shaped parcel and smiling sheepishly.

"I thought you were a long time in that stable," I said.

"Ah yes. By stable I meant shops."

"You drove into town? You're kidding? My God, I didn't even hear the car." I handed the baby and the bottle to him and he swapped them for the present.

"Go on, open it." He went to sit with Isla in the crook of his arm and tipped the bottle to her mouth.

"You don't have to do that, you know. I don't need presents. What is it, choccies?" I tore off the paper. Not chocolate. Not chocolate at all. An iPhone.

"Mikey!" I gasped. "You – you can't. These cost a fortune and we've only just moved."

He grinned. "I know you miss your old one. I've set it all up for you. The camera's really good. I've taken a photo of my knob so you can look at it while I'm away."

I laughed and hit him on the arm, threw my arms around his neck and kissed his cheek. I'd dropped my old phone down the loo in Glasgow when I was changing Isla one time. I'd been making do with my old Nokia brick ever since. "Thank you."

"I've put my number in there, under Mikey Offshore." He pushed me away a little, took the phone, went into contacts and pulled up his number. "See? I can't take my mobile out there but that's the number for the rig. For emergencies only. But I'll call you. Every day." He looked into my eyes. "Are you sure you'll be all right?"

"You sound so Scouse when you say 'all right'. You sound like Ringo Starr."

"Shona?"

I waved my new phone at him. "Bring me some oil back, will you?"

We got back to the nursery twenty minutes late. I'm never late so I was panicking. But Valentina seemed to take it all in her stride. *I don't give a flying fuck*, is exactly how she put it.

Once we got inside, the lass gave me a detailed rundown on the last two and a half hours. But I was distracted by Valentina talking to the manager.

"I won't book him in right this second," she was saying. "But I'll give you a call once I've spoken with my husband ..."

"We dinna give them vegetables," the lass had moved on to nutritional policy, which sounded less than promising. "Kiddies dinna like vegetables, ken?"

I opened my mouth and closed it again. No vegetables? Childcare costs more than money, I thought. No childcare at all and you pay with your mental health. Fabulous choice.

We made our way out and onto the Great Western Road.

"So you're taking Zac back there?" I asked Valentina.

"Nah," she said. "Truth be told, Zac already goes to Little Beans up in Rosemount."

I stood up, shifted Isla up and onto my hip. "So how come you brought him for a trial?"

"Free childcare," she replied then looked away as if her attention had been caught by something. "I'm kidding. I guess I wanted to check out the competition."

I offered her a lift home but she refused, said she would walk as she lived round the corner. I sensed she had grown cool with me. I'd been a stick in the mud about the speeding, I thought, she was bored with me already. But as we made to say our goodbyes, she seemed to change her mind.

"Listen, why don't we swap numbers? I teach on Tuesdays, Wednesdays and Thursdays but I'm free the other days." She inputted my number and sent me a text – no words, only a lobster emoticon with dancing eyes, a thumbs up and a glass of wine. "Maybe we can get together on Friday? Do you rollerblade?"

"Rollerblade?"

"Sure, you know, like skating? The promenade has heaps of space and the slopes are really fun."

There was no trace of teasing in her face and I didn't want to be a drip for the second time.

"I know what rollerblading is," I said. "I haven't done it for ages, that's all. I'm not sure my rollerblades still fit or if I've even still got them. Do we push the pushchairs as we roll?"

"Oh, I chuck Zac in the sling. I figure if I fall, I can always put my arms out. Protect his head." She crossed her fingers and pulled a silly face. "Hopefully."

"Right."

Zac started to whine. Maybe he understood more than he was letting on.

"Probably a bit crazy for you though, eh?" she said. "Mrs. Sensible."

I was right – she did think I was boring. "Are you being serious?"

She held my gaze for another few seconds before leaning back, pointing at me and laughing. "Gotcha."

"Oh, very funny." I laughed and shook my head. Couldn't believe I'd fallen for it – and so easily.

That night I couldn't wait to talk to Mikey.

"I've made a friend," I told him before he'd had chance to speak.

"That was quick."

"I know!" My God, I was full of it. "She's really cool and fun and she's funny, Mikey. She actually made me laugh. And I made her laugh too. She came to the cottage!"

"That's great. Good for you."

"She's got a little boy the exact same age as Isla so they'll be able to play together."

"What did you say her name was?"

"Valentina. She's Australian. She's a bit of a hippy – long skirts, long hair and all that, you know? She said something about crystals at one point. I thought I was going to laugh but she's nice with it. Husband works in a vintage record store and she's a yoga teacher. I might do one of her classes."

"Sounds perfect," he said. "Can't wait to meet her."

My mobile buzzed. A text from Valentina. I smiled to myself. That morning I'd had no one. Now, I had my partner on the line and my friend sending me messages. Form a queue, people!

Hi Shona. Great meeting you today.
Will be in touch about Friday.
Don't forget your rollerblades! Xxx

"Shona?" said Mikey.

"Oh sorry, babe. That was a text. From her. We're getting together again on Friday."

"I knew you'd find your feet." He sounded delighted for me and I felt a rush of love. That's what love was – nothing fancy – just two people rooting like hell for one another. "You're amazing. I was only saying to Bob, he's the Texan guy ..."

But I wasn't really listening. I was too busy texting Valentina back:

Great to meet you too.
See you then. X

I tried to keep it low key. Didn't want to put a load of kisses or exclamation marks or she'd pick up how excited I was to make one friend. Then she'd think I didn't have any. I wanted to tell her I had lots of pals, but that they were in Glasgow. I wanted to tell her I was a safe bet. But friendship is pretty much like dating at first: no matter how compatible you know you are – it's a dance.

SEVEN

The next day, almost happy to be on my own, I made my way up to the beach for a stroll. With Isla snug in the sling, I crossed the car park and headed into the funfair complex. Through the leaden rollings of the bowling alley I wandered, through the thick smell of sweaty shoe leather, the bloops and bleeps of the amusement arcade, through sugary pockets of candyfloss air, outside to the seafront, the tang of chip vinegar, the chill salt breeze. The wind blew the hair from my face like freshness itself, a spring-clean for the soul.

"Come on, Isla" I said, all gung-ho, putting on an Ozzie twang. "Let's seize this day by the bollocks."

Who wanted to be friends with those women at the swimming baths anyway? I thought. See her in the park? Her loss. I'd found a friend now. I'd found Valentina. The cold wind ran like liquid down the back of my collar, the sky was still the palest grey. The North Sea pushed itself into smoked, glassy peaks, smashed them against the shore. Out, past the violent waves and the flat ocean beyond, I fancied I saw the outline of an oil platform, the silk ribbon of a gas flame rippling in the sullen sky.

"Shout hello to Daddy," I said, pushing my finger into the soft claw of Isla's tiny hand. "Shout 'haste ye back.'"

She said nothing. Babies are lovely, don't get me wrong, but sometimes, when you could do with a bit of audience participation, they're a load of rubbish.

I walked along the beach, clambered over the groynes. It felt good to climb up and over the ravaged barriers, to feel the pull of hamstring and tendon, the spread of my ribcage, the stretch of my arms.

Isla slept, rocked to a peace she had not known at night for months by the warmth of my changed mother's breasts. I wondered if my body would recover, if the track marks on my belly would ever fade. I wondered, once I'd finished, what wreckage would be left of me. In bed, Mikey told me I was as gorgeous as ever, kissed all that damage with an unhesitating mouth. I wondered if he was lying.

At the end of the beach I climbed up the last set of stone steps and found myself at a collection of tiny houses. There was an official looking sign so I went over to investigate. Footdee, the place was called, also known as Fittie. Almost on the beach itself, the settlement's only defence was a simple harbour wall. I remembered this place from a news story – it had been covered in foam from the sea a few summers back. The spume had settled on and amongst the houses like a thick, dirty snowdrift – comical as too much washing powder in a cartoon, freakish as a plague.

I skimmed the history on the sign: the houses dated back to the fourteenth century, built originally for the fishing community. The humblest of dwellings but, as with many humble things, time had ennobled them. In 1968, the whole place had been declared an Area for Conservation, thank you very much.

I stepped through an archway to walk along the path that linked all the houses together. In their shelter, I realised how strong the wind had been, how much I'd had to battle against it. The houses were narrow, some lower even than our own cottage. The pathway ran around the square and cut diagonals through the centre. In a few of the gardens, junk sculptures struck poses and little gingham curtains hung in some of the windows. A curious community, permanent and makeshift all at once and unlike any I'd seen before.

"Come on then, little one, time to go." I held on once again to Isla's wee gloved hand. As I turned to go back, I noticed an old woman sitting on one of the benches. A silk scarf was tied around her head, knotted under the chin in the old-fashioned way. Her red anorak was zipped up to her neck and her glasses were tinted. I suspected the lenses were the kind that darkened in the sun.

"Bonnie loon you have there," she said as I drew near, barely opening her mouth for the words to come out. Even I, a Scot, had a job to understand her. *Bonnie loon*, I translated for myself: nice-looking boy. She nodded, once, at Isla, who was wrapped up such that only her eyes glinted out like wet stones.

"She's a girl, actually." I sat down at the far end of the bench. "Her name's Isla."

"Isla." She gave that singular nod again, her lips pursed with what looked like disapproval. "You settlin'?" she asked, after a moment.

Settling. She was asking had I come here to live.

I told her I'd come for a walk, that I wasn't living or planning to live in Fittie. "I have just moved up here though," I said. "From Glasgow. We're away towards Banchory."

"Affa pretty out that way, is it?" She turned her body a fraction towards me and I understood that she hadn't finished with me yet. I didn't mind. I was glad of someone to talk to.

"I was having a stroll about," I offered. "Bit of an explore, like. Get to know the area."

"I'm the last of the McClouds, ken?" she replied, as if that were the logical thing to say next. "My grandfather had number seven but I stay in number three. My daughter's moved into the town now. English couple bought hers." Her lips clamped again, as if she were suddenly embittered by this Sassenach invasion, before she went on. "She has a baby, like. Dinna know fit he does."

... Don't know what he does, I translated. It was my turn to nod – gravely. The thought flashed through my mind that I should call on her, this new mother who like me was not from around here. I could introduce myself. And maybe I would have, if I hadn't met Valentina.

"A lot of incomers here now," said the lady. "Oil people, like, ken?" She spat the last word as if it offended her, though I knew by now it was simply her way of speaking. "Used to hang the fish out the front. Now they hang out their washing, even on Sundays."

"Right," I said, humouring her.

"And tourists," she said. "Come in like Peeping Toms. Japanese, Chinese, Americans." She laughed. "Aye. They were here the other day. We should charge them to look in. A pound a peep." She gave a brief laugh and stood up. "Well, I'll leave you to it."

I smiled. "Nice to meet you."

And away she went, her feet planting themselves heavily and far apart, like a man's. She disappeared into one of the low, narrow cottages I assumed was number three.

I sat for a moment before getting up and making my way back towards the top end of the beach. I tried not to look into the windows but it was difficult because the path ran so close. I saw a man in his kitchen, chopping a cucumber on a white board, images of what looked like a soap opera on someone's television, a particularly lovely taupe-coloured throw over a sofa. But as I made to look closer at the beautiful fabric, a figure passed in shadow at the far end of the room. I backed away, ashamed. What the hell was I doing? I was like the old lady had said: a Peeping Tom. Staring in at someone else's life.

Mikey called in the evening.

"You always sound so clear on these lines," I said, trying to somehow speak through a smile. "Still can't believe I can't hear the sea."

He laughed. "We don't stand on the deck for two weeks growing beards you know. We do have such a thing as an office."

"Any funnies?"

69

"Trying to think. There's an American here that's good value. Texan guy. Tells the most sexist jokes I've ever heard."

"Oh yeah? Can't wait to hear those." I prayed he couldn't hear the strain in my voice.

"So," he said. "What've you been up to?"

"I went for a walk. Along the beach. Found a really cute place called Footdee. Sorry, Fittie. Actually I'm not sure which is right. Anyway, it was a cute wee place." I waited for a moment but he didn't reply. "Hello?"

"Yeah, hi, sorry, somebody came in there. Do you mean the place at the beach?"

"That's what I said. It's amazing. Dinky. Kind of boho, you know? We should go when you get back."

"Actually, I know that place. I mean, I've heard of it. They were talking about it the other day at work. They don't like people going there. Apparently everyone goes round looking in their windows."

"I suppose so." I remembered the figure darting out of sight, the old lady and her talk of Peeping Toms. "Maybe not then."

He didn't say anything in reply so I carried on chatting about nothing, trying to shake off what I can only describe as mild devastation, if that makes sense. I'd so wanted to tell him about that place, about my discovery of it. I'd wanted him to know I'd been out and about, not stuck at home with my chin on the floor. I'd wanted him to be proud of me for these small things. Would it always be like this when he was offshore? Would we no longer fit? This not fitting had something to do with only having one sense to work with, I thought. I wanted all five senses, all the time. Two weeks in four, we would have to manage with one sense alone. Two weeks in four, that was half the time. Half our lives.

That night, I'd got Isla to bed, I'd walked along the landing and switched on the bathroom light when, with a popping sound, the power failed. The cottage went black. I had never known darkness like it. No streetlights shone in through the windows; the orange halo that glowed over the city was miles away. In the country, the darkness is solid. It is tangible. But I stayed calm – maybe because actual catastrophe is better than the dread of the unnamed threat. I had made sure to find the fuse box before Mikey went away – it was under the stairs – I had to get to it without hurting myself. Easier said than done when you can't see the hand in front of your face.

I knew there was a light on my phone. Where had I left it? Mikey had told me always to bring it with me, in case of emergencies, and so it would still be in my bag because I hadn't taken it out since my trip to Fittie. My bag would be on one of the hooks by the door or over the end of the bannister. I figured the safest way to the top of the stairs, if I was going to avoid falling down them, was on my hands and knees.

I crawled, feeling for and finding the edge of the stairwell. I shifted myself onto my bottom and shuffled down the stairs one at a time. It was overly cautious, I know, especially for someone like me. I'd been a real handful in my youth. I lose count of the times I've woken up with no idea how I'd got home, all the dangerous situations I put myself in growing up – playing on railway tracks, hiding in the sidings eating Matchmakers we'd stolen from the corner shop, out in feral packs in the evenings with boys who sprayed their names on the precinct walls, who threw eggs at buses, bricks at street lamps. I had thrilled at the sound of breaking glass as much as the next teenager. But here was another thing that parenthood had changed in me. My own memories, which had once made me laugh, now made my blood run cold. I blanched at the thought of Isla doing what I had done. And if I looked after myself now, if I worked hard to make a home, shuffled at a snail's pace down these stairs, it was because she needed me to do those things, to be this person, to stay safe.

I found my bag on the bannister and used the phone to find the fuse box. Sure enough, one of the fuses had tripped. One quick flick and the hum of electricity returned, the lamp in the living room lit up. The digital clock on the hallway window ledge flashed zeros. I would be better-prepared next time, I thought. I needed to think about what I'd do if the problem was not one I alone could fix – if the boiler packed up for example. I would buy more candles, I decided, and make oil lamps. Belt and braces.

On the Wednesday or Thursday, I think it was, my mum and dad came up for the day. They couldn't believe the place.

"Oh, Shona," my mum kept saying. "I can't believe it. It's like something off the television."

Dad helped fix the back door where it was sticking; Mum helped me unpack the rest of the upstairs. I wanted everything to be sorted for Mikey getting back on the Saturday. I wanted it all to be perfect.

On Friday, Valentina and I took the babies to the swimming baths. She was slimmer than me and I found myself carrying Isla strategically in front of my belly. In the water, we whirled our babies around while they gurned at the splashes in dopey delight.

I didn't look at the other mothers that day. I didn't notice them.

As we changed, Valentina called over the cubicle wall. "Hey, Shona. Wanna grab some lunch and take it back to your place?"

She loved that cottage, couldn't get enough of it. She'd even driven out to pick me up in her old red Toyota, so while she hovered outside the store, I ran in to buy the smoked salmon and bagels she insisted on having. When I came back I could see she looked peeved.

"Bloody policeman tried to give me a ticket for being on the double yellows," she said as soon as I got in. "Bloody cheek."

"You should have moved on," I said. "You could have texted, I'd have come and found you."

"Don't worry, I sweet-talked him. He was putty in my hands."

"What? He let you off?"

"I might have flirted a little. I might have said I'd meet him for a drink." She started the engine. "I even took his number – check that for commitment, babe. You can have it if you want."

"Of course you did," I said archly, not believing a word of it.

Only, when I got out of the car, a torn piece of white card floated into the footwell. I picked it up. *John Duggan*, with a mobile phone number below. I threw it down, pretended I hadn't seen.

EIGHT

Back at the cottage, Valentina opened the fridge and pulled out the bottle of Sancerre I'd bought for Mikey's homecoming.

"This OK to drink?" she asked. But she was already screwing off the cap. And she had already taken off her coat and draped her raspberry-coloured scarf over the back of the chair as she had the first time. That was her: at home, right from the start.

"Sure," I said, not wishing to appear mean.

I dragged the travel cot from the stable and we set the babies up in there with some toys. She poured two large glasses, as if it were no more than plonk, and handed me one.

"I could get used to this," she said. "Up yours, sister."

We chinked glasses.

"I thought yoga teachers only drank water from mountain springs," I said. "Ate mung beans, drank soya milk, that type of thing."

She shook her head. "That's bollocks. I'd smoke too if I could. Don't suppose you have any dope, do you?"

I laughed. "Good grief, no. What do you think this is, a crack den?"

She smiled, pushed her thick auburn hair back from her face before shaking it out again. She took another long gulp of wine. "Listen, Shona, how would you feel about having Zac, just for an hour after lunch?"

"Sure. No problem."

"I have this private yoga session booked with a client. I usually take Zac but he can be such a pain and I'll be quicker if I go on my own. You don't mind, do you?"

"Of course not."

"I can have Isla another time, no worries," she said. "But thanks, you're a mate."

"To mates." I held up my glass. "Or as we say, pals."

As if pleasantly surprised, she smiled again, showing all those white sharkish teeth. She picked up her glass. "To pals."

At half past one, she announced she was late, that she had to go. She pulled her bag from the chair, kissed Zac on the head and rushed out. She'd drunk two large glasses of wine to my one; the bottle was two thirds empty. I knew she'd be over the limit, naughty girl. And how the hell she was going to teach yoga, I could not fathom. She was made of steelier stuff than me.

Once she'd gone, I put Zac in Isla's buggy and Isla in her pram and took them both into the garden. I spent a good fifteen minutes pushing both back and to, back and to, until I got them to sleep. Arms aching and back aching, I left the back door open and came inside to make a cup of tea. I was thirsty, fuzzy-headed after the lunchtime drink, already wishing I'd stuck to water.

The babies only slept for half an hour. When they awoke, I got a pit in my stomach wondering how I was going to keep them both calm. When I next looked at the clock I saw it was 2:30pm. Thank goodness. Valentina wouldn't be long.

At three o'clock, I wondered about texting to see where she'd got to. I left it, worried about coming across as nagging or uncool. She was only half an hour late after all – I calculated that the session was probably an hour and, adding on journey time, it was no wonder it had got to this time. At half past three I picked up my phone and wrote:

Are you OK? S x

I read the text and deleted it. The Brig O'Dee could get quite snarled up with traffic at certain times of day. The babies were watching a DVD now and seemed calm

75

enough. But for how long was anyone's guess. I still had the pit in my stomach.

At four o'clock I rewrote the text:

Everything fine here don't worry just wondering if you're on your way back. S xxx

Less direct. Friendly but still waving a flag – help. I sent it.

Zac began to fret. I picked him up – Christ he was heavy, it was like lifting a pig! I lugged him onto my hip, which made Isla cry. I picked her up too and put her on the other hip and lurched around the house like Quasimodo after a night on the town. By now I was pissed off. Where the hell was she? I'd give her a piece of my mind when she got here.

Anger turned to worry. She'd had two large glasses of wine. She hadn't replied to my text. What if she'd driven like she'd wanted me to the other day, tried to set the land speed record on the South Deeside Road and crashed? I didn't know where she lived, what her home number was. I didn't even know her last name. All I knew was that she was married to a man named Red who worked in a vintage record store.

Zac's face changed from pale to dark pink, a look of terrible concentration. I knew that look. Oh, and I knew that smell.

I carried both babies upstairs and manoeuvred Zac onto the changing table but lost balance and cracked my shoulder against the wall. I righted myself, ripped open the nappy and gasped. Ditch-water brown spray ran down his thighs, legs, up his back, all over his vest, his trousers. I coughed, swore, held my breath. I stripped him, cleaned his body as best I could. He was so much bigger than Isla, legs like hams, gut like a fridge-freezer.

Sat on the floor, Isla got louder, a desperate, abandoned sound. My hair fell into my eyes, stuck to the sweat on my forehead. I couldn't push it out of the way – my fingers were covered in shit. Still swearing like a sailor, I flattened one of Isla's nappies on the table. With my elbow, I held the nappy down, plonked Zac on top and pulled the tabs across. They stopped just short of one another – the nappy was too bloody small. Zac stared up at me, his big brown eyes unblinking.

"Where's your mummy? Eh?" I said in a sing-song voice. "Where's she gone? Where the bloody hell has your motherfucking bastard mother gone? Where? Eh?"

He smiled – obviously appreciating the quality swearing.

I pulled hard on the tabs, found a millimetre of connecting Velcro to take the strain. From Isla's chest of drawers, I found a vest, some grey jogging bottoms. But they were all, all of them, too small. Of course they were. Zac's birthday was the 27th February, only a week after Isla's, but I guessed, being a boy, he was thicker set.

I put him on the floor, naked apart from a too-small nappy: a mini Sumo wrestler, black hair, round belly and wildly chubby legs. Finally, I found an outfit, aged one, from my Aunty Moira on my mother's side: a baby pink sweatsuit with *Daddy's Girl* on the front in sequin letters. My Aunty Moira has a good heart, don't get me wrong, but her taste leaves a lot to be desired.

I wrestled Zac into the jogging ensemble. He looked ridiculous – but he was clean.

Still sweating, I picked up Isla. Her nappy was so wet that when I dropped it to the floor it landed with the thud of a dead animal.

All done, I scooped up both babies and shuffled downstairs on my bottom. I laid both kids on the rug to have a kick but Isla started whining straight away. I stretched out my back, hands to my kidneys, groaning like an old lady.

Never mind Valentina, I felt like I'd been in a road accident.

By five o'clock, I had sung so many nursery rhymes my voice was hoarse. I was bone-tired, aching and livid. Valentina had said one hour. She had taken more than three. This was an abuse of my generosity, no question about it. I would tell her so when she got here. I would not let myself get walked over in this way by anybody, not even her.

The doorbell went. Finally. I was away to open the door when Valentina stepped into the hallway. I was fired up to give her a row but her appearance caught me off-guard. Her hair was different – straighter. She'd redone her eye make-up too, I thought – and was that nail polish on her fingernails? She smelt of soap, as if she'd had a shower. All the things I'd had stored up to say evaporated.

"Hi there." She shook her head, her hair falling around her shoulders, catching the light, falling just so. She looked like Klimt's *Judith*. She looked relaxed on some deep, molecular level. I really should try yoga, I thought.

"You could have texted," I said.

"I left the damn phone in the car. I thought it'd be quicker to get on and get here."

"What happened?"

"Nothing." She looked at me in that very direct way she had, no arms crossed, no doubt at all in her body: a wordless, flagrant challenge.

"Nothing?"

"I underestimated the timings, that's all."

I waited for an apology. It didn't come.

"Have you washed your hair?" I asked.

"I always take a shower after a session. Especially Ashtanga. It's so ... vigorous." She was still staring at me, impassive, and I realised I'd seen her do this before, in the nursery.

"Zac did the mother of all poos." I indicated the living room with my head. "It went everywhere. I had to change him. It was a nightmare, to be honest."

"Oh God," she said, laughing. "He does whoppers. It's gross."

"Listen," I said. "If you're going to be longer than you say you need to let me know, OK?"

She saluted me with a smirk. "Won't happen again, officer. Didn't realise you were so touchy about it."

She strode into the living room and cooed in a baby voice: *Zac. Zackeeee. Zackee, angel.* I followed her to the door. *Please take him home,* I wanted to say. *Please go. I am too exhausted to be cross, too weary to know what just happened, what I feel about it.*

"I've put his other things in the wash," I said instead. "I'll give them to you next time. I know he looks like Kim Kardashian in her leisure wear but that was all that fit."

"Thanks," she said, turning to me. "You're so sweet."

"I'm away to give Isla her tea now so –"

"Wow, Shona," she said. "You really don't have to do that."

"Oh," I said. "I didn't mean ..."

"But I guess Red's not home till late on Fridays so that'll save me cooking two dinners." Out of nowhere, she leant toward me and stroked my cheek. "You have lovely skin," she said, before heading back into the living room. Through the open door I watched her sit, then lie on the sofa, Zac on her belly. "You're amazing, Shona," she called through. "Has anyone ever told you that? Absolutely amazing."

The next day, Saturday, the day of Mikey's return, I woke early as usual to Isla crying. But this day was different. I didn't groan, nor did my legs ache with deep fatigue. I felt OK. I felt light. I nipped out and bought scrummy things for tea and replaced the bottle of Sancerre that Valentina had drunk.

When I got back, I put my *Disclosure* CD on loud and burst into action cleaning the house. Honestly, it was like the 1950s, getting ready for a husband to come home from work – house perfect, wife perfect, baby perfect. But I enjoyed it despite all that, in a weird, postmodern, ironic way. I think.

At midday I heard the taxi from the kitchen. My stomach flipped over.

I ran to the door, as I'd imagined doing all week, flung it open and stepped out.

"Hey stranger," I called out.

He looked up, gave me a quick wave and continued to count cash for the driver, smiling and chatting in that way he had. I waited, hopping from foot to foot. I waited for him to come and fold me into his arms.

He patted the roof of the cab, picked up his kitbag and walked towards me with it dangling over his shoulder. Behind him, the taxi drove down the lane, out of sight. Anticipation built in my belly. His smile was different, I thought, almost bashful, his chin dark with stubble.

On the front step, he dropped his bag and opened his arms. "Look who's here."

"You!" I fell into him and he held me, buried his face in my hair.

"You smell like home," he said, his hold tightening.

We stayed there, neither of us able to move.

After a long moment, I pulled him into the house. "Isla's asleep." Up the stairs, into the bedroom.

He pushed me back onto the bed, lifted my t-shirt and plunged his warm face into my belly.

"Hurry," I said. "We don't have long."

He unfastened my jeans, pulled my underwear off with them. "I won't need long."

Isla started to cry as we fell back onto the pillows.

"Maybe you should put your bag down now," I said.

"I think it's still on the step. It might still be in mid-air." He kissed me, quickly, like a full stop after a lovely sentence and met my gaze with his. "That wasn't a very polite hello, was it?"

I rolled him onto his back, climbed on top of him, pinned him down by the shoulders. "Good afternoon, Mr. Quinn. How are you this fine day? I must say, you're looking affa fine. How's that for polite?"

"Spoken like a duchess."

"Affa fine means really well around these parts, don't you know."

The volume of Isla's cries grew like some out of control wah-wah pedal.

I huffed. "She's jealous I'm getting all the attention." I climbed off him and pulled on his t-shirt, grabbed my pants from the floor and waltzed out with them on my head.

In the nursery, Isla had reached crimson-faced fury, her tiny knuckles white against the cot rungs. I put my pants onto the correct part of my anatomy and reached out to her. As soon as I touched her she released her grip on the cot. I cradled her against my chest and shushed her. In the palm of my hand, her head still fitted: damp, soft and warm. She quieted as quickly as if I'd switched her to mute. I understood her. Sometimes, all it took was to be held.

Back in the bedroom, Mikey had propped himself up against the end of the bed and was buckling up his belt. A lick of black hair fell over his forehead. He blew at it, flicked back his head when it refused to behave. At the sight of us, he grinned and reached out. "Come here, baby girl!"

Isla squealed, mirroring his dark outstretched arms with her own. I passed her over and climbed up after her onto the bed. All three of us nuzzled into one another, Isla cooing and giggling against the tickle of Mikey's stubble. I thought I would cry with happiness. Mikey was home. We were a family. Not half a family now, but a whole.

"I'm parched," he said after a moment.

"I'll make some tea. You stay here with Isla."

I leapt off the bed, pulled on my jeans and ran down to the kitchen. As the kettle boiled I heard the creak of stair under foot. Mikey appeared, Isla in one arm, the other on the bannister. Like me, I thought, being super careful. At the bottom of the stairs he stopped, the way a person does when they hear a sudden, odd noise or smell burning.

"You all right?" I called from the kitchen.

"Yeah." He bent to pick up his coat from the floor, made to hang it up and stopped dead – again. "Whose is that scarf? Is it new?"

I followed his gaze to the coat hooks and laughed. "Don't worry, I've not been out spending. It's Valentina's."

"Oh." He hung up his coat, crossed the hallway with Isla and sat down with her at the wee table at the mouth of the kitchen area.

"At least it's not a man's scarf," I joked, setting down the two mugs of tea. "I hid that one."

He smiled and kissed Isla – one two three four five times. Both of them stared at me then and – for the briefest moment – I had a vision of myself on an iceberg, floating away, helpless. Tears pricked in my eyes, a fist of nameless anxiety clenched in my stomach. I turned away, to hide my face. This offshore business would, I realised, take a long time to get used to.

NINE

The next morning, Sunday, Mikey suggested we go out to lunch at a country pub he'd heard about while he was on the rig. With Isla in the sling on Mikey's chest, we walked straight out of our front door and into dense woodland. June's summer light filtered through the leaves, the air fresh on our faces. After ten minutes or so, we emerged into a field of rapeseed, acid-yellow, the sun creamy by comparison, outshone. We followed the field's edge up to the short length of road that led us to the Deeside Tavern.

Inside, red patterned rugs lay over stone floors, the furniture mahogany, solid, old – plaid cushions on the seats. In the hearth, where in winter no doubt they would have a fire, fat white cathedral candles burned with shallow flames.

We were shown to a table next to a couple who looked about fifty or so. Her greying hair was set in a tight curled style that was too old for her, his face was an angry red, veins broken with high living.

I took Isla to the Ladies' to change her. By the time I got back, Mikey had struck up a conversation with the couple. He always did this, everywhere he went, but today I didn't want him to talk to them – or to anyone for that matter.

The guy was telling Mikey he was an OIM.

"What's an OIM again?" I asked, sitting down.

"The big boss," said Mikey, winking at the couple, grinning, leaning forward.

"Offshore Installation Manager," added the man's wife with a pinched smile.

"Who do you work for?" I asked her husband.

"Maple Energy, for my sins," he said, placing one hand on his chest and blinking fast as if he had grit in his eyes.

"Mikey works for Maple, don't you Mikey?" I turned to Mikey, who was drinking his beer like a man dying of thirst.

The man brightened, sat upright. "Right you are, young man! Onshore or offshore?"

Mikey coughed into his hand – served him right for drinking his beer so fast. "Off. Which platform are you?"

"Fern, for my sins."

"You're on Fern, aren't you Mikey?" I said.

"Bracken," said Mikey, poking his thumb over his shoulder at me. "Honestly. As long as the money comes in, eh?"

"I'm sure you said Fern," I said. "I must've misheard." I winked at the man. "As long as I bring up the children and get the dinner on, eh?"

Mikey turned to me. "I wrote it down on that piece of card for you. With the number."

"Did you now? What, while I was changing Isla or hanging out your boxers?"

"That's Aberdeen for you," the guy interrupted, his chin puckering. "Can't fart at one end without someone smelling it at the other."

"Trevor!" His wife shook her head in disgust while I had a good belly laugh. I had not expected him to say that. "If you're an oil man," she said to Mikey, "you and your wife should join Kippie Lodge."

"What's that?" I asked.

Studiously avoiding me and her husband, the woman explained to Mikey with the air of someone in the possession of classified information she was, in her benevolence, prepared to share, "Oh, they have everything: a golf course, a café, a pool, you name it. You have your gym facilities, your classes, your yoga, etcetera."

"I have a friend teaches yoga," I said. "Valentina. I wonder if she does any classes there."

Still not looking at me, the woman nodded to Isla, who was on my lap, propped up in my arms. "You could take

84

the wee one for a swim when she's older. Away from, you know ..." she rolled her hand like the queen on a drive by.

"From?" I said.

"Crowds, you know. It's quieter there, more exclusive."

"I like a big pool," I said. "I like crowds."

Their food arrived, thank God. To my relief, Mikey bid them a *bon appetit* and we ceased our conversation. Our own lunches came soon after: mine, roast chicken dinner, Mikey, roast beef with all the trimmings. Starving after our walk, we tucked in. When the couple left, the guy slipped his card onto our table on the way past and gave me a wink. His wife gave a begrudging smile and walked out ahead of him.

"The oil industry's a village," I said, nodding after them.

"Certainly seems like it."

"That's got to be a good thing, surely?"

He drained his pint, replaced the glass on the table with a gasp. "Don't call me Shirley."

In the clean light, we made our way back across the countryside. Cheek to Mikey's chest, Isla dozed off in her sling. Our faces pinked, our hair ruffled. As we walked, I imitated the couple in the pub, to make Mikey laugh.

"I'm the big fat fascist boss, for my sins," I said, putting my hand to my chest and blinking over and over, then, "and you can take your rich children to our exclusive pool. That way, they don't have to swim with any of the commoners." I kept my mouth as tight as a purse, rolling my hand as she had done. "Then they can eat their caviar in the café-ey-ey without having their appetite ruined by the sight of paupers, don't you know." I returned to myself. "I should take her to where I grew up," I said. "There were no yoga classes there, I can tell you."

"Don't be so harsh."

"Oh, come on. These people assume that money and exclusivity's what everyone wants, don't they? They assume it's everyone's dream."

"These people. Listen to yourself, Shona. You don't even know anyone rich." He rolled his eyes. "Honestly, you don't half come out with some inverted snobbery bullshit sometimes."

Thinking about that conversation now, it sounds like we were arguing, but we weren't. It was no more than craic – at least, that was what I thought it was.

It was late afternoon by the time we got back. Mikey announced he was going to Isla's room to put up the shelves I'd bought for her bits and pieces. Two minutes later, headphones clamped to his head and pocket radio in his hand, he gave me a kiss and sailed upstairs. I knew he'd be ages – he always listened to the sport when he had a chore to do and somehow the chores always took the same length of time as whatever game happened to be on.

Left to myself, I decided to make oil lamps. I'd been meaning to make them since the fuse tripped but hadn't got around to it. Maybe with Mikey back, the cottage felt more like a home and maybe for this reason I found myself wanting to do something a real homemaker would do – something responsible and protective, something from my own childhood I wanted to bring to Isla's. We'd always made oil lamps when I was a kid. Me and my three brothers and my mum and my dad used to sit round their dancing flames in our sleeping bags, telling stories, jokes, sharing gossip. Looking back, I suppose that was to save on bills but I never felt that – it was something we did for fun. My dad taught us how to make them. He made the wicks from strips of old cloth. The bodies we made from empty jam jars.

I set out everything I needed on the little table, including Isla in her car seat, her archway mobile over the top. Fists in wee bunches, she stared at the mirrors and coloured pendants, placid enough for now.

"Now see, I used to do this with my brothers," I told her. "That's your uncle Gus, your uncle Craigie and wee

Davie." I screwed the lid tightly onto one of the empty jars I'd kept back from the jam then cast about for something to make the holes. Ah. Mikey had my drill. I dashed upstairs. Mikey's voice reached me before I got to him. Not the words but the tone: the accelerating rhythm and volume of irritation, as if he were arguing. I crossed the landing, stood outside the bedroom door.

"You knew the deal when we moved here," he was saying, his voice tense. "It's a bit late to start moaning about it now."

Any longer and I would be eavesdropping. I coughed and pushed the door a little way open.

"Wait," he said, placing his hand over the mouthpiece. His eyes were black – whoever it was had got under his skin, all right. I grabbed the drill and held it up.

He nodded: yes, take it, but he was still grim of face. "Mum," he mouthed and rolled his eyes, pointed to the receiver and made to push the door closed.

I gave him the thumbs up and backed out of the room. I'd never seen him so angry with his mother. If anything, his mother could do no wrong. But then, I hadn't seen much of his folks. Even though Mikey and I had a house and a child together, we'd been together such a short time. From what I'd overheard, it sounded like the argument had something to do with us moving here. She was upset, most probably, that we had settled so far away. Liverpool was a good six-hour drive away from here. And if they were flying in from Malaga, where they had their villa, they'd now have to get a connecting flight. Aberdeen was a long way from her Bonnie Prince Michael right enough.

I returned to the kitchen and, while Isla looked on, I made a dent in the jar lid with the bradawl then drilled a hole in the centre for the wick.

"Now," I said to Isla. "Thing about kerosene lamps is you have to vent them properly." I rummaged in the cutlery drawer and found the cantilevered bottle opener, which worked a dream. I held up the jar so Isla could see the air holes, let her touch the ends of her fingers to the jar. "If you don't make these wee holes, the pressure builds, see? If the hot air can't get out, it has to force itself through here." I pointed to the central hole I'd made for the wick. "So what happens then is, the flame gets longer and longer and ..." I took the jar from her and held it up, mimed an explosion with my hands. "Boom!"

After Isla went to bed, around ten, we toasted teacakes – we'd been too full for supper – and ate them with butter. I lit the oil lamps and put them on the mantelpiece, turned off the overhead light and went to lie on the sofa with my feet in Mikey's lap.

"So – what did your mum have to say?"

He took my foot in his hands and ran his thumb firmly up the middle of the sole. "She'll be fine." He twiddled my toes in his fingers one by one.

"They can come and stay whenever."

He shrugged, clearly not in the mood to talk about it.

"We all love you too much, you see," I said after a moment. "We all want a piece of you."

He continued to rub my feet, staring into the fire. We were so comfortable together, I thought. We could speak or not speak, it was the same. I watched him in silence. In his eyes, the flames danced about, small and distant as a gas flare in the cold North Sea.

Monday morning Isla woke at six. I dragged myself out of bed and took her downstairs so as not to wake Mikey. I changed her, fed her, lay on the sofa with her on my stomach and tried to close my stinging eyes for a few minutes longer.

At seven thirty, I heard him on the stairs. I forced myself up and went with Isla on my hip to find him in the hallway dressed in his shirt and tie.

"Where're you going all poshed up?" I asked him. "I was going to give you a long lie."

He stuck out his bottom lip, frowned – a bemused expression. "I'm going to work."

"What?"

He crossed over to the kettle, shook it. "I'm going into the office."

There was no sign of mischief, no giveaway upturn at the corner of his mouth. I shifted Isla around to my other hip. "But this is your two weeks off."

"Off the rig, yes." He plopped a teabag into his favourite mug, the big black one with the words *But You May Call Me Lord* written in white on the outside. Into it, he poured the boiling water. "But I've still got to go into the office haven't I?"

I stood and gaped, one step short of saying "but ... but" over and over like they do on the television. He was still going about the kitchen, grabbing cereal, sitting himself down, getting on with his breakfast. He looked up, raised his eyebrows. "Aren't you having breakfast?"

"I haven't had the chance."

He shovelled a spoonful of wheat flakes into his mouth. I heard the workings of his teeth and tongue, the crushing of the flakes against the roof of his mouth: crunch crunch crunch.

"You were off before you went," I said. "You were here."

"Yes. I booked the time off. I've started the rotation now. That's it."

"I thought when you said you'd be off, you'd be off as in off work," I said, my voice getting louder despite my attempts to stay calm. "As in – with me. I assumed ... I've been looking forward to it for two weeks. Us being together is all that's kept me going. It's all that's kept me sane. How did we not talk about this?"

His spoon lolled in his hand. "Shona, if I was a roughneck, yes, I'd be at home now. But I'm not, am I?" He took another spoon of flakes and held it below his clean-shaven chin. "It's not the same for people like me, Shone." In went the flakes: crunch crunch crunch.

"People like you?" I felt my eyes fill. "Why, are you special in some way?"

"I mean, people who have a career rather than a – you know, job job."

"A job job? Can't say I'm familiar with that term."

Isla started to fret. I bounced her about, swayed from side to side.

"Don't be like that, Shone," he said.

"I'm not being like anything. I was going to take you to the beach today. I thought we could maybe go to Ballater or somewhere another day – for a picnic or something. Or Balmedie Beach again, go rolling down the dunes. I was going to take you to the woods where Valentina took me, or anywhere, to do anything, I don't care what we do. But we're not going to do any of that, are we? I'm going to be on my own." I started to cry. "All day. Again. And again and again and again. Because what you're telling me is, this is my life."

He lifted his bowl, drained the milk into his mouth.

"Don't drink the milk from the bowl," I shouted. "It's disgusting."

Frightened by my shouting, Isla began to cry.

Mikey was putting on his coat. "Listen, I know you're upset but I can't talk about it now. Things will calm down, I promise, but I have to show the right attitude. Look, I really do have to go to work. We'll talk later, OK?" He made to pull me and Isla towards him. "Come on," he said. "My girls."

I shrugged him off, pushed him away. "No. You don't get to say that."

"Shona, I'm going to work now." His voice was firm, entirely without emotion. "I'm going to go into the office to earn money for us to live on. I have to do that, it's my job. I'll be back later and we'll talk about it then, OK?" He turned and began to make his way out of the cottage.

"No, it's not OK," I said, following him. "It's pretty far from OK, actually."

He opened the front door, stepped through and shut it behind him before I got there. I stood, Isla in my arms, the closed door in my face like a slap. A minute later I heard the car start up, drive off.

I couldn't scream or shout. I didn't want to frighten the baby any more than I had done already. I couldn't do anything at all except stand there facing my own closed front door, the taste of salt from my own pathetic tears leaking into my mouth. I had no idea what had just happened, only that in the space of one conversation my life had become one I had not chosen.

I went back through the house and sat on the sofa.

"It's OK, Isla," I said, trying to make the words come out in a sing-song. "Mummy's a bit upset. Mummies get upset sometimes and when they do they have a little cry and it doesn't mean anything."

Isla stopped crying. She had no idea what she'd been crying about. I put her on the floor under her mirror mobile and scrolled through my phone until I found Jeanie's number. My thumb hovered over the top. *Oh, Jeanie, it's all been a mistake*, I imagined myself saying. What the hell have I done?

My phone told me it was 8:15am. I couldn't call anyone. Not now. I would have to wait until a socially acceptable time and then – what? What the hell would I say?

I figured it was unfair to call Jeanie and dump on her – she was all the way in Glasgow, not a lot she could do about it. And the truth is, I felt stupid. What kind of journalist doesn't get the facts straight before she commits to the story? What kind of dumb hack doesn't even know for sure which platform her husband works on? One so sleep-deprived, one so wrapped up in babies and breastfeeding and all that goo that she can no longer function as an intelligent human being – that kind. Oh God, oh God, what had happened to me?

I was still sitting in a daze when Valentina called. It was half past eight. "Hey babe, this is your early morning wake up call. What're we up to later?"

I couldn't believe she'd called me when I needed her to, as if she'd picked up on my hurt through some psychic connection.

"Oh, Val," I said. "You'll never guess what's happened ..."

I sobbed down the phone at her like I'd known her for years.

"I can't believe I didn't realise that's what he meant," I managed to say, blowing my nose on a piece of kitchen roll. "It's like my brain has turned to mince. I don't take things in you know? And I thought the big advantage of this two on, two off deal was that he'd have all that extra time with us, doing family stuff. To make up for it. I would never have moved here for this."

"Struth," she said. "I can't believe he wasn't clear about that with you." Usually jokey and bright, she sounded sober – with shock – and I was gratified by that.

"And he's taken the car. How am I supposed to get around? I'm stuck, Valentina. All I can see is fields and trees and I've got no one to talk to and no way of getting out!"

"Do you think he deceived you intentionally?"

I hadn't thought about that – but now I did. "I don't know. Do you think he would do that?"

I heard her sigh, as if she was blowing out smoke from a cigarette. "I think men are capable of anything, Shona. They fix on what they want and they do it and to hell with anyone else."

"It's such a ... such a fait accompli. It's so ... I feel so ... helpless, you know? It's not like I can just move back to Glasgow now, is it?"

"You can do what you want, Shona. Don't let anyone tell you different. Why not try sending him to Coventry? Men hate that."

"Everyone hates that and it's – it's childish." I couldn't shake the thought of Mikey deliberately hiding the facts from me, hoodwinking me into living the life he wanted for no better reason than him wanting it. But his speciality was his power of persuasion, I thought, not his ability to lie.

"You could go back to your folks'," Valentina said. "Pack up and go stay with them for a few days. You should let him know you won't let him walk all over you."

I sniffed. The shaking sobs died down, my tears were drying, sticky. "I've never done anything like that. I usually stand my ground, have a good fight, you know? I don't run away."

"True that." She laughed. "But this isn't running away, is it? This is a protest, it's much more powerful. And I tell you what, if Red tips his reefer butts in the plant pot one more time I'll be coming with you."

I laughed. After a moment, I said, "He wouldn't know what'd hit him, would he?"

"Think about it. Really. Take action. If you act like a carpet, they will walk all over you. And they won't bother taking off their shoes. A girl needs bollocks in this life."

"You're right."

"I'm calling it the way I see it," she said. "Tell me to sling my hook if you want but I'm only being honest."

"No," I said. "No, I appreciate it."

That heavy exhalation again. I wanted to ask if she was smoking. But she couldn't be. She was a yoga teacher.

"Listen," she said. "I'm off today so I could come pick you up and take you to the station."

"You'd do that? For me?"

"Of course. No question."

"Thanks," I said. "You're a real pal."

TEN

Fifteen minutes later, I was sitting on the bed with my holdall on my lap. I had been so definite but now I was no longer sure. A horrid, stale feeling had lodged itself inside me, a feeling with its own sour taste, like a hangover. All this fury would make me ill, I knew. I didn't want it, I didn't want any of it – it was a poison I had to expel. But no matter how I looked at it, the only conclusion I could come up with was that Mikey had brought me here under false pretences. And now he expected me to live alone, a shadow in the darkness while he went about in the light. A housekeeper. A maid. For him, nothing had changed. For me, nothing was the same.

I went downstairs and began to clear away the plates and cups from breakfast. Other things, little things that had irritated me over the time we'd been together, surfaced. I remembered the first time I met him: he'd told me to have whisky when what I'd wanted was wine. When I moved in with him, he had already bought the flat he wanted – his parents had paid but he had chosen. I had moved into his choice. Once when he'd left his underwear on the bathroom floor I'd asked him, nicely, to put it in the wash basket.

"Don't," he'd said, so kindly, so softly. "Let's not become that. Not us."

And I had not known how to respond. He'd made me feel like something prosaic and sad. I had understood, had thought I understood that for me to ask him to do this was to reduce our relationship to something mediocre, something no better than everyone else had.

"OK," I'd said, still doped up on love, on sex. "I'm sorry."

And later, I'd picked up his dirty underwear and put it in the wash basket – since that was the only way to make our relationship special.

Outside, a car horn toot-tooted. Valentina. I ran to the living room window. The roof of her beaten up Toyota was drawn back and her red hair shone in the rare Aberdeen sun. She was wearing white-rimmed fifties style sunglasses, a cream mack and a bright blue silk scarf. My kookie, hippy friend.

Waving, I made my way with Isla to the car. On the back seat, the upholstery was solid, cracked with dried food. I had to wrestle with the clip on the seatbelt. The bloody thing wouldn't fasten. Valentina was already making her way back with the rest of my stuff.

"I'm sorry," I said. "I can't get this to clip in."

"I told you, it's a total bastard. Wait, let me throw this in the trunk."

And then it occurred to me: Zac wasn't there.

"Where's Zac?" I asked her.

"Red's got him."

"Isn't he at work?"

"He's in retail, remember? He's got to work this weekend so he gets today in lieu."

"Oh no. I've spoiled your family day."

"Not at all." She fastened the clip, gave me a kiss on the cheek then made her way back round to the driver's seat.

I got in next to her and pushed my face into my hands. "What am I doing?"

"The right thing." She started the engine. "It might seem dramatic but it'll make him think twice about steamrollering you again. When I left Zac, did I tell Red where I was going, when I'd be back? No. None of his goddamn business. I told him I needed him to look after his son, end of. I'm going into town for a coffee after I've dropped you. On my own."

I drew my hands down my face and looked at her. She'd pushed her sunglasses onto her head and was smiling at me.

I knew how drawn and stressed I must look. She, however, looked radiant.

"Trust me," she said, shaking her head. "The more you give, the more they'll take, without ever volunteering anything in return. They're not like us, Shona. They're not like women."

"I think maybe I should stay and hear what he has to say before I go raving off like this."

"You will hear what he has to say." She reversed the car at high speed around the edge of the picket fence and, with a spray of gravel, revved forward into the lane. "But you'll hear it from a position of power."

It was weird being back in Glasgow – like seeing it for the first time. My city seemed so built up, which of course it is, but living in the open space of the country had given me a new perspective. The sandstone was, I have to say, a welcome break from all that granite, the matt terracotta tenements flattened to card by an overcast sky. We crossed the Clyde, over into Govan. No granite here either, no glittering rock. Here, nothing would've glittered, even if the sun had come out. Nothing was claiming to be gold.

I got the taxi to drop me on the Govan Road. I didn't want my mum to see me pulling up in a cab. With Isla's car seat clipped into in the buggy base, I walked the rest of the way to Southcroft Street.

Davie let me in at the main door, barefoot, scant black hair sticking up all over the place. He wore only a thin white t-shirt and scruffy jogging bottoms over his skinny white frame. He was grinning as if he found the sight of me funny. "What are you doing here?"

I tipped up the buggy to negotiate the front step. "Great to see you too, brother dear."

He stepped back and held open the door asking how long I planned to stay.

"Hold on a second," I said. "Can I no' get in the door first?"

The hallway for the flats seemed smaller, awkward with the buggy – the faint whiff of weeks' old sick covered with something floral lingered in the stairwell. Someone needed to take that carpet outside and set it alight.

I followed Davie into my parents' ground-floor flat, into the kitchen. "Why aren't you at work?"

"Ach." He waved his hand over his head as if he were swatting a fly.

Once he'd made tea, we went and sat in the lounge. My parents have a white leather three-piece suite and a hideous pink leaf design accent wall where the gas fire is – for which I blame those nineties home design shows – my ma and pa were mad for those. The suite, the wall, all of it had embarrassed me the two times I'd brought Mikey here. I'm ashamed to say that now, but there it is.

"So how come you're here?" Davie asked.

I smiled at him, taking him in, his pinkish scalp visible through his tufty hair. "Are you going bald?"

He put his hand on his head. "Get to fuck, Shone. Yeah, I am. Twenty-four."

"Too much self-abuse. It'll make you blind too, you know."

He shook his head and smiled. Youngest of four. Never stood a chance with us lot.

"I'm here for a wee visit is all," I said. Lied. "Thought I'd surprise Mum. How is she by the way?"

"I've told her she should retire."

"She won the lottery and not told anyone?"

"Aye, right."

We gossiped, ran through our Gus, Craigie, my dad. Annie next door and her lot. Her oldest boy was inside for possession – it had put years on her.

"Aye, well, it does," I said.

"Yup." Davie looked away and I kicked myself. He'd seen the inside of a cell himself a few years back – the last thing he needed was me reminding him what it had done to our mum and dad.

"What about you anyway?" I asked.

He shrugged and looked at me once again. "Nae work just now."

"Mum never said."

"Aye, well." He sniffed, bit at this thumbnail.

"Do you want me to ask Mikey, see if he can get you something on the rig?"

"Nah. I'll be OK."

Davie didn't like Mikey. He'd never said as much. Never had to.

"Say the word," I insisted. "It's nae bother. The work's tough right enough but the money's good and you've only got half the time to spend it. Davie. Think about it."

He picked up Isla and sat her on his knee, let her pull his nose, poke him in the eye. I took a couple of photos of the two of them with my phone. We had a second cup of tea and I felt my insides thaw, felt the softness of my mum and dad's sofa under my backside. I yawned.

"I said I'd get something in for tea," Davie said. "Will I take Isla out with me, show her the sights? You look like you could use a nap."

"Thanks," I said. "Baldy man."

He rolled his eyes. "Your bedroom's still a museum piece by the way."

I went down the hall and pushed open the door to my room. My pink Hello Kitty jewellery box still stood on my rickety white dressing table, my cuddly toys lined up and staring at me from the top of my old pine wardrobe. My duvet cover with the lilac and pink hearts was still on the bed, my framed poster of *Casablanca* I'd thought so sophisticated when I was eighteen still on the wall. I hadn't lived here for ten years yet my cheap childish knick-knacks were, as Davie had said, preserved like precious antiques. Fully clothed, I got into bed. But it was weird being without Isla. The silence, the empty space had a shape to it and that shape was her. I breathed in the familiar smell of my mum's fabric conditioner, closed my eyes and tried not to think about Mikey getting home and finding me gone, finding the note I had left. At the thought of that note, I got a pit in my stomach, as if I'd done something very wrong. Valentina had said I had every right to make a stand but now that I was here, I felt less sure.

I woke to the sound of the key in the door. "Hello?" My mum's voice. "Anyone in?"

"I'm here," I called out.

"Is that you, Shona?"

"No, it's Elvis Presley, ma, who do you think?"

"Well, what d'you know? That is a nice surprise."

The bang and rustle as she made her way inside. Obviously carrying bags – she always was. Davie must still be out with Isla, I thought. Had probably taken her to Brechin's to show her off to his feckless ned mates. The crackle of the furred-up kettle drifted out from the kitchen; I knew my mum would call out in one, two, three ...

"Can I get you a cup of tea, doll?"

I was home.

We ate together in the living room, plates on our knees, in front of the news. Davie made chicken curry, which was all right, actually, and when I told him so he blushed so much his ears went red. Mum and Dad were full of questions about the cottage, about Mikey. I told them he rang me almost every night from the platform, told them about the electricity failing, how I'd had to bum shuffle down the stairs to find the fuse box. Basically, I made out that everything was peachy, that any problems were silly things, nothing more than a funny story to tell.

"D'you no get awful lonely out there?" my mum asked.

"Nah. It's beautiful, Mum. I'm always out and about. And I've made a pal. She's great – she gave me a lift to the station, actually."

"Aw, that's nice," said Mum. "Nice girl."

"Could Mikey nae come down the road with you?" my dad asked.

"Aye," Mum chipped in. "It's a long way on your own with a bairn."

"He's got a work dinner tonight," I lied. "The train was nae bother. And he's so busy I thought I'd clear out and leave him a bit of peace, you know?"

Davie, I noticed, was watching me, his plate empty, his fork still tight in his hand.

"He'll come next time," I added. "Davie, this curry is delicious by the way."

Davie laid down his fork. "You've already said that, goldfish brain."

After tea we went to watch television in the living room. When my phone rang at 7:30pm, I jumped. At the sight of *Home* on the screen, I felt my throat close.

"That'll be Mikey," I said. "He said he'd give me a buzz around now."

I left my mum, Dad and Davie to their programme. I closed the living room door behind me and went to switch on the hall light but decided to keep it off for fear of catching sight of my face in the mirror. If looked at myself, I thought, I'd lose heart. I answered.

"Hello."

"Shone?"

"Aye. It's me."

"What the hell's this?" He was almost whispering, as if he'd gone beyond speaking, beyond shouting. He sounded angrier than I'd ever heard him. "*Dear Mikey?*" he went on. "*I need some time to think ...* Really, Shona? Are we really doing this – this – soap opera?"

"Y'all right, doll?" came mum's voice from the lounge.

I covered the mouthpiece and shouted through. "Fine, Mum. Told you it'd be Mikey. He's away to his dinner."

"Shona," he said.

I couldn't remember anything I'd planned to say. Even if I could have, I couldn't speak for the fear I might cry. If Valentina were here, I thought, she would tell me what to say. It had sounded so clear, so right, when she'd said it that morning. *You'll be in a position of power*, she'd said.

"I told you we'd talk about it when I got in." His voice had strengthened but still had this terrible quiver to it, like there was a force beneath that would break through any second and leave us both screaming. "You can't go running off to your mum's every time you don't like something."

"There's a lot of things I don't like," I blurted, stopped, forced myself to whisper. The walls at my parents' house are thin. "I don't like it when you go offshore. I don't like being on my own. I don't like it when I've got no one to talk to in the evenings. This is more than a wee something. This is my whole life. It's not what you said. It's not what you promised."

"Oh, come on ..."

"Don't come on me. You've tricked me, Mikey, and it's a pretty big trick. I've come away because I cannae take it in."

"I've tricked you?"

"That's what it feels like."

"Do you actually believe that? You believe that I tricked you on purpose? What, like a con artist? Like a criminal? What a high opinion you must have of me, Shona." He gave a derisive laugh.

It was absolutely horrible. I felt horrible.

"I'm sorry, I ..."

"No, come on," he interrupted. "Let's play this out. Let's play this right out. I tricked you into moving here so that I could make you miserable, is that it?"

"No, I ..."

"You think that I enjoy going out onto a metal crate in the middle of a freezing cold ocean, that I relish the fourteen-hour days, the smelly bastard I have to share a bunk with and all the rest and then, when I get back, you think I love having barely two days to recover before I'm back on the treadmill? You think, you actually think, that I want to get up on Monday morning, still so knackered I can barely walk, and go into work?" He sighed. "Maybe you should change your focus, Shona. Maybe you should think just for one minute about someone other than yourself."

I started to cry – confusion or shame, it was hard to tell. Both, probably.

"I did tell you," he said. And, thank God, his voice had lost its edge. "I did, Shona. I can remember the conversation. I said I'd still have to go into the office sometimes, I asked you if you could cope. You said as long as I was coming home at a reasonable time, it was OK. I did tell you, babe. Of course I did. I'd never have kept that from you. Think about it. What you're saying is – it's quite mad actually."

I tried to picture his face. He could easily have been offshore right now for all I knew. That was the thing about phones. He could have been on the moon. Had he told me? It was possible. Of course it was. Of course he'd told me. Only, there had been so many arrangements, so little sleep. I had jumped to a terrible conclusion. How could I have let myself think this way about him? He was my Mikey, the man I had fallen in love with, my life partner, the father of my child.

"Where are you?" I said.

"At home."

"I mean whereabouts?"

"In the kitchen – I'm at the little table."

"Have you eaten?"

"I'll get myself something in a minute."

"There's eggs," I said. "You could make an omelette. I think there's some oven chips in the freezer."

"Thanks, I'll find something." He gave another sigh.

"I'm so sorry, Mikey," I sobbed. "I was so disappointed, that's all."

"Hey, don't cry. Don't cry, Shone. Let's not start blaming each other. This has all been a misunderstanding." He paused. The excited blare of adverts from my parents' television bled through the thin wall.

He had told me and I had not heard or not digested the information. He had told me and I had agreed to the plan or had appeared to agree – maybe given a nod he'd interpreted as agreement, maybe when I was seeing to Isla or thinking about something else. He had thought I'd got it. It was all a horrible misunderstanding. He was shocked too. Oh God, and now – now I was standing in the dark and the cold in my parents' hallway wondering how I could ever find my way back.

"You couldn't even remember which rig I was on the other day." His voice was soft, full of sympathy. "Don't feel bad. I'm not criticising. It's normal. I do understand. Totally. You're not getting enough sleep. You've had a tough time. Isla's been up at night. You haven't made many friends yet. Not all the millions of friends I know you will make. It will get easier, you know." His words had a rhythm to them, a gentle lull, like the patter of a hypnotist. "And it's not forever."

"I'm not getting enough sleep," I said. "Isla's been up at night."

"That's what I'm saying, Shone." His soft Scouse burr. "Come home to me, baby. Come home."

"I just needed to work it out."

"I know, baby. I know."

In the background I heard a voice.

I sniffed, dried my eyes. "Did you get the TV working?"

"It's the radio."

That'd be Radio 5 Live, I thought.

The background went silent – he'd switched it off. I wiped my nose on my sleeve.

"Do you want me to come and get you?" he said.

"No, it's all right."

"I'll come and get you right now. Say the word."

"No, it's fine. I'm fine."

"You're not going to leave me are you? I'll make it right, Shona, I promise."

"I won't leave you, don't be stupid. But I'm going to need a car. I can't be relying on Valentina for lifts and the buses are one an hour if you're lucky. And we need to sort the WiFi. It's rubbish."

"Of course. We'll get you a car as soon as we can afford one, I promise. We'll look back on all this and say – how did we ever manage?" He laughed. "In the meantime, I'll get the bus to work or you can run me in, OK? You will come back tomorrow, won't you?"

"I'll spend some time with my mum and I'll come back tomorrow night." I brushed the tears off my face. They seemed to be falling quite independently of me, I was barely aware of them. I pictured him in the kitchen, looking out onto the back garden, seeing only himself reflected in the darkened pane. I heard him sigh yet again – that heavy exhalation – and wondered what it was about the phone lines today that made everyone sound as if they were smoking.

"It'll take some time to get used to, that's all," he said. "But we can do this, Shone. Me and you. We're a team aren't we?"

"Valentina got me all fired up." The moment the words left my mouth I regretted them. Valentina had tried to be a friend and here I was, using her as a lightning rod to deflect the blame for my ridiculous petulance.

"It's none of that woman's business."

"She was only being kind, Mikey. She didn't say anything bad – it was me. I wound myself up."

"I'd be careful if I were you. From what you've told me, she sounds unhappy. Unhappy people can be very dangerous, don't forget that."

"At least she's around." I bit down hard on my lip, cursing myself inwardly.

"That's not fair."

"No," I said. "You're right, it's not. I'm sorry. I'm so sorry. I seem to be making a mess of everything."

Silence. Another heavy exhalation.

"Valentina cares for me, that's all," I said. "Tell you what, I'll invite her and Red over for dinner when I get back. That way you can meet her properly and get to know her a bit, OK?"

"OK."

"You'll like her, I promise".

After the call, I stood in the dark with my fingers pressed against the wall, listening to the low mumbling of the television, the peaks and troughs of TV presenter speak. I wanted to feel at peace but I didn't. I didn't know why, but I felt worried – but in a general way I could not have named. It did not occur to me that it was me, after all, who had said sorry, not Mikey. If any conscious thought came to me at all it was that, in the evenings, Mikey always listened to music. He only ever listened to talk radio at the weekends if there was a big match on. But you never know anyone as well as you think, do you?

ELEVEN

Davie drove me back to the station in Mum and Dad's car. He parked up and came all the way to the train, helped me on board with Isla and the tripper and my bag.

"Right then," I said. "Better see if I can find a seat." I blew him a kiss but as I threw out my hand he caught it in his.

"Anything you need, Shone," he said, holding my gaze. "I mean it."

I had no idea what he meant. I pulled my hand away but not without giving his fingers a wee squeeze. "Sure thing, Davie."

I reached Aberdeen at nine. Mikey came to pick me up at the station: red-eyed, unshaven. He'd been up late, I thought, fretful, not sleeping. And now he looked like hell. Because of me.

We said little on the way home, as if the car did not afford us the privacy we needed to finish our recovery. By the time I'd got out of the car, Mikey had taken my bag and the buggy from the boot. He waited until I'd lifted Isla safely out before walking us both to the cottage. He pushed open the front door and ushered us in first.

He'd left the heating on, and the soft electric lamp in the kitchen. There were flowers in a vase on the table and a card. Beneath the perfume of the flowers, another smell. I couldn't say exactly, couldn't separate out the components of that smell but I knew it was us, our family, our home.

"Welcome back," he said softly.

I put Isla in her car seat on the floor and let him lift me up. I wrapped my legs around his waist and sank my face into his neck.

"Don't ever, ever leave me again," he said.

"I won't."

He lowered me down, kissed me softly on the mouth and handed me the envelope. Inside was a plain piece of card upon which he'd written:

> *I could not go, not anywhere, not even for a moment,*
> *if you were not here when I got back.*
> *I love you, Shona, always will.*
> *M.*

I was crying – of course I was. The whole episode, the shock, the anger, the strain of hiding all sign of trouble from my parents, and of course the guilt over my selfishness, had left me raw.

Mikey held my face in his hands and pushed my tears aside with his thumbs. He kissed me again – harder this time, slower, before leaning back.

"This is what I love about you," he said. "It's all here, all written on your face."

"I wish I was mysterious."

"Don't even think about becoming mysterious."

I pulled back from him and looked him in the eye. "I'm going to look for a job. Soon."

He smiled and rubbed the tops of my arms as if to warm me. "You've had a shock. You've got yourself into a state." He took my hand and led me to the chair, eased me down into it. He crouched down in front of me and took both my hands in his. "I think, for what it's worth, you need to stop putting pressure on yourself. I can look after us financially but I'll be away a lot over the next year or two. You're not sleeping properly yet. If it were me, which I know it isn't, I would take it easy. You're Isla's only point of stability here. Two weeks in four, you're all she's got. I would wait for, say, a year, wait until you're properly settled, and then think with a clear head about what you want to do next. Make the decision for the right reason."

I sniffed, nodded.

"Maybe we should try for another?"

"Maybe – not right away."

"No, but soon. No point hanging about, eh?" He let go of my hands, slid his warm hands up the inside of my thighs and back again. Tiny electrical pulses ran down to my toes. "Besides, we'll have a great time trying." He knelt up, brought his face close and kissed first one eye then the other.

"Don't leave me," he whispered. "And don't listen to that Valerie woman again."

"Valentina." I laughed, wiped his cheek where my tears had wetted his skin. "She was only trying to help."

She was only trying to help. These were the words I said.

Three days later, Valentina invited herself over for lunch. I was still trying to make it up to Mikey – small attentions – more effort on my appearance before he came home, to be better company, maybe put a little more thought into what was for tea, that kind of thing. We called each other two or three times a day. Oh, and he'd decided to cycle to work and, Mikey being Mikey, had bought himself all the clobber. When winter set in, we hoped to be able to afford a small second-hand car.

Shaky as I still was, I looked forward to seeing my friend. Her intention had been only to help strengthen me or at least remind me of my strength and I was still grateful for that. An evening back in Govan with my family, or with some of them anyway, a night in my childhood bed, had given me time to think and to compare the Shona I was now with the old one, the one who had slept every night under that low ceiling in a room no bigger than a store cupboard. That girl had got into all sorts of scrapes growing up. That girl was strong – would never have stood for injustice or cruelty, not on her turf. But where I grew up, cruelty took the form of punch-ups in the playground, at the bus stop and in the battered play-park, bruises paraded like trophies. Where I grew up, cruelty lay on the surface, where you could see it.

At around midday, Valentina arrived. I was washing up when I heard her come in and so, wiping my hands on the tea towel, turned to see her striding in with Zac fast asleep in his car seat. She set him down on the floor tiles, brushed her hands together and smiled.

"Hey, you." Her patchwork skirt reached down to her ankles. She was rummaging around in her cloth hippy bag and after a moment produced a bottle of white wine and a long hand-rolled cigarette with the end twisted shut. Both she held out to me. "Presents."

"Is that what I think it is?"

"It's wine, yes," she said, kissing me on the cheek, pulling me into an embrace and holding me tight.

"Very funny. You know I don't mean that. The other thing."

"If you think it's a doobie then yes it is, Sister."

"You're kidding?" I took both from her, sniffed the joint along its length.

"What are you, some hokey cigar connoisseur now? Do you need to put it in the humidor?"

I laughed. "I haven't had this stuff for years."

"Thought you could use it." She took off her coat and went to hang it up. I noticed her scarf was still there on the hook. I thought I'd given it back but I must have forgotten – yet another thing that had slipped my mind.

Valentina was back in the kitchen, already pulling two glasses from the cupboard. She picked up the bottle, held it up and sighed. "Fuck," she said, and began rifling through my cutlery drawer. "It's got one of those synthetic corks. Where's your corkscrew, babe?"

"Should be in there," I said.

"I tell you what," she replied, her back straightening. "I'll do this in a sec. I'm actually dying for a pee. Won't be a tick." She ran up the stairs. Her footsteps sounded on the ceiling above me, the closing of the bathroom door, the clank of the loo lid hitting the cistern. A minute or two later, the flush, her footsteps again. But they didn't come down, not immediately. They fell softer, slower, in the direction of mine and Mikey's room. I stood motionless, ears pricked, unsure of what to think. A second later, the footsteps padded back along the landing, the creak of the top stair, another second and Valentina reappeared, hands deep in the pockets of her swishing maxi skirt.

"Phew. Needed that." She crossed the room and began searching once again in the cutlery drawer, clearly desperate for a drink. I wanted to ask her why she'd been creeping about upstairs in my house but I couldn't find the words. I was too embarrassed, I suppose.

"Do me a favour, would you, babe? Take Zac's hat off for me? He's going to overheat in here."

"Sure." I squatted down to the baby, unfastened his chin strap and pulled off the funny wee deerstalker hat he was wearing. He woke up and moaned a little, so I picked him up and kissed his head. "Hey wee man, that better?" He stopped grizzling straight away. "That's right, it's all OK. Your Aunty Shona's got you now, darling."

"Eureka," came Valentina's voice behind me. "Found it."

I stood, Zac on my hip, to find her working the corkscrew.

"I thought they were all screw tops now," I said.

"Not this one. This is special. Montrachet, ooh la la." The wine splashed into the glasses, the palest liquid honey, pure-looking, clear. The glasses broke out in perspiration. I still got a thrill from us drinking like this so early in the day. In Govan, you'd have to be a wino or a homeless person or both to drink at this time, but here in the cottage it was decadent – classy, even. Two educated women sipping cold white wine.

"Hold on a second," I said. I carried Zac into the living room and put him in the playpen with Isla. They loved lying in there together, the two of them. I went back into the kitchen where Valentina was waiting with my glass held out in front of her.

"Bottoms up," she said. "I thought we should celebrate you growing a pair of bollocks."

Glass to my lips, I took in her lovely white teeth, her lovely long salon hair. What had been her upbringing, I wondered, to afford herself, on a part-time yoga teacher's wages, such teeth, such hair, such assumptions about me and my status – bollock-wise? What did she know, what could she possibly know, about me? My fist, quite involuntarily, clenched.

"You'd be surprised," I said, carefully. "When I was at school, this lassie, Marjory McMasters, threatened to beat up my wee brother, Davie."

"Oh yeah?"

The two of us took our seats at the kitchen table and drank wine so delicious it almost made me lose my thread.

"Yeah," I said. "Happened a lot where I grew up. We walked the same way home anyway, me and this girl. So one day, I caught up with her and I grabbed hold of her and I pushed her to the ground." I smiled at the memory, my school friends' faces appearing in my mind's eye – *go on Shona, kill her.* "I got on top of her and pinned her arms down with my knees. I didn't shout or anything like that, but I went in really close, you know? Like this ..." I stood, put my face to Valentina's, our noses almost touching "... and I said, 'if you go near our Davie again, I'll finish you, you scabby old dog.'" I pulled away, sat back in my chair and took a good long drink of the special Montrachet. Ooh. La. La.

Valentina gave a hollow laugh. "You sound like you've got a real temper."

"When enough's enough," I said, "yes, yes I have."

It must have been about half past two in the afternoon by the time we ate but the more we drank, the less I cared. I'd made crusty rolls with brie, bacon and cranberry – I needed them to soak up the alcohol. I hoped she didn't expect me to share the joint. I'd be sick.

Over lunch, I explained about Mikey and what he'd said, how we'd made our peace.

"It's tough on both of us," I told her. "Not just me. It was selfish of me not to see that. And if anything, it's galvanised me into looking for work sooner rather than later. I was thinking about calling the *Press and Journal* and seeing if I could set up a meeting and I'll maybe give the BBC a call too."

"Good idea."

"Enough about me, anyway," I said. "How's Red? Have you got a picture of him by the way? I don't even know what he looks like."

"Sure." She rummaged in her bag and pulled out her phone. She thumbed the screen for a few moments. "Where is it ... ah, here it is," and handed the phone to me. "Hardly heart-throb material, I'm afraid."

He didn't look like I'd expected him to, not that I'd expected anything specific. Red was a proper carrot-top, like Jeanie, with pale skin and eyes screwed up against the low Aberdeen sun. His checked shirt hung from his shoulders almost as it would from a coat hanger and he was holding Zac in his arms and smiling – laughing possibly. He looked happy. He looked proud of his wee boy. I guess I'd thought she'd go for someone seriously good-looking, maybe I thought he'd have a trendy hairdo or something, with him being a musician. I swiped the screen and another photo came up: Valentina, him and Zac – a selfie.

Valentina had stood up and was holding out her hand. I realised I was being rude, flipping through her photos like that.

"He looks like a nice guy," I said, handing back the phone. "Genuine, you know?"

She sat down again, finished her wine and poured herself some more. She offered me some but I shook my head, wondering how the hell she was going to drive home.

"Things are ... they're not good actually." She sniffed and covered her eyes with her hand.

"Hey." I reached over, covered her other hand with mine. "Don't cry."

"I'm not," she said, though her voice was high-pitched. "He's ... I don't think I can take it much longer."

I didn't know what to say. I wasn't like her. I wasn't full of advice.

"I'm so sorry, Val," I said after a moment, laying my hand on her arm. "I'd had no idea things were so bad. Can you talk about it?"

She shook her head. I was about to ask if she needed to stay the night when the key sounded in the front door and who should step in but Mikey.

"Mikey!" I jumped up, felt the colour rise to my cheeks. Obviously, it was a surprise to see him at home in the middle of the day, but it wasn't surprise that had sent me springing to attention. Here I was, tipsy with my friend in the middle of the day while he was out working hard, earning our living. I had been rumbled.

Valentina too had shot out of her seat. Partners in crime, I thought, not without a twinge of childish excitement. What a pair of naughty schoolgirls we were. But the colour drained from Mikey's face. He began to cough, his hand shot to his chest.

"Oh my God, Mikey, what's the matter?" I rushed over to him but he fell to his knees, still coughing, still holding his chest. My throat tightened. I sank to the floor beside him, tried to loosen his tie. "He's choking," I shouted, turning to Valentina, who was already carrying a chair from the kitchen over to the front door. She set the chair down beside him.

"I want you to sit on this chair for me," she said.

"Mikey, talk to me," I cried out. "Are you having a heart attack or something?"

He raised his hand, sputtering horribly like the victim of tear gas.

"Shona, calm down," said Valentina. "He is not having a heart attack, don't be ridiculous. Now help me get him into the chair." Chastened, I took one of Mikey's arms and together we eased him up and onto the chair. "I want you to focus on breathing in and out," she said to him. "Can you do that for me? Breathe." I was aware of myself kneeling on the floor, of her moving around, coming and going in my peripheral vision. "Shona, do you have a paper bag?"

"Yes," I said. "In the drawer next to the cutlery. I keep them back from the bread."

"Right." She caught my eye, held my gaze.

"I'll get it," I said. "Sorry." I rubbed Mikey's leg, told him it was going to be OK. I ran to the kitchen, grabbed the paper bag, ran back and handed the bag to Valentina. Mikey's breath came in rasps – staggered, terrifying.

"Here." Valentina held the opening of the bag tight and placed it to Mikey's lips. "I want you to blow into this bag for me." She handed me some water and, having freed her hand, placed it at the back of Mikey's head. Slowly the bag inflated. "That's good. And again. Keep going."

The bag ballooned and deflated, ballooned and deflated. Once he was breathing regularly, Valentina took the bag away.

"Drink this." She took the glass from me and put it to his lips. "Sip."

He made to take the glass from her but his hand was too unsteady. Valentina held it still: one hand on the glass, the other on the back of his head. Of course, I thought. She's a yoga teacher. She's done this before.

"There you go," she said. "Nice bit of H_2O. You'll be right."

Feeling useless, I knelt down again, on the floor by his feet. "Mikey, what happened?"

Valentina pressed the glass again gently to his lower lip. He drank a little more, waved it away. He leant back in this chair and sighed.

"I took ill at work," he said. "I thought I'd be OK to drive but ..." He coughed again, into his hand. "It's nothing, just some fluey thing. It's going round the office."

I reached up, pressed my hand to his forehead – it was clammy and a little cold. "We need to get you to bed."

He nodded. He could walk, just about. I helped him upstairs. Thankfully, Valentina did not follow. I wanted to do at least one useful thing for my own partner. Once we got into the bedroom, I sat him down on the bed. I pulled off his shoes, his trousers, his tie, unbuttoned his shirt, eased the cuffs from his wrists. His breathing had regulated but he still looked clammy. "I should call a doctor," I said.

"Don't," he whispered and lay on his side, unable apparently to get under the duvet. I ran and fetched blankets from the cupboard in Isla's room and threw them over him.

"Are you warm enough?" I said.

He nodded. He had closed his eyes. His colour was coming back, I thought.

"Do you need more water, darling?"

"No. Thanks."

"Shall I leave you to sleep?"

He nodded.

I pushed his damp hair back from his forehead and kissed him there, my lips registering that he wasn't in fact running a temperature. "You sleep now," I said. "I'll come and check on you in a bit."

I went downstairs. In the kitchen, there was no sign of Valentina but I could hear the television blaring from the living room.

"Well, now you've met Mikey," I said as I went through. "Wasn't exactly how I'd imagined it but ..."

But there was only Isla, wide-eyed in front of seven cartoon dwarves on the screen. I went back through to the kitchen, round into the utility space. The secret back door clattered against the outer wall and came swinging back shut with a bang. I heard a car starting up out front.

"Valentina?"

I ran up the path at the side of the cottage, reached the front garden in time to see her pull away, the silhouette of her wavy hair dark against the fading afternoon light.

TWELVE

By around half past five, I had given Isla her tea and was sitting on the living room floor with her. I was building a tower with those huge Lego bricks that decorate your entire home when you have wee ones when I heard the soft pad of Mikey's footsteps on the stairs. A second or two later, he filled the doorway.

"Hey babe, sorry about that." His hair was sticking up at the back, his eyes puffy. He'd thrown on an old sweatshirt and some jogging bottoms. His feet were bare, bony and white.

"Are you OK?"

"Yeah. Funny turn, that's all. Stress, most probably." He lifted both arms up and leant against the doorjamb, his sweatshirt rode up to show the black line of hair that trailed down his abdomen and disappeared into his waistband. I had a flashing urge to put my mouth to that place.

"You need to get to a doctor," I said. "Tomorrow."

He huffed and puffed, walked silently over the carpet and came to sit in the armchair. One look at his daughter and his face softened into a smile. I have to tell you, Mikey's smile could melt an ice cap.

"I'm fine, Shone," he said. "Don't fuss."

"Ach, don't do that," I said. "Don't pass out then say there's nothing wrong. That's macho bullshit. You're a father now, don't forget. It's not just about you any more."

He waved his hand in front of his face.

"Don't give me that 'shut up little woman' gesture either," I said, angering. "I'm serious."

"Shona, don't. Leave me be."

"*Leave me be?* What the hell's that about? I'm not going to mop your brow, carry you up the stairs and feed you

117

chicken soup for you to get up and waltz out of here saying, *oh, it's OK, I'm fine now*. I'm not your nurse. I'm not your bloody mother."

He shot out of his chair. "Stop nagging. For Christ's sake."

I jumped up too, stood close, looked up into his face. "Don't you raise your voice to me – you're too tall and you're too big. And besides, you're not doing that thing that men do."

"Oh, and what's that?"

"Act totally unreasonably then turn around and blame the woman for nagging. What's nagging anyway, in the Gospel according to St. Michael? Anything that involves telling you to do something you don't want to? We all have to do things we don't want to, Mikey, that's life. Fucking hell, is this how it's going to be? I make one small demand and you throw your toys out of the pram? You drag me up here, stick me in this cottage, get on with your life as if nothing ever happened and meanwhile my life, my life, Mikey, is upside down, back to front and inside out. I don't know who I am, what I'm doing, what day of the week it is. I'm doing all this for you and a lot of it doesn't suit me, frankly, but I'm doing it – for you, for us. So don't you baulk at taking one trip to the doctor, all right?"

"OK." He raised both his palms and stepped back. "All right."

We stared at each other. He blew at his fringe and gave me a sheepish grin. "You might be pocket-sized but you can be very scary when you want to be, d'you know that?"

I shrugged, anger evaporating like boiling soup. "You knew that from the start. Bit late to start complaining about it now."

"You don't have to fly quite so far off the handle though."

"Better out than in where I come from. And call me old-fashioned but I can't stand it when people aren't fair with each other. And my husband's no exception."

"Husband, eh?" He grinned, stepped forward, slipped his hands round my waist and kissed my neck. "Husbands have rights."

More kisses. The stubble on his chin scratched my neck.

"You're not my husband, not in law," I said, smiling.

He pulled open my shirt, kissed my collarbone. "We don't need no certificate." Kiss. "From the council." Kiss. "To keep us together." Kiss. "Do we?"

"All right, all right, old man." I was laughing. "But that's not how the song goes and, besides, the floor has eyes."

We turned together to look at Isla, whose construction technique consisted of staring at the bricks as if to attempt the world's first telekinetic building project.

Mikey took the back of my head in his hands, pushed my face to his and kissed me so hard my insides surged. I pictured his stomach, that trailing line of dark hair.

"You," he said, "are a firecracker, d'you know that?" He took my hand, placed it at his hard crotch.

"I am the Firebird." I kissed him again. When we broke off I lifted Isla into her playpen, cooing at her, talking to her all the while. I set her up with her electronic plastic train that played music and, seeing she was content enough, I took Mikey's hand and led him away.

Around nine o'clock that same night, I called Valentina. I guess I wanted to check she was all right. No. That's not true, I'm not being honest. I was phoning her because I thought she'd behaved strangely – driving off like that without saying goodbye. I couldn't think of one reason why she would do that.

I went through my contacts on my iPhone and punched her number into the home phone, which I had never, would never, get around to programming. One ring and it went straight to voicemail.

"This is Georgie," came the drawl of a well-to-do English voice. "Leave a message and I'll get back to you pronto."

119

I rang off, laughing to myself. I'd got so clumsy since Isla was born. And who the hell said pronto? I punched the number in again, more carefully this time. Valentina answered.

"You'll never guess what I've just done," I said. "I called the wrong number."

"Did you get a toffee-nosed English bitch by any chance?"

"Yes! How did you guess?"

"For fuck's sake. I'm changing my goddamn number. This happens at least three times a week." A clicking sound came down the line, followed by a pantomime suck, like the sound you'd make if you were imitating a fish. Then came the intake of breath, the heavy exhalation. No mistaking this time. She was definitely smoking. "I'm sick to death of it," she said, her voice reedy, croaky.

Some yoga teacher – I couldn't help but laugh.

"Don't," she said. "It's a frickin' nightmare."

"We used to get people ringing for pizza at my folks' place. There was one digit's difference between us and a Margherita with extra pineapple. I'll leave a message next time – tell her to get off the line there's a train coming." I waited, unsure of what to say next, whether to ask her if she was smoking – make a joke of it to show her I didn't disapprove – or whether to go straight in and broach the subject of her rather premature departure.

"Listen," I ventured. "I was calling to see if you were OK."

"Oh, yeah. Thanks, babe. I was going to call you before actually but I didn't want to wake Michael. I'm sorry I rushed off like that. I only realised halfway down the road how bloody weird that must've seemed but I just wanted to get out of your hair, you know? I thought you guys might need a bit of space." Another suck, another blow, the thin voice returned. "Last thing you want is some Aussie hippy around the place when you're trying to have a heart attack, right?"

"Don't be silly, I was glad you were there to help. That trick with the paper bag was impressive."

"Oh that? An old yoga trick. It's psychological more than anything. Some people think it makes it worse – you're basically breathing in your own carbon dioxide so I kept the bag loose until he'd calmed down."

"Well, it worked, whatever it did."

Mikey appeared in the open hallway in a loose, open shirt and jeans, his hair wet. He raised his eyebrows in question. I covered the mouthpiece with my hand.

"Valentina," I whispered.

He nodded, put a hand on my shoulder on his way through into the kitchen. The smell of shower gel trailed after him. I was aware of him opening cupboards, filling a glass with water, drinking it down. I turned away, so he couldn't hear what I was saying.

"So is that a joint you're smoking?" I kept my voice low.

"A little one."

"Is Red with you?"

"Who do you think rolled the fucker?"

I laughed out loud – out of relief partly, that we were back on track. I said goodbye, hung up and yawned hugely, like a dog.

"Wow," Mikey said, leaning back against the sink, crossing his feet. I noticed he was wearing his trainers. "You are one tired mummy."

"I'm always one tired mummy," I said. "But not forever, eh? And she's worth it. Think I'll go to bed actually." I stayed where I was, too pooped to move.

He checked his watch. "Listen, if you're going to hit the hay, I might nip back to the office."

"What?" I looked into his face to see if he was joking. Apparently, he wasn't. That was why he had his trainers on. That was why he'd pulled on his Superdry hoodie.

"I've left my wallet there. At least I hope I have. I can't find it in my briefcase and it's really bugging me."

"But you've only just raised yourself from the dead."

121

"I've had a shower. We've eaten. And the rest." He wiggled his eyebrows, puckered his lips stupidly. "Honestly, Shone. I feel fine."

I shook my head, scrutinised him. "What the hell do you need your wallet now for?"

"I don't need it." He turned, filled his glass again with water and drank half of it down. "I know I won't sleep unless I know it's not lost. If it's not in the office, I'll have to cancel the cards. I'm worried about the cleaners."

"Oh, of course. Cannae trust the cleaners."

"Shona, please. Not this. Not now."

I folded my arms. "My mother never stole so much as ten pence in the ten years ..."

"God, you're relentless, do you know that? You'd worry too if you'd left your purse somewhere, don't pretend you wouldn't." He turned back to the sink, topped up his glass once more.

"You're dehydrated," I said. "You're not well enough to go driving about. It's at least a half-hour round trip. More like forty minutes by the time you've had to park up and go in and all that jiggery-pokery."

"Look, I've had a drink of water. I'm rehydrated." He rolled his shoulders, stretched his neck to the left and right. "And I'm antsy. I've knocked myself out of whack with that sleep this afternoon. I could do with a drive or something before I go back to bed."

How lovely, I thought, to have energy on a top-up system instead of some gaping deficit a mere nap could not hope to repay. "You won't be long, will you?"

"An hour, tops. You go up. Warm the bed for me." He kissed me on the top of the head on his way past, grabbed his coat. The front door swung open, clicked shut. The jeep fired up, roared into life. The beam of the headlights swung across the living room wall, the gravel percussive beneath the rolling tyres. Off he went, man on a mission. Raiders of the Lost Purse.

I climbed the stairs with heavy legs. Mikey was right, I was tired, dog-tired. I was already thinking of my pillow: how soft it would be when I laid my head, how soft, soft, soft.

What happens to time once a baby is born? It vanishes – that's what. Add in an offshore rotation to that and it disappears even faster: hours, days, weeks – pouf! Magic. The tap of wand, the clap of hands, the starry curtain drawn swiftly back and look! The lady's been sawn in half ... you wake up on a Monday spooned against your husband, you go to bed and search for him once more under the covers. You wake up the next day and it's two weeks later, it's Saturday, and he's already dressed, already leaving for the North Sea. It's a month later, two: your baby can sit up now, she can roll, grab, jabber away; he's packed his enormous kitbag; he's putting on his boots and he's walking down the stairs and you're trying to remember whether this is the third trip or the fourth. You follow him to the hallway and find you have no right words to say and he's kissing you on the mouth, kissing your baby on the head. His tea is still cooling in its mug and the taxi's honking its horn outside your window and all of it has come around too quickly. He's at the door, he's outside at the picket fence, waving. Your tears run onto the back of your baby's head, you bury your face in her fleece pyjamas and sniff hard, sniff yourself into a braver face, one you can hold up and say brightly to your daughter, *wave to Daddy*. In this way you hope to teach her to act the way your parents taught you. To be brave. *Tell him haste ye back*, you whisper in her ear. *Tell him be safe. Tell him he's lucky he gets that helicopter ride, eh? That must be exciting, mustn't it?*

The taxi pulls away. You picture it, weaving down the lane, long after you lose sight of it. You imagine it, pulling out onto the South Deeside Road, revving through the gears on its way out to Dyce Airport. Half an hour later, you ask your baby daughter what she thinks Daddy's doing now.

"Will he have on the funny yellow safety suit?" you ask her. She's six months old now, she can sit up but she cannot reply. "Will he be walking across the airfield like a big banana, climbing into the helicopter with the roughnecks? They'll be huddled together in the big metal fly, won't they? Taking off like this, they'll be." You imitate the sound of the rotor blades:

Chuckachuckachuckachuckachucka. Baby laughs. You do it again. Chuckachuckachuckachucka. She squeals.

"Again? Chuckachuckachuckachucka."

Chuckachuckachuckachucka. That's how the helicopter goes. Chuckachuckachuckachucka. That's the noise the helicopter makes.

Chuckachuckachuckachucka. It's enough to drive a lonely person insane.

Time. Mikey away in his great Meccano teapot in the middle of the ocean, Val and me whiling away the months. When it rained we spent afternoons indoors, chatting about everything and nothing, or we went into town together in the jeep, in and out of shops, stopping for coffee, sometimes sharing a chocolate muffin, laughing at ourselves, making faces, calling ourselves pigs. In rare sunshine, we whiled away those afternoons in the garden, lying back on a picnic blanket, drinking dry white wine. Summer cooled into autumn but still, out of habit, we sat out as much as we could. I spent so much time with Valentina, sometimes it seemed like I spent more time with her than I did with Mikey.

"I wonder if finding a friend in a new place is actually more important than finding a husband," I said once.

An October afternoon, a picnic blanket afternoon, the two of us lying on the vast lawn behind the cottage. Sweaters and coats on, scarves and hats, for the sake of being outside. White wine sweating in its chiller jacket, kids asleep in their prams – hedonistic, but still ...

"Of course it is," she replied. "It goes: friend, hairdresser, husband. In that order."

"You're a wicked, wicked woman." I laughed, hauled myself up on one elbow and rested my cheek on my fist. "Do you keep in touch with anyone back home?"

"Nah. Drifted around too much. I envy people like you."

"Me?"

"You've got Jeanie and Robbie and those guys, and I bet you still have friends from school. And your brothers of course. I don't even have siblings. You're lucky."

I was lucky. I felt it. Always had.

"I suppose being a yoga teacher's probably quite lonely," I said. "Now I think about it."

"I love my clients, they're sweeties. But yeah, not exactly rich pickings on the social front. Speaking of which, we should go out. You know, out out. Get drunk in town."

"But Mikey's away."

She raised herself up on both elbows. I couldn't see her eyes for her sunglasses. "Red can babysit. He's great with kids, I'll say that for him. You can bring Isla over to my place and Red can look after the two of them. Isla could sleep over. What do you say? It'll do you good to cut loose for a change."

"I'm not sure."

"Come on, Shona, shake a leg. How long is it since you've had a night out?"

"Nine or ten months, I guess. Maybe a year?"

"Bor-ing." She wagged her finger and tutted. "That's what you'll become if you don't watch out."

I winced. Couldn't bear for her to think I was boring. But to leave Isla with someone I didn't know? Someone who smoked dope?

"Maybe in a month or two." I got up, wandered over to the pond. A flash of golden armour – the biggest of the carp

– the one Mikey and I had christened The Knight. Valentina had lain back down on the rug. She had crossed her arms over her chest and become so still that when she spoke I almost cried out with shock.

"I could lie here all day," she said.

In the cobalt sky, high up, a bird soared over us, its wings wide, cloak-like. A kestrel, an eagle, a falcon maybe. In the garden, no sound, none at all. To speak was to break like a vandal into a haven. Above, the bird folded itself into an arrow and darted down into the trees. For some shrew or vole this was not a good day.

"Are things better at home?" I asked her.

She frowned. "Up and down, I guess. I've not had to tell him off in a couple of days."

She made him sound like a child. I stayed at the pond's edge, pushed the lily pad with my toe. I had never, I realised, invited her and Red for dinner after all. The intention had been lost in the spinning wheel of our new life, I suppose, in the joy of having Mikey to myself for two whole weeks. I guess, seeing him only half the time, I couldn't bear to share him – but if I let that continue too long, we'd become a couple of bearded hermits.

"Why don't you and Red come over one night when Mikey's next back?" I said. "Nothing fancy, mind."

"Sure," she said. "That'd be lovely."

The carp again, rolling down into the depths. There was black too in his scales, beneath the gold. We would have to find someone who could adopt the fish, I thought, when we got around to making the pond into a sandpit. Isla had started to crawl in the last week. So had Zac. The two of them were growing so close, following each other about like brother and sister, copying each other. I would tell Mikey to buy sand when he got back. We should fill the pond before something bad happened.

Time. I gripped my way through those two weeks blocks without him like a mountain climber on a steep cliff face.

One hand hole, one foot hole, shift up, rest, shift up. Isla became better company. Watching her grow and change was a pleasure in itself. Mikey and I decided that I would look for work once she had turned one. I was her only point of stability, he said, and I agreed. I got used to my stay-at-home role, got better at filling the hours, made small tasks last. One hand hole, one foot hole, shift up, rest.

The kitchen roof sprung a leak. I brought my tool kit from the garage and fixed it. Loose slate, nothing to it. I re-puttied the living room window which had been rattling since we moved here. To stop the cold air blowing in from outside, I bought and fitted an insulation strip to the bottom of the front door. These things I told Mikey on the phone, glowed when he praised my handiness.

I joined a playgroup, though I had difficulty connecting with anyone there. There were, apparently, grownup women who positively relished the singing of baby songs, who apparently could not wait to talk about their child's development, vegetable eating, digestive system. And if I'm honest, once I'd met Valentina, other women paled in comparison.

I went to the supermarket every day while he was away: relief from loneliness and boredom. Or existential despair for sale in coloured rows – depending on my mood. In the trolley, Isla thought she was on a ride at the fair, bless her. I pushed her and let go, pretended to panic as she rolled away. I ran after her, grabbed the handlebar at the last moment, making her jolt and giggle. I loved to make her laugh like that, her head flopping back then forward again as laughter made her weak. I'd spent a lifetime learning to make small thrills count. Of course, I wasn't poor any more but making simple pleasures out of nothing in this way was lodged in the very atoms of me. I went to town alone, called in at Markies. And who should I see there but Valentina. No mistaking that hair. You could have spotted it from a hundred miles away – or, in my case, from the end of the dairy aisle.

"Val," I called after her. "Hey, Val!"

It was the look she gave me when she turned around. They say people look like they've seen a ghost. Well, she looked like that. Like I myself had died and had come back from behind the yoghurts to haunt her.

"Shona." She pushed the trolley towards me, seeming to recover, digging in her back pocket, pulling out her phone. She was wearing tight black trousers, a silk blouse and some black high-heeled ankle boots. She looked a lot less hippyish than normal – not like herself at all.

She stopped her trolley bumper to bumper with mine. "I thought you shopped in the big Sainsbury's?"

"I do normally but – call me crazy – I fancied a change. Aren't you teaching today?"

"Lunch break." She checked her phone, frowned. "Sorry, Red's asking ... hold on a second." Her thumb twitched over the screen.

"Is he here?" I looked over her shoulder to see if I could spot him. "I'd love to meet him."

"Somewhere. I need him to pick up some peas, hold on." Her thumb pressed down again. "That's it." She looked up, her shoulders dropped an inch. "I'm making pea risotto."

"Yum," I said. "I might copy you."

We smiled at one another, neither finding anything to say. I'm no hippy but there was something in the air between us, something she would have described maybe as bad energy. I felt it as if it were a solid thing, something dense.

"Is everything all right?" I asked her.

"Sure, why not?"

"You look very smart."

She pinched up her blouse. "Oh this? Yeah. Corporate gig. Have to look the part before I strip off to the leotard and say ta-dah! Stiffies all round!"

I smiled, nodded, looked at the floor.

"Where's Red?" I asked after a moment. "I could say hello."

She wrinkled her nose. "Actually we're tight for time, babe. But the four of us are getting together for dinner soon, right?"

I winced with embarrassment. Mikey had been home and gone again since that conversation and still I hadn't organised the dinner.

"Yeah," I said. "I'll ask Mikey tonight when he calls, see what day is good. That way we'll get it on the calendar."

She looked in my trolley, at the six yoghurts rattling around in the bottom. "Petit Filou, eh?"

"Aye. No Petit Filou chez nous! Pity flew out the window. I need a petit f'lu jab – good grief, I'm gonna stop now." I laughed, felt myself blush.

She was smiling. Her canine caught on her bottom lip in the way it did, making her look almost coy. "Listen, we're still on for Friday morning swim, right?"

"Of course. Swimming baths at nine thirty." And now we were exchanging information we both knew.

"Don't forget your costume." She laughed, looked behind her and back again to me. "I love the way you Brits say baths instead of pool." Her phone beeped. She checked it and made to turn away. "Red's got the peas. See you Friday, babe. Better wax our legs, eh?"

"Aye, and the rest. See you."

I watched her go, didn't move until she'd disappeared into another aisle.

At the checkout, I looked for her to wave goodbye but couldn't spot her. I made my way out with shopping in one hand and Isla on the opposite hip. Outside, the rain was coming down in sheets. I found my keys, pulled my coat over the two of us and ran over to the car park. I threw the shopping in the boot, heaved Isla into her seat. As I tried to clip her in, my coat slipped from my shoulder. In seconds, the rain soaked my sweater. My hair flattened against my face but I no longer cared. I was as wet as West Coast Willy, as my dad used to say, and there was a certain pleasure in giving in to elements beyond my control.

I was about to make my way round to my side of the car when I saw, pulling out of the exit to the car park, Valentina's old Toyota. The passenger side was nearest me. Naturally, I think, I strained to get a look at Red. I was only curious. I must have been about ten metres away and I couldn't see well for the rain but from a distance I was pretty sure I could see that the man in the passenger seat had dark hair because he was talking to Valentina, his face turned towards her, the back of his head, then, towards me. Valentina had told me he was called Red on account of his red hair. I had seen a photo of him – there was no way his hair could look dark, not even from a distance, not even if he had got wet.

My guts flipped over. I climbed into the jeep and started the engine. Put the blower on high to clear the windscreen. I felt rushed, panicky. Guilty. I had spied on my friend and, as spies deserve, had discovered something I didn't like, something I had no right to know. She hadn't met my eye just now in the supermarket, had made conversation in the strangest way. It had been as if she were mimicking herself, but not getting it right. And now I knew why. Whoever it was she was with, I was pretty sure it wasn't Red.

I jumped into the car and started the engine. Valentina was already pulling out, heading for the roundabout. I tried to back out and keep sight of her car at the same time but it was so hard with the rain streaming down the windows. I almost crashed getting out of the car park, caught sight of the Toyota heading towards the lights. But I was three cars back already. At the lights she turned left as they changed from amber, leaving me stranded on the red behind a queue of traffic. I sat as high as I could, straining to see. But it was useless. Why was she heading left when she lived on Union Grove? Was she going to his place, with food and wine, to spend the afternoon there? The thought was too horrible. I was building it up into more than it was. I slammed my hand on the steering wheel and cursed. Whatever the explanation, I had lost her.

THIRTEEN

As planned, I met Valentina at Aberdeen City Baths that Friday. As planned, we took the kids swimming. We splashed about, we smiled at our children, eyes bright and pinked with chlorine, we laughed about the woman whose swimming costume had gone see-through at the back. We went for coffee. Chatted about this and that. Said goodbye.

At home, I made tea and sat on the sofa in my coat, Isla asleep in her car seat at my feet. Warming my hands on the mug, I sipped and stared at Isla's perfect face, the soft curved rim of her eyelashes, her damp, plump bottom lip. I should focus only on this, I thought: this child. She was all that mattered. But I couldn't focus on her, only on my unease. Something had changed between Valentina and me just now at the swimming baths, in the café, and it was that change, nothing else, which lay at the heart of how I felt now. I had not asked about the man in the car but why should I? What she did was her business, not mine. But this not asking had created a distance and I wondered if she felt it too. Today, we had enjoyed each other's company as we always did. So, on the surface, nothing had changed. But it was a surface, it seemed, neither of us dared to scratch. Was that wrong – not to have scratched? Isn't that what close friends did – told each other things – everything, sometimes?

But perhaps there was nothing to tell. The rain had been heavy. Red hair can look dark in a certain murky light. I hadn't seen him in profile. I couldn't have said whether it was Red or Billy or Bob. There was nothing, no secret, no mystery. I thought of Jeanie, how she always joked that the two of us could never fall out. If we did, she used to say, for reasons of privacy alone, one of us would have to murder the other.

In my memory, Mikey's homecomings take the form of one single event in which we fly into each other's arms. And yes, it was true – sometimes the second thing he did was put his bags down. But sometimes, we sat upright on the kitchen chairs, his kitbag a great black obstacle between us on the floor. On these occasions, we were solicitous with one another, almost formal, as if natural speech was or would not be possible until the physical conversation had taken place.

This was one of those times. Late October, the weather had turned for good, the air fresh, nippy. Isla was asleep in the living room when he came in and threw his kitbag on the stone tiles. But we did not rush at each other. Instead, we made tea and talked – no, not talked – we found things to say, both rigid on those stiff-backed chairs. He looked exhausted, face pale, black shadows under his eyes.

"You look so tired, honey," I said. "Your face is totally drained. You're working far too hard."

He smiled and closed his eyes. "I'm fine."

"Can't you take Monday off? Take a long weekend?"

"You worry too much, you do."

I reached across the table for his hand. He leant forward, pushed my hair behind my ear, let his fingers linger there. We stayed like that in perfect stillness, smiling stupidly at the small wonder of ourselves, until he scraped his chair across the tiles and brought his face towards mine. I can see him now, lips parted, eyes closing for our kiss. And then, from the living room, Isla's heartbroken wail sending us back, laughing.

"When you're a teenager you worry about your parents catching you," I said. "When you're a parent ..."

Mikey took both my hands in his, kissed the knuckles one by one with a kind of reverence. He was always so

132

adoring when he got back from offshore, worshipping, almost repentant.

He stood to fetch his daughter. "I'll deal with you later, Miss McGilvery. One thing at a time."

Time. Time to eat, to give the baby a bath, to coax her into her cot, into dreamland. Time to love. Delayed, our kiss became an event – with its own build-up – not something we could simply ... do.

We got into bed strange and shy, our pyjamas providing a kind of belated modesty. I lit one of the oil lamps I'd made with Isla.

"To remind you of your other home," I said, positioning it on the bedside table. "See the flame? That's the gas flare. The jar is the rig. You're in there somewhere, sleeping, in your wee bunk."

"I tell you, it smells too nice in here to be a bunk."

The miniature gas flare hissed. We watched its abstract theatre play out in shadows on the wall. I trailed my fingers down the soft hair of his belly, slid my hand into his pyjama bottoms.

"Bet your bunk mate doesn't do this." I kissed his neck, took a firm grip of him.

"I'd bloody kill him if he did."

"You could close your eyes and pretend it was me."

"Never." He rolled me onto my back, met my gaze with his: his face becoming hazy. His kiss came at last and with it my insides raced. He drew back, the kindness in his eyes replaced by an intensity that was almost cruel. "There's only you, Shone. You are a one-off."

Buttons can be unbuttoned. Strange can become familiar, shy can become bold, what has been shrouded can be revealed. Your lover's skin is your skin, his hands your hands, his mouth, your own – searching, finding, in the warm light of home. I fell into him, felt the heady release that falling brings.

"I love you," I said, gripping handfuls of his soft hair, sitting astride him, easing him into me. "I love you so much."

"I love you too." He sat up and closed his mouth around my nipple, took my buttocks in his hands and moved us both towards the edge of the bed. My legs wrapped around him, he stood and walked us over to the bedroom door. "I miss you every single day."

"Oh God," I managed, between gasps, my shoulder blades rubbing against the smooth wood of the door. "Oh God oh God oh God ..."

Sex is weird, isn't it? I only mean in the sense that sometimes, afterwards, the return to the mundane can feel surreal. One minute, you're as intimate as it's possible to be, the next you can be talking about, I don't know, what television programme you fancy watching the next night or whether the bins need emptying.

"I've invited Valentina and Red over for dinner on Wednesday night," I told Mikey once we'd snuggled down under the covers, my head on his chest, our legs intertwined. "I've finally got around to inviting them." I was hoping that, upon meeting Red, I would find in him some trace of the man I had seen in her car. I was keen to move forward from the awkwardness I had felt these last weeks.

"Who's Red?" Mikey asked.

I hit him on the chest. "Valentina's husband, stupid!"

"Oh. Yes. Right."

"I haven't met him, myself," I said. I was wide awake now. Sex does that to me sometimes. "I've seen a picture though. He's got proper red hair. That's why they call him Red."

"No shit."

I sniggered, kissed his chest. "Funny that they both have red hair, isn't it, with Zac being so dark? She didn't say whether we should call him Graham or Red or what. I'll have to ask her."

A deep, low breath. Another.

"Mikey?"

The rig always tired him out, poor lamb. He was dead to the world.

On Wednesday morning Valentina sent a text:

Red got man cold. OK to come me myself and I tonight?
No worries if you wanna cancel.

My first thought was that they'd fought. He'd found out she was seeing someone else and there'd been a showdown. My second thought was that she knew what I'd seen and knew that if I saw Red, I would realise he was not the same man as the one in the car. My third thought was that Red might have a cold. That there was no lover, no deception. I decided to call her.

She answered after a couple of rings. "Shona, hi!"

It was noisy in the background, like a café or an office.

"Shit, sorry, Val. I forgot you're at work. Are you in the middle of a class?"

"About to be. They're getting changed. Is that OK about Red? Did you want to cancel?"

"Of course not. I was just checking you were all right. I thought you'd had a fight or something, I don't know."

"Why would you think that?"

"No reason." I hesitated. I'd said the wrong thing. A phone rang in the background. It didn't sound like a mobile phone. "Where are you?"

"Church Hall. No one under eighty allowed unless accompanied by both parents." She laughed. "Yikes, think I might have said that a bit loud. I'll see you later anyway. Want me to bring anything?"

"No. Not at all. Yourself. And Red, obviously, if he feels better."

"Will do."

We said our goodbyes, rang off.

I'd bought ingredients for a lamb tagine. I'd never made one before and it felt like the most monumental effort to actually plan and cook something from a book. I cleaned the cottage and laid the fire, then, around six, started on the food. I was still chopping coriander with my apron on when Valentina's car pulled up outside at 7:30pm. I had said 8 for 8:30pm. I checked my appearance in the hall mirror and swore at my reflection. I was a total mess. Hadn't had time even to brush my hair or do anything that would make me look less like the wreck of the damn Hesperus. I had planned to make myself decent in the last half an hour – a half hour I no longer had. And the table hadn't been set.

I opened the door and stepped out.

"Hi there," I called across to her as she got out of the car.

She blew a kiss and waved – like celebrities do on the red carpet – and emerged from behind the car. She was wearing a white woollen coat I hadn't seen before with high spike-heeled boots. Here on my driveway stood a woman who would not have looked out of place at a law firm cocktail party or an elegant dinner in the world of high finance.

I looked down at my tartan slippers, covered in crusted baby food, at my apron, spattered with sauce. Thank God I'd thought to have a shower while Isla had her nap. At least I was clean. What kind of boast that was, I don't know. I reached behind me to untie my apron but found I couldn't unpick the knot. She was opening the back door of the car, pulling out a bunch of flowers from the seat.

She sashayed – she could do this, even on gravel – toward the gate, pushed through, kicked it shut behind her. She shook back her hair. It was super straight, shining with a high gloss even in the falling light. As she came forward, I could see she'd put on lipstick, the same colour as her hair, setting off her polished appearance to a kind of dusky, autumnal perfection. Yoga girl, high-polished executive: she had, I realised, a chameleon-like quality.

"Hey, babe." She kissed me on the cheek and handed me the flowers: three exotic, bird-like plants, bright, spiked heads like cock's combs. "These are for you." She bowled into the house.

I closed the door against the cold night. "Let me take your coat."

But she had already taken it off and was hanging it on the hook. She smiled and walked across my path, into the living room.

"Oh, you've lit a fire, how lovely."

I made my way back to the kitchen, laid the flowers on the counter and began to wash the last few pots in the sink. I should have offered her a drink but irritation had taken hold of me and, if I'm honest, powerlessness had made me resort to this pettiness: not offering her a drink yet. She was so early. Why? And why come at all when her husband was so sick he couldn't make it? Under the same circumstances I would never have come. I wouldn't have wanted to leave Mikey alone when he was ill. Valentina must, I realised, have been nothing short of desperate to come ... here, to this wee house in the middle of nowhere, for what? We weren't exactly the bright lights, Mikey and I, the big ticket, and yet here she was. Since I'd met her, I'd thought I needed her friendship more than she needed mine but that night I thought: maybe not.

She came to stand next to me at the sink, put her arm around me and kissed me on the cheek. I could see us both reflected in the black window: her, taller in high heels; me, a dwarf, in slippers. I moved away, went to get the nibbles, came back with bowls, a packet of nuts and a bag of crisps.

She was leaning back against the counter, her rather formal black dress opaque and fitted, showing off her yoga teacher's body every bit as much as her swimming costume did. I turned back to my task, tried not to notice that I was sucking in my stomach, tried not to admit to myself how pathetic that was.

"I hope I've got a vase big enough for those lovely flowers," I said, pouring out the nuts. "They look like they've been carved from wood. What are they, by the way, they're beautiful." And expensive, I thought but didn't say.

"African lilies," she said, turning to open the glassware cupboard, reaching out two flutes. "There's a spectacular florist off my road. I always ask for Rachel. She gets whatever I want for me." She pushed back a lock of hair that had fallen over her face and winked. "Can I do anything?"

"There's a couple of bottles of fizz in the fridge. You could open one of those."

"Now there's a job I can do." Her delivery dripped with suggestion, and it made me smile the way your naughtiest friends do sometimes. I couldn't help but watch her as she strode over to the fridge and flung it open – she had the unapologetic bodily confidence of an actor and my God her stomach was as flat as a chopping board. "Shall I bring these olives out too? Oh look, you've done little rolls of – is that Parma ham? God, I love Parma ham, yum."

"It's bresaola, actually," I said. "It's got rocket and Parmesan inside. Just a recipe I found."

Black against the white light of the fridge, Valentina tipped back her head, pinched a roll from the plate and lowered it whole into her open, waiting mouth. She closed her eyes and gave an indecent groan. "God. That. Is. So. Good." She swallowed, opened her eyes. "Where's Michael? Not had another heart attack has he?"

"Mikey? He's upstairs. He's settling Isla."

She nodded. "What a gem. I left Red rocking Zac in his car seat in front of the television."

I was staring at her, I realised, at her dress, her lipstick, her hair. "You're very ... poshed up," I said and turned away, embarrassed. "You don't look like you."

She looked down at herself, threw out her hands as if to apologise.

"Sorry," I said. "That came out wrong. You look lovely. I mean, I'm only worried the food won't measure up to your expectations. It's a glorified stew really. And I haven't even made pudding, I've only got some supermarket ice cream."

"Listen." She swaggered towards me, twisted the cork out of the Prosecco with a pop and began to pour. "I am sick of spending my whole time in a yoga kit or in clothes covered in food, sick, snot, you name it. I saw this dress in the wardrobe tonight – it must be a couple of years since I've worn it and I thought fuck it, you know? I'm wearing that sucker."

"Well, I'm sure Mikey will be impressed."

She handed me a glass, tapped her own against mine. In her eyes, something flickered. "Men never notice this shit, Shona. It's women. We notice each other. We appreciate each other, don't we? If I've worn it for anyone, I've worn it for you, babe." She leant forward, kissed me again on the cheek. It was not quite a peck – something slower, more purposeful.

"Well, I feel like a total scruff." I stepped back, a little flustered.

A creak from the stairs. Mikey. He appeared then in the hallway, seemed to aim his smile at me, only at me, like a secret gift. The roots of my hair tingled.

"Girls," he said, striding across the open hallway to us. I could smell the citrus eau de toilette he hardly ever bothered wearing. His slick, black hair was pushed back from his face, he'd changed into dark jeans and a dark sweater which suited him and, when he squeezed my shoulder and kissed me briefly on the mouth, I felt a rush of inappropriate and rather ill-timed lust.

He turned to Valentina and air-kissed her on both cheeks. "Pleased to meet you properly."

"Nice to see you on your feet, Michael," she drawled.

He stood back, clapped his hands, asked "So what were you girls gossiping about?" He was grinning, a little hyper, I thought. Valentina and I were both looking at him, holding our sparkling wine as if we were at a private viewing, Michael, the work of art, looking back at us with a kind of proprietorial satisfaction, as if we were the ones for sale, not him.

"This time you get to meet Valentina properly," I said, realising as the words left my mouth that Mikey had just said that.

"Oh I don't know," she said, fixing Mikey with a stare. "I think Michael's was the mother of all icebreakers."

"Call him Mikey," I said. "You know us well enough now. No one ever calls him Michael."

"Really?" She moved back to the glass cupboard and searched out another glass, quite at home. "I like Michael." She held up the bottle of Prosecco and looked intently at him. "Or would you prefer beer?"

"Don't call me beer, that's a terrible name." He leant against the countertop and crossed his feet, making no move to get it himself.

Valentina laughed, heading already for the fridge. "Very drole."

Mikey laughed after her. My God, they were both as bad as each other – two incorrigible flirts, met their match.

"Sorry," he said, watching her dip her face to the light of the fridge. "Beer's great. Thanks."

"I can only apologise for my husband," I joked while she pulled out a bottle of Budweiser. She strutted back, opened the bottle and handed it over. She didn't ask if he wanted a glass. Not that he would ever drink bottled beer from a glass but that wasn't the point. He might have wanted one. It was only then that I had to fight a flash of irritation at her – what? Over-familiarity, I suppose. I found it fake – this, *hey let me get you a beer, mate. We're all too relaxed for glasses, mate. G'day. Ripper.*

"Shona." Valentina had returned to my side and was bending close so she could murmur into my ear. "Why don't you tell me what you need doing and I'll do it while you go and do whatever you need to do, eh?" She held up her palm. "Not that you need to do anything, you look cute as you are."

It was a kind offer, one I didn't want to refuse. If I could splash my face, I thought, I would be all right – better anyway than this ridiculous, fraught woman I seemed to have become.

"That would be great actually," I said. "The table needs setting but don't let him charm you into doing it all. He knows where most of the stuff is. Although you probably know better."

"Off you go." She kissed me, again, on the cheek, her hand light on my waist.

I made to go.

"Stop," she said, catching me by the arm. She refilled my glass, to the top. Above it, bubbles winked and vanished.

I headed up the stairs.

"Now then, *Mikey*," I heard her say behind me. "Shona reckons you'll charm me into setting the table."

FOURTEEN

I went into the bedroom, shut the door and leant against it. My intention had been to change but instead I threw myself onto the bed and, for some reason, found myself blinking back tears. I jumped up, shook my hands in front of me, as if scalded. Dry your eyes, Shona. Dry them right now. Change your clothes. Get a life.

I slid open the wardrobe door and drained half the glass of Prosecco. Less than two glasses and already I was feeling it. What would my pals at work say? *Girl fae Govan gone soft.* Jeanie would be horrified.

Three or four minutes later, I was still rooted to the spot, still staring at my clothes. No matter how many times I closed and reopened the door, nothing new materialised. I hadn't bought anything in ... could it be a year? I couldn't remember, nor could I have said in that moment what I even liked. What suited me? Pass.

I pulled on some black jeans and, at the sight of the slack fold of post-childbirth belly pooling over the top, downed the rest of the fizz. My head spun. My belly was no longer my own. It had never been a washboard but now it had mutated into an amorphous, off-white, porridge-like mass.

The sound of laughter came from the kitchen. At least they were getting on – no awkward silences.

I dug through the wardrobe and found a loose top that was at least a bit shiny. It was the best I could do. *Not like I shop in Dolce & Gabbana.* Maybe, I thought now, maybe I should buy something new from time to time. What virtue could there possibly be in feeling like this?

At my dressing table, I applied a little kohl to my puffy eyes, some red lipstick I'd had since I was a student, which I then wiped off since it made me look like a corpse. I decided I looked as all right as I could, that, once I was sleeping all night again, I would look more like I used to, more like myself.

Reflected in the mirror behind me, the bed looked so white and so soft. Downstairs, those two were getting on fine – they would hardly notice if I closed my eyes for ten minutes. Fearing I might never get up again, I didn't lie on the bed but I did sit on the edge and close my eyes. I could leave them to it, I thought in that moment of sheer exhaustion, I could stay here and not have to serve any food, not have to make conversation, not have to make any kind of effort at all. I could float away, into oblivion. I could pop, into nothingness, like a bubble from a glass of fizz ...

"Hey."

I opened my eyes. Valentina was leaning against the bedroom door.

I felt my cheeks flush. "I was just coming."

"You look lovely."

"I don't."

"You do, don't be silly." She had brought the bottle up with her. She poured me another glass, sat down next to me on the bed.

"I'm drunk already," I said.

"That's impossible."

"I haven't eaten since breakfast."

"Ah. Maybe you are a bit drunk. But that's good isn't it? No point drinking if it doesn't make any difference, right?" She put her arm around me. "Michael, sorry, Mikey's adorable! Got yourself a keeper there, mate."

"Thanks."

"Better than my loser layabout. About time I traded him in."

"Really?" I said but she was standing up, holding out her hand to pull me up from the bed as I had done for her the first time we met.

143

"Shall we head down? Don't want to keep the master waiting."

"Sure."

I let her guide me out onto the landing where I stopped and took another drink. A faint headache had started but I ignored it. Drinking was a bad idea. But drink was what I wanted. I wanted, I decided, to be drunk.

Valentina moved so quickly that by the time I reached the kitchen she had already settled herself at the little table beside Mikey.

"We decided there was no point setting up in the dining room," she said, shaking the empty bottle at Mikey, who wordlessly made his way to the fridge for another. "Besides, it's super cosy in here." She wrinkled her nose, patted the chair next to her.

I had planned to eat in the dining room. But what did it matter? What did any of it matter? Who cared where we ate?

"Let me get the food," I said, stumbling, righting myself. "I need to eat something."

We ate. I had no idea whether it tasted all right or not, as if my taste for food had disappeared along with my taste for clothes. Did I even have an opinion on anything any more?

"This is delicious, Shona," said Valentina, turning then to Mikey. "She is amazing, your wife, isn't she?"

"Actually we're not married," I said. "Not officially."

"So you can still escape?" She laughed and stroked my arm. I sensed she was pulling me somehow into a conspiracy, two against one.

"I don't want to escape," I replied, reaching across the table for Mikey's hand. "What's a piece of paper anyway? It's not about ownership. Love isn't possession, is it?"

"Shona tells me you teach yoga," said Mikey, raising my hand to his lips, kissing my fingertips then, on glancing at Valentina, laying my hand back on the table, letting go. He was right – we shouldn't flaunt our happiness in front of her.

"That's right," Valentina was saying. "Salute the sun and all that bollocks."

"Can you do the lotus position?" Mikey was grinning now, flirting again. I would tease him about it later.

"Not in this dress." She returned his grin. "And you work offshore, I believe."

"I do."

"Which platform?"

He laughed and took a slug of wine. "Now, now, Valentina. Don't even pretend you're interested. I think we should move on to red." He stood up. I realised the second bottle of fizz was empty, that Mikey had already brought the red along with three larger glasses, and that he was pouring wine into these glasses. I finished my Prosecco, knew I was drunk but that I could get much drunker.

"What I bet you would be interested in," said Mikey to Valentina as he sat back down, "is how many terms for masturbation there are on an oil rig."

"Mikey!" I almost spat the rest of the fizz across the table. "I am so sorry, Val," I said, turning to her then back to Mikey, who was tittering into the back of his hand. "Behave, will you?"

But Valentina was laughing hard, a real guttural sound, almost a man's laugh. "And you'd be right. That is much more interesting."

We had coffee in the lounge. Mikey made it, brought it to us on a tray. I must have lit the fire. I know I laid it sometime in the afternoon and that the next day, when I woke up, it was burnt out but I can't remember being in its warmth, can't remember seeing it. The heat must have sent me to sleep before I touched my coffee cup. I woke up later, thirsty. I was in my bed, in the dark, Mikey's fingers tracing their way up my belly.

"What time is it?" I asked.

"Late."

"Where's Valentina?"

"I called her a taxi. She'd had too much to drink. She's gone."

"Oh dear. Oh no. I feel so rude."

"Not as rude as I feel." He pulled back my bra, ran his thumb over my nipple. It hardened, sent electrical currents down the length of me. I was still wearing my clothes, I realised, only because he was pulling them from me. I arched my back to help him, dipped my head as he drew away my top with the flourish of a conjuror. Slowly, he planted kisses over my belly, working his way down, taking possession. I ran my hands through his soft hair. He kissed – lower, lower, slid my underwear down, let his fingers trail over my skin. Lips to my thighs, his hands slid beneath my buttocks, raising me up. I scrabbled to get a grip on the pillows, on the bedstead and, for the briefest moment, opened my eyes. In the doorway, Valentina was watching, expressionless. I blinked. She was gone.

Light filtered blue through the curtain fabric, the clank of the radiators warming, stuffy air. I rolled onto my side. No Mikey on the other pillow. Was he offshore? No, he wasn't offshore, of course he wasn't. The dinner last night. Valentina. The drink. Oh God, the drink. The tang of stale alcohol, my tongue paper in my mouth. How much did I have? Too much, yes, but still ... enough to feel like this?

In slow deliberate centimetres I struggled into a sitting position, arms aching with the effort. My head spun, a wave of nausea washed over me, so strong I had to lie down again.

"Oh God," I said. "Oh God, oh God."

My shoulders were cold – I pulled the duvet up to my neck. I was naked. How had that ...? Oh yes. That. Mikey's mouth on my belly, my fingers in his soft hair. Valentina at the doorway, watching. No, Shona, Valentina had not been watching, you maniac. She had not even been there – she'd gone home in a taxi. I put the flat of my hand to my forehead and groaned. Get a grip, woman. Too much wine, too little sleep, my tolerance was shot, my own demons delusions in the night.

Mikey appeared at the bedroom door, Isla on his hip. Not a delusion, he was real, really there. He was dressed for work.

"Morning, boozer." He grinned widely, leant against the doorjamb.

"Stop smiling, it's offensive." I moved my hand over my eyes, peered out between the pink foggy edges of my fingers. "What time is it?"

"Half past eight."

"Oh God, is that all? Why can't I sleep in any more?"

"Your body clock's set for fascist baby o'clock, that's why. And some of us have got to go to work. Do you want a cup of tea?"

I smiled at him. "That would be great."

He padded out of the room. I pushed myself down under the covers. A second later, the creak of the top stair, his footsteps receding. An urge to pee. I sat up, threw back the covers and stood. But my vision swarmed, a blackish kaleidoscope, spinning. I had to stop and put my hands to my knees until the dizziness cleared before moving again but stayed hunched as I walked, stepping carefully over the tangle of my clothes on the bedroom floor. In the bathroom I kept my eyes away from the mirror – the last thing I wanted to see was myself.

I peed: the short, strong stream of the seriously dehydrated. I shuffled back to the bedroom, pulled on one of Mikey's t-shirts from the back of the chair and crawled back into bed. Downstairs, Mikey was talking to Isla. The childlike rise and fall of his words reached me. My eyes were sore, even when closed. Oh, why had I drunk so much? What had I been thinking? Beyond nine or so, the night was a blur. A memory came, of Mikey lying me down

147

on the bed. Me getting up, protesting, him pushing me back. "Shona, sleep it off. You're wasted."

The irresistible softness of the pillow beneath my head.

He must have returned downstairs. To her. At dinner, they had been flirtatious with each other, nothing outrageous, nothing I could complain out loud about without sounding like a jealous witch. And then I had left them alone together in front of a log fire, mellow, woozy and warm. I should have stuck it out, waited for her to leave. But no, I was being paranoid. Mikey was just being Mikey: charming, cheeky, full of mischief. He was like that with everyone – women, men, old, young – it was his way. And as for Valentina, didn't I already know she was an incorrigible flirt? Hadn't she drawn me in with her drawling, wicked humour, her intense green eyes? She had escaped a parking fine by promising to let a policeman take her out, for goodness sake.

I sat up, clutching my head. The policeman. He had given her his number. I had found it in the footwell. Had she called him for that drink after all?

Last night, Mikey had said he'd put her in a taxi. I thought I remembered him muttering something about Valentina being too drunk to drive, his voice all smoky and late night.

I threw my legs over the side of the bed, stood carefully this time, rolled my head slowly up. I shuffled over to the window and looked out onto the driveway.

Her car was gone. A creak on the stairs.

"Room service."

I turned to see Mikey carrying a breakfast tray into the bedroom.

"I've put sugar in your tea," he said. "And extra marmalade on the toast."

"Oh, you wee darlin'. Thanks." I climbed into bed and propped myself up with pillows, took the tray from him and set it on my knee. The toast smelled good: sugary, restorative. "Where's Isla?"

"In her high chair, talking to a marmite soldier called Steven." He kissed me on the head, sat down on the edge of the bed and looked at me intently. I wished he would reduce his energy levels. He was too bright. I had to screw my eyes up to look at him. "Sore head?"

"I feel like ten pounds of shite in a five pound bag." I took a sip of tea. It was too hot. I put it back on the tray and nibbled the toast instead, closing my eyes for a moment at the vivid sweetness.

"Valentina's car isn't on the drive."

"So?"

"You said she got a taxi."

"Did I? When?"

"Last night. You said you'd put her in a taxi."

He frowned. "Did I?" His face cleared. "Yes! I did. That's right. I did put her in a taxi." He made a silly face. "God, how much did we have to drink?"

"Too much. We're debauched." I took another small bite of toast. "I can't believe you said that thing about the oil rig – about the masturbating. For Christ's sake, Mikey, you barely know her."

He laughed, threw back his head. "Give over. She loved it."

"I know, but she might have been offended." My head pulsed – a shot of pain at my temples. "Oh God, I need a painkiller."

"I'll get it." He left the room, came back with a glass of water and a foil wrap of pills. "Your wish is my command."

I wished he'd stop smiling – he looked smug, as if he'd won a bet.

"How come her car's gone?" I asked him.

"What d'you mean?" He sat again on the side of the bed, his weight causing me to lean awkwardly towards him.

"If she got a taxi," I insisted, straightening myself up, "how come her car's not there?"

He shrugged. "She must have come back for it early this morning."

"In what?" I said. "They've only got one car, I think."

"Maybe she got another cab or got a lift." He stuck out his bottom lip – non-plussed. "Listen, I'm really late for work." He kissed me again on the head. "Anyway, I think you might have taken advantage of me last night." He kissed my cheek. "I'm feeling violated, frankly." My neck. "You are very ..." My mouth. "Sexy."

"That's what they say." I picked up my mug, my face mirrored on the surface of the tea, no more than an odd light and shadow pattern, unstable fragments: an eye, a nostril. "If only I could remember."

He left. I sipped my tea, puzzling over the empty driveway. A cab both ways would cost a fortune but she did spend money like water. Those flowers too. A lot of dosh for a yoga teacher. A lift, then. In a police car?

Later that morning I texted Valentina:

> *Too much to drink! Sorry I caved.*
> *Hope Mikey didn't keep you up too late. C u soon. X*

She replied:

> *I k r? Thanks for having me over, babe. Food great.*
> *Michael so nice! Sore head today.*
> *Hope I didn't stay too late? V*

I read the text two, three times, deliberating. Then I thought: fuck it.

> *You didn't drive home, did you?*

I'd barely put down the phone when it bleeped:

> *Christ, no! Grabbed a cab back over at 7.*
> *Surprised you didn't hear – it was a diesel lol.*

I smiled, impressed. Here was me, a shambles in my dressing gown, barely functioning. She meanwhile was up at dawn, saluting the sun as if she'd hit the hay at ten with a cup of camomile tea and a good book. The woman was made of steel.

Is Red any better?

I wrote.

Red mad as hell. Am officially in doghouse. (Crazy, fuming devil emoticon, gritted teeth face and a pile of steaming shite.)

I laughed. She had won the last word – with a picture.

***

People who play with fire end up getting burnt. Only now, with the smell of freshly combusted phosphorous clinging to her frozen fingers, does the cliché form itself in her mind. People who play with fire ... she wonders why, given the circumstances, she hasn't thought of it until now ... end up getting burnt. But isn't that what boring people say to keep their kids from having fun? Play safe, risk nothing, shrink back, be good. Hasn't she always yearned for more than that? Hasn't she always dreamed? How else did she get here?

People who play with fire ... These leaden-faced alarmists wouldn't know a good time if it came up and smacked them in the mouth. They have never risked, never thrown themselves in with their eyes closed and their hearts tight with heady thrill.

Or maybe they have. Once, long ago. Maybe, if pushed, something in their memory would kindle and they would be able to recall a time when blood ran high in their veins and love and sex were one and the same thing and life was raw and every bit as all-consuming as the flames they try to keep you from today. Maybe their fires have simply gone out, maybe they are used to their own diminished states by now. Not her. She is still glowing among the coals, no more than a charred remnant who once lived and loved without fear, who played as near to the flames as she damn well felt and, of course, got burnt.

***

FIFTEEN

During those months, I felt sometimes that if I blinked, Mikey would be here, that if I blinked again, he would not, that all I had to do was this: open my eyes – he was here, close my eyes, not here. Here. Not. Here.

Not. I woke up and this time I really was alone. Monday. Mikey had left as usual on Saturday but here I was, two days later, still waking and expecting him to be there, still feeling the soft punch of dismay when he wasn't. It was 6:30am, Isla for once still asleep. Too tired, too lazy to go and get myself a cup of tea, I lay in bed and ran through the day ahead. Valentina had said she would come over as usual for lunch, so that was something to look forward to – although I looked forward to our time together less than I had a month ago. On Friday I had seen her but only briefly. She'd had a private client, had dropped Zac over for a couple of hours but had not come in for a chat.

She had less time to chat these days, I thought then, and more private classes. Were they private classes? Or was she seeing him, leaving me holding the baby? The thought was horrible. I knew I shouldn't even be thinking that way about her but now I'd had the thought, I couldn't get it out of my head. No matter how many times I told myself there would be a completely reasonable, even boring explanation, the man in the car was lodged in my psyche. He had by then taken the borderline comic form of a policeman in uniform, a domed helmet, a whistle. *Let's be 'avin' you.* Was it possible she was lying to me? I knew people functioned fine on lies: their own, other people's, it didn't matter – they could glide around like swans on a lake, shaking untruths like water from their oily feathers. God knows, I'd met enough of these people in my time at *The*

Tribune – politicians, white-collar criminals, a church minister once – big lies, big secrets. You'd think the smaller lies of love or friendship might matter less in the greater context of the world. But they don't. They matter more.

Isla cried out from her cot. I threw back the covers and went to her, found her flushed, irritable, her brow singeing and damp against my hand. I ran and fetched the Calpol, injected it with the medicine syringe into her wailing mouth. I carried her around, shushing, soothing, singing to her. She refused milk. Clamped her lips at the sight of Weetabix, cried at it, turned her head away. I carried her around the cottage, trying to comfort her but by ten o'clock, she was sicker than I'd ever seen her, her eyelids swollen, her forehead hot as lava. She would not stop crying, even in my arms. I added baby ibuprofen to the cocktail, stripped off her clothes and bathed her with cool water. Still she raged, despairing, wailing. I tried to take her temperature but she was thrashing about so much I couldn't hold the thermometer steady for long enough without dropping her. And then gurgling, a foul smell. I took off her nappy to find it covered in inhuman, greenish, liquid shit.

"Oh, my wee girl," I said over her howling cries. Nothing, nothing strikes into your heart more than that sound, that plaintive look in your own baby's eyes: help me, Mummy. Help me.

I'm trying, baby, I'm trying.

"Shh, now," I cooed. "Mummy's here. Dear, dear, dear, let's get you cleaned up."

Her cries escalated, as urgent and frightening as ambulance sirens in the dead of night. Somehow I managed to put a clean nappy on her, to pull on a fresh romper suit. I picked her up, rocked and bounced her on my hip, trying all the while to soothe her into quiet.

I had to call Valentina. There was no way she could come today. I searched for my phone but Isla gave another howl and exploded again. I cleaned her a second time, ran cold water into the bath and dumped the soiled baby clothes in there before pacing up and down the landing, singing as softly and as calmly as I could.

"Ally bally, ally bally bee,
Sittin on yer mammy's knee,
Greetin' for a wee bawbee,
Tae buy some Coulter's Candy."

She calmed down a little but still each one of her cries pierced the skin and bones of me. She was still so hot, her head lolled back against my arm. Was she simply sleepy or was she becoming listless? Feeling terribly alone, I dialled Valentina's number.

As always these days, she answered straight away.

"Val," I said, halfway to crying. "Isla's sick. She's really sick. She's shitting green, it's like soup and I can't get her temperature to go down. I'm going to have to cancel. I won't get out for food, I won't get out I don't think all day, I ... I think I need to take her to hospital."

"Shona. Shona?"

I made myself shut up.

"Shona, listen. You're right, you do need to take her in. It's going to be OK, but she might need a saline drip, maybe antibiotics, and you need to get her checked out. Are you listening?"

"Yes."

"Good. Now keep listening. I'm in my car, do you hear me? I'm already in my car. I'm driving over right now and I'm going to take you to the hospital."

"I've got the car. I can take her."

"You can't drive. You're hysterical. Shona, stay there, I'm on my way."

"Oh God!"

"Shona, listen, babe. Listen to me. You don't need to panic, it's going to be fine. Are you listening to me, Shona? I'm coming over. I'm going to drive you to the hospital. Stay where you are."

155

Isla fell asleep before we reached Aberdeen Royal Infirmary, exhausted by her own crying, by pain. When I told them it was the baby I was there for, they put me to the front of the line, told me I'd go straight through.

"You should go," I told Valentina, who was sitting on one of the red vinyl seats flicking through an ancient copy of *Saga* magazine. "I'll get a cab home."

"I'm staying right here," she said. "At least until I've finished this mag. It's gripping."

I smiled. Now that we were in the hands of the hospital, I had calmed down at least enough to do that. "Has Zac shown any sign of illness?"

"Nah."

"Where is he by the way?" I hadn't thought. It was her day off – she should have him.

"I dumped him with Red at the shop. I was in town when you called."

It occurred to me the illness could have come from Red – via Valentina. But Valentina had showed no sign of even the merest sniffle.

"Is Red better?"

"Hmm?"

"He was ill," I prompted. "Must be better if he's back at work, eh?"

She shook her head, waved her hand. "Oh, you know what men are like, it's kiss-me-Hardy as soon as they have to blow their frickin' nose. Then the game comes on and suddenly they've recovered."

"Isla McGilvery Quinn?"

I turned to see a stout nurse in heavy-framed glasses smiling benignly at us. I raised my hand to her and bent to kiss Valentina on the cheek.

"I'll be right here," she said.

"Thanks," I said. "I don't know what I'd have done without you."

The doctor diagnosed a nasty strain of gastric flu, common in babies. It came with this specific type of diarrhoea, he told us. At eight months old, well fed, she would have been able to fight it off but we'd been right to bring her in. He wrote down the name of an electrolyte drink to help her recover her salts. Valentina stopped in town, hovered on the double yellows outside the chemist while I ran inside.

"Lemonade," I said when I got back in the car. "Flat lemonade. Or ice pops. That's what we always had after a bug. Electrolyte drinks are a wee bit over the top if you ask me."

She didn't reply. Her eyes flicked to the rear view and she pulled out onto Union Street.

"What about you?" I went on, a little wired after the stress, wanting to chat about anything, nothing, whatever. "Did you have flat lemonade or is it a Scottish thing?"

Again, she said nothing. I looked at her, her face set, her eyes still fixed on the road.

We stopped at the traffic lights.

"Val?"

She blinked and turned to me. "Oh, sorry, what?" She seemed to have come out of her daydream, back to the present. "What did we have after the shits, is that what you're asking?" Her eyes drifted to the lights as they changed from red to amber. She engaged first, accelerated through amber to green. "I really can't remember." Her tone was cross or bored or both, as if I was getting on her nerves. "My father left when I was two," she continued, "so I have no idea what he did, shit-wise or otherwise."

"I'm sorry," I said. Why hadn't she told me this, I wondered. The information felt too big, in a friendship like ours, not to have been mentioned before.

"Don't be sorry," she said, eyes fixed on the road. "I'm not. There's nothing to say."

"And your mother was a teacher, you said?" I couldn't remember her telling me this either, but I knew it so she must have at some point.

"Comprehensive school. Pretty thrilling all round, I think you'll agree."

"What did she teach again?"

"Good grief, Shona," she glanced at me and rolled her eyes. "What do you want, a resumé?"

"No. Sorry. I was curious, that's all." I fell silent for a second, afraid I'd upset her. But I couldn't keep it up, I was too antsy. "Do you see them?"

"They're both in Aus, so both too far away. In every sense of the word."

"I thought your mum was coming over to see you? The day we met, remember? You said she was coming over? You were worried about Zac swearing?"

She shook her head. "I was joking." She glanced at me and smiled thinly before returning her eyes to the road. "I was trying to impress you."

She didn't appear to be joking now.

"Impress me?" I said. "Why would you want to impress me? I'm just some hack who got herself pregnant a wee bit earlier than she meant to."

"Don't say that," she snapped. "Don't devalue yourself like that, Shona. Really. Honestly, you Brits think this self-deprecation thing is so charming but it isn't. It's a disaster. It's what women do or feel they have to do to get people to like them and I hate it." She was almost shouting, not looking at me, her knuckles white on the steering wheel. "All that *oh, don't feel threatened by me 'cause I'm no good at anything at all.* What is it, unfeminine or some such bullshit? To be good? I teach yoga. I'm a frickin' great yoga teacher. So what? Do I have to go around saying I'm the worst teacher in the world, tell people my clients come back year after year because they like my frickin' leotard? It's pathetic, frankly." She took the roundabout on two wheels.

I wanted to tell her to slow down but thought better of it. My cheeks went hot, my eyes prickled.

"I'm really grateful you took us to hospital," I said. "I know thank you is not enough but ..."

"I don't mean you," she said – more quietly, more kindly, nudging into the build-up of traffic towards the Brig O'Dee. For a moment neither of us said anything.

"I didn't realise you felt so strongly about it," I said.

She shook her head. "I'm trying to get you to value yourself a bit more that's all. I know you Brits don't like to blow your own trumpet but what's the point having a trumpet if you can't blow it? Pretty pointless trumpet if you ask me."

"Where I come from," I said, "that's not really our style. But I take your point."

We crossed the bridge, headed right onto the South Deeside Road. The route was as familiar to me now as my own teeth. Across the Dee, on the golf course, I could see men in tweed caps. I wished Mikey were here, in the driving seat or that I'd taken Isla to the hospital myself. I wished I hadn't called Valentina. She had dropped everything to help me this morning but perhaps she resented it. It wasn't the words she said – they were good words, solid and sisterly – it was the way she had said them, the anger in her voice. Did she secretly see me as pathetic? Now that we knew one another better, did I in fact get on her nerves? I wondered if the kinder words that had followed her outburst were no more than leaves hastily thrown down to cover her tracks. Perhaps there were other things about me she despised. And if she was harbouring an armoury of secret irritations like this, what would it take for her to blast me again?

Back at the cottage, Valentina unlocked the door and headed upstairs to use the bathroom. Inside, a sepulchral cold, colder somehow than outside. I put Isla, who had fallen asleep again, in the living room and came back into the kitchen to set about making Valentina and me something to eat. It was after three and I was cold and starving hungry. Shivering, I put the heating on, emptied some soup into a pan, thick sliced a white loaf I'd taken out of the freezer at dawn and slathered it in thick butter. I was still wearing my coat.

I need to stop a second and say something. I just realised, the way I'm telling you all this, you must think I had no other friends, but I did. When Valentina was giving classes on Tuesday, Wednesdays and Thursdays, I saw other people quite a bit. There was a baby music group on a Wednesday and I always went out for coffee afterwards with the girls from there. I joined Aquababies down at the baths, took Isla there on Thursdays and there too I made friends with three great lassies who came in from one of the housing estates at the other side of town. But the thing is, none of these pals come into this story and besides, I didn't connect with them like I did with Val. She and I shared the same dark sense of humour, and we were both outsiders, incomers. That's what I would have said at the time.

Valentina reappeared and told me I should put Isla into her cot, where she could rest properly.

"OK. Yes, I suppose you're right." I fetched Isla and carried her upstairs. She didn't stir. I laid her in her cot, placed a thin blanket over her and stayed a moment so I could look at her. Her skin had a soft pink blush now that the storm in her had passed. Her eyelashes curled upwards, tiny blonde spokes, her hands closed into two miniature fists. I sighed and, for the first time that day, relaxed. I stroked her cheek with my finger and whispered to her. "I love you so much, little one."

I stayed there a moment, composing myself, before returning downstairs. Valentina had laid the table, poured the soup into bowls and was waiting for me.

"Are you OK?" She took a big, almost bestial bite of the fresh bread. "Do you want a drink?"

"Not just now." I sat down and looked her in the eye. She smiled, her lips touching, her canine tooth catching on her bottom lip in that way it did. The closeness between us seemed to return. Maybe I had only imagined a degree of separation, because of what I knew or thought I knew about her.

"Who were you with that day at the supermarket?" I said.

"When?" She held my gaze with her intense green eyes and for a moment I thought I would falter.

"At Markies." I had to look at my knees. Her stare was too intense. "When I saw you. You said you were with Red but, I don't know, you were so strange with me and you wouldn't let me meet him and then I – I know I haven't said anything about it, I didn't want to ... what I mean is, I saw you. Going out of the car park with ... well, it wasn't Red, was it?"

When I looked up I knew I had been right. Her cheeks had flushed a little and she was staring into her soup.

"I'm not judging," I added, keeping my voice gentle. "But I don't want us not to be able to talk about things."

She thrust herself backwards, her chair scraped across the stone tiles. "You want to talk about it?"

"Yes," I said. "Don't you? Otherwise we've got this whole 'thing' between us. I don't want it to drive a wedge into our friendship. And, as I said, I'm not judging."

She was looking at me, unblinking, as if I was mad.

I reached across the table, tried to beckon her forward, to take my hand, but she didn't move.

"You're not out of your mind?" she said. "You're not going to strangle me with your bare hands?"

I shook my head. "Why would I do that? We're friends. We're not here to punish each other, are we? Whatever's going on, I'm supposed to help you bury the body!"

She gripped the edge of the table with both hands, as if to stand or, perhaps, as if to stop herself from sliding off her chair.

"You can tell me, you know."

She screwed up her eyes, seemed incredulous, suspicious even. "Are you fucking with me?"

"No!" I was panicking. I had pushed her too hard. I smiled, to show her I meant it kindly. "Is it the policeman?"

She shook her head a fraction, as if in hesitation. Her right eye twitched. I was watching her so closely, trying to gauge her reaction – I was afraid of scaring her, and yes, to my eternal shame, I was thinking of myself. I didn't want her to up and leave and never come back. Without her, my world, reduced as it was, would disintegrate.

"The policeman from outside Markies ... Marks and Spencer's, you know? The one who tried to give you a parking ticket. I thought it might be him. The guy who pulled you up for waiting on the double yellows. John. Douglas, was it? Duggan? He gave you his number?" I laughed. "I thought you were joking, but I remember finding it in the footwell – so when I saw you I thought maybe you'd held onto his number after all and, oh, I don't know ..."

Her eyes searched mine. Looking for trust, to see if she could trust me, is what I thought.

"Yes," she said. "John Duggan. Yes." She put her face into her hands and let out a long groan.

"Oh God, that's a relief."

I reached out, laid my hand on her arm. "It's always a relief to tell the truth."

SIXTEEN

Things with Red had been patchy since before we'd met. This she told me while I made tea. I rested my hand on her shoulder when I placed the cup in front of her on the table. These tender gestures I made, these small loving acts of friendship.

"I checked his phone," she said. "This is ages ago. And I found out he'd been on one of those websites where you post pictures of yourself. Of your private parts, you know?"

"My God. That's pretty seedy." I knew people did this but even so I have to admit I was shocked. "I mean, not seedy, but it's a bit anatomical for my taste. But it obviously floats a lot of boats otherwise people wouldn't do it, would they?"

Valentina produced a packet of cigarettes from her bag and pulled one out. I wondered if she would ask before lighting up and when she lit up I wondered why I'd ever thought she would ask.

"Seedy," she said. "You said it. Men are pigs. Animals. So I drove to the beach and I parked up. I don't know why I went there, I guess I wanted to be alone, have a smoke, whatever. I was leaning over to get my ciggies from my bag I saw that scrap of paper in the footwell. John Duggan. He was a nice guy, I thought. Good-looking too. Fuck it, I thought, you know?"

I nodded even though, to be honest, I couldn't grasp what she was telling me. No matter how mad at Mikey I got sometimes, I had no idea what it felt like to want to cheat, or how it felt to be cheated on for that matter. The whole idea made me want to put my hands over my ears. But I didn't. I listened and I believed.

Did I? I certainly told myself I believed – maybe that's nearer to the truth, because if I'm honest I would say that it was at that moment, down, low down in my guts, I began to doubt her. I wonder now if I'd always doubted her, right from the start, on some subliminal level. Why else would I have felt a sudden urge to burst into tears for no apparent reason the night she came for dinner with her African lilies and her black dress? But I did not face the rumbling unease within me. I ploughed on, hoping perhaps that I was wrong, and that it would all work out.

Winter came. I'd spent October and November shrugging my shoulders, wondering what all the fuss was about. The Aberdeen winter – how they'd teased us about it back in Glasgow – yet in those early winter months, the weather really wasn't so cold as all that. I'm not saying I was running around the back lawn in a bikini but as long as I put my gloves, hat, scarf and coat on I was toasty. And it wasn't like I'd moved from the Bahamas.

We spent a quiet Christmas at the cottage – holed up with plenty of food and drink and of course a raging fire in the hearth. I went to Glasgow for New Year as Mikey was offshore so that was a low-key affair too: me, Davie and my folks. My other brothers were off with their families. As seasons of goodwill go, it was a wee bit dull to be honest but I didn't mind, I knew I'd be back to big Hogmanays soon enough.

January came and with it the sub-zeros. I saw Valentina less but we texted each other in flurries a couple of times a week, met up once or twice a fortnight. The cottage froze – ice patterns like thick white flock wallpaper on the windows in the mornings. I had to run the heating at night as well as all day to stop myself having to walk about with my shoulders hunched, my arms crossed. I kept the fire going twenty-four seven, woke up early to rake it out and lay it again, sometimes doing nothing more than rekindling the embers still warm in the grate. At that temperature,

164

there was no question of simply popping out to grab more wood from the stables. Not without a full set of arctic exploration gear. No such thing as bad weather, they say. Only inadequate protection.

On Radio Scotland they forecast snow, ten centimetres falling in the north. I knew I should prepare to be snowed in, alone. I could lose phone contact, power, the lot. That was the only time I thought about staying with my folks for the whole duration of Mikey's trip. I could have stayed on after Hogmanay but I didn't want to make extra work for my mum and now my confidence was coming back a little I relished the challenge, in my eyes, of the wild.

For twenty-four hours I stayed holed up in the cottage for fear of getting stranded outside with no way back home. But the snow stayed shy in its cloud and I, meanwhile, stayed indoors, trying to teach Isla to walk, trying not to bounce off the walls. When there was no word from Mikey that night, I assumed the phone lines were down. The next day, seeing little more than a thin, greyish slush, I decided the forecasters were exaggerating and that I would brave the roads no matter what. By that stage, getting stranded in town looked like a better option than going stir-crazy. I could always stay at Valentina's over on Union Grove in an emergency.

A trip to the shops required a survival kit: candles, matches, blankets. I packed chocolate biscuits as well. By the time I'd done all that, it was three o'clock in the afternoon and the light was all but gone. I decided to stay cosy indoors and go to town the following morning instead.

I woke to whiteness, phantom light. A childish excitement rose up in me at the sight of all that snow – thick white stoles bending the branches, softening the line of the ground with all that glittering white. Perfection. Out here, no feet to vandalise the surface. I wished Mikey were there to see it – so much I got a pain of longing in my chest.

I dug out the car and left the engine running to warm the interior. I cleared the driveway up to where the lane had

165

been gritted. By the time I finished I was sweating, my back and shoulders ached. I went to fetch Isla from the playpen. She had on her new snowsuit and looked like a marshmallow. I ran to pick up my keys and turned – turned and saw her, Isla, walk two steps towards me.

I fell to my knees. "Isla! Clever! Come to Mummy!"

She fixed me with her eyes and gave a toothy grin, wobbling a little. She regained her balance, took three more steps then fell down.

"Clever girl!" My eyes filled with tears. She was walking.

She got up, held onto my finger while I led her, step by slow step, towards the door. I led her outside, saw the incomprehension in her face.

"Snow," I said. "This is snow!"

Isla's first steps. Isla's first sighting of snow. Our first snow at the cottage. Mikey was missing so much.

"No!" Isla pointed, eyes wide, forehead creased in wonder. "No!"

"Snow! That's right!" I grabbed my iPhone from my bag. "Snow," I said, taking a photo of her holding the snow up to her face, another of her licking it, another of her wrinkling her nose in delight at its delicious coldness. "Snow, snow, snow."

I filmed her then: two steps and down, four steps and down, giggles, picking herself up, determined. Snow in her hands, eating it, blowing it, finding it hilarious. Like that she moved and tasted and fell towards the car, while I took way too many pictures. After a minute or two, she held up her hands and whined. Her tiny fingers were dark pink. I ran back into the house and grabbed her gloves from the trunk. I took the gloves out to her, breathed warm breath into them and put them on her little ice-cold hands.

She let me pick her up and strap her into the jeep. I drove slowly, no more than ten miles per hour along the lane, hooked like a blind woman over the steering wheel. There's a line of pines opposite where the track hits the T-junction.

166

They block the view so at first you can't see out onto the fields. When I drove out from behind them, the sight took my breath away. There was nothing else on the road so I stopped the car. White, as far as I could see. No sign of my lone horse, my houyhnhnm. And vast. The vast whiteness of countryside under snow, the vast white sky.

Snow. In Iceland they have fifty words for it, don't they? Here, we're reduced to fitting adjectives around our one inadequate little noun: thick snow, white snow, snow like foam, foam-like snow. Snow that creaks like polystyrene underfoot, snow that melts to dirty slush at the roadside, snow that covers everything, that makes even the grimmest landscape look pure.

In town, the ruined snow lay scooshed up against the roadsides in dirty brown cornices. Rudimentary snowmen gesticulated with stick arms in some of the gardens, where kids had been too excited to wait until they got back from school to start building. Later, they would race to the slopes and the parks, dragging their plastic sleighs along behind them. They'd return home, blue with cold, shivering, asking for hot chocolate. At the thought of them, these unknown kids, I felt a rush of something warm and unnamed – a formless idea of the future took solid shape in my mind: Isla, a walking, laughing girl coming in through the back door of the cottage, flushed with cold, bright with her life's adventures, and some other child, a brother perhaps, trailing in behind her, cheeks flushed like hers, snow in his duffle coat hood. How lovely that would be – to warm their wet hands in mine, to peel off their ice-flaked jackets, sit them by the fire and bring them hot chocolate.

The roads in the centre had been cleared by sheer volume of traffic. My aim was no more specific than to while away some time, to make a trip out of nothing. I decided to call in at a new deli that Valentina had told me about. John had introduced her to it. It was at the top of Market Street, she'd said, where the picture framer's used to be. It was called

The Grocery and they had the best fresh Italian bread – John was half-Italian – brands of oil and wine you'd never heard of, delicious fresh savouries displayed in a clear chilled counter. Apparently this arrangement was based on the American idea of a village store. According to John.

So I went in. And that's when I saw Mikey. Nothing unusual about seeing your partner in a deli – unless of course he's meant to be in the middle of the North Sea.

I saw the back of his head first. I knew better than to react. I was used to seeing the back of his head, his profile, him, everywhere. I'd called after him once or twice, only for that person to turn to me and not be him – to my eternal embarrassment. This was what missing someone meant sometimes. It was a kind of grief. So when he did turn, when he did see me, when it was him and when his face spread in shock, I too reeled.

"Dada," said Isla from the sling, her voice seeming to come from my heart.

"Shona." He put up his hands as if he were under arrest and blushed. I tried to think if I'd ever seen him blush about anything before.

I cannot remember exactly what I did. Perhaps I took a step back, perhaps my mouth dropped open – but nothing came out.

"Red-handed." His face creased into a smile.

"What ...?"

He emitted a strange avuncular chuckle, still shaking his head. "Caught me. Red-handed." He pulled me to him and kissed my head before crouching to kiss Isla in her sling. "Caught Daddy in the act, haven't you?" He rubbed her nose with his. She giggled. "Now, don't tell Mummy, but Daddy got sent home at seven o'clock this morning so he was picking up some scrummy bits and pieces for a surprise." He pushed his finger to his lips. "Shh. Don't tell."

"Shh," said Isla. "Dada."

"I'm right here, darling." He stood straight and kissed me on the cheek. "That's a shame. I was hoping to arrive like Prince Charming with a luxury hamper."

"But you're on the rig."

He threw out his hands, his mouth a flat line. "Compressor's gone. The gas compressor. They've had to send for the suppliers to fix it so they've moved to skeleton staff. There's a whole squad flying over. They need the beds so here I am – booted off!"

I met his eye. My head felt wrong on my neck, like I was holding it at an odd angle but couldn't stop myself. "How come you didn't phone?"

"What's the matter?" He frowned, tucked a strand of my hair into my woolly hat. "You don't seem very pleased to see me."

The pink in his cheeks was receding. The lady at the counter was asking him if the olives in the square plastic tub were enough. Through the glass cabinet, on the other side where the lady was serving, I could see a wrap of cold meat, a small box of four designer chocolates and a bottle of Prosecco with an orange label: Valdobbiadene. Superiore. D.O.C.G. Valentina was right, I thought. I'd never seen that brand before.

"I tell you what," Mikey was saying, "I won't tell you what we're having. At least that bit can be a surprise."

I'm not confident I can tell you the rest. Maybe I should say nothing more. But I'm almost there, so I guess I may as well finish.

Mikey suggested grabbing a cup of coffee. I let him take my hand and lead me to a small café near the dock. It was a greasy spoon place, with linoleum floors and Formica tables. The kind of place folk like Mikey go, due to some perceived notion of authenticity. Me, I hate those places. Authenticity isn't something I've ever felt the lack of.

"I'm gonna have the full Scottish," he said. "May as well now we're here, eh? What about you, Shone?"

"Just a cup of tea, thanks." I fussed over Isla, looked at her, looked at the floor, looked anywhere but at him. Why I behaved like this, I had no idea at the time. If you'd asked me then, in that moment, I'd have said strangeness. Strangeness was all I felt.

"Sure?" Mikey was saying. "Go on, they do great sausages here. Real cheap shiny bangers. God knows what they put in them, probably ground up eyeballs but I love them, they're brilliant."

"I'm sure they are." I pulled off my woollen hat, unwound my scarf. My nose was running, my eyes streaming in the heat of the caff.

"Here." Mikey handed me a paper napkin from the table. "Freezing, isn't it?"

Isn't it. He had pronounced the t hard. The effect was fake. He never pronounced his ts that way, they always hissed a little. It was one of the first things I'd noticed about him, one of the things that made me fall in love. He got up and went to order at the till. Pulled his wallet from his back pocket. Paid up. Came back and took his seat.

"Are you OK?"

I nodded, met his eye. "So this thing sent you home."

"The gas compressor, yeah. Bloody disaster. Not for me though." He took my hand. At the touch of his warm skin I realised how cold my hands had become.

"Does that mean you'll be here all week, then the following two weeks? So you'll be at home three weeks in total?"

"I'm not sure." He tapped his fork against the table's edge. "We had to go straight to the office from the heliport. I've got to go back in now, after this. Find out what's happening."

"So, what? You'll know by tonight?"

"Yeah." He leant back to allow the guy from the café to put his plate and my tea down on the table. I nodded my thanks, Mikey said cheers and carried on talking.

170

"Hopefully they'll let me stay home. I'll have to see how it goes."

"OK."

I watched him eat. He carved through the bacon, made a great pile on his fork: egg, sausage, white pudding, black pudding, bacon – a real heart attack of a mouthful – and shoved it all in. He stopped talking then, his mouth was too full.

"Didn't your mum ever tell you not to put it all in your mouth at once?"

He grinned, swallowed it all down. "I like to have it all at once."

On the way home, I stopped the car and googled 'gas compressor' on my iPhone. I saw immediately that it was a vital piece of kit, skimmed the listings, eyes landing on 'dangers' and 'fire'. After a moment, I looked up the number for BP – I was too paranoid to call Maple so I called BP and asked to speak to a drilling engineer, and after a few bars of lift music was put through to a guy who told me his name was Pete.

"Oh hi," I said. "My name is Diane. I'm a researcher for the BBC drama department ..."

"Oh, aye?"

"I wonder if you could help me, it's a small technical enquiry actually." I laughed. "I'm working on a short drama series about the oil industry and I need to know what would happen if the gas compressor were to break down. The main character works offshore, you see, and we need him to be evacuated from the rig, for the purposes of the story ..."

"Right, well, in the event of the compressor blowing, yes, that would be ..."

He talked a lot. People love talking about what they do to someone who appears to be interested. They would call out to the suppliers, he explained. Evacuation was highly likely in the event of a big problem.

"... bunk space is tight, you see, and repairs can take days. Does that answer your question?"

"It certainly does," I said. "Thank you, you've been more than helpful."

I hung up. It was true then. My chest sank with relief.

Later that morning, Mikey called to say he was stuck in the office, that he would bring the goodies for supper instead of lunch. That night he came home and announced that he could stay the full three weeks. Due to the rota system, it had to be that way. He had brought with him the basket: the olives, some fresh pasta, some home-made (by someone) wild boar ragu, which he prepared once he'd put Isla to bed. And the chocolates, of course. The Prosecco was too warm to chill in time. We drank supermarket wine instead: Hardy's Shiraz. Red. Australian.

He washed up, seemed determined not to let me do anything at all. Like a guilty person, I thought, then felt guilty myself for thinking it. But winter, isolation, all that business with Valentina and PC John Duggan, had shaken my faith in my own relationship. At least that's what I'd say to anyone if I had to justify that, when he excused himself to go to the loo, I spent one long minute staring at his phone on the countertop before grabbing it and scrolling through his text messages. I couldn't believe I was doing it even in the moment but I was. But there were only texts from me, a football-related banter trail between him and Robbie and one from George Maple, a colleague I presumed, asking if he'd completed some request or other. Nothing. I opened the photos – all of me, Isla, him, all three of us, one of Isla with his parents, Isla, Isla, Isla. I put the phone back, adjusted it to what I thought was the exact position it had been in when I picked it up. My insides burned with shame. Still I stared at his phone, knowing that even though no one had seen, I could not take back what I had just done.

A second later, I heard his footsteps on the stairs.

"Hey." He came up behind me and ran his hands over my shoulders, up my neck. He leant down and kissed me on the cheek. "Shall I light a fire?"

I took hold of his hand and kissed it. "No, it's OK. I'll do it."

We drank the rest of the red in front of the fire. The stress of suspicion had tired me out. I ached all over, as if I'd been in an accident. So, when he laid his hand on my neck and told me I was beautiful, that I was his, that he loved me, when he pulled me to the floor and covered my mouth with his, I had neither the strength nor the will to stop him.

SEVENTEEN

Two weeks on. I blinked. Two weeks off. I blinked. He was here. I blinked. He had gone.

On Monday Valentina came over as usual. I had not seen her for a few weeks. She breezed into the cottage in her usual way, proffering wine and some red tulips, which she presented to me with a shy smile.

"Thanks," I said, "but you don't need to bring flowers for me."

"Trust me, I do," she said, taking hold of my arm before I could turn away, her eyes glowing green.

The kids played – if that's what babies do at eleven months or so. Zac wasn't walking yet so he sat in Isla's bouncy chair while she toddled around him, passing him bright bricks, plastic lorries, toy figures.

"Ta," she said, holding out whatever it was, her face set in hope: accept my gift.

Valentina sat down at the kitchen table: a sandwich lunch, a few crisps, white wine. Though, actually, I barely drank. Isla was sleeping better and I was sick of feeling woolly-headed.

Valentina took out her phone and held it up, her expression coy.

"What?" I asked.

"I thought you might like to see a picture of John."

I didn't, not really. It was the first time she'd mentioned him since our conversation before Christmas. I found it odd that she would bring it up out of nowhere like that.

"Sure," I said and took the phone from her.

On the screen was a picture of the pair of them together. It looked like a selfie, taken in the centre of town. They were smiling away, in broad daylight.

"Don't you worry Red might find this?"

She snorted. "Ha! He's too doped up to notice me, let alone my phone."

"He's good-looking," I said, moving on. "Lovely dark hair."

"His father's Sicilian."

"You said."

"And yes, he's easy on the eye but so dull, bless him. Better than nothing though, eh?"

Red, then, was nothing. As if he did not exist.

"So what do you guys talk about?" I asked, feeling less comfortable by the second. "Does he like the same films and books?"

She laughed. "God, no! Shona – it's a bit of fun. It's just sex, you know? Not like we're going to break each other's hearts or anything."

"Ah. OK."

"And I've been so low lately I guess I felt like I deserved some fun for a change. You can't help how you feel, can you?"

"No. I guess you can't."

I felt a little bit sick. But I listened, because that's what friends do. And wasn't it me, after all, who had urged her to take me into her confidence, who had wanted intimacy above all else?

"Last week we went to the new place up by the golf course. You know that hotel? We ordered room service and when it came we were, you know, in the throes." She clapped her hand over her mouth to suppress her shrieking laughter and rocked back and forth. "So he picks me up – he's inside me, right? I had to wrap my legs around his waist while he carried me, like that, to the frickin' door." She gave another shriek.

175

I composed my face into a smile that said: well, I never. Fancy that.

"He stops off halfway to grab his wallet from the chest of drawers. He pulls out a note and hobbles over to the door and he says, 'Hello?' And the guy says, 'room service' and I'm laughing so hard at this point but I'm really trying to hold it in and John has me against the wall but his knees are buckling, poor guy. He's smaller than me." She giggled. "And he opens the door a crack, pops his head round. He's got one hand under my butt and with the other he gives this guy a tenner tip and says, 'leave it there,' except his voice is really strained so it was more like ..." She repeated what John had said in a strained voice, her glee palpable. She poured the information over me, like hooch from a jug. I guess she must have thought, now I knew about the illicit brew, that the two of us could get blindly, secretly, gloriously drunk.

"I thought you said he was dull," I said.

"Oh, he is. But not in that way." She laughed and shook her head. "Oh, Shona."

Watching her laugh, feeling the joy that came off her, it occurred to me not for the first time that I must be her closest friend and that perhaps she, like me, had been lonely when we met.

"So," she said coyly, nudging me with her elbow, narrowing her eyes. "You never talk about you and Michael. I bet he's no slouch in that department."

I felt myself blush. "Er ... he's ... yes. I've no complaints."

She leant forward, poked me in the chest. I realised she was a little drunk. "Come on, Shona, don't be so secretive. You're not a prude, are you?"

"I'm not," I said, flustered. "But I can't think of anything to say without ..."

"Without what?"

I shrugged, felt my face grow hot. "Without ... betraying him, I suppose."

She threw herself back in her chair. "Oh, for crying out loud, Shona! Chill. Out. We're only talking." She took a slug of wine, gesticulated with the glass in her hand. "What about when he, you know, in the moment when he ..." she raised her eyebrows, smirked.

I nodded. "What about that?"

She shrugged. "I mean, come on, does he do or say anything in particular?"

"Like, 'I'm coming', you mean?"

"God, you're hilarious!" She laughed so loudly I felt myself relax a little. I was being uptight. Women had these conversations all the time, I supposed, people had flings. It was the way of the world. Maybe I was weird or, like she said, prudish. Maybe I did need to loosen up.

"I suppose," I said, taking a swig of white wine. "I mean, he gets this look in his eye – like he's taking a dump, you know?"

She laughed again, arms wrapped around her belly, feet planted together on the floor to support all that hilarity. I wanted to join in but couldn't. I felt horrible, dirty, wrong.

So I didn't say any more. Instead I listened to everything she had to tell me and said *hmm* and *oh yes* and I drank the wine and did not mention the growing discomfort I felt. What could I have said? There was nothing to say. It was a feeling, to describe it in words would have been like trying to screw smoke to a brick wall.

At three o'clock, Valentina checked her watch and gasped.

"I need to pee," she said. "Then I'll get my shit together and leave you in peace."

She disappeared up the stairs, singing. After a minute or two, I got up to clear the plates. On the floor, Valentina's bag had turned upside down, half its contents spilt over the stone tiles. I put the plates back on the table and bent to tidy her things. Her beaded cloth purse had fallen out along with an official letter, unopened. On the front of the letter I read, couldn't help but read:

Ms. G. Smyth-Banks,
14, Fittie Place,
Fittie
AB11 5BT

"I think you're out of loo roll," came Valentina's voice. She was halfway down the stairs.

I thrust the letter back in the bag, my face hot. I looked up as she was crossing the hallway. She glanced from the bag back to me.

"Your things had fallen out," I explained, felt I had to explain.

She took the bag from me and pulled it onto her shoulder. Her movements had slowed. She appeared to reconsider her action, and placed the bag on the chair.

"That reminds me," she said, pausing between each word. She turned towards the front window, as if she'd heard something outside, then back to me. "I've got to get to the post office before it closes."

I took hold of our wine glasses, headed for the sink, ran some hot soapy water. With my back to her, I said, "Got a package to pick up?"

"No, it's this damn letter." I heard the chink of her keyring on keys. She was rooting – or pretending to root – in her bag. Why, I wondered, would I think she was pretending?

I plunged my hands into the hot water. Of course, I thought, the letter was from her to someone else. Why had I not realised that immediately? What other possibility was there? I was a nervous wreck.

"Got to post it?"

"Sort of." Her voice came quieter and louder as she moved about the kitchen, the strain and ease of it as she bent or straightened to collect hers and Zac's stuff. "Postman delivered a letter addressed to someone at the other end of town to my flat in Union Grove. Can you believe that? Brainless idiot."

178

Not from her to someone else then.

"Can't you redirect it?" I squeezed the cloth. My hands glowed red.

"What do I do, stick it back in the post box?"

"Um, yeah. You underline the name and write *not known at this address* on the envelope." I turned, intending to look her in the eye but found myself staring at my own hands, wiping them on the tea towel. "That's what I always do anyway."

I made myself look at her.

She did not look away. "Maybe I'll do that then. Probably got stuck to one of my letters in the sorting office and got carried like a stowaway." She smiled, her tooth catching on her bottom lip. "Cute, when you think about it."

"I suppose. Otherwise why would your postie even have it in his bag? Which reminds me, I don't have your address."

"That's right."

"If you give me your second name ..." I took out my iPhone and looked up at her.

"What?"

"Your name."

"The name of the street? I told you, Union Grove. Seagull paradise."

"I meant your name. Your surname."

"Oh," she said slowly, light dawning. "Sure, right. My second name as in my surname. It's D'Angelo."

I typed it in. "Is that Italian?"

"I guess. Somewhere along the line. But listen, I'll write it down and give it to you next time, eh? Unless you've got to have it right now, like, urgently? What're you going to do, write me?"

I can't put my finger on why but I had the feeling I always used to get at work when an interviewee was dodging a difficult line of questioning – like whatever I

179

asked would bounce back and I would still be none the wiser.

She pulled her bag onto her shoulder and headed into the living room to fetch Zac. I followed her to the doorway, watched her thread Zac's arms through his jacket.

"Are you on Facebook?" I insisted. "I could send a friend request."

"Why bother?" She buttoned up Zac's coat. "We're not Facebook friends, are we?" She stood, picked up Zac and plonked him on her hip. When she reached the doorway, she planted a kiss on my cheek and smiled. "We're real friends."

I waved her off from the front door, as I would normally, wishing she wouldn't drink and drive like that. When her car had disappeared behind the trees, I returned to the kitchen, picked up my iPhone and touched the browser icon, any worry for her safety replaced now by a deep unease. Something was not right, more than not right. Something was wrong, I felt it in my guts. Perhaps it was as simple as the imbalance of Valentina knowing where I lived without me knowing where she lived. But then, I had never asked her to be more specific than the street. That she and I always hung out at the cottage, I had taken as the natural order of things. The cottage was a pleasant place to while away an afternoon with small kids, whereas she lived in a small flat with no garden. Here, there was an acre of green space in summer, a cosy fire in winter – and it was safe, if you didn't count the fish pond.

She had said she would write her address down for next time – fine, she was in a rush. She had a letter addressed to someone else in her bag. But that was a postal error. All of it could be explained. But I had suspected that the man in her car had not been Red. And I had been right. Now I suspected her of, if not outright lying, then evasion of some intangible sort. In the supermarket, she had not said, *yes, Red is here with me*, she had simply said she was texting him to buy – peas, was it? She had presented the tip of a scenario and let me arrive at the implied conclusion myself.

There was still no signal on my phone. My next thought was to call Mikey from the landline. But he was offshore and anyway I was not sure what I would say. In an emergency I could contact him. But this wasn't an emergency.

It was nothing, nothing at all.

In the end I called Jeanie and was lucky enough to find her at her desk.

"Hello stranger," she said. "I was away to send a search party."

"It's so good to hear your voice," I said. Oh, and it was. How was it possible I'd left it so long? On my highly intermittent internet service, we'd managed to email each other a few times these last few months. But I hadn't liked to call her at work even though we used to call each other all the time, one desk to the other. And at night, by the time I'd finished with Isla and the dishes and all of that, I was always too tired.

"When are you going to invite me to stay anyway in your country hideaway?" she was saying in her dear voice, the accent of my home town.

"Don't give me that," I said, half-choked. "You know you can stay anytime you like."

"Aye, right. Maybe I will. Everything OK, doll?"

"Ach, we're up and running now. I'm fine, really." I paused. I wasn't fine, wasn't that why I was calling my best friend? My other best friend? "Actually, I wondered if you could look someone up for me. The signal is having an off day. It's having an off life, actually."

"Here's me thinking you were after my scintillating repartee. Go on."

I laughed. "I was wondering if you could get any information on Valentina D'Angelo. She's a yoga teacher up here – has her own business."

"Is that the lass you've got friendly with? The Australian? Whereabouts in Aus, do you know?"

"I don't, actually." I'd only just found out her second name, I almost added, but didn't.

"Is D'Angelo her married name?"

"I'm not sure. Maybe. No, I think she said it was her family name. Sorry, shite journalist, aren't I?" I thought for a second. "She lives on Union Grove. Not sure which number though."

"OK," Jeanie said, slowly. "You're sure you didn't make her up? Is she your imaginary friend? Come on, Shona, you can tell Aunty Jean."

I laughed again. "Aye, right. She lives at the bottom of the garden."

I had dropped Valentina off once in Union Grove, about halfway down, but she had stayed on the pavement, waving me off. I had found that charming. I had thought: what a nice girl. But as Jeanie tapped on the keys, I thought about how I had no idea what pictures were on Valentina's walls, whether she had carpets or hard floors, paint or wallpaper, what crockery she used, what books were on her bookshelf, what food was in her fridge. Apart from Zac, I had not seen anything of her life.

"There's quite a few on Facebook," said Jeanie. "What does she look like?"

"She's got red hair and green eyes. Kind of hippyish, you know? A wee bit New Age."

I waited.

"Nah," said Jeanie, then, after a moment, "they're all either Italian or American. Wait, one here with red hair here but sunglasses ..."

My stomach muscles clenched. "Australian? Yoga teacher?"

"Lives in Treviso, Italy."

"Not Aberdeen, Scotland."

"No." She tutted – the tap tap tap of pencil against teeth. "Let me try another search. You don't have an Australian address, even a town?"

"Nah. Sorry. It's just that she had a letter addressed to somebody Smyth-Banks in her bag, Smyth with a y, you know? Ms. G. – Grace maybe? Gloria? It's put the willies up me a bit. Probably nothing though – think the countryside's driving me a bit nuts, to be honest. I need to get back to work."

"LinkedIn, let's see ..." The flurry of keys, the heavy tap: Enter. "OK. Medico, Grafica, these are all Italians ... business analyst, mental health professional, no job specified but that's Italy again ..."

Valentina had said she needed to go to the post office to return that letter. She wasn't stupid enough to have thought that necessary. A lie, then. Possibly.

"There's nothing here," said Jeanie. "Obviously not a big online presence."

"That's funny. She's got her own business and she's very confident – can't imagine her being a shrinking violet when it comes to publicity. Or in any other context for that matter."

"Some people are luddites, Shone."

"Aye, I suppose she's a bit hippy dippy. Probably not very techie."

"I'll keep digging. I'll give you a bell if I find anything, OK, hen?"

"Ring me on my mobile," I said. "I'm going for a drive."

On Union Grove, I slowed the jeep, scanned the cars parked up along one side. I counted four red cars but none of them were her old Toyota. She had said she was going to the post office so maybe she had gone there after all, to hand it in. I drove on, looking for red cars, for answers.

Why I seized on this letter, I had no idea at the time. It wasn't the letter, I think now, but the same feeling of confusion as when I'd met her in the supermarket, the same bouncing ball of deflected questions. Then as in my kitchen earlier she had slowed her speech, her actions had become more deliberate. In both instances, her behaviour had been like that of an alien disguised in the unfamiliar skin of an earthling. Could it be something to do with the law-enforcing Italian lothario? Maybe he was married and she had told me otherwise because she had been too ashamed to admit it. Maybe it was he who had left the letter in her flat by mistake. Maybe John was his nickname, maybe he was Geoffrey or Giovanni – I had a hunch that was Italian for John? No, it was Ms. on the envelope, not Mr. Maybe the letter was for his wife and he'd dropped it at Valentina's flat? Gayle. Gaynor. Gabriella.

I pulled in, turned off the engine, wrenched up the handbrake. Palms pressed flat to my face, I made myself stop and think clearly. You're a journalist, Shona. Avoid speculation. What are the facts?

The letter had been in Valentina's bag. Fact. It had been addressed to a woman in Fittie.

The GPS took me to Fittie a different way, to the other side of the settlement, near the docks. With Isla strapped into her backpack, I walked by the harbour wall, past the lighthouse, until I came to the same set of squares I had wandered around that time with Isla. The whole way here I had tried to bring to mind the house number on the envelope but couldn't. The name I could recall: Ms. G. Smyth-Banks. And I was pretty sure it had said Fittie Square. Or was it Place? I had been hoping to find someone and ask, the old-fashioned way, but there was no one about. And there looked to be three squares. All I could do was start at one end and walk slowly past the windows in the hope that something would jog my memory.

I can't remember how long I paced around before I remembered the darting shadow behind the window, only that as soon as I thought of it, I headed for that house. It had creeped me out at the time, I knew it had no meaning but I went anyway because I had nothing else to go on. The sign on the wall of the square read: Fittie Place. I could see the house on the far side of the green. I crossed, not bothering with the path. My shoes sank into the wet grass. My socks soaked up the water, became heavy. I got closer. Something on the ledge defined itself, as did the number: 14. 14 was, or could easily have been, the number on the envelope. The something was an ornament. It was a stork. It was a stork exactly like the one Mikey had given me. With a sick feeling, I stepped up to the window.

Peeping Toms, the old lady had said. A pound a peep. Well, sometimes, you need to peep – sometimes you need to pay your pound and find out what the fuck is going on. Still, I looked around me, cagey as a burglar, before putting my hand like a visor to my forehead to cut the glare from the glass. I leaned in and I peeped for all I was worth.

The window looked onto the living room. The sofa with the throw over it filled most of the floor. It was too big for the room; there was barely space for a wee coffee table and a television in the far corner. I pushed as near to the pane as I could, the glass cold against my nose. Immediately below the window was a sideboard, with photos in frames. But they were facing inwards, all I could see were the backs. I peered further in, made out a painting on the opposite wall of what looked like fishermen carrying an upturned boat over their heads, only their legs visible, their feet in rubber boots. On the grate was a thick white candle, half burnt down, unlit. In a frame on the mantelpiece, another photograph.

Of Mikey.

EIGHTEEN

Isla was crying.

"Hello?"

Someone was saying hello. Isla was crying. Someone was pulling at my arm.

"Hello? Can you get up?"

I opened my eyes. An old woman with tinted glasses was peering into my face.

"You fell," she said. "I think you might have fainted. I saw you from across the way, ken?"

I sat upright, the pathway cold and gritty on my hands. My head was spinning. The woman was grabbing at my coat sleeve, trying and failing to pull me up. I raised my hand – it's OK, I can manage – stood slowly, keeping my head low. The woman was bent over, baby-talking to Isla. I put my hand to the wall to steady myself. After a moment, Isla stopped crying.

"That's it, you wee soul," said the woman to Isla. "Who's a brave girl, eh?" She straightened up, looked into my eyes. I recognised her. "Can I give you some tea, dear?"

She was the woman I had spoken to here some months ago – the one who sat out on the bench and watched. I imagined she'd been over here like shot – I was probably the most exciting thing that had happened to her in months. "Thank you," I said. "But I have to go."

I walked away, step by slow step, waved off her concerned pleas for me to sit down awhile and drink some sweet tea. I kept my hand to the walls of the houses, girded my loins to breech the windows, before stopping, backing up a little.

"Excuse me," I called to the woman. "Do you know who lives in that house?"

She almost smiled. "English lassie. Affa posh. Oil, I think. Incomer, y'ken?"

"Thank you. Goodbye now."

I waved and continued on. As I became surer I would not fall, I took my hand away from the wall. My steps quickened but I was still walking very slowly. I reached the jeep and leant on the bonnet, closed my eyes, opened them again. An English lassie. A posh English lassie who worked in oil. Who the hell was she? And why did she have a picture of Mikey on her mantelpiece? And why did Valentina have a letter for her in her bag?

"Drive safe," I said to no one. "There will be an explanation."

I put Isla in her seat and started the engine.

The harbour had grown dark – no more than monstrous oily shapes. Foot shaking on the accelerator, I pulled out of my parking space and hit the road.

The old lady had said oil. The woman who lived in that house worked in the oil industry. That first time, the old lady had spoken about an English couple. They had a baby, didn't they? No, it couldn't be them. She would hardly have a photo up where her husband could see it. The house would have to belong to a single woman, a woman who knew, who had her sights on Mikey. Either that or Mikey was ... no. The thought was inconceivable. I couldn't say it, couldn't even give silent voice to it in my head. Not Mikey. He was too loving, too warm, too damn *there*. And the way he was with me when he got back from offshore – the air of holy awe about him. He did all but fall to his knees before me. I would read it in his eyes if he was ... And anyway, when would he find the time? When he wasn't offshore, we were always together. That left only a lunchtime sex tryst. No. No. That wasn't him at all.

Focus, Shona. What are the facts?

A letter bound for this address had been in Valentina's bag. Fact.

Valentina had claimed it was misdirected post. I no longer believed that. I believed Valentina knew this person. Conjecture.

It had said Ms. on the envelope. This person was a woman. Fact.

The photo. This woman knew Mikey. Fact.

The woman worked in the oil industry. More than probable. Perhaps the woman was a colleague of Mikey's. Perhaps she had cut his photo out from the office newsletter or something. A creep. A lonely creep. She had developed an obsession with Mikey – understandable – he was funny, talented, charismatic. Hadn't I had a crush on him too? Didn't I still? All conjecture.

But how did Valentina know her? Some dark reason she wasn't prepared to divulge – an abortion, a lover? A female lover. Was that possible? She could be very sensual in the way she touched sometimes. No. But something. Conjecture conjecture conjecture.

Valentina knew this person knew Mikey. Conjecture.

Did Valentina even know this woman? Was that fact? No, actually. It was circumstantial, nothing more.

One of those wacky serendipitous sequences of events perhaps? You heard stories like that all the time, the papers were full of them: whole series of global connections that left even hardened cynics shivering with the heebie-jeebies, a burgeoning belief in the afterlife. Possibly.

So. Facts. One photograph on a mantelpiece, one letter to someone I'd never heard of. Few facts, no case, only questions: what was Valentina hiding, who the hell was G. Smyth-Banks, and why did she have a picture of my husband on her mantelpiece?

I got back to the cottage, stripped off my freezing cold, soaking wet socks and changed into some cosy fresh ones and my slippers. Once I'd done that, I picked up the phone and dialled Jeanie's work number for the second time. I held the receiver in the crook of my neck while I peeled off

Isla's coat and set her in front of an old *Singing Kettle* DVD.

When I was one I'd just begun the day I went to sea
I jumped aboard a pirate ship and the captain said to me
What did he sa-ay?

I shoved a rusk in her hand to keep her going. Still, Jeanie didn't pick up.

I cracked an egg into a saucepan and added some butter. I put the gas on low and ran to grab the laptop from the sitting room. I ran back and, stirring the egg with one hand, fired up the computer. Please God, let there be a connection. Please God, you owe me one.

I shoved some bread in the toaster. The egg scrambled. The toast popped. I scooped Isla up from the living room floor and wedged her into her high chair. I wiped her hands and mouth with the dishcloth even though it was stinking, slimy. I buttered the toast, cut it into fingers and put it with the egg onto her plate.

"Come on, come on," I said to the computer screen, absently spooning egg into my baby's mouth.

My screen wallpaper appeared: me, Mikey and Isla, smiling, taken at the top of Scolty Hill. Look at that picture, I thought. It was impossible Mikey was seeing someone else. I remembered that day as if it were the week before. We'd taken a flask and some bacon sandwiches up to the top of the hill, so we could see the view. It had been his idea: to survey the wider canvas of the life we were going to build together, he'd said, to find ourselves in that picture, to see ourselves as part of that landscape.

"Look," he had said, sweeping his hand over the horizon. "How gorgeous is this? Imagine the kids toddling off to the village school, twelve in a class, all that land to play in, trees to climb." He kissed me on the head. "I'll build a treehouse. A fort. God, they'll be so free!"

They. Not one child but two, maybe three. That's what he wanted. Me and kids – plural – were what he wanted. I trusted him. We were still happy, still pals, still lovers. Our imagined future was one we loved to imagine – our dream. We were normal. He would be heartbroken if he could see me now, imagining – imagining what? I couldn't even think it. Look how devastated he'd been when I'd taken off to Glasgow. And all I'd done that time was accuse him of not telling me the full truth. He had pleaded with me to come home, wrote me that note, made love to me with tears in his eyes. He was a family man, a loving, kind man who deserved better than this toxic doubt. He deserved trust.

There would be some reason for that photo, I knew it. The more I thought about it, the more some nutter with a crush on him made sense. A stalker. The person I no longer trusted was Valentina.

I opened the browser. Connection, for once.

"Yes!"

Isla shouted,"Oi!"

"Sorry, baby," I said, fed her some more egg while googling Valentina again, myself, to see. Nothing. Only the other Valentinas – the Italians and the Americans. No Australians. Even I had Facebook, my old profile at *The Tribune*, the Twitter account I once used daily. Who under forty wasn't online?

I deleted the letters and typed: G. Smyth-Banks. Pressed search.

The screen went white: *Error. You're not connected to a network.*

I tried again. Nothing.

I yelled, swore, slammed the laptop lid down.

Isla whined, a low, plaintive howl.

I fed her the rest of the egg. "There's no one I can talk to," I said miserably. "I can't talk to Daddy because he's away. I can't talk to Valentina because ..." I stopped, choked.

The landline rang. I jumped up and answered before the second ring.

"Shona?"

"Jeanie, thank God. I was away to call you. You know I told you Valentina had that letter? Well I went there – to that address in Fittie. I've just this second got back. I went there, Jeanie, and I looked through the window ..."

"Shona ..."

"And anyway would you believe it there's a photo of Mikey on the mantelpiece? I don't know what's going on, but something weird is happening."

"Shona."

"Sorry. I'm in a bit of a state."

"Shona. Are you sitting down?"

I sat down. Of course I did. "What?"

"I've been trying your mobile for the last hour. Have you even checked your email?"

"I can't get any connection in this fucking place and when I do it craps out before I have time to read anything."

"Get your iPhone and take it into the garden. Go as far as it takes to get a signal. Call me back." She hung up.

I looked at Isla. She was sucking on a buttered toast finger, singing soft nonsense to herself. I had five minutes.

I ran over to the coat hooks, found my phone in my jacket pocket. I'd put it on silent earlier when Isla was sleeping. There were five missed calls: four from Jeanie, one from Valentina. I walked back through to the kitchen and stared out through the back window. At the far end of our land, the tall trees loomed, black and huge against the deep blue of the sky. I kissed Isla's head, put on my coat and headed out of the back door. Holding my phone in the air, I crossed the patio, strode past the pond to the end of the flagstones. Still no signal. I looked back to the house. I couldn't see Isla from here. But she'd be OK. This wouldn't take more than a minute. The grass ahead was wet, muddy. I had on only my slippers. Shivering violently, I stepped onto the grass, felt it squelch, felt the cold wet soak through the fabric to my feet for the second time that day. I walked on as fast as I could.

191

By the time I got signal, I had almost reached the leylandii. It was spooky up there, the dark thicker somehow in the farthest reaches of the lawn. At the other end of the garden, flanked by trees, one square of light at the kitchen window. I should get back to Isla, I thought. I downloaded my emails, jumping from foot to foot: spam, mostly – ah, the one from Jeanie, sent half an hour earlier, with an attachment:

You should see this. Then call me right away. J.

I opened the attachment. It was a page from St. Matthew's Parish newsletter. I shook my head.

"What?"

At the top of the newsletter was a blurry, badly photocopied photo of about twenty people, all in theatrical costume. The headline read:

PETER PAN FLIES INTO ST. MATTHEW'S

Mikey's panto – over two years ago now. Jeanie must have dug it out from archives. The photographer had evidently decided to prove his originality by snapping the cast mucking about instead of in a serious thespian pose: there were headlocks, karate kicks, one guy was lying across the front of the stage with his head propped up on his hand. Why was Jeanie sending me this?

I scanned the faces, recognised Mikey, aka Captain Hook, grinning away in his eye patch and beard – the quality was terrible – he was holding up his hook, one knee slightly bent. Robbie too, next to Mikey, his arms thrown out, partly obscuring a tall blonde girl. That would be Wendy, I thought. Mikey's ex-girlfriend. The geologist, the hill-walker, the classical musician with perfect skin. She had known him, once, like I knew him now. I hated the thought, stood there as I was in the lonely dark, my feet dead and damp and cold. I stared into the image, cursing the poor quality of the reproduction. Wendy had both hands on Robbie's arm, as if trying to push it away so she could smile for the camera. He was laughing, his head turned towards her, apparently having a great time blocking her chances of parish-wide fame while he, Mr. Smee, hogged the lens.

Underneath, the print was so small I could barely read it.

Members of 'Said the Actors to the Bishopriggs' Community Players go mad after their smash hit performance of *Peter Pan*.

Below was the article.

Congregations have been full to bursting these last few nights at St. Matthew's ...

What did this have to do with anything? I looked again at the photo. Jeanie obviously wanted me to see something there. I couldn't see it, whatever it was. I called her.

"Jeanie?"

"Have you read it?"

"I've seen the pic. It's the panto."

"The article."

"Jeanie, hon, I've got Isla half a mile away in the house probably choking on a toast finger. I need to get back to her. Can't you tell me quickly?"

"Mikey's ex – she was Wendy do you remember?" Her tone was flat, almost tired-sounding.

I pushed back into the trees. The needles scratched the back of my neck. "Of course I do. So?"

"I hate to be telling you this," she said. "When you said about the letter, something about that name rang a bell. I remembered Mikey's ex-girlfriend was called Georgia so I called our Robbie. Shona, you're not going to like this. Her last name is Smyth-Banks."

"Smyth-Banks ..." I began. "The letter."

"I recognised the name, you know," Jeanie was saying. "When you said it before, I thought I'd seen it somewhere and I remembered looking at the programme at the panto

193

when we were trying to find out who Captain Hook was, remember? So that's why I looked it up. I was trying to get a picture of her but no joy so far. She lives in Aberdeen. Shona. I'm sorry."

Mikey's ex-girlfriend lived in the Fittie house. She was G. Smyth-Banks.

"I'm sure there's an explanation," Jeanie said. "But you need to talk to Mikey."

"Yes," I said. "Yes I do."

"You OK, doll?"

My mind raced. An ex-girlfriend. His ex. Of course.

I laughed with relief. "Actually yes I am. It's the only thing that makes sense, Jeanie! It makes perfect sense! I mean, what else explains why there's a photo on the mantelpiece? The woman's obviously still in love with him, poor lass."

"You don't think he's ..."

"What, Mikey? No way!" I laughed. "When would he have the time? Unless he's shagging her in his lunch break. No, Jeanie, I'd be surprised if he even knows she's in Aberdeen."

Back at the house, Isla was whining. I knew I should deal with her but I let her whine, shushing her half-heartedly as I ran around looking for my address book. I kicked off my wet slippers and socks, found the book in the kitchen drawer where I kept the odds and sods. I flipped through to M as fast as I could. There was only his office number. His emergency number wasn't there.

"Of course," I said. He'd programmed it straight into the phone. He'd put so much stuff on there, so many apps hovering in their neat squares on the screen. I scrolled through my contacts. Found his emergency number under Mikey Platform. Phone in the crook of my neck, I pulled a Petit Filou out of the fridge and took it over to Isla. Stomach tight with nerves, I pressed call. This was all I would ever use this phone for, I thought, as it bleeped

194

through the numbers: its original purpose, to call. When the hell would I have time to post, play games, Tweet? What the hell would I Tweet anyway?

A pause. I spooned a mouthful of fromage frais into Isla's waiting mouth. Down the line came the familiar sound of three rising, slightly off-key notes and the message:

Your call has not been recognised. Please try again.

I tried again. Same three tones, same message. I tried again. Same.

There must be a digit missing. Or a wrong digit – Mikey must've punched it in incorrectly or maybe – maybe what? I did not know. All I knew for certain was that I would never get through to any rig anywhere with this number, there was no way of guessing how to correct it. Unless I called head office ... Shona, stop. I made myself breathe, told myself to calm down. Mikey would call later – at the latest tomorrow. And actually, maybe it would be better to calm down, think through everything logically, get my head straight before I spoke to him. If I called, it would signal distrust, panic, madness. If I waited for him to call me, I could simply drop Georgia into the conversation and take it from there. Yes, it was better to wait. I was, despite the relief, still raw. I didn't want my voice to carry even a trace of suspicion, since suspicion kills trust. On both sides.

I gave Isla another spoonful, tried to talk to her in a soft, level voice. A maternal voice. But I could not keep the pantomime out of my head – all that happiness, all that larking about. How he'd come into the pub afterwards, all teeth and wit, and I'd pulled his beard and nearly died of embarrassment. Then, I thought, then was the moment I had fallen for him. Captain Hook, line and sinker. It was in those slow rolling seconds as if everything else had faded away, leaving nothing of any real importance for me but him. And then he had thrown her in like a grenade – Wendy, Georgia, whatever she was called – and hope had been blown to shrapnel around my feet.

195

I pressed the browser icon on my phone and waited. One bar of signal – enough maybe to call up the search engine. I typed: Georgia Smyth-Banks. The buffer took an age, swirling around like a roulette wheel in a casino. I waited for the ball to land. Finally, under listings, came her Facebook page.

Hallelujah. Let's see what you look like, you mad stalker bitch.

I clicked. It was slow to load, so slow. My knee jiggled. I spooned more pastel fruit gunk into Isla. Still the roulette wheel buffered. Place your bets. I wiped Isla down and lifted her from the high chair. She toddled off into the living room, to her toys. If I had a moment, it was now – she was always contented after food.

I looked in to where she was playing. I thought about grabbing the travel cot from the stable but she was talking to herself, quite happy with her bricks. This time I put my leather boots on. I ran out, all the way up the garden to the leylandii, and stared into my phone. My breath came fast and shallow. The page loaded.

"Fucking come the fuck on!" I shouted at the phone.

The profile photo was a cartoon of Marilyn Monroe. Marilyn Monroe, for fuck's sake. Someone had a high opinion of herself. There must be a photo on her page somewhere. I clicked albums. It wouldn't let me look.

"Bastard privacy settings." I threw the phone onto the grass, howled and swore over and over. What the hell did it matter? There was no one to hear. I could swear all I wanted, as loud as I wanted. I was alone, completely alone, and never had I felt it more than now.

I crouched down and buried my face in my hands, wailing to no one. After what must have been a minute or so, I picked the phone from the wet grass and ran back to the cottage, tears of frustration making everything swim. I should call Valentina, I thought. I could not think of anything else to do. I should call her and ask her what the real story was with the letter. *How do you know Mikey's ex?* That would be a good starting point – since she obviously did. I could at least find that out. Or I could drive back to this Georgia woman's house and do my own little stakeout. Sit on that bench in the square and wait, wait until she came out, march right up to her and tell her to stay the hell away from my Mikey.

The back door was open. I thought I had slammed it shut. I had. I had slammed it. But too hard. It must've bounced off its latch.

"Isla?" I stepped into the kitchen and headed straight for the living room. No sign of her – only the bright plastic bricks she'd been playing with a moment ago. I ran upstairs calling her name. She could crawl up here if she wanted to, although she never had before. I had never left her long enough, would never normally leave her at all. I checked her room. Nothing.

"Isla," I called. "Isla?"

She wasn't in the bathroom, the spare room, or mine and Mikey's room. She wasn't in the airing cupboard, she wasn't in the wardrobe, she wasn't in the bath. My heart hammered. Warm sweat ran down the sides of my body.

"Isla?"

I almost threw myself downstairs. At the bottom, in the hallway, I stopped and made myself listen. One coo, one small noise and I would know where she was. I called her name and waited. Nothing. I checked the living room again, behind the sofa, the armchair. Nothing. In the kitchen, I looked inside the oven, knowing this to be insane even in the moment, banging the door shut. My throat blocked.

The back door banged against the outer wall.

"Isla!" I headed out into the dark. Outside, I hesitated, the pale blue light from my phone a fuzzy halo on the paving stones. Left into the garden or right into the lane?

The pond.

I ran left, gasping for air. "Isla! Isla! Where are you?"

On the surface of the pond, the lily pads lay undisturbed. But still. I jumped in, slipped on the bottom, fell backwards. My elbows cracked on the stone border. My phone clattered into the flowerbed. The cold water sucked at my thighs. I kicked around, felt small bodies. Fish. Not her, Shona. Fish, not her.

I heaved myself out, half-weeping, half-shouting. My wet legs froze in the cold air. I grabbed the phone, ran down the side path, jumped over the picket fence. My soles crunched on the hard gravel. My socks squelched in my boots.

"Isla!"

All was darkness. Again the choice: left, up to the house half a mile up the track, right to the uninhabited new builds. Or straight on, down the lane. Surely she couldn't get far? She'd only just learnt to walk.

"Isla?" The metallic taste of blood filled my mouth. My lungs went cold, my nose and eyes streamed. I took one step then another towards the lane.

"Isla! Isla!" Between words, I heard myself moan. A horrible lowing, like a cow.

A noise. I made myself stop. Stop moving and listen.

The noise came again – a soft moan, like my own, but higher pitched. A baby calf calling for her mother. Isla. I turned slowly, arms out, eyes wide. Where are you, baby girl? Where are you?

"Maaaaaaaa ..."

Ahead. Not far. In the lane.

"I'm here, darlin'," I shouted. "Mummy's here. Wait there, my love. Mummy's coming."

I ran to the mouth of the lane. She was there, no more than three metres from the cottage.

She was there at the end of the lane, her tiny silhouette backlit by starlight, her golden hair in static wisps. I ran to her, tripped, almost fell on her, saved myself with my hands against the pitted gravel track. I knelt up, grabbed her and pulled her tight to me. She was moaning softly over and over. Wet faces pressed against each other's necks, we shook into each other's embrace.

"Mummy's here," I managed to say, my voice strange in the still night. "Mummy's here darlin'."

"Mummy."

The bones of her were so very small, her wee shoulders no wider than the bone handle of a knife, her baby arms, her tiny neck. Her head pressed its warm weight against my open hand. She smelled of strawberry yoghurt, of cold air and of the stinking cloth with which in my carelessness I had wiped her tiny mouth and hands. I kissed her cheek, her nose, her sticky hair. I held her tight, told myself to stand, to pick her up, that I should stand, that I should pick her up right now and get her back into the warm.

"Mummy's got you," I managed to say. "Let's get you home."

NINETEEN

I drew a bath, bubbles like crazy meringue. Isla had warmed up, had stopped crying and seemed happy to coo at the foam as I lowered her in. I scooped up a handful and blew it at her. Closing her eyes against the flurry, she squealed with delight. I shivered, my teeth chattered as if I were not in fact safe and warm and in my home but still outside, in the cold. I stripped off my wet clothes, pulled on Mikey's robe. His smell comforted me, the XL size wrapping around my body, the nearest thing I had to his embrace. I was shaking, couldn't seem to stop shaking. I hugged myself, tried to imagine him there with me, watching our baby in her bath.

She put up no fight at all when I took her to bed. I'd expected her to be fretful, to want me to stay with her while she went off to sleep but she closed her eyes and appeared to be drifting off even as I said good night.

I pulled the door to and headed back to the bathroom. My eyes and hands stung, my legs and back ached. I ran steaming hot water into what remained of Isla's bath, peeled off my torn wet jeans, my sweater, and lowered myself inch by inch into the suds. The water soothed me. I lay back, let the heat penetrate my shoulders and neck. Tears ran into my ears. Excess water, that was all. I was too exhausted, too confused to cry.

Flannel over my eyes, I tried to make myself relax. What was important here, all that was important, was Isla. Isla was all that mattered and in all my paranoid chasing about I had forgotten her. That was unforgivable and, at the thought of her alone in the lane, my cheeks burned with shame. I had got myself into a state – about Mikey and about his silly, obsessive ex-girlfriend – without waiting for an explanation. I had neglected my own daughter and suspected my own partner, and for what? I had treated him as less than the accused in the dock. Even those accused of murder got a fair trial. By not asking for an explanation first, I was treating my partner – and my best friend for that matter – like convicted criminals, and in so doing had surrendered responsibility for my own child. She could have been run over. She could have developed hypothermia. She could have fallen into a ditch, wandered off, got lost in the darkness of the woods. Stop. But still, images of disaster leaked from my subconscious, the flash cards of post-trauma: Isla at the side of the road, traffic roaring, her stepping out; Isla in the mud, her legs bent the wrong way; Isla ...

I sat bolt upright, panting, nauseous. I took the flannel from my face. On the side of the bath, the hand mirror had frosted with steam. I wiped it and met my own glowing face, a horrid, diseased-looking red, bloodshot eyes, black hair slicked back. I looked like Dracula.

"Stop it," I said aloud. "Calm down, Shona. Calm down and think."

My shoulders were cold. I lay back once more. What were the facts? The question was becoming a mantra. Not fantasies, not frantic ravings, Shona, only hard, journalistic facts. One: in her bag, Valentina had been carrying a letter addressed to someone I now knew to be Mikey's ex-girlfriend, Georgia. Two: Georgia lived in Aberdeen. Three: she had a photo of Mikey on her mantelpiece. This was all I knew. This was all I actually knew.

So to the first: letters didn't stick to other letters, not that I'd ever heard of. Letters didn't reach the wrong address, only the wrong person as a result of the right person once having lived at that address. Conclusion: either Georgia had once lived at Valentina's address or Valentina did in fact know her and was not telling the truth. Which would point to her knowing that Georgia and Mikey had once been together. I had been brought up to think the best of people.

Valentina was my friend. She had come to me when I was lonely and vulnerable and brought light and laughter into my life. She had taken me to the station when I needed to make a stand, to the hospital when Isla had got sick.

OK, so she was cheating on her husband with a man she found dull but she was kind too. She was funny. People were complicated, they bore scars we could only guess at and her love life was not my concern. To me, she had been a good friend who, for whatever reason, had not told the truth and I was determined not to judge her nor suspect her until I had spoken to her. Until I had asked her, directly, for the truth, for her reasons for not telling it.

I picked up my phone from the side of the bath and scrolled through the contacts until I got to her name. I put the phone back on the side of the bath. Not now, not now. More than a conversation with Valentina, I needed sleep, needed to recover from Isla's Houdini trick. I was too shaken to call her, especially if the conversation proved difficult. I would call her tomorrow, when I had rested, when my mind was clearer.

Now to the second: Mikey's ex-girlfriend, the love-struck geologist. Aberdeen was the centre of the oil industry in the UK. It was likely, inevitable even, that she would settle here in this city. It was entirely possible this city was the only place which could provide work for such a skill set. So she lived here. So what? I had no proof that Mikey even knew that.

Third. She kept Mikey's photo on display. If she held a candle for him, that made her a threat. Did it? Did it really? Mikey and I had a child together now. We had a home, which was so much more than somewhere to live; it was the bedrock of our dreams for our life together. One photo on its own was not enough to distrust Mikey. Even if he knew the woman was in town, it was entirely possible he hadn't wanted to tell me. No one wants news of their partner's romantic past thrust in their face and I was no exception. He would know that about me. He would never want to upset me – he was too kind.

I regretted having even attempted to call him. Thank goodness the number had been wrong. I would have sounded so needy, and that was enough to send a guy like him, maybe any guy, running for the hills. Mikey deserved a capable, resilient woman alongside him, not someone who would fall prey to delusions, become a snivelling neurotic the moment events proved difficult to explain. There was always another side, always. He had three days left of his trip. I decided I would not ask him about Georgia when he rang – it was difficult enough to discuss even routine domestic matters when he was in the North Sea, let alone anything emotive. I would not, this time, end up back in my parents' dark hallway, I would not wake up tomorrow to the horrible knowledge that I had poisoned our relationship with baseless suspicion. I would wait until he got back. He would explain everything and, instead of making myself ridiculous, I would learn the truth like a calm rational woman, a woman still in possession of herself.

I was about to go to bed, when Jeanie rang again.

"Shona? Are you OK?"

"I'm fine," I said. "I'm going to talk to Val tomorrow. I can't face it now. There'll be an explanation, I'm pretty sure."

"Right-oh." She paused.

I knew she had more to say – I could sense it. "If you're worried about Mikey, don't be. I know it's strange he hasn't said anything about Georgia, but I don't even know if he knows she's in town."

"I'd be surprised if he didn't, Shone."

"Oh aye?"

"I did some more digging." She sighed heavily. "Thing is, she's at Maple Energy."

"Right." My stomach turned over. "As in works there?"

"That's where Mikey works, isn't it?"

203

"Aye," I said quietly. "It is."

I hung up. It was nine o'clock. I felt more tired than I ever had in my life. I checked the window locks, locked the back door, locked and bolted the front. I made myself some hot milk and honey, added a dram of brandy to help me sleep. On the stairs, my feet fell like rocks. I dug into Mikey's dressing gown pocket, pulled out my phone and composed a text to Valentina.

Coffee tomorrow?

First things first. Let me see what she had to say.

In Caffè Nero, Valentina was scooping chocolaty foam from a babyccino into Zac's mouth while trying to read a magazine. It occurred to me that she never, or hardly ever, looked at her child, almost never spoke to him. I felt nauseous at the sight of her and realised I could not delay asking her what I needed to ask. I could not have formed one coherent sentence of small talk anyway.

I sat down opposite her at the table, put Isla on the floor with Zac. "Hi."

"Hi, babe." She looked right at me. "Aren't you grabbing a coffee?"

"No."

She cocked her head, her brow furrowed, her intense green eyes still on mine. "Everything OK?

"Not really." That was it. That was all I had to do – start. "I need to ask you about that letter. Thing is, last night I got a very interesting call from my friend Jean. She had some information for me – about a Ms. G. Smyth-Banks. Georgia. So, what I want to know is, how come you've got a letter to my partner's ex-girlfriend in your bag ..."

"Shona, I'm sorry," she said. "I lied to you."

"Oh."

She shook her head, her red hair cascading down her back. She glanced at me, looked away. "You weren't meant to see that letter."

I sat back in my chair and folded my arms. Beneath them, I could feel my own heart beating. "Clearly not."

"It's not what you think."

"They say that on films, Val. Why don't you tell me the truth then we can get on with our lives, eh?"

"All right." She sighed, frowned. "Georgia. That's the name of the girl who that letter was for."

I exhaled heavily. She was telling the truth, quite unprompted.

"She's a student of mine," she went on. "Former student. We became friends. I don't normally – usually have a rule against that but we got on well and I didn't see the harm. Anyway, turns out she was totally obsessed with this ex-boyfriend of hers."

I almost jumped in and said Mikey but thought better of it. She did not know what I knew. Let's see if her truth fit mine.

"Georgie told me he, Michael – she called him Michael, that's why I call him that – I can't get out of the habit." She smiled. I thought I detected nerves.

"Go on," I said. "I'm listening."

"Georgia told me this Michael guy was moving up with his new partner and their baby. She was very jealous, mad with jealousy in fact." She took a deep breath. "So. This is difficult. She asked me to check you out, see what you were like." Again, her eyes flicked up and met mine before darting away.

"Check me out? What for?"

She shrugged. "I don't know. Listen, she's a bit – unhinged, I guess you'd say. But we were friends and I said I would. I didn't know you then, Shone. I didn't see the harm." She glanced at me and again looked down. "I was going to call on you, on some pretext. But then I met you at the nursery and when you told me your name and all about the cottage and everything I just knew you were *the* Shona. It was a coincidence, I guess."

"So, hang on, what are you saying? You were planning to spy on me?" My chest burned. "You did spy on me? Is that what you're saying?"

She raised her hand, her eyes welled. "Please, Shona. Listen. I did do that. I can't change that I did that. As I said, I'm sorry. And I didn't know you then. And that's all I was going to do. But you were so nice. And you seemed so lost. And I thought, fuck it, you know? I can go back to Georgia and tell her that you're a great woman, that Michael is very happy and that she should stay away. I thought I could tell her all those things then get her to drop it. And I didn't see why I should miss out on being friends with you." She met my eye for longer this time, smiled doubtfully. "I liked you."

"You lied to me," I said, but even as I said it I knew I believed her now. "From the beginning."

"I know. Trust me, I know. I should have come clean straight away. But I was still friends with Georgia, I'm not any more, and I thought, oh well, it'll blow over, you know? It was one lie. One. It didn't, it doesn't, have to mean everything. I didn't think I would ever have to admit to it, I didn't want to, I was afraid it would spoil what we had. Still have, I hope?" She drained her coffee cup. She looked so miserable that with every second I thawed a little more. "And I didn't know Michael then either."

"His name is Mikey." My voice had an edge.

She sat back, shocked. It was not a side of me she'd seen. Few people ever do.

"Don't be like that, Shone," she said. "You know what I mean. And I did tell her to stay away. Told her to look elsewhere and as far as I know she did. We kind of drifted after that. She was nuts."

"She has a picture of him on her mantelpiece. She works at the same company. Hardly staying away."

"I didn't know that." Her voice had taken on a pleading quality. "I don't see her any more."

"None of this explains why you had the letter."

"It was a bill. She never paid me for last term and now we've lost touch or cooled or whatever you want to call it, she's stopped coming to yoga and I guess she thought she would get away without paying. That would be just like her. Did I mention she was mean?"

"So why didn't you say it was a bill? Are you a compulsive liar or something?"

She closed her eyes a moment and when she opened them again she looked like she might cry. "A terrible liar, more like. I can't do it – the lying thing. Some people can but I can't. I felt guilty by association and I ... panicked, I guess. What I said was ... it was ridiculous. And I knew it was ridiculous. And then you texted about coffee and I thought, right, I'll tell her everything then, face to face."

Neither of us spoke.

After a moment, I said, "You lied about John too. How am I supposed to believe a word you say?"

She groaned and covered her face with her hands. "Oh, Shona. Yes I did. I am so sorry. I couldn't tell you. I'm not seeing John that often any more. And I thought the whole Georgia thing would go away. I thought it had gone away." She leant forward, took my left hand in both of hers. I let her, even noticing that her nails had been freshly painted: a dark, chocolate brown. "Shona, one thing you've got to know is that Michael – sorry, Mikey – has no interest in Georgia. He told her to leave him alone or he would call the police."

"How do you know that?"

"She told me, of course. She was hopping mad about it. Tried to blame it on me!"

"Is that right?"

"Yes. I think he threatened her with a restraining order."

A group of four mothers, all with papooses, came and sat at the next table, bright with their own chatter, their new baby friendships. I pulled my hand from Valentina's but not without giving her fingers a squeeze.

"When did she see him?" I asked. "How exactly did he threaten her?"

She sat back in her chair, coiled a lock of burnished copper hair around her finger. "I don't know. I don't even know how I know he did. I guess they still had each other's numbers. Maybe she showed me a text once, I've forgotten."

"Have you ever been to her house?"

"What? No. Why would I have been to her house?"

"No reason," I said. "Just never knew you were backwards about going to your friends' houses that's all. Or staying there all day, for that matter. Maybe grabbing some free childcare." I stood to go. I was already saying things I would regret later.

"You're not going? Come on, Shona, you're making this into more than it is."

I picked up Isla. "Actually, I am going. I can't think straight. I need to be on my own."

"But you haven't even had a coffee."

"I can't manage one." I fastened Isla into the sling, grabbed my bag. I could not look at Valentina, could not bear the green of her eyes. Even though I knew she was telling the truth, the fact of her, her words, even the pitter-patter of her summery voice, was suffocating me.

I crossed over to a tacky clothes boutique called JuicyGirl. Inside, miniskirts hung from the plastic hangers, glitzy crop tops, glitter cherry motifs; there were jeans skinny enough for dolls, bodycon dresses, playsuits and, by the till, was a display of coloured glassy jewellery. The shop assistant looked me up and down as I went in, asked if I needed help. What she meant, we both knew, was *what the hell are you doing in here, you big scruff?* I said I was just browsing but stood in the doorway, looking back at the café. I could see Valentina through the passing crowds, through the window of the café, through the group of women who had sat down next to us. I don't know what I was expecting now that I had left her like that – was I hoping that she would have thrown herself down, that she would be weeping on the floor? Not really. I suppose I thought she would at least look troubled. And I guess she did. Her brow was furrowed, her mouth set in a tight line. She was cleaning Zac's face with a baby-wipe, phone in the crook of her neck. As I watched, she began to talk. To whom, I had no idea.

So Mikey's name had been cleared before he even knew it had been muddied. But even so, the next few days waiting for him to come home were among the worst I'd known since the move. I had started this journey alone in this cottage and now here I was, more alone than I had ever been. In essence, there was no change. Except there had been a change. I had found a friend and I had loved her. I wanted to still, but no longer felt safe enough to love her as I had. I believed everything she had told me but still the ground beneath me had cracked, as if after an earthquake. I needed to move forward but I knew, or sensed, that I should tread with caution. In the café, Valentina had confessed – more than that – she had volunteered her confession before I had asked for it. She had told me the truth, something she could only do by admitting to her lie. That had taken courage. And I believed her. She wouldn't admit to lying only to replace the lie with a half-truth, would she? I wanted to call her and talk it through once more – if only to stop myself endlessly revolving the subject in my own head – but I didn't call her, I called Jeanie. Jeanie, who picked up on the first ring, who listened to all I had to say.

"It's all perfectly feasible," she said. "The problem is, when someone you're close with lies to your face, it's hard to believe what they say even when they do tell the truth. It's the old cry wolf thing, isn't it?"

"It's possible isn't it," I replied, "that she was protecting me? It was her after all who said she'd lied, not me. She came right out with it."

"Aye," she said. "I suppose. Is she still friends with this woman?"

"She says not. And Mikey doesn't know anything about Georgia's friendship with Val because Val was lying to him too, effectively." In the background, I could hear phones ringing, tapping – Jeanie's fingers on the keys, possibly. I wished I was back there, with my colleagues, trying to write the truth about the big stuff, not here trying to find out the little truths of my tiny, insignificant life.

"Contact me if there's any more weirdness, OK?" Jeanie was saying. "In the meantime, I'll see if I can find anything else on this Georgia psycho bitch."

I laughed – for the first time in ages. "Thanks Jeanie. You're a pal."

TWENTY

By the time Mikey got back, I was in knots. When he called to say his helicopter was delayed due to poor visibility and there was a chance he would not make it home till the next day, I had to bite the back of my hand to suppress a wail. But he got off, thank God. The taxi finally came, its diesel engine rattling. I ran to the window, saw the diffused yellow halos of headlights coming up the lane.

I waved from the window, ran to the door.

Kitbag in hand, he crunched over the gravel, through the patches of greying ice slush.

"Hi," I said, stepping aside, pulling back the door.

"Hey." He grinned, bowled in. He was so male, I thought, compared to Valentina. So dark, so other. "What are you doing standing in the shadows?" he said. "Come here and give me a kiss right now. I demand it." Without warning, he lunged for me and picked me up, kissed me hard on the mouth. He smelled of coffee, of vanilla – the cab air freshener, maybe. He planted me back on the floor and hugged me to his chest, bent to my ear so he could mutter into it. "God, I've missed you. Can we sneak upstairs?"

"Isla's watching TV," I wriggled out of his arms, backed away. "Isla," I called. "Daddy's here."

"No," she shouted. "No Dada."

I smiled at Mikey. "That's what we call 'the terrible twos' come early."

"She's not even one yet." He reached for my hand, let his fingers trail through mine.

"She will be," I said. "The week after next. You'll be away."

Blink. Here. Blink. Gone.

It took me until Isla had gone to bed to ask about Georgia Smyth-Banks. And even after two days of careful planning as to how I would broach the subject, I still made a complete mess of it. We had eaten together. We were in the kitchen. I had put on some soft music and I was loading up the dishwasher with our dirty plates. Maybe the job, having something to do, somewhere else to look, helped me to find the words. Pity I didn't say them calmly – like Valentina doubtless would have done. Pity that, as soon as I opened my mouth to speak, emotion sent my voice wavering out like the strained tones of an old lady trying to sing the high notes of a particularly challenging hymn.

"Why didn't you tell me your ex-girlfriend lived in Aberdeen?"

"What?" He was still at the table. I had topped up his wine, told him to stay put after the meal. I had wanted him to rest after his exhausting fortnight in the North Sea.

"Georgia Smyth-Banks." I rinsed the cutlery, dumped it into the holder with a crash. "Ring any bells?"

I had done precisely what I promised myself I would not do: let the poison of suspicion leak into my words, asked a question designed only to trap him. I barely recognised myself. Neither, it appeared, did he. His eyebrows knitted together in confusion as if to say: who are you?

"Where is this coming from?"

I pressed my back to the countertop, and made myself look at him. "Mikey, Georgia lives here. She works for the same company as you. Don't tell me you didn't know. Were you ever going to tell me? I only know because of the letter."

"What letter?" His eyebrows moved even closer together, his lips pursed.

"Valentina had a letter addressed to Georgia in her bag. That's how I found out. Valentina used to teach her. She lives in Fittie."

"Fittie?" he said. "As in Footdee? Who lives there? I thought you said Valentina lived in Union Grove?"

I slid the tray into the dishwasher, pulled up the door and turned to face him once more. "No. Georgia. Georgia lives in Fittie. You must know that."

"Shona, stop." He jumped up, strode the two paces it took to reach me and grabbed my wrist.

"Let go." I had not meant to shout. But I had. I saw the hurt in his eyes.

He let go, as if he, not me, had been burnt, and held up his hands. "OK. Sorry. Look. Sit down. Let's sit down. Let's talk about this properly. You've gone flying off God knows where. Sit down, come on. I bet you've been thinking about nothing else, haven't you?"

I nodded, blinking back tears. Damn tears. Why couldn't I punch a hole in the wall like a man? Shout, slam a door, knock back a whisky and throw the glass to the floor? He was so right – I had thought of nothing else – and for some reason I found that humiliating. Stuck out here, no friends, no job, no one I could trust to talk to, yes, I had nothing else to think about. But now I wanted the truth – not any old truth, but one from his lips, one I could believe enough to stand on, no more shaky ground.

Mikey was pouring more red wine into my glass. He was ushering me into my chair.

"Come on. Sit with me," he said, his voice unchanged. "Let's talk about this."

"I've got to finish cleaning up. There's a laundry load I still haven't ..."

"Shona, sit. We'll do that after. Together. Or I'll do it. Sit down."

I lowered myself into the chair.

"Right." He sat down opposite me, laid his hands flat on the table. His nails had grown while he had been offshore, I noticed; they were long and rounded, like a guitarist's. "So Valentina had a letter – which we'll get to in a minute."

"Why in a minute? Why not now?"

He threw up his hands. "OK. Now. Whatever you want."

I shook my head. "No. I've spoken to her. Georgia used to do yoga with her, that's all."

"So how come Valentina had a letter addressed to her then?"

"It was a bill. For some classes she didn't pay for."

"She told you that?"

I nodded. I didn't say that she'd lied at first, told me it was a postal mistake. I didn't say Valentina had befriended me under false pretences. Mikey already had such a low opinion of her. Nor did I add that I'd driven over to Georgia's house, like a raving lunatic, that I'd peeped through her windows, fainted on her front step. And I certainly didn't tell him she kept a photo of him on her fireplace. I don't know why I kept these things to myself – perhaps I was trying to keep some shred of dignity.

"So Valentina tells you that she knows Georgia, she used to teach her? And she lives here in Aberdeen," he said, slowly, as if he was working it out for himself. Then Jeanie phones you and tells you Georgia's my ex. My God, I can see how ... two plus two, eh? What the hell did you think?"

"I don't know. You left out the bit about you and Georgia working together."

"And that, of course." He smiled. "Let me guess. You thought that, because my ex-girlfriend is in the same city, even though you know she's a geologist and that Aberdeen is probably the only place she could get a job in the UK, the fact she lives here and works for Maple automatically means she and I are having some sort of affair? Is that the gist?"

"It's not as defined as that." I hated my voice. It was still warbling all over the place, frail-sounding, weak. "It's bad enough that Valentina knew this woman and never told me, then I find out that you knew her too ... more than knew her ... and you didn't tell me she was here. I guess it's about realising that there's something your husband isn't telling you. It's – it's ..." What was it? What was it, exactly? Why now, faced with him, didn't I know what it was? "I mean, it's not devastating, I'm not saying that. More like I'm trying to stand up but I feel like I'm going to fall down."

He rubbed his hand over his chin and frowned. "I can see that." His fingers splayed across his mouth. He looked down at his lap, seemed to see some speck of dirt there, brushed it off. "And meanwhile you've had days and days on your own with it all going around in your mind. It must've driven you mad. It's enough to drive anyone mad." His voice was unaltered, compassionate. I was glad – I guess because I took his flat calm to be a sign of a man with nothing to hide. There was no politician's rhetoric here – he had spoken almost as if he saw the whole thing from my point of view.

The tears came thickly then. Along with the shaky voice, out they rolled, regardless. Before Isla, this would never have happened. Never. I'd been as strong as steel. You could have made a ship out of me. Now I was little more than a leaking bucket.

"Don't cry, baby." He leant forward, brushed my tears away with his thumbs.

"I'm not." I sniffed. "I'm tired."

The music faded and stopped. Outside, black silence pressed against the windows. The silence out here is like nowhere else.

"She was here before we moved up, I think," he said, after a moment. "But I didn't know she was at Maple when I took the job. We weren't in touch."

I waited for him to look at me, which he did, with a cool, level gaze.

"Are you in touch with her now?" I asked. "Do you see her?"

"Where would I see her?" He scratched with his thumbnail at the leg of his jeans. "I spend half my life offshore."

"But you do go into the office?"

"The office is massive, Shone. There are hundreds of people working there, it's not as if she's in my team. I've never seen that guy we met at the pub that time, remember the one with the snobby wife? Never seen him and I don't see her. And even if I did, I'd keep away." He puffed out air and shook his head. "She's a bit nuts."

I knew this to be true and my heart seized upon it. I had seen the photo on the mantelpiece. Valentina had said she was crazy, obsessive. I had said neither thing to him and I suppose that means I still at that point held the smallest residue of doubt, enough to test him.

"In what way?" I asked instead.

He shrugged. "Oh, you know. She did sort of stalk me for a bit. After we split up."

"She's only human." I smiled – not at him but at the fact I knew he wasn't lying.

"This is it." He smiled too. "What woman wouldn't go mad for me, eh?" He lunged for me, tickled my belly.

I shrieked, pushed him away. We both laughed. And sighed. The silence leaked back into the cottage.

"Actually, I had to tell her to sling it in the end," he said. "It got a bit nasty. She couldn't cope with me moving on. I actually ended up telling her I'd call the police." He reached out and squeezed my knee. "Hey. Are you OK?"

I knew all this to be true.

"I think so." I took a deep breath, stretched my neck, tried to ease the stiffness in my body.

"I didn't tell you because I didn't want to upset you," he said. "And then she stopped bothering me and then I – I forgot. I forgot because she means nothing to me, Shone. You and Isla. You're everything. You're my family, my home. You're absolutely everything." He grinned. "Besides, when would I have the time for anyone else, let alone the energy? Half the time I'm on a piece of Meccano in the middle of the bollock-freezing ocean." He laughed again, took my hand, kissed the back of it. "Bloody hell, Shona. The last thing I need is another bloody woman to keep up with."

Later, we sat top to tail on the sofa listening to *King Creosote*, talking sometimes, sometimes not, lost to the peace, the pulsing fire, our home. Later still, I followed him upstairs, changed into my nightshirt and climbed into bed next to his warm body. I bent my knees into the backs of his and wrapped my arm around his solid man's torso. His hand came back to find me, running over my hip, sliding down my leg.

"I can't," I said.

"Of course."

"I'm still a bit all over the place, you know?"

He turned over, pushed me onto my back and kissed me on the mouth – not a sexual kiss, but still one a lover would give: tender, his lips soft and unrushed. "I love you, Shone. You're my home, you know that don't you?"

My eyes brimmed, overflowed – more tears, for God's sake, pooling inside my ears.

"You're my home too," I said. "You're the only place I feel safe."

Waking on Sunday morning I felt as if someone had lifted a heavy weight from my back. The catharsis of the night before had brought this lightness and, as if in sympathy, the sky treated us to a bright winter sun. In bed, with the sky still dark blue, we had turned to each other, still sleepy. We had kissed, he had pushed his hand onto my breast, when Isla woke up and shouted "Mamma!"

Mikey groaned, let his forehead drop on my chest.

"We have two whole weeks ahead of us." I said, taking a fistful of his hair, scratching his scalp with my fingernails. "Plenty of time for *that sort o' thing.*" I left him there and went to fetch our wee baby.

"We need to think about a party for Isla," I said as I came back into the bedroom with her, nappy changed, all fresh. "We should have it this week or next. I know that's not on her actual birthday but you'll be offshore and I think we should celebrate while you're here." I put Isla next to

217

Mikey and stood back to look at them both sat propped up against the white pillows. There is something so tender about the sight of your life partner and the baby child you have made together sitting in a big white double bed. Her in her pink Babygro, thin infant's hair rubbed into soft fuzzy knots at the back of her head, him bare-chested, dark, both swathed in white cotton. It was something more than precious, it was holy, almost, something that must not, must never, be desecrated. I guess you'd call it a moment of clarity: these two human beings, there on the bed, were all and everything I wanted. They – this – was home.

I found I could neither move nor speak.

After a moment, I turned away, went over to the bedroom window and pulled the curtain across enough to see out. I looked onto the vast green, the regiment of leylandii at the far end. I had stood in the dark against those scratchy branches, lost in a nightmarish storm of doubt. Now the sun had come up and nothing looked scary any more. Beyond the trees, braids of churned soil lay fallow for the winter and beyond that again, though I could not see it from here, the back road out to Stonehaven, where the dual carriageway headed south.

"What do you think?" I said, turning to face them. "I could ask a couple of babies from the nursery over – might be a way to meet some other mums. And I know Zac's birthday is near Isla's so maybe I'll ask Valentina if she wants to do a joint party."

He nodded, though he was taken up entirely by Isla. Happy to be invisible to them both, I slipped away to make tea, leaving them to their love-in.

When I came back upstairs, Mikey had put Isla on his knee. He was nuzzling her nose with his, making a funny buzzing noise, making her laugh. When he pulled back, she grabbed his nose with her tiny fingers and he gave a loud *ow*!

"Her nails are sharp, right enough." I set his Lord mug on his bedside table and took mine around to my side. I climbed in and kissed Isla's head. She wriggled, threw herself down into the duvet and laughed. She pulled herself up and giggled again before pausing, her body set in the tension of expectation. I pushed gently on the side of her head. She threw herself down again onto the bedding, this time hysterical. Two seconds later, she hauled herself up again. I pushed her down. More giggling.

"This could go on for an hour," I said to Mikey.

She rolled, pushed herself back up. "Dada," she said.

I nudged his elbow with mine. "She wants you to do it."

He barely had to connect with her – in fact, I bet he never did – before she collapsed once again, beside herself with laughter at her own talent for physical comedy, but still managing to pull herself up for one more go.

Mikey pushed her down again.

"I think it'd be better if we had a party just for Isla," he said. "Just us, I mean." He brought his tea to his lips, seemed to reconsider, lowered the mug. "I think we should maybe keep our distance from Valentina. She's a bit, I don't know, intense."

"But you guys got on really well when she came," I said. "So well, in fact, that it was me that went to bed and you two that burnt the midnight oil." As I said the words something inside me shifted. The lightness I had felt on waking was replaced by a cloudy, heavy feeling.

"I think Isla's party should be just us," he said. "The three of us. That's all."

"Can I at least invite wee Zac?" I said. "They're so close, that's all."

"I'd rather you didn't if that's OK." He reached for my hand and held it. "I understand what you're thinking, and I know it's hard for you to understand this but when I'm offshore I miss you two so much. You're all I think about when I'm in that bunk. Even in the day, even when I'm busy, I catch myself looking out towards the land, and I want to come home so badly." He pulled my hand up to his mouth and kissed it. "I want it to be the three of us. She's only one after all."

He looked into my eyes. The cloudy feeling left me as quickly as it had come. That's what happens when what you see in your husband's kind brown eyes is love. I had not thought about, knew nothing about, what life was like on the rig, apart from what Mikey told me. I could only imagine how grim it must be to be woken in the middle of the night by the grunt of a stranger shitting, wanking or snoring, to be out for hours on the cold oily deck, the North Sea wind whipping your face, staring back to shore. But I felt the melancholy of it then, as if I myself had been there with him. If he and Isla together in the white bed represented something pure for me, I thought, then that must count doubly so for him.

"Ignore me," he said. "If you want to have a big party for her, that's fine. Honestly. I'm being selfish."

"No, you're right," I said. "Of course it's OK just the three of us. I was being selfish."

He closed my head in his hands and kissed me on the nose. "You're amazing. You get it, don't you?" With a comic old man groan, he turned away and got up. Rearranging his boxer shorts, as he always did, he wandered towards the bedroom door. He was whistling happy birthday.

We never celebrated Isla's first birthday. My God, it's hard to keep hindsight out of this, it's nigh on impossible.

TWENTY-ONE

Having agreed not to invite anyone to Isla's birthday party, I asked if I could invite Red and Val over again, as a compromise. Initially reluctant, once he'd agreed, Mikey's enthusiasm bordered on the evangelistic. Not only did he offer to cook – I was only too delighted to let him – but, before I knew it, he'd ordered a rotary barbecue affair for the back garden and a whole rabbit from a butcher in Banchory. I couldn't help but laugh when he announced all this the moment he got home – like a kid with big news.

"Bloody hell," I said. "You never do things by halves, do you?"

The day came. It was the middle Saturday of his time at home. I was happy to get out into the garden and prepare the fire, which I did in the very early evening. It was – well, it was fun.

"We need red-hot embers," I told him, once I'd got the fire going, finding him in the kitchen with his chef's pinny on. I went over to where he was standing at the counter, put my arms around his waist and laid my head on his back. "You know, to roast the poor, innocent beast."

But he didn't hear. Headphones on, too busy doing things with rosemary and cider marinades. I left him to it, singing *Bright Eyes* at the top of my lungs, and carried Isla upstairs to bed.

And this is where I have to stop. I have to stop what I'm telling you and say this.

Had I known that this was to be the last happy moment of my life, the last time I would ever feel safe, or loved, or like I even had a home, I would have made sure I lived that moment second by precious second. I would have held Isla for longer. I would have sung her one more song. I would not have been impatient to get back downstairs and start the party. I would not have rushed her to bed. In fact, if I'd had any control over the world, over time and space and the cosmos, I would have stayed upstairs, closed my eyes and held onto her forever.

So.

I was still on the landing when I heard Valentina's voice, the conspiratorial sound of her throaty chuckle.

The two of them were in the hallway. I saw them from halfway down the stairs. She was standing close to him, her hand laid flat on his chest, her left foot kicked up behind her. She was giggling. I remember that most of all. Her, giggling.

The cloudy feeling in my gut returned. No, I thought. No. But what I knew was: yes.

All that had gone before came back in one wordless rush and, as the air left me, I gripped the bannister tight. My husband and my best friend were not the casual acquaintances they claimed to be, not any more. They were something much more intimate, something that violated me, that ripped the heart from my entire life. Did I have it as clear as that in my mind? Not in that moment. The knowing was bodily, as it had always been, only now that knowing came stronger, filling me up with a kind of white heat.

"Hello," I said. I was still polite. Still friendly. Still holding onto the bannister for dear life.

Why, I have no idea. Conditioned response, maybe, of a working-class girl brought up to be nice, or maybe I was simply newly and badly injured, bleeding out, waiting for the pain to start. "What are you two up to?"

Valentina swung round to face me, all smiles. "Hey, babe. Michael reckons he's burning a bunny in the backyard."

"Nice alliteration." Is it possible I could have said that? I remember myself saying it. I was on the bottom stair, one foot in the hallway with no idea how I had got there. I could feel my legs trembling and wondered if she could see. Upstairs, Isla's wind-up toy plinked its plastic lullaby. "Where's Red?"

She threw up her hand in a stop sign and rolled her eyes. "The bastard double booked. Frickin' idiot. I am so furious with him right now I can't even go there. He was meant to book the babysitter and he couldn't even manage that. I've had to bring Zac with me, I hope you don't mind. He's in the living room, out for the count."

"Let me get you some of the wine Val brought," said Mikey. "It's sparkling Shiraz. It's red but you serve it cold, apparently."

"Sure," I said. "Why not?" I took the drink, drank half a glass in one go.

"Wow," said Mikey. "You were thirsty. We haven't even toasted."

I held up my glass, meeting Mikey's gaze. "To you, my darling, love of my life. To us."

"I'll drink to that," said Valentina.

A loaded silence lowered like mist. Or maybe not – maybe it was just me, my own private mist, my own loaded silence.

Mikey headed out into the garden, saying he had to turn the rabbit. Valentina helped me fetch the salads from the fridge. She was chatting about something – it hardly matters what. I could hear the interrogative rise of her Australian accent, see out of the corner of my eye her languid, confident movements, her arms reaching out when she spoke, her teeth, the way her hair moved as one fluid, shining thing. There were baked potatoes in the oven, a French stick on the table. I had set the table that afternoon, for four. A centrepiece posy, cloth napkins, napkin rings. Valentina readjusted the bowl of home-made coleslaw, straightened the glasses, picked at the vegetable crisps.

"This table is awesome," I heard her say, then, "a real art." Then, "Homemaker." And, "Such an eye for detail."

Charm. That's what they had in common, her and Mikey. Both funny, both so affectionate, both a little bit irresistible.

"Are you fucking my husband?" I asked her.

She made no reply, moving instead towards the wine bottle, picking it up, pouring wine the colour of pomegranate seeds. I realised I had not said the question aloud.

"Excuse me," I said. "I've left something in the bedroom."

I ran upstairs. Breath catching in my chest, I rummaged around in my bedside table for a packet of tissues. I began to cry. I cried silently, suppressed the gasps that I knew would be heard downstairs. I can think of no reason now for wanting to spare them the sound of me crying beyond not wanting to spoil the evening.

My iPhone was on the bedside table. On the screen, the WiFi signal indicated half strength. Had I ever tried to connect up here in the bedroom? It was possible I hadn't. I usually kept my phone in the kitchen – if I came upstairs during the day it was only to change Isla. I thumbed my way into my email account and watched twelve little white envelopes download. All of them junk, apart from one, from Jeanie, with an attachment. I checked my text messages – there was one from her – sent that afternoon at 5:13pm.

Check your email now.

I opened Jeanie's email. It said:

FYI. Finally found a picture of Georgia Smyth-Banks aka Wendy. Got in touch with the photographer from the parish newsletter and he had some head shots. Stroke of luck, eh? Recognise her at all?
J xx

224

I downloaded the attachment. I opened the attachment. It was the face and shoulders of a woman with long blonde hair – or rather, a wig – in ringlets. She was wearing a blue dress with a white old-fashioned collar. She was caked in the same dreadful orangey foundation Mikey had worn the first time I met him but her eyes were bare of make-up, her white eyelashes barely visible, her face almost unrecognisable because of that. But her canine tooth caught on her bottom lip and that, yes, I did recognise. It was a photo of Georgia Smyth-Banks. It was a photo of Wendy.

It was a photo of Valentina.

I sat down on the bed.

I got up.

I was about to be sick. The urge became a need. Heaving, I ran into the bathroom and retched into the loo. I was gasping for air, my knuckles white on the toilet seat. I stood, dipped my face under the tap and drank some cold water, let the water run then over my forehead. I gripped onto the sides of the sink and looked at myself in the mirror. My eyes were bloodshot, my skin grey. I looked older than I was, much, much older.

I walked out of the bathroom and into the bedroom. I sat on the bed and read the email again. When I had confronted Mikey about the letter, about Georgia, he had told me what a shock that must have been for me. *Jeanie called you and dropped that bomb*, something like that, he'd said. But I hadn't told him how I'd found out. I had not mentioned Jeanie. And the only person who knew about the letter, apart from Jeanie, was Valentina.

"No," I said, my voice high and strange. "No."

From the garden, I heard her laugh. I looked at the photo. I wanted so badly for it not to be her but there was no room for doubt. Her eyes were big when made up heavily in black but in the photo, without black paint to define them, they were small, almost beady.

The woman in my garden with Mikey was Georgia Smyth-Banks, his former lover. No, not former. His lover.

The two of them had rekindled their relationship right under my nose. She, she had not sent someone to come and check me out. She had come to check me out herself, had come into my house not to meet me, but to meet him. Again. Disappointed with her own lacklustre husband, she had come here to seduce mine, to lure him back into her bed, her life. That – that was why, when he had come home early and found her here, he had collapsed. It had not been a heart attack, it had not been flu, it had been shock. She had not been shocked. She had walked slowly across the kitchen floor, put a paper bag to his mouth and told him to breathe.

And then? And then later he had gone to her. Of course. He had not left his wallet in the office. He had gone to her. That's when it must have started. But how could he even think about doing that to Isla and me? How could he risk us and everything we had together? The Mikey I knew would never do such a thing. I did not know him. Who was he?

And what now? What the hell happened now?

I stood. My legs shook so much I had to lean against the wall for support, trace my way out of the bedroom like that. I was crying, I think, my breath was ragged, my insides in flames. One hand tight around the handrail, I lowered myself onto the first stair. Then the second. My legs were shaking too much to continue. I was not sure I could go down without falling. I gripped the handrail with two hands and stepped sideways, got two feet onto the third step. The fourth. Slowly, I reached the bottom. Mikey and Valentina – whoever they were – were still outside. I could hear the crackle of the rabbit, smell the aromatic flesh as it cooked. I reached the back door. They were chatting in low voices by the brazier, at ease with one another. Of course. They had put on their coats against the chill of the February night.

I went out, pulled my cardigan around me. It was cold. A midnight-blue darkness had fallen. Above the glowing coals, the rabbit hung from the pole, tied on by its paws. It looked like it was clinging on for dear life. One sharp knife to the string and it would drop into the fire.

"What have you done?" I asked them. I had my phone in the palm of my hand.

They looked at me, both of them, but it was her I was looking at.

"Why? Because you can, is that it? Because you're free and easy and you teach yoga?"

"Shona?" Her voice was edged with caution, her head cocked a little to one side. "What is this? Are you all right?"

I took a step nearer, held the phone out in front of me. "Because you're not bogged down in his crappy domestic life? Because you never have to ask him to take out the rubbish, is that it?"

"Shona." She took a step towards me, her brow furrowed – the image of concern.

"Because you and he never have to be *that couple*?" I was shouting, my voice chaos. I turned to Mikey. "Because you've got me to raise your child, haven't you, while you two fuck in hotels? Like dogs shitting on the pavement – because they're animals and they don't care who steps in it?" I lunged forward, prodded him hard in the chest, stepped back, afraid of the tremor of murderous violence I could feel rising within myself. I met her eye. "Do you dress up? What do you do, fuck him on his lunch break? Because you can do that, can't you, while I'm here looking after his child? Looking after yours too, eh? Oh God! Private yoga session? No wonder you have to take a shower before you come back. I bet you're dynamite in the sack, aren't you? I bet you can get your feet behind your head, you treacherous bitch."

"Shona, stop." She was a metre away – her face still composed, almost questioning.

Mikey stood, impassive, a little behind her.

"It's weird," I said. "You both *look* like human beings. Legs, arms ... the resemblance is uncanny. But you're not ...

227

you're not are you? You're monsters." I began to laugh. My nose was running, I wiped it with the back of my hand. "What am I saying? You don't even teach yoga, do you? I can't get my facts straight, great journalist I am. You're not a yoga teacher. You're Georgia. You're a geologist." I pointed behind her, to Mikey, but did not look at him. "You took a job up here so you could wheedle your way back into his life and steal him back, is that right? You came to the nursery. My God, I thought ... but no, that was before he left his wallet ... that was before ... you even said you were there to check out the competition." I dropped forward, rested my hands on my knees. I was panting. I couldn't see. Only darkness, my feet no more than shapes. "That wasn't a coincidence at all. You knew I was going there because he told you."

"Shona, listen to me." I heard her say.

I forced myself to stand up. My head spun, I staggered, laughing, regained my balance. I was still laughing, I couldn't stop. "You can drop the Aussie accent now, I think." My God, I could hardly speak for laughing. "I think the time for play-acting is finished, don't you, Wendy, Georgia, Valentina, whoever the fuck you are?"

"Shona, stop this." Mikey came forward now, out of the shadows, his face pale in the light from the kitchen window. He still had his drink in his hand. Sparkling Shiraz, a red you serve cold.

"Don't you say a word," I said to him. "Your words mean nothing. They're just – they're just noise." I turned back to her, seeing and hating her supercilious expression, hating her hair, her teeth, hating everything about her. I stepped forward and slapped her with all my might in the face. With a shriek, she staggered backwards. Mikey caught her in his arms.

"Shona, please," he said. "Let's go inside. Let's talk about this properly. Let's work this out."

I looked at him then, met his eye, saw worry. Was that all? Worry?

"Talk about it? Aye, right, that'd be nice. She followed you here and seduced you. Must've been nice having someone go a bit crazy for you, turn up at your house, make friends with your wife, stalk you into having them back? Big thrill, was it, having a bit on the side?"

"It's not like that."

"Not like what? You said ..." My vision blurred. My chest hurt. I could taste snot running into my mouth, down the back of my throat. I wasn't laughing now, not any more. "You said we were your home. Me and Isla. You said that the other day." I lunged forward and grabbed Valentina by the chin, held it tight. But I was still looking at Mikey. "Offer you a hot date, did she? We can all do that, you know, when someone else is cleaning the fucking house."

Mikey pushed me off her, held me back, his hand against my neck. "Look, Shona, calm down. Let's talk about this properly, like grownups."

"Grownups?" My chest filled, emptied. "I'm the only grownup here. I'm the only one who knows I can't have everything. Only six-year-olds expect to have everything at once."

Valentina – my God, I was still calling her that in my head – held up her hands. "Shona, please, calm down and listen to us."

Her accent knocked the breath out of me. Pure home counties, cut-glass, straight from Merchant Ivory.

I wanted to hit her. I wanted to tear her hair out, thump the white teeth from the lush mouth. I could not push aside the thought of her, naked, with him, her flesh on his, hours after, or maybe minutes before or after he had been that way with me.

"I won't calm down," I said, my voice shaking. "How can I calm down? Do you have any idea how ridiculous you sound? You've taken away my whole life. So you're fed up with your husband, so you want mine, is that it? Or is it more? You want to trade? Red for Mikey? So he can come and look after you and your child – make a better job of it than your pothead record-peddling shitty loser husband?"

"It's his child," she said, stepping forward.

"What?"

"Zac is Michael's child."

She took a step nearer. In her face I saw no remorse, only something superior, almost sneering: victory.

"Georgie, stop," said Mikey, grabbing her arm, pulling her back.

"But he's mine." I was pointing at Mikey – as if no one could see him but me. "He's my home. He's my life. He's mine."

"I'm afraid he's mine," she said. "If we're talking possession here. He's my husband, Shona. In law. We're married."

I looked from her to him. He had covered his forehead with his hand, stepped back into the shadow – all I could see clearly were the ends of his shoes.

My mouth filled with a sour taste.

"Don't be ridiculous," I said. "How can that even be possible? When would he have time? He works offshore, for Christ's sake."

"Again, no, Shona," she said. "I really think Michael's right. I think we should go inside and sit down and discuss this like adults."

"I'm fine standing right here."

"All right." She tipped her chin back. "Shona? I want you to listen carefully. Michael lives with me. He works with me. We're married. We have a son together, Zachary, who you know as Zac."

"Georgie, please," said Mikey, stepping out, striding forward, taking her arm once more.

But she shook him off and walked towards me. I backed away but she followed. My back hit the garage wall. She came in close, the outside lantern catching the wet sheen of her eyes.

"When you think he goes offshore," she said softly. "He doesn't. He has never been offshore, never been in a helicopter as far as I'm aware. On Saturday mornings, he takes a cab not to the heliport but to our home. 14 Fittie Place, I think you know it. On the way, he gets his other little phone out of his pocket and texts me. *Put the coffee pot on*, are the words he usually uses, since you seem so keen for information. And then? Well, we spend the weekend together doing all the things that a family does and on Monday we go together into the office where we work, as normal, and instead of coming to you, he comes home with me in my car. He lives with me, in my house, with our son, Zachary for those two weeks. Understand this, Shona: I am his wife. Zac is his child." She smiled. "You, Shona. You are the mistress. You, not me. So I would put your moral outrage away if I were you because you are, I'm afraid – how did you put it? – the *bit on the side*."

***

What does it mean to belong to someone, she wonders, the tip of her nose blue on her clenched face. Is it wrong to regard another person as yours? The language of love is the language of ownership, this is what occurs to her now, here in the dark. This is what strikes her as so damn ironic. She has used these possessive terms as often as the next person, in her mind, aloud, without giving them a second thought. He is mine. I am his. Oh yes, she has let herself believe, utterly, that she belonged to him. And, as she'll tell you herself, she never even entertained the possibility that he wasn't, that he wouldn't, be hers alone. She never for one second doubted that he understood this as profoundly as she did, not a cerebral understanding but something deeper, down low, in the guts, where love lives. If she's got it so mixed up in her mind, if she's got it so wrong, then someone please explain the Valentine's day cards that line the shelves year after year. They're in the shops now; she saw some in the supermarket only today: Baby be mine; I'm yours; Take me home and keep me.

Love.

Ownership.

Belonging.

Inside the fairy tale cottage sleep a man and woman she loved generously and freely; two people she wanted only to love and be loved by in return. But they did not love her, not at all. And now here she is: outside.

Whatever, it is pointless thinking about it all now. She must move on – which she will do, in a moment. Right now, she must focus on the task at hand. Sure enough, there's a faint glow pulsing at the front window. The fire has not yet reached the living room but from the hallway it has cast its solid orange light far enough to be seen from here, beneath the trees. It is not the light itself she sees but the echo of it, she knows that. She knows too that they won't be able to get downstairs, not now. Even if they wake, they will not be able to reach the phone.

And what of the baby? Oh no. Oh no, no, no. She can't think about the baby now.

***

PART II

TWENTY-TWO

This is ridiculous. I'm not going to stand here and be painted as the wicked witch to Shona's simpering *Belle Dormante au Bois*. Please. This isn't some nasty little affair, it isn't the story of a sumptuous office Lolita tempting some flaccid grey-faced executive into her petal-strewn bed. Any half-decent looking woman can offer a touch of forbidden silk to a man whose wife is familiar to him as an old woollen sock. Especially once you throw a baby into the equation. Christ, who wouldn't want to escape that kind of shit-soaked hyperreality? So no, I didn't bat my eyes at someone else's man because I couldn't get one of my own. I had someone of my own. The point here is that Michael was mine. He was mine first.

OK, so we were breaking up around the time he met her. Had broken up. But it was only temporary. What you have to understand is that Michael is a very difficult man, a very selfish man. But difficulty and selfishness don't stop you loving someone, do they? And we understand each other, Michael and I, always have. We see the world in the same way. We feel things the same way. And you can't help how you feel, can you?

I'd only ended our relationship because he needed to know what it felt like to lose me. He needed sharpening. I suppose I realised I'd handed it all to him on a plate. Michael has a way of making you do that. Casts some kind of Shamanistic spell and before you know it you're bringing him breakfast in bed with a gooey expression in your eyes and a broom up your backside so better to clean the damn floor. And then the inattentions begin. Little things. He complains when you ask him for a foot massage. The flowers, because it's Friday? Forget it. When it's his turn to cook, out go the spices ground by hand in the marble pestle and mortar, gone is the chilled Sancerre, the home-made tiramisu. In comes the takeaway chicken tikka masala, the supermarket plonk, the tub of Mackies ice cream if you're lucky. The sex gets lazy, the foreplay predictable, but still afterwards you tell him how you don't know how he does what he does but, my God, you've never lost control like that before. If not, he takes offence.

So I was sick of it. We were both nearing the end of our MScs at Heriot-Watt, he in Petroleum Engineering, myself in Petroleum Geoscience, we both had a lot of work to do. I know we girls have to do everything backwards and in heels but a girlfriend has a right to a certain amount of attention, not just the dregs. I'm really not a dregs kind of girl. Even if Michael's dregs are better than most men's finest, creamiest head.

"I am not the harbour where you moor your fucking boat," I think were my exact words when I threw him and all his stuff out of my flat. "Come back when you're ready to commit."

I should have known he would never do that. Commit properly, I mean. But I did know he would come back. I knew I would win him. Because, you see, there is no one quite like Michael and me. We are made for each other.

So when I saw on Facebook he was seeing someone else, a positively indecent two days after we'd split, I did have a fleeting moment of ... doubt, I suppose, not to mention irritation. Two days. Was it possible to meet someone so quickly? I doubted it. To be romantically entangled so soon, he must have met her when we were together. Had he cheated on me? It was possible, more than possible. It would be typical of him to put the heating on before he got out of bed. Michael can't stand a single minute without someone adoring him, besides himself of course.

I gave her a week, maybe two. I was studying hard so it was easy to distract myself, in between checking his posts. A month later, he was still posting. No photos, no names, but rave reviews. It was all for me, I knew that. With a connection like ours, we can communicate in code. The whole world can be listening but only we will know what is being said. Of course, if I'd accused him of writing these cryptic messages for my benefit, he would have thrown up his hands and said: *what*? He's clever.

But then so am I.

It got to late May. He was still with her. Things were not going according to plan. And so, when I bumped into Robbie on Sauchiehall Street, it was the ideal moment to catch up. After the endless *how's it goings* Glaswegians seem to favour and some pantomime-related small talk, I cut to the chase. I hadn't seen Michael in a while, had he, Robbie, seen him at all? Yes, yes he had. And was Michael still with that girl he'd met? Yes, yes he was.

"Heavens," I said, feigning surprise, placing my shopping bags on the pavement. "That's weeks now. She must be an absolute goddess."

"Well, she's no' bad ..." He eyed the bags. "Three pairs of shoes, eh? That should see you right."

"I'll be starting work soon," I said. "Can't exactly go into the office in Converse and jeans, can I? So, do you know her?"

"She works with our Jeanie. They live together, like, you know?"

I smiled, told him that sounded nice, that I was glad Michael was happy.

"Anyway, so ..." He took a step back. I always thought he might be afraid of me, as short men often are. "I'd better get off."

"That's a great shirt, Robbie," I said, reaching forward, touching the tips of my fingers against his chest. "Very ... fresh looking. What is it, Ben Sherman?"

He looked down, stuck out his bottom lip and pinched the fabric between his fingers. "I don't know. Probably Markies, to be honest with you."

"Well, it suits you."

"Aye right." He blushed.

"So," I said. "What's she like, this, what did you say her name was?"

"Shona."

"Shona?"

"McGilvery."

"Shona McGilvery. Good Scottish name."

"Aye, well." He shifted from foot to foot. "She's fae Govan so."

"Govan." I smiled. "Michael will like that. Very authentic."

I left him and headed for Frasers. I bought some capri pants and two silk blouses from Mango (for the office) and, as a treat for the stress I'd gone through, a gorgeous dressy-but-not-too-dressy LBD from Max Mara. I was so weighed down with bags I had to get a cab back to my flat. Once inside, I kicked the door shut and opened the first bottle of white that fell out of the fridge. I lit a joint and threw myself on the couch. The couch where he and I had ... I stopped myself. So her name was Shona, was it? Shona from Govan. He'd gone out and found himself a nice working-class girl. A real pulled-herself-up-by-her-bootstraps, salt-of-the-earth, have-a-go heroine. He'd come over all wanna live like those much revered common people, and had found a bright wee local lassie with just enough about her to swim out of the swamp.

Classic rebound.

I sucked on the joint, imagined her, Shona. Small, I thought. A ready smile, a gutsy, girl-next-door type, someone that people found charming. I pulled out my iPhone. Facebook ... let's see ... Shona McGilvery ... here she was. Dark, straight, short hair, a vaguely Inuit look about her, really rather boyish. The ready smile was there. Pale blue eyes with, I'll admit, a certain intelligence in their regard but even so, what, frankly, did he see in her? Education: University of Glasgow, English Literature and Journalism. Hadn't travelled far from Mummy and Daddy for her degree. A homebody, then. Maybe she had a mother with nervous trouble or, more likely, couldn't afford rent. Work: *Glasgow Tribune*. Yes, that was right – she was a colleague of Robbie's sister, what was her name, Jayne? Joan? Shona McGilvery would be a journalist of the morally righteous variety, no doubt, armed with the swords of truth and justice. How unspeakably dull. I closed the page, took another hit, a long slug of white. Whoever she was, she had come in and stolen Michael when he and I were simply enjoying a brief hiatus.

She. Shona. Opportunist.

So I did what any woman in love would do – I set about getting him back.

Drastic action was required. Danger. Nothing a man like Michael loves more. Makes him feel alive. Makes us both feel alive. Shona could never give him danger. She could never understand him like I did. Michael and I are two sides of the same coin, cut from the same cloth, members of the same tribe – choose your metaphor. No matter what she could give him now in the short term, I knew in the long term she would bore him into his grave. What makes you feel safe ultimately limits you, and it's not like they were married, is it? They weren't even living together at that point, so don't you look at me like that.

Don't you dare look at me like that.

And if I happened to catch Michael outside Robbie's flat that was hardly my fault. And if I suggested a drink I can hardly be accused of overstepping boundaries. We'd had something together, something special, something rare. It was only natural we would go for a drink and a chat. To catch up. We were coming to the end of our studies. And it was good to see him.

"You're looking well," he said, once we settled in our seats.

"Thanks." I'd spent a fortune with Frank at Toni & Guy that morning. I should hope I did look *well*.

"What've you been up to?"

I shrugged, crossed my legs. One high-heeled tan mule half-slipped from my foot, a louche surrender to the sticky day – the type of early summer heatwave that sends half of Glasgow to hospital with third-degree burns. I don't get that British obsession with tanning. And fake tan, don't get me started – who wants to look like they've covered themselves in gravy browning all summer? Patchy ankles, orange palms? What's wrong with alabaster skin?

"I may go to France for the summer," I said. "I need to plan my next move."

He took a long drink of his lager, looked around the bar, back to me. Laid his hand on my thigh. "You really do look well."

"Thanks. So do you."

"Robbie's out. He won't be back till later ..."

And if in the passion of the moment I forgot my pill, I'm sorry. It was a mistake, one many before me have made and will make again. They call it the oldest trick in the book but, as I've said, it was a mistake.

After finishing his Master's, Michael got a bar job – wanted to *chill out*, he said, which I found curiously unambitious. I picked up some contracting work through an old contact of my uncle's so I didn't go to France in the end. I thought I'd hang around for a bit, see whether our *embryonic* relationship would take shape. Michael was still with Shona but I knew that was for form's sake more than anything. Habit. It was complicated now they'd moved in together, he said.

"It's my flat," he explained to my reflection as I applied my mascara in my dressing table mirror. We were about to head out for dinner. "I can't exactly turn her out onto the street, can I?"

"I hardly think she'd be on the street Michael," I replied, eyeing him leaning on the doorjamb behind me. I picked a clot of black from the end of an eyelash and proceeded to search in my vanity case for my lipstick. But when I looked up, he'd gone. I ran my hand over the hard curve of my belly. What did it matter if he didn't get rid of Shona immediately? He would soon enough.

And in all the push-me-pull-me-will-he-won't-he, what I have to say to you is this: for me, things were good. The attentions had returned. I found I adored being the other woman even though, of course, I was the main woman, if that makes sense. It was a revelation – like syphoning off the creamy head. The dregs, well, she was welcome to them.

So. Turns out I am really rather fertile. One shot hits the spot. I didn't want to announce the glad tidings just like that. I wanted him in the right mood. And there's a particular, very specific moment when men are receptive to anything.

I arranged a rendezvous in our favourite dark bar round the corner from my flat. It was a kind of shorthand between us for what might lie ahead. He told her he had to work a double shift and met me at six. It was July but cold and rainy, the usual disaster of a British so-called summer. The sooner we fled to hotter climes, I thought, the better. Oman would be nice. Maybe Malaysia. Some cushy expat deal. We ordered gin and tonics. A vigorous bout of kissing soon became a get-a-room situation, a rather hurried canter down the street, a racy trajectory up two flights of stairs before we staggered, clothes half-off, into my sitting room. That, Shona, is what men want: sex. Not some washed out little pixie in food-encrusted slippers.

When I waved away the post-coital joint he asked me why.

"I think I'm pregnant," I said.

"What do you mean, think?"

"I think therefore I am." I smiled, decided to take a puff after all. How much harm could one toke do to it anyway?

"I see." He did me the courtesy of trying to hide his shock, of not asking if he was the father. And, as I explained, it wasn't such a disaster as all that. We both had good prospects, we were in love and, for goodness' sake, he and Shona had only just moved in together. Nothing that couldn't be undone.

"You can move back in once you've told Shona," I said. "And don't worry, I will be going back to work after it's born."

He was already pulling on his jeans. "It's after seven," he said. "She'll be wondering where I am." He knelt on the bed and leant over.

I pulled him onto me, kissed him hard on the mouth. "Tell me it's going to be OK, Michael." I let my voice crack, let the tears well in my eyes. "Tell me you love me more."

He held my chin softly in his fingers. "I do love you, you know that. Don't worry about any of this. There's no one like you, Georgie. You're a one-off."

How was I to know she'd be waiting at the stove with news of her own?

I hadn't seen that coming.

She had, I must confess, out-manoeuvred me. I almost admired her for it.

I considered a termination. But wasn't that like throwing away my best card? And over the weeks that followed, Michael was, if anything, more attentive than ever. Flowers when it wasn't even Friday, chocolates for no reason, a white gold necklace which must have cost the earth.

But he didn't leave her. He just didn't.

Whenever I hinted at him moving in, he changed the subject, suggested going to a movie, initiated love-making. It was like trying to catch a bar of wet soap. But I didn't push. He wouldn't do anything unless he felt it was his own idea. That's the trick with Michael. Always flatter, never criticise. And always stay one move ahead. That's what I mean about us understanding one another. So I didn't mention her, I didn't complain and was instead – perfect, I guess you'd say. Regular trips to see Frank at Toni & Guy, to this great manicurist he recommended who also, despite my burgeoning bump, gave me the rudest Brazilian wax I'd ever had. Drove Michael wild. Things were good between us. I relaxed in the knowledge that, even if he didn't leave her straight away, he would tire of her soon enough, baby or no baby. She was, I felt – no, I knew – too small for a man like him. She was not *enlightened*. If there was, ultimately, to be a single parent in this *ménage à trois*, then it wouldn't, I felt, be me.

But Michael isn't like anyone I've ever known. Michael had his own plan.

It was a little after Christmas which, by the way, I spent alone. I must have been around seven months gone when he took me to dinner at The Grill Room.

"You should have steak," he said. "For iron. For the baby."

I laughed at him. "Dear God, Michael. You'll be offering to come to NCT classes next."

"I will if you want me to."

"Spare me the earnestness, please. You'll get wrinkles on your lovely forehead. Even I'm not going to NCT classes. There's one exit, as far as I understand. Pain relief is available. And I'll be taking everything they have. I don't think I need to sit in some draughty church hall listening to some woman with frizzy hair and bad shoes boring on about massage techniques for four weeks or however the hell long it is."

"OK," he said, laughing. "No NCT classes. I'm having the sirloin, what about you?"

"Fillet mignon," I said. "Rare. And a large glass of the Bourgogne."

"Are you sure you can drink?"

I did not deign to reply.

He leant forward, his menu bending against the table edge. "I love that you always know exactly what you want. You don't muck about, do you?"

I scrutinised him a moment and said, "If you want something, what's the point in not getting it, frankly?"

We ordered, talked shop briefly, but only briefly. Our wine arrived, our steaks on rustic chopping boards – someone's idea of a sophisticated plate replacement. The steaks were adorned rather alarmingly with twin tomatoes, blanched and peeled and sitting close together like googly eyes; at the top, a mop of watercress hair.

"Everything OK?" he asked, seeing my hesitation.

"I'm not sure. I think I might recognise this person."

When he didn't laugh, I should have known he was building up to something. Halfway down the bottle, he pitched.

"So," he said, placing his glass carefully on the dark, high sheen of the wooden table top. "I've got an idea. About how this is all going to work. You, me, the baby. Shona, the baby." He picked up his glass, took a long slug, placed it back on the table. He exhaled heavily, looked up and fixed me with his cavalier spaniel eyes. "I reckon I can get Shona to give up work."

"We're here to talk about Shona's maternity arrangements? How nice."

"Let me finish." He drank again, deeply, and topped up his glass. At this rate, I thought, he'll have passed out before he's finished his big speech. "So," he said. "There's a position for a Junior Drilling Engineer going at Maple Energy. I have a good chance. More than a good chance."

"Maple are in Aberdeen." A flutter of concern – mild concern – passed through me. I'd pictured us somewhere a little more exotic, at least while the baby was little. "You'll visit us at Christmas, is that it?"

"Please, Georgie. Hear me out." He reached for my hand, which I, naturally, withdrew. "You and I will end up in Aberdeen whatever. We can't stay in Glasgow, there isn't enough work here and you know that as well as I do."

"I've managed to pick up a contract. It's you who's working in a bar, darling."

"I know. But that won't last. You know it won't. My idea is that we all move up. I mean, you, me, and the baby, Shona and the baby too."

I narrowed my eyes at him, waiting for him to point and say *gotcha*! but his expression remained the same ... perfectly serious. "You're insane."

"Listen. Now here's the plan. I tell her I'm going to work offshore. Except I don't. I spend the two weeks she thinks I'm on the rig with you. She knows nothing. You get a job – possibly with me. We work together. I spend two weeks living with you, maybe even working with you, two weeks with her. You spend more time with me than she does because we'll see each other at work. I'll put her out of the way, in the country or somewhere, where she can't bump into us." He threw out his hands. "Everyone's happy."

I took a sip of wine and levelled my gaze at him. He was still earnest, his eyebrows twin arches of misguided optimism. It had a certain amusement value, I suppose, watching him set out his ridiculous argument – like watching an expensive lawyer defend a rich but guilty client.

"You're out of your mind," I said.

"No, I'm not. I'm very much in it. Think about it – but think about it carefully – with an open mind." His eyes shone, his hands making clouds in the air. "You're like me, Georgie. Unconventional. You can see the bigger picture. One, you don't like being tied down. It bores you, you know it does, I know it does. This way, it would always be fresh between us. We'll never end up like that couple who have nothing to say to each other – stale, bored to death, finishing each other's sentences. That's your biggest fear, George. This way you don't have to settle." Rather alarmingly, he had begun jabbing his finger into the table for emphasis. "Husband and two point four kids." Jab. "DIY at weekends." Jab. "Sunday roast." Jab. "Two weeks in the sun every summer, getting fat and bored, bored, bored." Jab jab jab. "Come on!" He sat back in his chair

247

and pointed at me. "That's death for you. Or am I wrong?" He leant forward – good God, the man couldn't keep still. "Think about it, Georgie. This way, you'd have the freedom you need. But! You'd have security. You'd have me plus that little element of risk you – well, we both, love so much."

I stared at him, again waiting, waiting for him to laugh. He didn't. I felt for the napkin on my lap, screwed it up and threw it on the table. "You're being ridiculous. Even if I agreed, which I obviously won't, we'd never be able to keep it from her."

"Yes we will." He held up his forefinger. Next he'd be repositioning the crockery by way of demonstration, making me the condiment holster, Shona the water pitcher, himself the wine. Please.

But I let him talk since he clearly wanted to so very badly and, as I said, it was entertaining.

"I've figured it all out," he went on. "Check this. I'll give her a brand new iPhone. As a moving present. I'll put Spyware on it. She'll be a walking GPS system. I'll be able to follow her every move. Her old iPhone's buggered but she won't buy a new one for herself – she's not like that."

"What a perfect saint," I said. "You're making me cry."

"That way," he continued, ignoring me, "I can locate her wherever she is." His eyes widened. "It's totally doable, Georgie. You and me. Freethinkers, risk-takers, visionaries – like all the great pioneers. We could have the life we actually want instead of the life we're conditioned to think we want. You want freedom but you want me. I don't want to lose either of my children."

"Or your women," I added. "How big of you."

He grinned. "Very bigamy, I say."

"Oh dear God."

He shrugged, laughed at his own joke. "You'd be in the superior position. You would know everything. It's not like I'd be cheating on you, is it? Honestly, this is what makes you so amazing. You're the only woman I know with the vision to see that this is a brilliant idea." He was back to jabbing the table.

I savoured my last mouthful of steak. I love meat. Love its fibrous, bloody taste. I drained my wine glass and got up.

"Michael," I said. "Call me when you have a real plan. And by real, I mean one which doesn't come from a Hollywood film and which, more importantly, doesn't include her."

I walked out. He didn't shout after me, didn't chase me. In fact, I have no idea how he reacted. If I had to guess, I'd say now he probably poured himself the rest of the wine, maybe ordered the tiramisu.

I went home outraged. *Georgia doesn't want me to herself. Georgia is only interested in a part-time lover.* This was what he believed. For Christ's sake, I had only given him that impression so he would worry enough to give me more. More, not less! I had played it cool – a tactic that had never failed me before. Why are people such imbeciles? Why can they not do what we want, when we want, exactly as we want? He had believed my façade but, instead of worrying himself back into my arms like a wounded little fledgling desperate to be let back into the nest, he had flown off in a whole other direction.

That night I didn't sleep. Michael's plan was preposterous. I will admit I found the idea of having him around only half the time immediately appealing, so long as he spent more time with me than with her and so long as I could guarantee his regular return. The last few months had been exciting, the sex passionate, the arrivals and departures emotional, dramatic. There had been not one instance of dirty socks left on the bathroom floor. He was offering to leave me free to do what the hell I wanted while having all the advantages of a relationship. He would have his Shona, if I wanted a second lover to fill the gap, so to speak, he could hardly object. What? Oh, don't judge. Don't be so parochial. And don't tell me you haven't wanted the same, haven't stared at the ceiling and wondered how much longer you can cope with the tedium of it all. A change, here and there, a little chilli in the dressing, we all want it, but most of us are too cowardly to take it. I was young, attractive, financially independent. Why should I have less than him? It was his plan, after all, not mine. All I was doing was securing a future for our child. I was simply not ready to enter a convent quite yet.

But even if I did accept, I thought then, we could never keep it up. Shona would see us together eventually. One heard about such secret arrangements but they took place with families in different cities, with men who travelled for a living. One heard about teenage children meeting up at university, discovering somehow that they're actually half siblings. But Aberdeen was one city, and a relatively small one. The oil industry was a village. She would hear about us, at least about him, within months. No, it couldn't last.

I rubbed my swollen belly and sighed to no one. Too late for a termination. What was I going to do?

I got out of bed, made hot milk with honey to try and abate the acid reflux brought on by the steak and the red wine. Pregnancy was playing havoc with my usual resilience. At the window, with the shutters open, I stood and sipped my milk. Below, the street shone black with rain. No cars, no one about. How quiet it was here, in the small hours of the night. From the dresser, I picked up the stork ornament he had given me, twirled its thin stem leg. Its plump body twisted this way and that. This kind of loneliness I liked: peace, sleeping when I wanted, drinking when I wanted, staring out at slick abandoned streets when I wanted. I could do whatever I pleased. Loneliness you can end isn't loneliness, not really. If I called Michael, if I called him right now, he would come. Loneliness like this was control.

But he was not with me. He was with her. They would be asleep, together. They would wake up, smile at each other, she would bring him coffee, run her hand through his thick, soft hair. I placed my mug on the top of my belly. Beneath, the soft *kick kick*, making ripples in the surface of the milk. With the birth of this kicking little mite, all silence would end. In its place would be chaos, screaming and shit. Another kind of loneliness altogether. A lack of control. Was this, actually, what Michael was offering – not the best of both worlds but the worst: insecurity, jealousy, uncontrolled loneliness, two weeks out of four?

But if I refused – I wouldn't even get the two weeks. She would get him four weeks in four. If I pushed him, threatened suicide, took a posting in Malaysia or Oman, he might not come with me. Or he might, but he would become resentful at the loss of the other child – the relationship would sour. He would leave, go back to her. She would still get him four weeks in four. I would still have lost, in the most complete way. She, the girl from Govan, would have won.

I went back to bed, lay down. I closed my eyes, tried to regulate my breathing, trick myself into sleep like I used to at boarding school. And then something occurred to me, something so obvious I couldn't believe I hadn't thought of it before. I sat bolt upright, rigid with purpose. Here I was worrying that Shona would find out.

But what if she did? *So what if she did?*

I laughed out loud, clenched my fists. If Shona discovered the truth, as she surely would, wouldn't that be the best thing that could possibly happen?

I got up again, ran back to the window and looked out onto the rainy street, half-insane with the revelation.

If I fought now, I might win, but for how long? If I rang Shona and told her, forced his hand, made him do something he was not ready to do, he would, ultimately, throw it back in my face. The blame for his losing Shona, whose limited charms were apparently still fresh, would fall upon me. But! If I waited it out, if I played along like a lovestruck fool, she would still find out – it was inevitable. And she would go mad. Insane mad, yes, and furious mad.

She would, would have to, leave him. The girl who fought for truth and justice would have no choice. Hell, she'd probably piss off back to Glasgow.

I was cackling by then, hysterical with the crystalline clarity of it all. She would have lost. I would have won and, in Michael's eyes, I would be blameless. Blameless and humble and ready to accept the prize.

Back in bed, I slid a pillow between my knees, lay on my side and closed my eyes. It was too easy. A few months – that's all it would take. A woman like her against a woman like me? I didn't need to see her in the flesh, I'd seen her on Facebook – tiny little pipsqueak of a thing. I knew from the snippets Michael had let slip, from my conversation with Robbie, that there was no contest. She was, I had gleaned, physically and intellectually inferior – and she was governed by some misguided, outdated notion of integrity, some unutterably dull working-class moral code. Let him move her and his other child into the stinking countryside. Let her believe his lies, the fool. If she was idiot enough to believe his shaggy dog story in the first place, she deserved to be duped. I would simply ... sit it out. That's all I had to do until she found out, flipped out and fucked off out of our lives forever. Smug fools deserved all they got. The more I thought about it, the easier it became. I would agree to the plan he thought so elegant. And I knew what my condition would be.

TWENTY-THREE

It was a quiet ceremony. Not one of our acquaintances knew about it. Robbie didn't even know we were together, so he was hardly going to be the best man. I agreed to keep Michael's parents out of it since they already knew that Shona and he had moved in together; mine were both back in Melbourne. So no parents and no parents-in-law – talk about the best of both worlds. For the honeymoon, Michael told Shona he had a business trip and away we went on a fact-finding mission to Aberdeen. We stayed at the Craigendarroch in Ballater, flipped through property schedules in the four-poster bed, ordered room service: champagne, beef and horseradish on soft white bread. We made love, made plans, made calls to estate agents.

When I saw the two up, two down in Fittie, it struck me as a perfectly adequate temporary hideaway. I sold up in Glasgow and put in an offer. Ironically, it was me, not Michael, who got the first job. Any position Michael could get would have to be onshore and onshore work would not let him have the two-week holiday every month he would need to keep up appearances. So I was bailing him out. It was tough, tougher than I thought, but I was keeping the long game in mind.

Once Zachary was born, I took up the part-time position with Maple and moved. Simple. I can remember my first day in Fittie – trailing my hand along the white walls of that minuscule kitchen and thinking, yes, this is somewhere I can ... wait it out. Michael pretended he had to travel, that he had to do all sorts of training courses, survival weekends, you name it. He simply kissed his Glasgow mistress goodbye and travelled up to his wife in Aberdeen.

I put Zachary in Little Beans nursery up in Rosemount, fixed up the hideaway as best I could. I had everything organised more or less as I wanted. When he was in town, Michael and I lived together at the Fittie house. We were lucky. When the time came, he walked into a job at Maple and out came the property schedules once more.

The cottage was a dream, of course. As soon as I saw it I knew it was mine, would be mine, once I'd dealt with the issue at hand.

"It's perfect." I said to Michael. "For Shona, I mean."

It wasn't easy. The day he moved her up, into the cottage that would be mine, that was mine, I couldn't concentrate. We had been so free. No GPS tracking devices, no subterfuge. Now she was here, things would have to change. My work suffered. I left early, pleading a migraine.

In the end, after hours imagining them half-deranged with happiness, cooing over where to put the Welsh dresser or whatever hellish crap they owned, I cracked. I had to find out if this loneliness really was the controlled state of affairs I believed it to be. Could I get him to drop everything and come to me when I needed him?

It was about 9pm when I sent him the text message. He wouldn't have his other phone on him, not on the day he moved, so I knew I would have to contact him on what I called his Shone. He'd put my contact in that phone as George Maple so I knew I had to write some kind of work-related code that he would be able to unpick. My long-term intention was to blow his cover, of course, but I had to make it look like it had happened by accident otherwise I would lose. And that wasn't an option. So I put something like:

Present drilling requirements at HR office asap.
Regards, George.

Again, God knows where that came from – funny, how your mind shoots off on tangents when you force it to invent.

He was at my door thirty-five minutes later. I calculated that he must have left the cottage within minutes of receiving my message and I was gratified by that.

"I came to present my drilling requirements," he said, grinning, stepping in, lifting me up and carrying me until, bang, we hit the back wall of the living room.

"Good," I said. "I'm in urgent need of some drilling."

We knocked a picture off its hook, a photo of the two of us with Zachary when he was a week old. The frame broke, the glass smashed. Clothes still on, we fucked up against the wall, fell onto the floor, sweaty, flushed, exhilarated.

"That," he said, "was unbelievable."

That, I thought, was exciting. What would happen to that once Michael became mine alone? What would I have to do to keep *that?*

Once he'd gone – out over the quadrangle, muttering about fish and chips, threading his arms through his jacket sleeves in his immediate and perhaps tactless return to the mundane – I lit a joint and opened the front window, stared out into the night.

Did I even want to blow his cover? I was no longer sure. Maybe this could work. Maybe this was a good deal more exciting than real life. Maybe this was *better*.

And then on Saturday morning I got his text:

Put the coffee pot on.

And there he was, fifteen minutes later, at the door. We spent the weekend together. The Spyware worked as well as he'd said it would. She was in his pocket or on his desk, right in front of him, all the time – a small orange dot with no idea she was being watched. He knew and I knew that she was there alone in that cottage. We were in Fittie, safe, in our love nest.

I would have stuck it out, kept to myself, but I was too curious. I'm only human – any woman in my position would have felt the same, done the same. I'd seen a photo of course. In addition to the one on Facebook, I'd found several on his *Shone* so I'd seen her and the baby. The baby was curiously fair, considering it was the issue of such a dark-haired rake as Michael and his little Celtic pixie. But a photo wasn't enough. I wanted to meet her, find out what she was like.

So, that first night, while Michael slept, I sneaked out and drove to the cottage, half-mad with some need I could not name. At the end of the lane, I stopped, the cottage walls bright white in the glare of the headlights, and almost fainted when I saw the bedroom curtain twitch.

I killed the lights but almost in the same moment realised what a stupid idea that was. I turned the headlights back on and drove up to the old farmhouse at the top of the track, turned the car around and drove back slowly – no rush, ain't nothin' dodgy goin' on here – a wrong turn on a midnight cruise. So I saw nothing and I have no idea what she saw, only that she didn't see me. All in all, it was a disappointing, pointless and extremely tiring trip.

In the days that followed, I tried to think of a way I could casually call in – not so easy when the cottage is miles from anywhere. Could I pretend to be a canvassing MP? Mobile something or other, make-up consultant, image consultant, personal shopper? *Madame, we're doing complimentary grooming sessions in the Aberdeenshire area today as part of our introductory offer ...*

No. That wouldn't work. I'd never keep a straight face.

The solution came one evening. I was in the kitchen of our Fittie hideaway, preparing Zachary's bottle while Michael indulged in one of his tedious phone calls to her – part, he said, of the plan's authenticity: *if I really were offshore, Georgie, I'd ring her daily wouldn't I?* He'd told her they weren't allowed mobiles offshore after one of the roughnecks had been driven insane by his wife calling him and threatening to sleep with someone else if he didn't get himself home that instant. That was actually true – he'd heard the story in the office. So, not that I was listening, but I couldn't help but hear him say the name of the nursery. And the time. Blue Moon. Monday. Two o'clock.

Monday was my day off. Michael cycled to work and I went straight to Monsoon and spent a fortune on a maxi skirt I didn't even like. In Oxfam I found a pair of ghastly red leather shoes that positively screamed orthopaedic. I went home, put on the shoes and the skirt with an old t-shirt of Michael's, which I knotted at one side. I studied my reflection and laughed like a drain. Here was one thing I hadn't considered: that this would be so much fun.

At The Blue Moon, dressed in my ridiculous get up, I made out like I'd been trying the doorbell. A chance meeting, that's what I was going for. If it's easy to avoid someone when you know their exact location, it's even easier, when you set your mind to it, to meet someone by chance. And then, in the nursery, I only had to brazen it out with the staff. Of course there was no appointment! But faced with a weak mind, a strong mind will always win.

I had every intention of leaving it there. I'm not a pervert and I'm not a stalker. This wasn't some sinister plot. All I wanted to do was see her, maybe speak to her, try and figure out what she had that I didn't. And yes, I should have said goodbye and walked away. My plan, after all, was only to sit and wait. That's all it ever was.

But here's the thing. I had hated her – for over a year. I had wanted to hate her. But, when I met her, I didn't hate her at all. I actually liked her. I don't know, I think I'd imagined some rictus grinning homemaker, all baby charts and absolutely zero sense of humour. But she wasn't like that. She was sarcastic and open and honest. She was darker in spirit than I thought she'd be and, now that I'd met her, now that I'd gone to so much trouble, I thought it might be nice to hang out. What harm could it do? Michael would never know. I had no other friends, I needed company on my days off and besides, this way I could help things, at a pace controlled by me, towards their inevitable conclusion.

And so I got a lift from Shona and put myself, metaphorically speaking, in the driving seat.

I couldn't believe it when she agreed to let me come to the cottage. She couldn't get the front door open, I had a better hang of the key than she did. Can't say I liked what she'd done with the place. The pictures on the walls were a clueless hotch-potch of prints and photos and her crockery was that cream, raised fruit design favoured by people who don't know their own taste. But it was easier to fake enthusiasm, fake everything for that matter, in an Australian accent. There's a sense in which you're not in your own skin. You're not yourself. You can get away with anything. I spent my childhood in Australia. Tourak, a wealthy suburb of Melbourne. When my father left, we came back to the UK, to be near my mum's family in Hampshire. I told Shona my father left when I was two but actually I was twelve, old enough to understand the immediate effect if not the long-term damage. My mother's family is rich, I may as well get that over with so you can get on with the judging. Silver spoon, all of that. Go ahead, get it all out of your system. My grandparents paid for my education and, because they were paying, they got to choose the convent school I so loathed. That was when I decided I would never again let anyone pay for anything on my behalf. I would never sacrifice my financial independence, never be beholden. I would be in control of my own choices.

So fill your boots, judge all you like. What do I care? I could bleat on, in my defence, about my mother's depression at the hands of a cold academic husband, her spineless acquiescence in the face of my being posted off to boarding school, as if I were her ward and not in fact her own daughter. I could rant and rave about her move back to

Aus the day I went to uni as if she had been waiting all my life for the freedom to leave me. I could wipe away a tear and tell you about my father – the esteemed Melbourne University Professor of Geophysics – who could be in a room with you and still be so absent you would begin to wonder whether or not you were really there. But I won't.

So I got into the cottage, I drank her Scottish tea, ate her mother's recipe cake and got her to show me upstairs. Seeing the picture of Michael on the chest of drawers was a kick to the solar plexus, I will admit.

"That's us at my parents' silver wedding," she said, in that self-satisfied way, as if happy marriage was in her genes or some similar smug self-delusion common to the terminally glass-half-full types. I had to throw myself on the bed to get her to shut up.

So we started to hang out – when I wasn't teaching yoga – again, where that came from I have no idea. I think someone might have asked me if that's what I did once, on account of my slim figure, perhaps my dancer's posture. It's possible I should have kept my distance but it wasn't like I had better things to do on my days off, now that I had Zachary. Being with Shona was a little like being a stay-at-home mum except that, instead of the crushing boredom of polite exchange, I got to invent a whole other life for myself while someone with half a brain cooked my lunch. I loved eating her vegetable soup, staring around my future home and imagining all the changes I would make. The back wall would come off the day I moved in. The house was begging for picture window sliding doors where I would sit and gaze out at the lawns, the trees, the vast, vast space.

I don't know where Graham came from, let alone Red. I'd had a dope smoker boyfriend at boarding school. He went to the boys' school over the field. We used to meet – there was a dell where kids used to go to fuck. He was wild, sexy in a clumsy kind of way, but no, he didn't have red

259

hair. I think that came out because my own hair is rich auburn but once I'd said it I knew I couldn't go back. I knew I'd have to find a red-haired guy. Not that we go round showing our friends pictures of our husbands, but it was possible I would have to provide photographic evidence, casually, if she ever asked. I'd seen a guy in Fittie who lived in one of the really small places like mine. I was pretty sure he worked offshore because I'd noticed him around, sometimes with his kids, sometimes not. Turned out he didn't work offshore at all. He was divorced, only saw his kids at weekends and during the school holidays. I found this out when I knocked on his door and asked him if he could spare any milk. I was hoping to get from there to a photo, which was ambitious.

"Hi, I'm Georgia," I began. "I live opposite?" I waited.

"Hello. Er. Colin."

"Colin. Lovely to meet you." I giggled, shook his hand awkwardly. "Listen, I've just got back from the supermarket." I shifted Zachary on my hip, making heavy work of it so he could see how awfully heavy my baby was. "I only went out for milk. I've spend fifty quid on all sorts of stuff I don't need and guess what I've forgotten?"

He smiled, blushed. "Er. Milk?" And then he was standing back, ushering me in. I was trying to think whether or not he looked like a musician. His hair was red, yes, but rather nondescript, not what you'd call trendy. Might he be geek chic, I wondered. The kind of guy that wore nineteen-seventies metal-rimmed glasses and parted his hair at the side in a kind of ironic way – a beyond-fashion kind of style? So square he's cool? Possibly.

It was dark in his place, no pictures on the walls, a television on a cheap birch veneer unit, a can of Fosters on the coffee table. The whole place smelled of stale cigarette smoke but you can't smell a photo, can you?

I followed him through into the kitchen. He was wearing long khaki shorts and thick ski socks pushed down over his thin white shins.

"I've seen you around with your kids," I said. "I didn't really know who to call on. I don't know anyone here, you see."

He opened the fridge door, pulled out a pint of milk. While we talked about his divorce, his kids, his ex-wife, he set about the painstaking process of finding a Tupperware tub, emptying a measure of milk enough for perhaps two cups of tea – big spender – and closing the lid so that it sealed, which required what looked like preternatural amounts of strength.

"There." I shifted Zachary to the other hip. "That was an effort and so kind of you. I didn't mean to put you to so much trouble." Too much? Did he spot the sarcasm? I don't think so. Not like I said, *25ml? Are you sure? No, it's too much, your generosity is overwhelming. I might weep.* "I'll make sure I drop the tub back when I've finished," is what I limited myself to.

He shrugged. "Aye. Great."

I led the way out. His house was beginning to make me feel depressed. OK, so you're divorced, I wanted to say. Do you need to be quite so central casting about it? Put some damn pictures on the walls, for Christ's sake, hell, buy a throw. You see, don't you, how restrained I had to be?

"Hey listen," I said, once we were on the threshold. "Sorry to be an absolute bore, but could I ask you another favour?" I took his shrug for yes. "I need a photo of Zachary to send to my mother. She's nagging me about it and you know what it's like in the evenings ... by the time my husband gets home, I'm tired, I forget, you know? You couldn't hold Zacky for me could you while I take a quick pic? The light is so much better during the day."

"Sure."

Well, what was he going to say? I couldn't believe I'd ever worried about getting something as simple as a snap. Any old tourist can ask for a photo and people usually do what I tell them so why would Colin be any different? I handed Zachary over and dug my phone out of my pocket.

Smile. Click. Smile again. Click. How about a selfie with all three of us. Tralala. What fun. Thankyouverymuch.

It was a blast, making all that up. And I wasn't doing anyone any harm. People are so limited in the things they say and do, the way they live their lives. People are so damn dreary. Michael and I had vision, that's all. We were just trying to do something different.

After my first meeting with Shona, I felt so much better about the arrangement. When Michael got in and hung up his coat and came to kiss me in the kitchen, I thought: I know something you don't know. You think you're so clever with your two lady puppets dancing to your tune. Little did he know that there was someone new pulling the strings.

Later, when he was on the phone to her, I went into the bedroom and texted her at the same time. Well, that was a riot, pure and simple. *Valentina*, I heard him say. *I knew you'd find your feet*. What a laugh. What a pair of idiots. Later still, when we made out on her sofa, I knew my gamble had paid off. Now, when he went to her, instead of sitting and waiting, resentful in pathetic compliance, I could really start to enjoy myself. From now on, things would only get more interesting.

There were other advantages. When Michael came to me he too needed to cut loose after two weeks of cloistered domesticity. I hired a marvellous babysitter from the nursery. She brought Zachary to the house straight from there, bathed him, fed him, put him to bed. We were free to go to the cinema, to dinner, we even went to a club one night and stayed out until three. We were freer than we'd imagined. In fact, sometimes it felt like we didn't even have a child. And all the time, she was out in the countryside so there was no way she'd be in a restaurant, a pub, a club. How could she be? Someone had to look after Isla while Mikey was offshore. Even if she did eventually get around to a social life, my decision to befriend her so soon after her arrival would pay off handsomely. If she ever cobbled enough friends together for a girls' night out, I would be the first to know, since I would be not only her friend but her oldest friend, her best friend.

Only once in that entire first fortnight did I think Michael might back out. That was the time he came off the phone the colour of stone.

"She was here," he said. "Today."

"What do you mean, here?"

"In Fittie."

"Christ, I was here." I heard the panic in my voice and immediately shut up. He didn't know she and I had met, it was important to remember that. "But that's OK, isn't it?" I said, calmer. "She doesn't know who I am so even if she saw me it wouldn't matter."

But he was still fazed. "I was in a meeting. I didn't check my phone. I need to be more careful – she could see me."

I kissed him, slowly, began to unbutton his jeans. "But she didn't."

He stayed my hand. "We need to come up with a story – something I can say if she ever catches me onshore."

"That's easy," I said. "Blame the weather. Say you've been emergency helicoptered back. Play up the danger, make her feel afraid. Say there was a fire, a mortal accident. Say you barely escaped with your life." I finished unbuttoning, slid my hand inside his boxers and stopped talking.

As did he.

At the end of those first two weeks together, Michael and I were exhausted! I didn't care. I knew I'd have two weeks off, as it were, to take it easy, go to bed at nine o'clock if I wanted to. This was perfect. While he was here, I could go out on dates, have regular sex late into the night, enjoy a limited amount of domesticity. While he was with her, life didn't have to dry up altogether. There were lunch hours, there were hotels, and Fittie was not far from the office. While he was with her, I had my own space. I could read, shave my legs, eat digestive biscuits for dinner if I wanted to. I could take another lover, if I wanted to. This is what it meant to think big, bigger than the worker ants who spend their lives chained to convention. Two weeks in four, he lived with me. Four weeks in four, I did exactly what I wanted. I was happy with him, happy without, and I had my own little game of jeopardy going – only for my own self-respect, you understand. My life had never felt so balanced. Isn't that what everyone wants, balance?

TWENTY-FOUR

And yes, I did leave Zachary with her while I went to meet Michael. That first time, as a test to see if she would, then several times after that. I'm sorry, but I cannot allow you to feel pity for her. Let's not forget whose husband he was, not to mention who put up the deposit for the damn cottage. And while I was holed up in some minuscule hideaway, the North Sea battering against the walls, she was wandering the vast green lawns – *aren't the leylandii lovely, Mikey reckons we should make the pond into a sandpit* – offering me, me, her hospitality like the lady of the fucking manor. Have you any idea how irritating that was for me? And the expense was crippling. It was a good job I was cushioned, financially, and that Michael's parents were such a soft touch. We'd never have been able to afford it otherwise. That's another thing that was so annoying about Shona – she was always telling him not to ask his parents for money. Never taking it upon herself to go out and earn some, you understand, but always pointing out how she was 'managing', how she 'didn't need much'. God knows, everyone hates a martyr.

So if I did let her look after her own stepson while I was a bit naughty with her boyfriend, so what?

Let's not forget: I was his wife.

Looking back, I was nothing short of a saint putting up with it all. Sundays were terrible – endless. I called him once, desperate to talk to him, to someone, only to find out he'd taken her out into the country for Sunday roast.

"We need that money, Michael," I said. "I can't believe you're taking her out while I'm stuck here on my own."

"But I take you out."

"Michael, no one takes me out. I'm not a dog. We go out together."

"But if I never take her anywhere she'll get suspicious. I can't pretend we're that skint."

"I had to pay her damn nursery bill last month and there you are, swanning off to country pubs. Tell her to sling a damn chicken in the oven. Tell her she can't have any more childcare until she's got a bloody job."

"I don't want her getting a job," he hissed – he was trying to keep his voice down, hiding in Isla's bedroom like a crook – it was all so seedy, so bedroom farce, now I think about it. "If she goes back to being a reporter she'll be zipping about all over the place. Even with Spyware, it's too risky."

I sighed. "Convenient."

"Look, you knew the deal when we moved here," he said. "It's a bit late to start moaning about it now."

There was an edge to his voice I recognised. I knew I could push him no further. I took a deep breath – theatrical, perhaps – and reminded myself of the long game.

"OK," I conceded, forced a conciliatory smile into my voice. "You're right. I miss you, darling, that's all."

My phone rang at 8:20am on Monday. Michael's work number came up on the screen.

"Georgie, thank God." He sounded shaken.

"Michael? Are you OK?"

"Shona's gone mad."

My throat went tight. This was it, game over. I wasn't even nearly ready for the fun to end quite yet. "Why? Has she found something out?"

"No, it's ..." He was so stressed he could barely talk. "I've just had to have the conversation. The one about coming into the office when I'm onshore."

"You're always onshore."

"You know what I mean. Don't joke. I told her she knew I'd have to go into the office, like you said, but I don't think she bought it. I know she's spaced out but she's not stupid. She's saying she only agreed to come here in the first place because she thought I'd be off work for two weeks." He gasped, a kind of throttled sound. "Oh God, I remember the conversation."

I waited a moment, to be sure he'd finished with the histrionics, before beginning softly, "Michael, we discussed this. Think it through. She has no reason not to trust you. Why would she start looking for clues? She has no idea, remember? None. We don't go around worrying that everything we know is a lie, do we? We'd have a nervous breakdown. We accept the reality with which we are presented unless there's a very good reason not to. You've seen *The Matrix*, haven't you? *Plato's Cave* ring any bells? There is nothing, nothing about Shona's existence that doesn't fit her belief in what that existence is. So if you tell her what the arrangement was, she will believe you, doubt herself. Don't use too many words."

"If you say so."

I almost said – leave it to me, I'll talk to her. But of course, he had no idea we were friends. But I did call her afterwards. I knew how she was feeling, knew it before I picked up and dialled. And when she told me how she was feeling, how hurt and hoodwinked, I was ready with the words to console her. I was there to make the suggestions a good friend would make and, after I'd dropped Zac off at Little Beans for an hour, I could drive her to the station, put her on a train to Glasgow and wave bye bye.

That evening, when Michael's home number appeared on my mobile, I knew what he was going to say before I answered the phone. Oh, the trip. It was like being psychic. It was like being God.

"You're not supposed to call me from the cottage," I said, my voice edged with caution. "What if Shona hears you?"

"She's not here." He sounded furious. Tearful, possibly. "She's left me. She's written me a fucking note. I never thought she'd do something like that. I didn't think she had it in her. It's unravelling, Georgie. The whole thing's unravelling." He sniffed. Good God, he was tearful.

"It is not unravelling, don't be silly. Wait there. I'm coming over. Do not call her until I get there."

"OK," he said. "Thanks."

I packed an overnight bag, for Zachary and myself. I thought wearing her nightie would be a step too far, although there was, potentially, some erotic capital in it. When I got to the cottage, he'd barely opened the door before he started blithering on and on about this friend of Shona's, this *Valentina* – he almost spat the name. She was leading his partner astray, he said. She was a shit-stirrer, she was trouble, she was turning her against him. She was a bitch.

"She sounds like trouble," I said. "But nothing we can't handle. We'll deal with her later. Now, let's run through what you're going to say."

Once I was satisfied he would stick to the script, I rolled a joint and handed it to him while he called her and talked her through it. When I asked – quietly – if he wanted a glass of wine, he shooed me away, panic in his brown eyes. I poured a large glass of Bourgogne, slid it across the table to him. God knows, he needed it. The man was a wreck.

I left him to it. I could hear every word from the living room. Eventually, I heard the beep of the phone returned to its holster and duly returned myself to the kitchen. He was bent forward in his chair, face in his hands. "She's coming back tomorrow night."

"That's good, isn't it?" I knelt at his feet, put my head in his lap. He stroked my hair. I ran my hands up his thighs and felt him stiffen against my head. I stood, took his hand and pulled him upstairs, grabbing a second bottle of Bourgogne, two fresh glasses and the corkscrew en route.

He sat on the bed while I opened the wine.

"She apologised." His smile was wretched, his eyes sad. He took the glass from me and drank.

"Don't think about it. It's sorted now. Let's think about us."

We burnt the midnight oil that night. The kerosene, to be precise. What was it with those funny little lamps? Some survivalist shit? They cast a lovely light though, I'll admit. And they gave off an old-fashioned aroma, like how I imagined a gypsy's caravan might smell or a hideaway shack in the outback. When he started up again, fretting about *that Valentina woman,* I rolled on top of him, kissed him hard to shut him up, kissed his chest, his navel, his hips, took him in my mouth and, yes, he stopped talking then. He shut right up. When, later, we let each other go, I lay beside him and stroked the hair on his chest and wondered how soon I would be in this bed for good. My moods on this subject came and went. Sometimes I wanted to stay where I was, to remain independent with benefits, sometimes, like that night, I wanted to be here, in my rightful home, and to have all that went with it. He loved me more, much more than her. That much was obvious. He simply didn't realise it yet.

Shona came back. On my next day off, I went over to the cottage, where I had spent Monday night. We had lunch and I let her tell me what I already knew. Not before I'd rescued the corkscrew from upstairs. The bloody thing had slid under the bed, thank God but even so, it was too close a shave and I must confess I did not enjoy the panic. It felt ... low, a little grubby. But as she spoke, as she confessed to her shame and her selfishness, I saw in her eyes that she trusted me absolutely. And trust is halfway, more than halfway, isn't it, to love?

And then the damn door clattered open and who should be standing there but Michael, one hand to his chest and looking like he'd seen the Wicked Witch of the West out in the front garden. There he was, shocked beyond reason to discover that this troublesome friend of his mistress, this Valentina woman he had raged about the night before in

269

bed to his wife was in fact – er – his wife. If I too hadn't been so stunned to see him I would have cracked right up. Looking back, it's a wonder the vicar didn't arrive, trousers round his ankles, followed by a busty wench in provocative underwear and spike heels. It was quick thinking on my part, though, I'm sure you'll agree – all that nonsense with the paper bag. Shona never suspected a thing. As for me, I got out of there pretty damn quick. I knew Michael would be furious.

He was. But with anger comes passion.

He came over to the Fittie place at about 9:30pm – but, wait a minute, that's right, not before Shona had reached my blasted answering machine. Christ, that required some quick thinking. I couldn't believe I'd been so stupid as to leave my name – not a mistake I could repeat. As soon as she rang off, I deleted that sucker, I can tell you, and replaced it with a brief Australian: *G'day, leave a message folks!* To anyone else who asked, I could say it was a joke. Hilarious, that's me, a real prank a minute.

Anyway, Michael arrived about half an hour later, full to bursting with fury. I was smoking a joint and sipping a lovely crisp Sancerre in front of *The Apprentice* when I heard the firm thrust of his key in the lock.

I had bathed, I had removed every hair from my body, moisturised so thoroughly I needed a sign: *caution, slippery surface.* I had put on a loose kimono and turned the heating up high.

"What the hell do you think you're playing at?" In one stride he was bearing down on me, hands on hips, glowering. He was really quite ... menacing.

"What do you mean, what am I playing at?" I raised my shoulders, the kimono slipped from one of them. "I'm making things more interesting."

"You're crazy," he said. "You've gone insane. You're going to blow this whole thing, you're going to ruin it." He put his hand to my long white neck and squeezed.

270

I did not budge, did not take my eyes off his. "I'm not." The pressure of his thumb was choking me. My voice sounded strangled, like a robot's. "I'm making it better, baby. I thought you'd see that straight away. This is for us." I leaned forward, put my hand to his crotch. He was as hard as granite. "See?"

His eyelids became heavy, his grip loosened. "You ..." He straddled me, pulled my hair, bit my collarbone. "... Are a piece of work."

I had not imagined there could be another level to all this but, clearly, there was. I had never known fulfilment like I shared with Michael that night. There was a moment, the coffee table upended, ash scattered, white wine soaking into the cream rug, when I genuinely feared for my sanity. I was touched in every possible way: emotionally, intellectually, physically. I was flying. I could feel the heat of the sun on my feathered wings. It was heady, fearsome, irresistible and in that moment I knew I could not possibly end what I had started. I had to fly higher.

Months passed. I never thought I'd enjoy being the wronged wife so damn much. And then, of course, just when I'd decided to string this whole thing out for as long as possible, she fucking well caught us in the supermarket. And yes, it was my turn for a near cardiac arrest. It's one thing understanding inevitability, quite another when the thing you know must happen actually goes ahead and happens.

Basket pushed close to her trolley, I looked right into her eyes and texted Michael:

Get out now. Shona in dairy aisle.

Told her I needed peas. Peas and quiet, more like. Some goddamn space. What the hell was she doing in Marks and Spencer's Food Hall for Christ's sake? Shona the frugal. Shona, the *don't mind me, I'll manage*. I thought I'd got away with it. But still I could barely maintain eye contact. I knew she'd picked up on something but I was hoping she'd put it down to that tiny embarrassment you can feel when you bump into someone you're close to in unexpected circumstances. I know now that she saw someone in the car, but not that it was Michael. Did she see us, chuckling like maniacs at our near escape? Who can say? But when I saw her at the pool that Friday I did what I always do: waited for it to blow over. If she had noticed anything, found my manner a little strained, let her be the one to mention it.

She didn't say a word. And when she invited Red and I to dinner, I became pretty sure she hadn't seen a damn thing. *Are you and Red free on Wednesday to come over for a bite to eat?*

Who the hell's Red? I almost said. But I did have a good laugh the next day in the office with Michael.

"For crying out loud," I said to him, "where the hell am I going to find a red-haired musician at such short notice? Most people have to rock up with nothing more than a bottle of plonk."

But Red caught a cold. So I, naturally, texted Shona to let her know. Poor Red. Poor music-loving, pothead, sickness-prone Red. What a dog's life I led him – not letting him come out to play, making him work in some dreary vintage record store with no hope of success. I wondered if she'd cancel, but I didn't want her to. The evening promised to be so interesting and besides, who doesn't enjoy a cosy night in with their husband and their best friend?

What I didn't bank on was her calling me at work. She never called me while I was 'teaching'. So I hadn't factored in her hearing the open-plan office in the background. Bloody hell. But – wonderful thing about someone believing your lies so utterly? The handy way they have of providing your alibi for you. *Are you in a yoga class?* Ah – *yeah, Shona. Sure I am.*

By 6pm, I was ready. I had put Zachary in front of some mindless baby television (How do those presenters do it by the way? How do they avoid complete nervous collapse?) and had had a hot bath. I had put on my Max Mara dress to remind him of our wedding day. At seven, half an hour early, the babysitter from the nursery arrived. I didn't see the point of waiting around in Fittie stone-cold sober and alone – so I went.

And, by God, she looked like hell. Some women can really relax with their partners. I admire that, I really do. But personally, I'd have to be terminally ill to let myself look like Shona did that night. I'd have to be most of the way to death. I'd made an effort, sure. For myself. It's a question of pride, after all. What is it with these women who, once they've had children, develop a sudden penchant for elasticated waist trousers and walking boots or, God forbid, Birkenstock sandals? What's that about?

Sorry, where was I? Oh yes, the dinner party *à trois*. When Michael and I had popped back to the Fittie house for lunch that day, I'd made him lay a bet with me that one of us would catch the other one out. Upping the jeopardy, you see? He loved it.

I soon dispatched Shona upstairs to fix herself up – she needed to, believe me. While Michael set the table, I poured a quarter-pint bottle of vodka into the remaining Prosecco and took it up to Shona. She looked a little better – she'd taken off her slippers at least.

"Here," I said. "Let me top you up."

Later, when she'd passed out, Michael carried her up to bed and came down to find me. I was – ready, let's say, by the fire. I do enjoy the sight of a man's eyes popping straight out of his head.

"Put your clothes back on," he said.

"Why? We're married aren't we?"

"She might come down. She might see you."

I propped myself up on my elbow. "Michael, she's drunk God knows how much wine. I don't think she'll be getting up anytime soon."

"This is madness," he said, trying to pull me up from the floor.

I knelt up, unbuttoned his jeans. "Isn't it?"

Afterwards, he went to fetch some water and I lit a joint. When he came back into the living room, he practically broke into a run. He looked ridiculous, knock-knee'd with panic, desperate to set the two glasses of water down. Honestly, he was becoming a neurotic old woman.

"Put that out," he hissed. "She'll smell it."

"You need to grow a pair of bollocks, my darling," I said relieving him of one of the glasses and taking a long drink. I was parched. And I was still enjoying the warmth of the fire on my skin, the illusion of being in my own place. "Tell her I had a cigarette, can't you?" I pulled him close, blew the smoke into his open mouth. "I'm the guest. You have to accommodate my wishes."

"We shouldn't have done that," he said.

"What?"

"That. Here. It's wrong."

"Please. What difference does it makes where we do it? Spare me the guilty feelings, Michael. You're being very small."

"Thing is," he said, lifting the joint from my fingers and taking a pull. "I don't feel guilty. I know I should. I know objectively that this is wrong but I don't feel it."

We smoked in silence.

"I've got an idea," I said after a moment. "I want you to go upstairs and do to her what you did to me. I want to see you do it. I want to watch."

"No way."

"Come on! Don't be a spoilsport. I won't watch the whole thing, just enough to get a flavour."

"You're sick."

I laughed. "All right, all right." I threw the joint into the fire. "If you're going to be boring, I'm going home."

He called a cab. I sent the cab away, waited on the driveway, twirling the keys to the cottage in my hand. It may have been the drink, maybe the sheer mischief of it all, but I could not stop laughing until I'd let myself back in and climbed the stairs. Taking care, of course, to step over the last one.

She saw me. I know she did. And she never even mentioned it. What? I can feel you looking at me through narrowed eyes. I can feel the judgement. But don't even try to argue that you haven't thought about watching your husband make love to someone else, or that you haven't fantasised about making love with him somewhere you shouldn't, knowing you could be caught at any moment. And what about her? Do you seriously think she thought I was – what – a trick of the damn light? Please. Though I guess, conceivably, she could have believed that when what she'd actually seen was so very far from what she was telling herself she believed. The trouble with Shona is the same as the trouble with most people – a total lack of honesty. And if you're not honest, you're not living, as far as I'm concerned. You may as well put yourself in a straightjacket, dope yourself up on morphine, plug yourself twenty-four seven into a virtual reality game. Michael and me? We were honest. We were living.

I'm aware in all of this that I sound as if I was against Shona. I was, of course, at first. But I did like her. And over the months, I grew to like her a lot. She was kind to me. She was sweet, loyal, not unamusing. And she was clever, even if she was letting herself atrophy as so many women do once they have children. But more than all of this: as our relationship developed, I believed I could get her to love me.

"I wonder if finding a friend is more important than finding a husband," she said once.

In the beautiful grounds of my future home, with our babies leaving us alone for once, something in me – melted, I suppose you'd say. When, despite my protestations, my mother packed me off to the convent school, I learned – quickly – to keep my Ozzie accent hidden. How I begged my mother for contact lenses but no, she made me wear the ghastly, thick-rimmed spectacles I hated. She would not pay for the braces I needed for my teeth, leaving me with one tooth permanently snagging like a rogue wolf fang. She was determined perhaps, like Snow White's wicked step-mother, not to be outshone. Except she wasn't my step-mother, she was my real mother. Still, I tried to belong. I made jokes, clipped my speech with the best of them but even when I got a Saturday job and bought my own goddamn contact lenses, even when I learned to enhance my glorious red mane with Clairol's magic tints and emerge like the ugly duckling into a swan, there was still a colour of nail varnish I didn't have, a pair of shoes I wasn't wearing, a CD I wasn't listening to. There was always something, some indefinable wall, I could not penetrate.

Ironic, then, that the moment I let my mother tongue back out in all its Ozzie glory, the moment I scruffed down and let rip with the g'days and the rippers and the struths, I found the first decent friend I'd ever had.

What this meant for my plan, I did not know at first, but I began to feel it was imperative that Michael and I keep our situation secret long enough for Shona to love not just him, but me. I had Michael where and how I wanted him for now. But I was beginning to want Shona too – not in that way, although, hey, let's not rule anything out, here – I liked this whole friendship thing. It was cosy. Intimate. New. I realised that, like Michael, I too could have both. Why not? I had learnt so much these last months. I had learnt that life was simply a matter of presentation. I had presented both Michael and Shona with a version of reality and they had bought into it without hesitation. Why wouldn't they? Why wouldn't anyone? In playing along with Michael's plan, in letting him think he was in control, not only had I secured him, his child, his wedding band on my finger and my future home but, with the creation of Valentina had come a passion that risked consuming both of us in its flames.

But it could not last. I knew that. We would need to mutate. I had seen a flash of rage in Shona when she told me about her school days. I had seen a spark. And I was beginning to understand something of her capacity for love. If I could make her love me enough, as much as she loved Michael, could I persuade her to accept whatever discovery she might eventually make about the truth of her life? Could I get Shona to love both Michael and I so much that she could not bear to lose either one? Could I get her to *join* us?

TWENTY-FIVE

When you're constructing your own narrative, there are always roadblocks ahead. You worry you will never find a way over or around them and then, when you hit them, lo and behold, a solution presents itself. That, at least, is what I have found.

Isla fell ill.

I could not believe my luck.

"Isla's sick." Shona was crying down the phone, something about green shit. "I can't get her temperature to go down." She sounded raw. When she mentioned hospital, I knew it was serious.

"Shona, listen," I said. The voice of calm – this was who I could be – to both Michael and Shona. "You're right, you do need to take her in. It's going to be OK but she might need a saline drip or some antibiotics and you need to get her checked out." I told her I was getting into my car right that second and that I would take her to the hospital.

She was still too stressed to listen. I carried on talking, talking and soothing until, eventually, she did calm down and, after much persuasion, agreed for me to take her to Aberdeen Royal Infirmary.

Some people get off on a crisis, don't they? I understand that, I really do. It's empowering. I called Michael at the office, told him in serious, compassionate tones, that his daughter was sick and that I was taking his mistress to the hospital. He cycled straight over to the Fittie house. I waited at the window and saw him arrive on his bike, jump off, chain it to the drainpipe.

I opened the door before he knocked, furrowed my brow. "Zachary's had a bottle and I've changed his nappy."

"How bad is she?" he replied, kissing me on his way into the house.

Leaving the door open, I grabbed my keys from the kitchen counter and threw on my jacket.

"She's fine. But it'd be unrealistic not to go and help and you can't go because you're *offshore*." I stood in the doorway and smiled at him. He was still a little flushed from the ride. "And I do care for her, you know. Shona, I mean."

"Do you?"

I met his gaze. "Of course I do. I care for her very much. I care for both of them very much." I kissed him on the mouth, gave the neighbours a good eyeful. "I'll call you and let you know how she's doing."

I drove to her. But my mind was on Michael and what I had seen in his eyes.

Isla was fine, of course she was. No more than a bad dose of the shits and a high temperature. She is not what I remember most about that day – what I remember most is that I nearly lost the plot. My plot – yes, I'll admit, it had become a plot by then. Sitting in the kitchen after the hospital trip, there was a moment, a second, when I could have admitted to everything: Michael, Zachary, the whole damn deal. Because, for that second, when time seemed to slow down, I thought she knew.

After our encounter in the Food Hall, I had assumed she had seen nothing at all. How was I to know she'd seen me drive off with Michael in the passenger seat of my car – albeit, in her eyes, with an unidentified man who didn't have a single red hair on his head? So when we got back from the hospital and all was calm, and she came out with the whole *I know you weren't with Red and I think we should talk this through* spiel?

Well, you can imagine.

I thought I would pass out right there, the faint trace of *you got me!* on my frozen lips as my head hit the stone tiles. But for the second time, Shona provided the alibi.

John Duggan. I honestly had no idea who she was talking about. For Christ's sake, she had to explain to me who my own lover was. I'd say it was funny – but it wasn't, at the time. It was heart-stoppingly, throat-tighteningly terrible. It was not the way I wanted the information to come out – the truth had to be grafted on carefully, so that the body would not reject it. It's only now, looking back, that it's funny. Her proposing we calmly talk through the fact of me sleeping with her partner, me almost choking on home-made soup.

Now it's funny. Now it's downright hilarious – a real comedy of errors.

There she was, holding my hand over the kitchen table, her eyes the palest, shining blue, "It's always a relief to tell the truth."

A relief to tell the truth? You should try the relief of thinking you've got a Go Directly to Jail and Do Not Pass Go card, only to reach for the pack and turn over a Get Out of Jail Free.

I can barely recall what lies I told in the immediate aftermath. Something about Red's marijuana habit spiralling out of control. At least that built on what I'd said about him before, I guess. I was riffing, I will admit. Took me back to my university days – all that improvisation. Trick with improv is to relax totally, see yourself not as an inventor but as a conduit for what you, or rather what your character already knows. The cleverer you try to be, the less true it sounds. All that stuff about the sex pictures? I already knew it. Somewhere. Red was a seedy, low-down love cheat, obsessed with his own gratification with no regard for the feelings of others. He was without honour, without scruples, without morals.

Not long after his next trip *offshore,* I think that was when Shona caught Michael in the deli. And away went not only my two weeks with him but also my very expensive, romantic supper.

It was around 1:30pm, I was tucking into my sushi tray for one when he rang me on my extension and relayed the grim news.

"I didn't check the GPS," he said. "I forgot."

"You forgot?"

"It's OK, though. I told her the gas compressor had blown like you said. She believed me. She did. She definitely believed me."

"For fuck's sake, Michael," I hissed. "Do I have to do everything myself?"

"Thing is," he went on, his voice smaller with each word. "I mean, it's not the end of the world or anything but … I'm going to have to go back to the cottage now. For the next three weeks. Otherwise, she'll suspect."

Well, at that point I lost it, as you can imagine. I'm only human.

"Three weeks?" I tried to keep my voice down but it was a trial, it really was. "This is *my* time, Michael. *Mine*, not hers. What about *our* plans? What about the damn tickets for *Madam Butterfly*?"

I slammed the phone down, but barely had I done that when I composed myself, redialled his extension and told him to meet me at the coffee machine. There was no need to panic – I had rehearsed Michael as to what he would say in such an eventuality and he had at least stuck to the script, knowing by now to trust me when it came to lies. And this was the only reason he hadn't completely fucked everything up. As I had anticipated, the flaming, mortal danger scenario had dampened Shona's nascent suspicion rather nicely. But, frankly, things had to change. The moment had come to broach what I had seen in his eyes some weeks before.

In the kitchen area, Michael was still visibly shaken. I made two espressos, sweet and strong.

"This will end soon," I said, handing him his coffee. "You know that."

"It won't. It's OK. She believed me."

"She believed you today. But this will happen again. You can't expect to keep track of her twenty-four seven and you know she won't believe you a second time." I touched his arm, gently. "We can't keep this hidden, Michael. She won't be losing sleep forever and she will want to go back to work. She's already mentioned it to me."

"What are you saying?"

"Nothing. I'm only telling you what you already know. I love you, you know that. I wouldn't have agreed to this crazy scheme otherwise. But there's a difference now, and you know what that is."

He pouted, folded his arms.

"Come on, you do." When he said nothing, I continued. "Back in Glasgow, Shona and I weren't close, we didn't even know one other. But we're friends now. She cares about me. She won't want to lose me."

"What are you saying?" He took a sip of coffee, winced, poured the rest down the sink.

I took a step nearer to him. "I'm saying we have to be clever. We have to anticipate this whole thing coming out and when it does we have to control it. It's all about presentation."

"What?"

"We have to present the situation as we want her to see it." I took hold of his hands. We had agreed never to do this in the office – we were work colleagues who got on well, nothing more, but I was sure it wouldn't be long before we could come out, as it were. "The only difference to her life will be knowledge. And knowledge, the truth, finally, has got to be better than nagging suspicion."

"No," he said, panic in his voice. "No, we can't tell her. We can never tell her."

I squeezed his hands, made him look at me. "Michael, listen. I think we can persuade her to live exactly as before."

"No. She will never go for that."

"You underestimate her. She has the intelligence. She has the spark. We need to find out if she has the imagination. She could have the happy family she dreams of. You, me, Zac, Isla. Perhaps not quite the nuclear family she comes from but something else, something better."

"Never. She knows that's not right."

"Who's to say what's right and what's wrong? Why does this have to be wrong? Why can't it be simply different?"

"She'll see it as wrong, I know she will." He looked like he was about to cry. It was an appalling sight in a man I had thought so strong, and disappointment coursed through my veins like poison.

"Michael. Michael? You did this with the best of intentions, with the interests of your children at heart. Shona will understand that. Don't you know right from wrong too?"

He pulled his hands from mine and pushed them through his hair. He was looking at the floor, apparently searching the linoleum squares for answers.

"I only know it in my head," he said miserably. "She feels it, Georgie. It's in her body, the blood and bones of her. I've seen her take on a bunch of men late at night – absolute meatheads, you should've seen them – while I was hiding in the shadows. She doesn't think, she bursts. I know, I've seen her. It's ... it's elemental."

"I don't really see what other choice we have." I drained my coffee. It was cheap, bitter.

So Michael wasn't ready. Yet. But you can't say I didn't try to keep the charade going. You can't say I didn't do my bit. I even found a tourist and persuaded him to have his picture taken with me. I needed a John Duggan now that Shona had put him in my bed and that's what I was reduced to in the name of evidence: propositioning strangers on the damn street. Luciano Sarti, bless him, over visiting family in Glasgow, strayed north for a day trip with no idea what awaited him. Thirty-three, thin but nice-looking and such a good sport. I suppose he didn't look like you'd imagine a policeman to look but then I didn't need him to walk the beat for me, did I? And the thing about Italians is, they really know how to talk to women. They know how to take them for lunch, make outrageous suggestions about how to fill an afternoon without anyone having to feel sordid. I had to text Shona:

Sorry, babe, won't make it over this afternoon – urgent police business!

I had worked hard to find a decent PC John Duggan and, now that I had, it was only fair to let him take down my particulars.

Sorry, couldn't resist that one.

It was only that one time, I swear. Just a bit of fun, as they say. No children or animals were harmed etcetera. By way of distracting Shona from, if not home truths then truths nearer to home, I shared the John gossip with her – although I have to admit some of the more risqué details did come from Michael and me. What? There are only so many yarns you can spin from one afternoon and I don't think Luciano, slight as he was, could have tipped for room service in such physically demanding circumstances.

But that distraction wore thin fast. Michael was still set against Shona finding out, still convinced we could carry this on forever. I was becoming restless. The whole double life scenario had run its course. There was nothing more to be gained. And Shona was ripe, she was ours for the taking. We had to make sure we took her instead of letting her go screaming off into the night. The time was coming for her to join us in a real life, an honest life, one which soared above everyday existence in ways only we could show her. Only we could free her from the kind of blinkered drudgery only a lobotomised chimp could endure. Only we could save her.

The next phase would be the trickiest. How does one foil one's husband's plans whilst appearing to support him every step of the way?

I wonder now, when Shona saw the letter, whether I let her see it. Subconsciously, of course. I'm not a mean person. I would never hurt anyone intentionally. But I'd realised it was down to me to move things on. This is what women are good at – getting things done. Need a fridge, a television? Ask a woman. The next day you'll have your fridge, your television. A man meanwhile will still be lost in pages of research, signing up for *Which?* magazine, price comparison websites, not a domestic appliance in sight. So I got on with it, told a lie so pathetic, so dreadful, you'd have to be a total imbecile to believe it. The letter must have hitched a ride to Fittie on its way to Union Grove? What was I on?

It worked. Shona did not let me down. The blinkers of trust were falling away; the horse could be led stumbling to water. Something was iffy about that G. Smyth-Banks. To put it mildly.

I spent that night preparing my story: Georgia was my former yoga student, a friend. She had an obsessive crush on Michael and had asked me to be complicit in her schemes. Schemes which I, upon meeting Shona, had rejected. I was quite proud of that. It explained away everything and at the same time was dubious enough to unsettle Shona. If it worked as well as I hoped, the 'truth' would drive her even further into my arms. Had I not protected Shona from this terrible woman?

Meanwhile, I could fill Michael in on my small mistake. I could tell him how ingeniously I had put it right. I could share with him Shona's every thought and doubt so that when he got back from 'offshore', when Shona, tearful and anxious, confronted him with what she 'knew', he would be able to back me up one hundred percent without hesitation. A lie told by two has a much more solid base than a lie told by one.

When another invitation to dinner materialised, I knew we were back on course. On the phone, Shona's voice had acquired a repentant softness.

"I want to say sorry," she said. "I should've known there'd be an explanation. I didn't know what to think, that's all."

"That's quite all right, babe," I said, sliding into Valentina's sunshine drawl. "No worries. I'm sorry too. I should have told you ages ago. I don't know why I didn't."

I rang off. We'd had our first fight, I thought. Like lovers.

But now it was time to put our love to the test, whether Michael liked it or not. To help things along, I took Zac. He'd been grisly all day, hadn't given me any peace to get ready. I'd ended up rushing to get out of the house in the hope the drive would knock him out. Once we got there, all he'd have to do was see Michael, shout "Dada," and we could all, finally, progress.

As it was, Michael really went to town, buying that rabbit. It was almost as if he knew this was the big one, the night we all held hands and jumped into the flames.

She was upstairs when I got there. I cornered Michael in the hallway and kissed him full on the mouth. He pushed me away, but I pushed back, laughing.

"Hello," came her voice from the stairs.

"Hey, babe," I said, turning, my face composed into innocence itself. "Michael reckons he's burning a bunny in the backyard." He'd been on his way to pick it up when I spoke to him. I even knew the ingredients in the marinade.

When I told her Red hadn't come with me I saw doubt flash in her eyes. I almost faltered. She was so sweet, so damn trusting, it was possible the final revelation would kill her. I had hoped to edge her towards revelation – as one edges hot crockery into cold water. Now I feared I had regained her trust a little too thoroughly and that, plunged headlong into the truth, she might crack. And that would be a shame. The fact was, we had all of us come this far.

Either we joined together tonight or one of us would go home empty handed. And that wasn't going to be me.

When Shona went to powder her nose, I wandered into the garden to see the hallowed beast.

"I think you need more friends," I said to Michael, kissing him again by the light of the flames. "We'll never eat that, the three of us. Think your eyes might be bigger than your belly, Mr. Quinn."

"You have no idea how much I can eat," he said. "My appetite is limitless." He bit my earlobe, making me laugh. We muttered like that for a little while, flirting with danger. Michael was nervous she might come out and catch us. I was determined she would.

And when I looked up and saw her across the glow, I knew she wouldn't need to catch us, knew I wouldn't have to do anything more. Her jaw hung oddly, as if it were broken. Her eyes sagged at the edges, as if in the time it had taken her to go to the bathroom she had aged ten years. I knew then without any doubt that she would not join us. I had been a fool to think she would.

"What have you done?" she said.

Indeed, I thought. What have we done?

When she ran upstairs, presumably to pack her bags, I ran through the argument with Michael, made him repeat back to me what I needed him to say. Remember, I had to play this like it was a disaster for me too or risk losing him forever. And now that Shona was lost, he was all I had left. He went into the hallway. Through the French windows I watched, hidden in the shadows. He reached for her, knelt before her, as I had told him to do. I waited and watched, resisted the overwhelming temptation to go in there and do it myself. Eventually, unable to bear the impotence any longer, I walked away, up onto the lawns. After a few minutes, he stepped out and called my name. I headed back towards the cottage and found him on the patio.

"She's taken the keys to the Fittie place. She's going to sleep on it." His eyes shone with what looked like jubilation.

"What?" I said. "But that's my house. She has no right to go in there. You have no right to give her my keys. They're mine." I grabbed him by the neck and pushed him against the back wall of the cottage. His face, half lit, half in shadow.

"Georgie, stop," he said. "It's all right. She's upset but she's going to think about it."

I let go, stood back. "And you believe her?"

"She said she'd think about it. But she needs space. She's taken the car and she's going to stay at yours tonight. She won't wreck anything, don't worry. She's not like that."

"Not like what? Are you stupid? She's just found out her whole life is a lie and you're trusting her with my house? She could torch the place."

He laughed, sniffed. His face crumpled. He put his head in his hands. "Oh God, what've we done to her?"

"To *her*? Michael, this affects all of us. She's no worse off than we are. Don't you see, we're all compromised here. Come on, baby, you must see that."

"You don't understand." He stared at me, his eyes wild. "You don't know her like I do."

"Are you sure she won't damage my house?"

"Is that all you care about?"

Yes, actually. There was no way I was letting her trash my house. I had to persuade him to let me go there. "You don't think she'll do something to Isla do you?"

He was still looking at me like I was the devil. "Of course she won't hurt the baby. The only monsters here are us, Georgie." Good God, was he crying? "We're monsters."

"Hang on a second, why all the guilt all of a sudden? We're in love, that's all. We're simply trying to figure out what's best for everyone. So we can't do the two point four kids thing, so what? Doesn't make us monsters. You know that. I know that. And Shona will realise that eventually.

She'll be fine. I'm concerned about her, that's all, and wonder whether I should go and talk to her. I'm her friend after all."

"She needs somewhere to sleep," he said, almost absently. "She said if I text or call or do anything she'll never let me see her or Isla again. I can't risk that. I need to give her space. She knows I love her, doesn't she? When you talk, you know as girls, does she tell you she loves me?"

"Of course." This conversation was beginning to make me feel sick.

"I can't lose her, Georgie," he whined. "Please tell me it'll work. Tell me she's coming back. She will come back won't she?"

Er, no.

I shrugged. "She took it better than I thought she would."

"She did, didn't she? She won't be angry forever, will she?" I couldn't see him clearly for the dark, his head was bowed, but I was pretty sure he was still crying. "She'll come back, won't she?"

"Of course she will," I said, knowing she would never come back, wondering how the hell he could not see that for himself, how he could even begin to believe what he was saying. He was, always had been, deluded. "She just needs a good night's sleep."

I had to get away from him. His wretchedness was getting me down. I stepped through the French windows, back into the cottage and ran myself a glass of water from the tap. I drank it all in one go, felt the cool trajectory down into my body. My body felt empty, as if the water was all that ran inside it: no bones, no blood, no organs, merely water, running forever down, without ever reaching my feet.

Outside, the rabbit burned, no more than wasted meat. On the table, Shona's little touches, a woman's touches – undervalued, unappreciated, unused. I had lost her – perhaps the only friend I'd had and all Michael could do in the darkness, out of my sight thank God, was snivel in the face of his own failure. He had played us, Shona and I. Shona more than me but all the same, I had been played too. I had allowed that to happen. I had convinced myself I could somehow come out on top, that I could manufacture a satisfactory outcome to suit my own needs, but I saw now I could never have Michael or Shona, let alone both, in the way I wanted. Shona was too strong and Michael was weak. I had believed her to be a pathetic victim but she was simply ignorant of the facts. A lack of facts was all that had kept her here whereas I, with all the facts at my disposal, had played along – as brainwashed as a teenage girl in a sect. She, armed with the facts at last, had walked away, without hesitation, wanting no part of it. She had said no. And that took strength. He, meanwhile, like a spoilt child upon hearing he can only have one ice cream not two, had fallen to pieces, broken shards on the patio stones. Not a visionary, not at all, but a greedy little boy too spoilt to choose.

I had changed my mind. I no longer wanted the three of us to live in an alternative idyll out here in this place. I should have known this had never been on offer. Shona had left me forever and as a parting gesture had handed Michael to me and told me I could keep him. He was her cast-off, her broken toy. And now I no longer wanted what at the very beginning I had set out to get: Michael, to myself. Had I ever really wanted him? Now I had him, now he really was mine, I saw him for what he was: worthless and weak. All I wanted now was the freedom to live without people, people who, no matter how brave and interesting you thought them, were no braver and no more interesting than anyone else.

The cottage. That was all I wanted now. Not a third of it, not a half. All of it.

But that too would take some planning.

PART III

TWENTY-SIX

I left Valentina and Mikey in the garden. I staggered upstairs, half-blind with fury. I can't remember much about those moments, to be honest. I threw nappies, clothes, whatever I could lay my hands on into a bag. I remember weeping. I remember that all I could think about was getting out. I had to get away from the toxic cloud of them both.

Isla barely woke, simply nudged into my shoulder with her sleepy head. I can't believe now that I managed to hold onto her, that I managed to pack – but I was in life-saving mode, I think, the ultra-efficient autopilot setting, the tunnel vision of the undiluted crisis state. Her in my arms, I made myself walk back down. There was after all no other way out.

Mikey was standing in the hallway, hands on hips, teeth gritted in angst.

"Shona, don't go." His voice had a pleading tone to it.

I stepped off the bottom stair, stood in front of him with our baby in my arms and looked into his eyes.

"I don't know who you are," I said. "I have literally no idea."

"Shona, give me one minute. Please." He grabbed the tops of my arms, hard.

"Take your hands off me," I said. "And if you touch Isla I'll kill you."

He raised his hands in the air. He stepped back.

"Talk," I said, keeping my eyes on his. "Go on. Say what you've got to say."

"Can't we sit down?"

"No."

He exhaled heavily and shook his head as if *he* was in some sort of despair.

"Is she still here?" I asked him.

"She's in the garden." His brow furrowed, he looked at his shoes. I supposed he was going for contrition.

"Talk," I said, swaying from side to side to try and keep Isla calm.

"Look," he began, spreading his hands while I imagined ripping out his lungs, his spleen, his black husk of a heart, blowing it from the flat of my hand and watching it scatter and settle like ash. "I know it's a lot to take in," he went on. "It's been hard for me too but I never meant to hurt you or harm you, Shona. That's the truth. The truth is, it was all about us – you and me and Isla – but I found out George was pregnant on the same day I found out you were. Honestly, it was unbelievable how it worked out."

"Mikey – for Georgia to become pregnant with your child you would have to have had sex with her. I don't mean to be crude, but you'd have to fuck her, which you clearly did while we were living together. It's not unbelievable. It's nature. Take some fucking responsibility for yourself."

Isla had grown too heavy for me to hold. She was hard off to sleep and I was glad of that at least. I lowered myself into the armchair under the stairs. "Don't let me stop you."

He nodded and again held up his hands. "You're right. I did sleep with Georgia while we were together. And yes, that's how we – that's how we have Zac. But we were all so young, Shone. We still are, we've got our whole lives ahead of us. And – and – we're not like other people. If you give this a chance, if you open your mind, you'll see we have something really special, the three of us. Think about it. You love Georgia – the name and the posh accent don't make any difference, do they? And I know you hate her now but she does care for you, you know. Very much. All I've done is try and figure out a way to make this all work." He knelt on the floor by my feet and I had a fleeting memory of when I first met him, a grinning Captain Hook, the black beard, my own inability to distinguish between what was real and what was fake.

"It was for the kids more than anyone," he was saying now. "You must see that. Isla and Zachary need us to be together. They're so close. They could be brother and sister. I was going to suggest it to you, the whole set-up, but I knew you wouldn't go for it, not at first, so I kept it a secret – but I was going to broach it in time. Honestly. I was waiting till you were ready." He threw out one arm, gesturing towards the garden. "Georgia's been happy. She likes her space. She's a very unconventional thinker."

"Is that another word for psychopathic bitch?"

"Shona, stop." He scratched his head and for the second time let out an exasperated breath as if I, not he, were the unreasonable one. "Don't, baby. Come on. Don't do this. You always do this. You let your emotions get the better of you. Don't let that happen. Open your mind for a minute, that's all I ask. The only difference between now and half an hour ago is that you know. That's all." He laid his hand on my knee. "You know. Nothing has actually changed and knowledge is better than ignorance, isn't it?" He ran his hand up my thigh and back again, the way he did when I was upset or tired. I shook him off before I'd even processed the presumption in him doing this. His hand flew back, as if singed. "I know you're shocked, but take the emotion out of it for one second. I know what I'm offering isn't normal, it's not what normal people do but that's because they're normal. People like us, Shona, we can live differently. Shone?"

I could see only his knees, clothed in black denim, black jeans resting on the terracotta tiles of the kitchen floor. He was talking, talking, talking, but I could barely hear him above the roar of my own raging blood. He was talking about taking the emotion out of it. He was talking about how nothing had changed. And I – I was looking at his black jeans on the tiled floor while in the periphery of my grasp hovered the knowledge that nothing about my life was, had ever been, the truth. The information was coalescing, somewhere near me. From the gloom it was taking solid shape. And I was staring at black denim, at the stone tiles of my kitchen floor, and I was trying to figure out how it was that I did not know, had never known, the father of my child. I did not know my closest friend.

My life, my love, my home, had been violated.

Her life, her home, meanwhile, was at peace.

Well, we would see about that.

"Tell you what," I said quietly. "This is what's going to happen. You're going to give me Georgia's keys and I'm going to take Isla to Fittie and I'm going to think it over, OK? Like you say, we need to be calm and think things through. I can't think here. I can't even breathe."

I felt him stand up, heard the click of his knees. "Shona, you shouldn't be alone. You should stay here."

I made myself look up at him. "You can't ask me to do that. And you can't tell me not to sleep in another person's house. What would you have us do, sleep in the gutter? Just give me the fucking keys, you lying, pathetic excuse for a human being."

He nodded quickly and held up his hand. "All right."

I watched him walk over to the coats, dig into his own coat pocket, pull two keys from his own key ring. I had never noticed the two extra keys, I thought. There were so many things I hadn't noticed.

"Here." He held the keys out to me. "It's number 14."

"I know what number it is."

"Sorry. Of course." His eyes were still as deep and as brown as that first night in The Crow when I had seen, or thought I'd seen in them mischief and kindness and possibility. I steeled myself against those eyes and spoke.

"Now," I said. "Let's be clear. If you so much as try and follow me or disturb me in any way, if you call me or text me or let that bitch come anywhere near me, that will be the end. There will be no negotiation, nothing. I will take your

296

daughter away and you will never see me or her again. Do you get that?"

He nodded. "All right."

"Because it's very important you get that."

"I get it." His face was grim. I had noticed how tired he had looked this last year and had felt sorry for him. I had thought it was the offshore life sapping his resources. But it wasn't. It was the strain of two lives. His expression softened to sadness.

"Are you going to be OK?"

I took the keys from his open palm, stood up and shifted Isla further onto my shoulder. "What a ridiculous thing to ask."

The door to number 14 was stiff. I had to hold the key and give the door a kick at the bottom. It opened directly onto a tiny kitchen. On the draining board was a flowery china mug, upside down, one teaspoon in the cutlery drainer. I closed the front door behind me and immediately noticed her smell. She had, I realised, a very particular scent – spicy, aromatic like herb oil or dried grass and there was another note in there too – vanilla. Vanilla, that I had smelled on Mikey and thought it was air freshener from the cab. I had thought her a hippy, come day go day, a free and rebel heart. I had thought her a friend, with all that word meant. I had loved my friend, little realising she was no more than a lie, a fictional character, the imagining of a cruel mind. I had loved no one, then, no one at all.

A thin doorway to the right led onto the living room I'd seen through the window months before. I put on the overhead light. Its dull glow threw little more illumination than a candle at first. But, slowly, it brightened. The sofa was ours, I saw that straight away. It was the one Mikey had told me he'd put into storage. There was a small rip in the back where they'd caught it on the doorframe trying to squeeze it into the cottage. On the mantelpiece, the photo of him was still there; on the table under the window, the pictures I had only been able to see from the back. I saw them now. In one, Mikey and Zac and her, on a beach. Dunes – was that Balmedie? Looked like it. They were sitting on a blanket, smiling. The photo had been taken recently – this past summer. Zac will have been five or six months old: bonnie, smiling. Beside them was a sandcastle, a sandcastle he had made no doubt for his son, even though he was too wee to appreciate it. Zac. Isla's half brother. I thought of them together in the swimming baths, the look of wonder on their faces, their wet eyelashes clotted into tiny spokes. Mikey had taught his son to splash the water the same way he had taught his daughter. Did he believe himself, while he did this, a good father? He may have taught little Zac to walk, let him fix his baby's grip onto his strong father's forefingers, coaxed him to put one foot in front of the other, picked him up and comforted him when he fell. He may have done all this while a few short miles away I was teaching his daughter to walk, alone.

I stared at the photo. Zac looked so like Mikey, I saw that now – same impossibly straight hair, same mischievous expression. How had I not seen?

In the other photo, Mikey with her, in what looked like a register office. She was wearing the same black dress she had worn for dinner, her burgeoning belly a discreet fecund bump under the stretchy fabric. Black fabric. Odd choice for a wedding.

I sat on the sofa in my coat. Outside, I fancied I could hear the whistle and whoop of the funfair. But I was no longer sure of anything that I, Shona McGilvery, could hear, smell, taste, see, touch. I did not know, if I stood up, whether I would feel the floor under my feet, or whether I would keep on reaching with my toes until I fell through into oblivion. I did not know, I think, in that moment, if I was even real and, if I were, what possible reason there was to continue to be real.

Isla gave a shout, almost an *Oi!* as if to tell me that she – she was the reason. I picked her up and held her to me. She babbled away, unaware of anything at all, apart from me. She was with her mother, she was awake, that was all. I cradled her to my chest and carried her into the kitchen. At random, I opened cupboards. Pans, plates, wine glasses, tumblers. Tea, coffee, tins – chopped tomatoes, kidney beans, jars – apple compote, piquillo peppers in oil, artichoke hearts. It was all so normal – the assorted tins and jars of a middle-class professional working couple who liked to eat well.

In the fridge, there was milk in the door alongside the butter. There was salad, cod loin in cellophane packaging, carrots ... what did these things matter? What did I expect to find – a rosy red apple ripe with poison? No one thinks of a witch's groceries.

"Pea risotto," I said aloud, pulling the fish, the butter, the eggs, onto the floor. "Fucking pea risotto."

I had seen her with someone in the supermarket. She had told me it was Red. I had known it wasn't Red because he had black hair. Black, like Mikey's. Like John's, the imaginary policeman. Let's talk about it, I had told her. I had wanted her to trust me and she had taken my trust and held it like a beating heart in her hand. And she had reached for the knife. No. I had handed her the knife. Here, I had told her. Cut right through it.

And then: *Is it John?* I had asked, feeling the crease of concern in my brow. And she had looked at me blankly, not a clue who I meant. *John Duggan*, I had insisted. *You know, the policeman?*

I covered my mouth tight with my hand to stifle the roar that came out of me. I pulled the food from the fridge and threw it onto the floor. I opened all the cupboards, reached my arm around the mugs so as to sweep the whole lot out and send it crashing.

No.

These houses were close together. Someone would hear, they might call the police.

At the front of the cupboard, a mug I recognised: Black, with white writing. *But You May Call Me Lord.* He must have bought two. I picked it up. The first time she had been to the cottage, I had joked about putting peanuts in his coffee – *you mean so he chokes, right?* she'd replied. Of course, she knew about his allergy as well as I did. Mikey had told me this mug was from a business trip but maybe he bought it, bought both, when he was with her – maybe she bought them, as a joke. *Here,* she might have said, *one for your home, one for your mistress's cottage in the woods.* She liked dark jokes, didn't she? And the biggest, darkest joke of all was on me. How the hell could she have agreed to the set-up? A woman like her, who could surely have anyone – why share?

I was still holding the mug. I could line it with peanut oil, sneak it back into the cottage, swap it for the other one. And wait. That's all I would have to do.

No.

I carried Isla through the wee house, found two bedrooms coming off the hallway: one, theirs, taupe-coloured bedding, scatter cushions in pinks, lilacs, acid-greens. By the window, a small bureau, closed up, a dull brass key poking out of the lock.

I turned the key. Opened the bureau. The space was so tight I had to sit on the bed to be able to open the desk all the way. Inside were pens, a silver letter holder stuffed with bills, a chequebook: Ms. G. Smyth-Banks ... Nothing of interest. What was I expecting to find? Not like it could get any worse.

In the wardrobe, her clothes – some I recognised, like the patchwork skirt with the pockets, a cheesecloth smock top; some, more formal, I did not. On the top shelf, box files, one labelled *House.* I tried to pull it down but couldn't manage with one hand. I put Isla on the bed and dashed back, pulled the box down with both hands. It was heavy. I placed it on the open bureau. The popper catch was stiff but I prised it open. Inside, official documents: gas bills, electricity, same kind of thing as the bureau ... I looked at the address: Burns Cottage ... and the names: Mr. M. Quinn and Ms. G. Smyth-Banks Quinn. How many fucking surnames did the woman need? And why were her names on our utility bills?

I checked back with the bills in the letter holder, some I saw now were bills for the Fittie house, all with her name on, other bills with her name alongside his. Bills from the cottage.

A fist of pain in my chest, I flicked through the documents in the box file. Papers scattered over the duvet, floated down to the floor. Towards the bottom, in a plastic sheath, I found the deeds to the Fittie Place. In her name only, thank God. Lower in the pile, another document, also in plastic: the deeds for the cottage. With shaking hands I examined the names on the document: Mr. Michael Quinn and Ms. Georgia Smyth-Banks Quinn.

"Oh God," I said, sitting on the edge of the bed.

In my hands, the document shook so much I could no longer read it. But I didn't need to read it again to know that I didn't own my home. That I had never owned it.

Don't you need me to sign anything?

Don't you worry, Shone, babe. You're exhausted. I've sorted everything.

Caught up in the baby and all her needs, befuddled by exhaustion, by love, by trust, I had taken him at his word. Having a child had been the making of the man, is what I had thought. But now it made perfect sense. Why indeed would Georgia agree to share? She wouldn't, that was the answer. She never had. She had never seen the cottage as the mistress's cottage in the woods. She had seen it as hers. Because it was hers. She had never seen Mikey as her lover. Because he was her husband. Why agree to a husband only half the time? Why not? Isn't that what I'd done? But another woman? Who would agree to that?

I carried Isla back into the living room and sat on the sofa, rocking gently, madly, making this awful, keening sound over and over, as if, along with all my rational sense, all language was beyond reach. I don't know how long I sat there until I became aware of Isla's fingernails sharp in my nostrils, and a deep cold come through my coat into my bones. I was shivering. My face was sticky and when I stretched it, the skin under my eyes felt like it was cracking.

"OK," I said to myself. I stood up. "OK."

I found the nursery, a box room. White cot in the corner with a circus mobile hanging above it. There were acrobats, elephants, a ringmaster. I laid Isla on the mattress. The back of my head brushed against the mobile, making the circus people swing. The bed smelled of Zac, of the washing powder his clothes were washed in. Did Mikey pull his clothes from the washing machine? Did he hang them out to dry in the breeze that blew over the sea wall? Did he love this family more than us? My tears dropped, wetting the covers. I tucked Isla in, soothed her, but she was restless. I wished I was still breastfeeding – for myself as well as her.

"Stay there, my darling," I whispered. "I'll get some milk."

I found Zac's bottles, made up one for Isla, heated it in the microwave. I could hear Isla starting up for a cry. The microwave bell pinged.

"Isla, darling," I called softly down the short dark hallway. "Mummy's coming. Mummy's here."

Mummy was right here. Mummy wasn't going anywhere. Isla needed me, now more than ever. Her home, her safety, her life, was down only to me now. I would hold her while she drank this milk. I would hold her safe in my arms until she slept and I would make a plan: something that would make things fair. Something that would settle the score such that they would regret what they had done for the rest of their sad and sorry lives.

Once Isla was asleep I went back into Georgia's bedroom. Georgia and Mikey's bedroom. I dug my phone out from my bag, sat on the bed, my breath quickening. In the midst of this maelstrom, one thing I could be sure about was that I could not bear for his name or his face to appear on this phone. If he dared call or text, I would throw this phone against the wall, I would jump on it over and over until it lay in pieces at my feet. I switched it off. But instead of bringing me even a grain of peace, as the screen died all the tranquillity I had conjured for Isla's sake melted away. In its place a fizzing current threatened to bubble over my head and drown me. I was gasping for air. My chest heaved with the effort of simply trying to breathe. A plan had half-formed in my mind but there were too many holes in it and now I could not think clearly enough to plug the holes, to finish the plan. I stood and opened the wardrobe. I pulled out her clothes: four, five hangers at a time. In the other half of the wardrobe I found his clothes. A blue sweater I thought had gone missing in the move, a pair of stripy socks I hadn't seen for months and some old jeans he'd told me he'd thrown out. All of them I heaved onto the bed.

In the living room I pushed the photos one by one until they lay face down on the table. In the kitchen I emptied the rest of the food out on top of the pile of fish and butter and cracked eggs. I stood back, admiring the slimy mass that oozed over the grey linoleum.

Still breathing heavily, I marched into the bathroom, scanned it frantically for damage possibility. In the mirror, my reflection scowled back. I could not stand to look at it, could not stand the hate in its eyes. I cast about, looking for something heavy. There was a metal loo brush holder on the floor. I picked it up and with all my strength rammed it into the mirror, sending out icy spider legs. My reflection splintered into shards.

I looked around for more to do, thought maybe I could take a shower, wash some of the filth from me. And then I saw her phone. On the side of the bath, propped up against a bottle of shampoo. I imagined her lying in the suds, her red hair tied up in a loose, sensual knot, composing love texts to Mikey, Michael, whoever he was.

"Hang on," I said aloud, my fingers closing into fists.

The phone was the key. It was the plug to the hole. I lunged for it and pressed the on button. A photo of her, him and Zac bloomed before my eyes. Ghosts, that's all these people were, phantoms. I slid to unlock and got the Enter Passcode screen.

"Fuck."

I tried her birthday. No. I tried Mikey's. No.

I was frantic. I had to find the passcode. Four simple digits were all that stood between me and what I had to do.

Zac's birthday was 27th February. I typed in: 2702.

It opened and I cried out: *yes*. But as I opened the message file and saw the trail headed Michael the word died in my throat.

They weren't the love notes I was expecting. The messages were like the house: the normal, everyday, private lives of a married couple. *What's for dinner? Lunch out?* And then, one that made my heart tighten: *Booked Treetops for Thursday lunch. Let's get room service!* The Treetops was the hotel by the golf course. Room service. She had told me all about the room service. And I had sat and listened while she told me which sexual position they were in when it arrived. Her and John. Not John, of course, but Mikey. She was telling me all about my own partner. She must have been getting off on it, probably went home and told him, let him get off on it too. Oh God, oh God.

In my clenched hand the phone dimmed. But I could get back into it now, whenever I wanted, use it for whatever call I wanted to make. I did not know much about police procedure but I was pretty sure the police would be all over this place, should I find the courage to go through with what I had planned.

By then, they would be looking for incriminating evidence.

I would have to clean up every scrap of mess I had made.

TWENTY-SEVEN

I finished cleaning at around 4am. Exhausted, I lay on the sofa and tried to sleep but could not. I made myself a strong espresso coffee with milk and drank it in the living room. Two hours melted to nothing; 4am became 6am.

I prepared milk for Isla and woke her, changed her nappy and left. As I was away to close the door, I saw her trainers on the shoe rack. An idea came to me. I picked them up and packed them. Out on Fittie Place, there was no one around. It was too late for the fishermen, too early for the lady who liked to sit out on the bench and watch the comings and goings of the square.

On the way to Govan, I stopped at The Horn, the famous greasy spoon on the A90, for breakfast. I ordered the full Scottish and ate every bite. In my constant plotting, I'd had a panicking thought about CCTV cameras, so as I carried Isla to the café and back again to the car, I kept my actions as breezy and normal as I could. I was acting, I suppose you could say. See me, a tired but happy mother with her wee girl, taking her time, away to Glasgow to see her folks.

At around 11am, I parked at the end of our street. I'd left the buggy in the boot, thank God, so with Isla heavy on my hip, I pulled it out and shook it open. It had started to rain – fat drops. I took off my coat and draped it over her to keep her dry. The rain quickened. By the time I reached my parents' front door, my hair had stuck flat to my head, my clothes were dripping.

Davie opened the door. His face fell at the sight of me, his mouth recomposed itself into a grim, set line. I guessed he must be mirroring my own fallen features. I had collapsed on the outside – having nothing left inside to support the façade. The cold rain ran into my eyes.

"Shona?"

"Can I come in?" I said.

He shook his head, once, as if to break out of a stupor.

"Aye, 'course." He pushed open the door, helped me in with the pushchair. He went ahead then, through the hallway, into the flat. "Ma and Pa aren't here, so. I'll put the kettle on, eh? Actually, I'll get you a towel." He ran upstairs.

Only when he'd made tea, when he'd wrapped the towel around my shoulders and sat me down in the lounge, did we talk.

"So what's goin' on?" He took Isla and bounced her on his knee. She sucked on her rusk and cooed. Ignorance is bliss.

I began to cry. Davie put his arm around me and told me to shush, to cry as much as I liked, that everything would be OK. When I'd calmed down, I told him everything.

"So he wants you to be his second wife?" Davie asked. "What's he starting, a cult? What have you told them?"

"Said I'd think about it."

"And are you?"

I looked at him, met his eye. "What do you think?"

He got up and walked over to the gas fire and stood with his back to it. He shifted Isla in his skinny arms, nuzzled her nose with his, pretended to bite her rusk. She squealed with delight.

After a moment, he said, "I'm going to kill him."

"No, you're not."

For a moment neither of us said another word.

"Davie," I began. "Remember when I got on the train last time you said anything I need?"

"Uh-huh."

"Well, I need."

"Anything," he said.

"I need a car that can't be traced to me or you, can you do that?"

He screwed up his eyes. "What you gonna do?"

306

I shook my head. "I need you not to ask. I need you to look after Isla tonight and I need you to cover for me while I'm away up the road."

"Shona, what're you going to do?"

I fixed him with a stare. "I need you not to ask."

"You're not going to do anything mad are you?"

I shook my head. "I need to settle things up, that's all. But I don't want the jeep on any cameras between here and Aberdeen. I stayed here tonight, all night, if you get my meaning. Can you get me a car or no?"

"Aye." He nodded, frowned at his feet, bit his thumbnail. "What?"

He met my eye but only for a second. "I'll need a ton."

I gave him fifty quid, told him I'd get him the rest. We didn't say much else. He's my kid brother. We've never needed a lot of words.

I brought up Google maps on his phone and began fiddling about with the zoom.

"Here," he said. "We need a bigger picture." He went over to the bookshelf and grabbed my dad's RAC map of Scotland. He spread it out on the table and leant in beside me. I felt the heat from his head next to mine, smelled the tobacco on his breath.

"I can leave the A90 here by Stonehaven," I said, tracing my finger up the road.

"On the way back," he said, "you should take the road all the way out to Stonehaven then cut down and drive to Montrose. If you join the A90 later, maybe as far down as Forfar, that should be OK. But you'll have to drive fast."

"Aye, right. And Davie," I folded up the map, "we cannae even go near telling Mum and Dad. I'm just visiting, OK? Like last time. Everything's peachy in my life, do you get me?"

He nodded.

"Then when it all comes out tomorrow or the day after, if the police come here, I didn't know he had a wife, let alone another child." I stood up, began to pace about. "He told me he had a work dinner. That's why I came down the road. Everyone here will back me up – that's going to be my story. I was here all night. I was calm. I was normal." I stopped, threw out my hands. "What d'you think?"

"What are you going to do, Shone?"

"Criminal damage will be involved, that's all. I don't want a criminal record."

His head dropped.

"Sorry, Davie, I didn't mean ... I'm a mum now."

"It's OK."

I grabbed his hand and squeezed it. "If I get found out, I did this on my own, OK? You cannae tell a soul."

"Let me get down the pub," he said. "See if Dougie'll let me have his van."

"I'll chum you." I stood up, took Isla from him. "I need to walk anyway. I need to get you your cash. And I need the hardware store."

By the time my mum got home at six I'd prepared everything. I heard her key in the lock and was away to open the door for her, but by the time I reached the lounge she was already inside. One stripy carrier bag in each hand, she leant against the front door and closed her eyes. She only did this because she thought no one was looking. But I was looking, I was watching from the shadows, silently taking in the secrecy of her exhaustion. She looked tired, older. She lowered the carrier bags and let them fall the last centimetre to the floor. The thin striped plastic sagged, a can of baked beans rolled out and onto the carpet. I was flooded with love so deep it felt like shame. Every job she'd had to do to raise me and my brothers, every sacrifice she'd made and this, this crushing fatigue she'd kept hidden year after year. My father too, both of them good people, people who I had only ever trusted and loved all my conscious life. Outside this house I had been a fool to trust, yes I had, but why would I go into the world full of suspicion when I had been brought up by these good people, who had done nothing to disabuse me of trust? What was love if not total, blind, unquestioning trust? If my biggest failing was too much love then I would not apologise for that, not even to myself, since allowing even that small concession would be to let him, let them, change who I had been raised to be.

I know who I am, I thought. Who I am was never in doubt.

In this hallway I had whispered like a crook – to save face, to save him from my parents' poor opinion. Here, with remorse running through me I had said sorry to him for my failure to imagine his hard life out in the wilds of the North Sea, when all the time the nearest he'd got to the ocean was the damn coastline. Just shy of the sands, behind the sea wall, he had sat and laughed and eaten and loved and argued and lived with his other family, his real family. What were Isla and me now? The lover and the bastard, that was all. The toys. He'd claimed himself a man trapped by circumstance, a Mr. Rochester striving to do the honourable thing in a difficult situation, thinking only of his two women who needed and loved him. He'd claimed so many things and I had believed him without question. It had never occurred to me not to trust. And now I was the mad woman, an inconvenience he'd hidden away, out of sight.

Funny, when you realise the central truth you have believed about someone is a lie, everything else you believed about them falls away too. Every puff of smoke, every rabbit pulled from a hat, every mirror. Charm? Manipulation. An easy smile? An assassin's grin. You never saw Martin Amis on the bookshelf, never saw your husband read a single book. The past you shared, the present you live, the future you will share with each other? Nothing more than lies set to torment you for the rest of your troubled life.

With a groan, my mother bent to pull off her shoes while I stood, still watching her from the darkness, wondering how I would find my own lies, since lies were what I needed now to save her from the filth of my life.

I took a deep breath, thinking that, yes, people really did do this sometimes, people really did take a deep breath, draw back their shoulders and say things like –

"Hiya! Y'all right? Thought I'd surprise you."

At six thirty, Davie got back and gave me the smallest nod. His skin had a sheen to it, he smelled of alcohol and cigarettes but, judging by my parents' lack of reaction, this was nothing unusual. At seven o'clock we had tea together in the kitchen. Don't ask me what we ate, I can't tell you. I can't even tell you if I ate anything at all. I could think of nothing but the fact I had to get my parents away to their bed before eleven or I'd never make it.

Once Isla was down, I chatted to my parents about nothing while we watched the telly together. Again, don't ask me what we watched. Infusing my voice with pride, I told them how well Mikey was doing, how they really must come up and visit soon, now that the cottage was all set up. It was wonderful up there, I said. A real idyll. I told them I'd be staying with them for a few days this time, as Mikey had this dinner and had said he'd have to work late all week. Like mucus the words thickened in my throat but I spat them out all the same.

At quarter to ten, I yawned. "You guys not going away to your bed? You're usually in bed by ten, aren't you?"

"In a bit, aye," said my mother. "Seems a shame to go when you're here."

I yawned again, for emphasis. "Aye well, I'll be turning in just now. But I'll let you guys use the bathroom."

A quarter of an hour went by.

"It's after ten," I said. "Go on, you guys go first ..." But they didn't move. Time slowed, each second a minute, each minute an hour.

Eventually my mum glanced at my dad who said, "Aye, it's nearly half past right enough."

310

"You go, love," said my mother. "You'll be tired."

"I'm fine. You go. Go on."

At half past they finally went upstairs. I felt like I'd been through the shredder and I hadn't even got started. Davie and me sat in the living room in silence, listening to the scrub of their toothbrushes, the splash of water hitting the sink, the flush of the toilet. The bass notes of muffled conversation.

When all was quiet, I stood. Davie nodded, and stood up too. A surge of nerves rose up inside me.

"You get what you needed?" he asked.

"Aye. I got cash too." I handed him the fifty pounds.

He took it without a word, leant back to stuff the notes in the front pocket of his jeans. "I can do this for you, you know. Whatever it is."

"I need you here," I said. "If Isla cries, you'll have to get her quick. You'll have to keep her quiet. Above all else, I was here all night."

"I'll get her. I won't sleep till you get back anyway."

A little before eleven, I went upstairs and kissed Isla on her forehead. I took out my phone and switched it on, turned it to mute and laid it on my bedside table. I didn't know much about phones, but I thought maybe it might prove some sort of alibi. Then, I took some old coats that were stored in my wardrobe and arranged them in my bed along with my spare pillow. I pulled the duvet cover over them, pushed and shaped the mass until it looked vaguely like a body. I stood back to inspect my efforts, wondering how long it had been since I'd sneaked out at night. I went into the bathroom, did a wee, flushed the loo and washed my hands. My own hooded eyes staring back at me from the bathroom mirror, I cleaned my teeth with the door open so my parents would hear. Once I'd finished my for-show bathroom routine, I walked back into my room, sat heavily on the bed and was gratified to hear it creak. My hands tightened into fists. I stood slowly, silently. I switched off my bedside light, crept out and pulled the door to.

Davie was waiting in the kitchen. He handed me a flask and silver Thermos cup.

"What's in the cup?"

"Tea," he whispered. "Extra sweet."

We locked eyes. Then we did something we never do. We held each other tight; he swayed me from side to side and kissed my cheek. I knew he would taste tears and when I heard him sniff I knew he was crying too.

"I won't do anything too bad," I said. "I'll do enough."

"Just don't get caught, all right?"

"I won't."

When he let go we stood back a little from one another, wet-eyed, wet-faced in the dark.

"I'd better get going," I said.

He nodded and the two of us moved towards the hall.

"If you're not back by half seven," he whispered, "I'll take Isla out for a walk or something, tell them she wouldn't sleep, tell them you've gone on into town. I dunno, I'll think of something but don't be late, eh?"

"I won't. But if I am, tell them I've gone for teething gel."

We stepped out into the street. Davie walked me to the van, tapped the roof once I was inside. "Don't break the speed limit."

"I'm not that stupid."

TWENTY-EIGHT

After Shona flounced out all high and mighty, Michael and I left everything as it was and went to bed without exchanging so much as a glance. We did not touch. We did not speak, other than to ask if the doors were locked. You could say it was shock – if you don't count the fact that the merest glimpse of him made me want to throw up.

In the morning, Michael woke with eyelids like pillows.

"I haven't slept a wink," he said, his bottom lip pushed out and glistening revoltingly.

"Oh," I replied. Had I been awake at any point during the night, I guess I would have known that. But I'm a very deep sleeper and frankly, I was glad to have slept through the wailing and the hand wringing.

We ate breakfast. I put on Radio 1 to drown out the slop and crunch of him chewing. His eyelids had deflated; his beard had grown in ugly patches on his rather too large chin.

"We should clean up," he said.

"All right."

The rabbit was a blackened, dried out mess: a husk. I left Michael to prise it from the rotary pole while I sniffed the various bowls, wondering if they'd made it through the night. In the end, we threw away everything, every scrap. Michael lugged it out to the bin in a black plastic refuse bag.

By midday, Shona had not reappeared. Michael could not leave his phone alone.

"I can't even track her," he whined. "She must have turned it off. Oh God, she hates me, she really hates me."

"Actually," I said, "have you seen my iPhone? I haven't seen it since last night." I grabbed my bag from the kitchen floor and rummaged through it. No phone.

He appeared not to hear, too lost in his own phone, which he kept sliding unlocked, his face set in this wretched, angst-ridden expression so deep I wondered whether it would ever change.

"Oh, never mind," I said.

I searched through my coat pockets but it wasn't there either. Fuck. I must have left it ... I'd had it with me in the bathroom ... I must have left it on the side of the bath when Zac started whining. Fuck. Fuck. Fuck.

"Why won't she text?" He wailed.

Erm, maybe because her phone is switched off? "I really don't know, Michael."

"Maybe if I send her a message ..."

"Don't," I said, crossing the kitchen to him so I could physically stop him if I had to. "She was very clear. If you text her now after she expressly asked you not to, you could lose her forever."

He'd already lost her forever, I knew that. We both had, which was a shame. But, my God, I wanted him to leave his fucking phone alone. And I needed to get hold of mine. It was OK, though. She didn't know the passcode.

Unable to bear Michael's expression any longer, I turned away. I made lunch, made myself sit opposite him and composed my face into the very picture of sympathy. But there was something else in his eyes now, besides the misery, something worse. Hope. He had not let go of the hope that, if he bombarded her for long enough with messages of love and contrition, she would crumble and come back and all would be well. But last night from the garden I had watched her leave. She would not, I knew, crumble and come back. Michael could talk, God knows, he could charm the proverbial birds out of the trees, but there would be no talking now. I couldn't say this to him of course. It was tragic enough being around him as it was.

My main concern, frankly, was the mad woman currently in residence in my other house and what she might be doing.

"If you're going to sit waiting for a reply," I said. "We may as well go and see her. She must have calmed down by now. Maybe we can talk to her."

The door to the Fittie house swung open at the lightest touch of my finger. As soon as I stepped into the tiny kitchen I knew something was not right. The floor and countertop were spotless. Everything had been put away in the cupboard, apart from Michael's favourite mug, which was on the draining board, right way up. *But You May Call Me Lord.* That, I'll admit, gave me the shivers.

I wandered into the living room. Same: vacuumed, immaculate. Eerie.

"See?" Michael's voice came through from the kitchen. "I told you she wouldn't trash the place."

From the mantelpiece I picked up the photo of Michael. "You're right. She hasn't."

No, she hadn't wrecked my house. But why the hell had she cleaned it? Another shiver passed through me. I rolled my shoulders and shook my head against an inchoate case of the heebie-jeebies.

Michael came into the living room, holding Zac and smiling like an idiot. "She just needed somewhere to stay," he said.

"But where is she?"

He looked around, as if he expected to find her standing by the window, ready to play happy families. "She's probably gone for food. Maybe taken Isla for a walk."

"You think?"

"Yes. Along the beach." The hopeful set of his eyebrows made me want to scream. This man, this face, would murder me by stealth.

I headed for the bedroom. Maybe Shona had cut the sleeves from my suits. I hoped so. Something, anything, other than this ... this weird perfection. In the bedroom, the bed looked strange. And then I realised. The duvet had been folded and tucked at the corners to make a kind of pleat. The cushions sat in a row, points down. They were completely central, as if she'd measured their position with a ruler. My jaw clenched. My breath quickened. I opened the wardrobe door. Surely ... but no. Nothing had been ripped or damaged in any way. I closed the door. Even the bedroom floor was spotless. Before leaving the house last night I had thrown some underwear down, two changes of clothes – they were in the wash basket. The curtains had been tied back, something I never bothered doing. The bureau was closed – had I left the key in the lock?

I headed for the bathroom. The shower bore no ghostly rings of dried droplets, no soap slime, no stray hairs. I looked around and shrieked.

"Michael!"

He appeared in the doorway. "What?"

"The mirror."

He came to stand beside me, the two of us fractured as a cubist painting: eyes doubled, random noses and ears repeated between the cracks. We were all wrong. We were freakish.

"I told you," I said.

"No," he said. "It will have been an accident."

"An accident? So, tell me, did a heavy object accidentally throw itself from the floor, across the room perhaps, and land smash in the centre of the mirror? Don't be ridiculous."

But he only shrugged and left the room. "Well, maybe she did do it on purpose. But it's only a cheap mirror. You're not superstitious, are you?"

No. But even so. Unable to look at my reflection, I stared down at sink. It gleamed, the scab of dried toothpaste I knew had been there when I left was gone. And my phone was no longer on the side of the bath.

"Michael, have you seen my iPhone?"

"Nah," he called from the other room. "It'll be at the cottage."

"I don't think so. I thought I'd left it in here." I bit my nail, tore a strip from it with my teeth and spat it out. "Don't you think it's a bit weird, how clean it all is?"

"She's proud, that's all. I think we should head back. She'll probably be waiting at the cottage."

I felt myself blanch. "The cottage," I said, joining him and Zachary in the living room. "What if she's there? What if she's trashing the place?"

"Now you're being ridiculous. She's solid gold, is Shona, she'd never do anything to the cottage. She loves it."

I could look only at Michael's feet, the white trainers I always hated.

"I need time to think." I said.

Oh, but he wasn't going to give me time to think, I knew it even as I said it. He wasn't going to give me space either. These were two things I would never have again. He was going to wait there with his fool's grin and believe that Shona wasn't as angry as all that. I had no idea what this pristine house, the smashed mirror or my missing phone meant, other than her possibly flipping out as I had predicted. And she had obviously, also as I had predicted, scuttled back to Glasgow.

"I think, actually, I'll get changed," I said, forcing myself to look into his hopeless, hopeful face. His designer hooded top screamed discount village. He actually believed style could be purchased in a brand name aimed at teenagers. How had I not seen him for what he was? I had thought him such a breath of air compared to the boarding school boys of my teenage years but now I saw he was nothing but vain, vain and more than a little stupid. I met his eye and smiled. "Darling, would you mind taking Zachary along the beach, give him a walk while I take a shower?"

"OK," he said, bewildered. "So, hang on, you don't think she'll do anything to the cottage then?"

"No, you're right, she wouldn't. It's like you said. Shona's solid gold."

Once the two of them were out of my sight, I sat on the sofa and wept with relief. Yes, wept. I made coffee and sat and sipped and plotted. They would be back soon. I had to think fast. I had to devise a plan.

They got back an hour later, Michael still wearing that pathetic, deluded optimism, the gurning, lobotomised half-smile of a mentally challenged game show contestant. I kissed him full on the mouth, stroked his chin. He smiled, a horrid, hoi polloi *Saturday night is sex night* smile. I smiled right back. Now that I knew what my next move was, I felt so much better.

On the way back to the cottage, Michael's energy slid away. He called Shona twice between Fittie and Sainsbury's but did not leave a message. He became morose once again, slid low in the passenger seat like a truculent spoilt schoolboy.

"What are we going to do if she's not at the cottage?" he said once I'd parked in the supermarket car park.

"I don't know," I said. "But you have to give her some space. She's had a shock and she needs you to let her come around. Tell you what, we'll have a nice dinner tonight and see where we are in the morning, all right? Curry, how does that suit you?"

"Shall I come in with you?"

"No, you stay here with Zachary. I only need a few things."

I kissed him on the cheek, left him like a cripple waiting in the car while I grabbed some food. I shopped quickly, but with care. A quick trip to the Ladies' is easily enough time to dump one bottle of oil down the sink and fill it with another kind of oil entirely.

"OK!" I said, throwing my goody bag onto the back seat. "One cheeky chicken madras to pick us up, maybe open a bottle, what do you say?"

318

It was five o'clock by the time we drove up the darling bumpy lane to the exquisite country cottage that was all but mine. As soon as I hit the kitchen I opened the red. We drank quickly, reached for our glasses, for numbness. We sank the first bottle before dinner was even on the table. Once Mikey had put Zachary to bed, I lit two oil lamps, turned off the overhead light and opened another bottle.

"Do you think I should call her?" His eyes were two sad pools of brown.

"Not again." I turned away, made great work of organising the cooking ingredients on the countertop. "Leave her be."

I couldn't see him but I knew he was checking his phone for the fifteen-thousandth time that day. "What do you think she'll be doing?"

"I really have no idea."

"Do you think she'll get in touch tomorrow?"

"Michael, let it drop now."

"Maybe she'll need a week or two. I need to know she'll come back." His voice had a nasal, whining tone to it. "She said she'd think about it. She said that. Did you hear her? Did you hear her say that?"

Oh, for Christ's sake, Michael, she's gone. "Yes. She said that. I did hear her say that."

From the cutlery drawer I pulled out the carving knife.

"Are you OK?" Mikey squeezed my shoulder.

Get off me. "I'm fine."

"More wine?"

"Great. Thanks." I could feel the tannin in the cave of my mouth, my gums thick, as if after a dentist's jab.

The lamplight glanced on the carving blade. There, on the scratched steel surface, watchful eyes blurred to no more than a dark strip. I gasped, seeing for a second Shona's eyes, staring back at me. And that was just it. Maybe she was gone. But she would always, always be here with us, watching, judging. This was the way it would be. Forever. If not spoken out loud, then shown in faraway

319

looks and heard in heavy sighs. This was why I'd had to sit down and think straight and make my plan B (well, plan C, technically), because Shona and Isla would live between us every single day, like restless spirits, the doomed souls of the undead. They would be everywhere, a chill air at the chimney stack where a fire once burned, a photo fallen from a drawer, a particular flavour of ice cream transporting him back to his *amour perdu*. Every look he gave me, every time we made love, every time we enjoyed anything at all – all of it would be underpinned by her and what he believed we had done to her.

On the handle of the knife, my hand tightened. Behind me I heard the slump of him sinking into his chair, a sniff. Oh dear God. I had married a whole man, for half the time. I had ended up with half a man, the whole time.

What use, frankly, is that?

Another bottle of red opened. A joint. Destination oblivion. The room began to spin a little but I needed the kind of courage only large quantities of opiates can provide. Somewhere in all of this, I made Indian chicken curry, extra hot, with the ingredients I had got. Michael joked about the latex gloves I'd bought.

"I need them to keep the chilli off my hands."

"Hey, I'm getting a bit nervous, here. You're not going to ask me to drop my trousers, are you?"

The naffness of the joke made me nauseous. "Maybe later. No, seriously, chilli on your hands is a disaster in bed," I positively chirruped. "You want fire in your loins, not your pecker, my love. Hey, can you twist off the top, baby?" I handed him the paste jar. "The booze has sapped my strength. Can you open the tinned tomatoes while you're at it, thanks." I laughed, merrily. "These gloves are making me clumsy."

I'm no cook but it wasn't bad. Hot as hell. A little oily perhaps.

Michael began to cough.

"Too spicy for you?" I asked, eyebrow arched for innuendo.

He pulled at his collar, took off his hoodie.

"Can't." Cough. "Stop." Cough. "Coughing."

"Really? Let's get you upstairs. I'll bring you some water."

He was coughing into his hand. I followed him up, sat him on the bed, ran to fetch some water from the bathroom. Cough cough cough.

"Here." I put my hand to his forehead, told him that his temperature was up, helped him out of his t-shirt. Perhaps it was the stress of the last twenty-four hours, I told him. He needed to calm down. He was coughing like an old asthmatic.

"EpiPen," he croaked.

"Sure." I threw up my hands and ran to get it. But, oh my, it wasn't in the bathroom cabinet. I searched all over the cottage, really I did, with him rasping and gasping from the bedroom, staggering and swearing on the landing.

"I checked the ingredients," I called from my relentless search, pulling a paper bag out of the kitchen drawer. "There's no way there were peanuts in the food."

I ran back upstairs, guided him into the bedroom. "Lie down." I put the paper bag to his mouth.

"Michael, lie down."

He wouldn't, couldn't lie down. He knocked the paper bag away, gasping, wheezing like a donkey. I tried to persuade him into the recovery position but there was no recovery, only the panic in his eyes, the violence in his limbs.

"She's poisoned me." The veins in his neck bulged. "Shona's poisoned me."

"Don't be silly," I replied. "She would never do that. She's as good as gold."

"I can't breathe. Georgie, I can't breathe."

I ran downstairs and pretended to call an ambulance. From upstairs came bangs, thumps.

321

"Shit." I ran back upstairs – this was exhausting – put my hand to his hot, wet brow. "They'll be here any second." He batted my hand away, lurched, staggered, banged into the dressing table, collapsed on the bedroom floor. He thrashed around, hands thrust between his legs.

I stood over him. I said nothing more. He bucked and flipped for dear life, hit his head against the dressing table leg. It was a ghastly sight but only when his limbs failed him, when he was gasping like a fish on the riverbank did I bend my lips to his ear.

"We could have been happy, Michael," I whispered. "You should have chosen me."

He bucked once more, and was still. After a second, he took the final, massive gulp. I looked away, put my hands over my ears and waited. When no more noise came, when all movement had stopped, I dragged him to a sitting position, hooked his arm around my neck. Michael is not an overweight man, in fact he is rather skinny but still, it was an absolute bastard getting him onto that bed. But I did it, collapsing on top of him as I laid him down, my cheek landing on his breathless mouth.

I stood up, sweating, panting for breath, swearing over and over. Once I'd composed myself, I pulled off his trousers and socks, left on his pants before rearranging him into a peaceful sleeping position. Once I was satisfied, I laid the covers over his body. It was terribly difficult, especially after so much wine. I really was sweating like a pig.

I checked him once more for signs of life. There were none: no breath, no pulse. I went downstairs, checked the kitchen for clues, filled the dishwasher and put it on. I left out the jar and the tins, everything he'd touched. I left out the lamps, to show that our last evening together had been romantic, poured the rest of the plonk down the sink. It was a really boozy night we had, officer.

Upstairs, I stripped off and got in next to him. He was still warm – like a hot water bottle that upon waking would be cold. What time should I wake up, I wondered. What would be the most normal reaction to have on discovering your husband stone cold beside you after an extreme anaphylactic shock?

We had eaten dinner, I would tell them. *We got a little drunk, very drunk actually. Yes,* I will admit, with a look of contrition, *we do smoke a little weed from time to time. We drank, we smoked, we ate. We were in the mood. He made his special curry. I can't understand it, he's usually so careful about these things. And then after dinner, he said he was tired, said he felt a bit ropey. I thought it was the drink or that he'd had too much to eat. He went upstairs. I stayed down to fill the dishwasher. When I got to bed, he was already asleep. He looked like he was out for the count. I kissed him and he was maybe a little hot* – at this point I will start to cry – *but I didn't think, I didn't think there was anything wrong. I was merely disappointed we weren't going to – you know – make love.*

And then, and then, oh, this morning when I woke up ...

And that, officer, is when I called 999.

***

It's one thing laying a wee fire in the grate. Quite another getting a whole house to go up. And that's without the added complication of making it look like an accident. You can't go using straw or kindling or anything like that. Firelighters, forget it. You have to think it through, back to the source, so that when the police trace the cause of the blaze it looks like an unfortunate domestic mishap: a candle falling over, say, or a badly made oil lamp. That's what she went for. Use what you know, they say. And it's like she said: if you don't vent them properly, the pressure builds. And that can be very dangerous.

***

TWENTY-NINE

Around two, not wanting to make strange tyre tracks, I parked up on the hard tarmac road that ran across the lane. I couldn't see a thing. Which meant the cottage was in darkness. Which meant they were asleep.

Out by the van I put on the latex gloves I'd bought at the hardware store and prepared everything. The head torch – another hardware store purchase – made it easy to pour the kerosene into the jars without spilling it, to assemble the lamps and put them on the tray. I took out Zac's baby bottle, filled it from the flask with the special milk cocktail Davie had warmed for me and set that on the tray too. My rucksack I grabbed from the back seat, took out Valentina's running trainers and, after pulling on three pairs of Davie's socks, put them on. They were still too big but it was too late now to do anything different.

I switched off the torch and shuffled towards the mouth of the lane. Lined by trees, the lane was as black as oil. I kept to the edge, picked my way over the grassy bit, avoided potholes, soft ground. The too-big trainers were awkward. I tripped twice, almost lost my balance both times – almost spilt the damn fuel. I was losing precious time. It took nine minutes in total to reach the cottage – longer than I'd anticipated. Despite the cold, I could feel rivulets of sweat running from my armpits down the sides of my body. My jaw was trembling. My throat had all but closed up.

I went first to the stable. I put the tray on the ground outside and pushed open the heavy wooden door. I had to do everything slowly, for silence, and that was hard on the nerves. Time waits for no man, as they say, and there was no reason why it would wait for me. Inside, I peered into the dark, looking for the travel cot. I reached my arms out but found nothing. Tentatively, I turned the head torch on. The travel cot was not there.

"Fuck," I whispered into the blackness, beating my head with my fists. "Fuck fuck fuck."

Nothing else for it and I could not waste any more time. I turned off the torch and felt my way out.

Inch by inch I edged forward until my foot finally hit the picket fence. I felt for the posts with my hands and climbed over, then went on like a blind woman until I touched the cottage wall. I kept my shoulder to the wall and traced my way around to the back. I felt with my toe for the rubber mat, with my fingertips for the lock. I still had the key, obviously but my fingers were cold, my grip clumsy. I dropped the key – it fell into a crack between two paving stones. I dug it out with my pinkie finger, swearing under my breath and, finally, unlocked the back door. As I pulled it open I lifted it a centimetre so the hinges wouldn't squeak, and stepped through. I was in the hidden part of the horseshoe of my kitchen. Above me, washing dangled its flaccid limbs from the pulley but the kitchen didn't smell of laundry. It smelled – strongly – of curry. Mikey will have made that, I thought. Chicken saag balti was his speciality.

Focus, Shona.

I put the plastic baby bottle on the countertop and, with the stealth of a burglar, tiptoed inside. This was no longer my house. It had never been my house. I was, legally, trespassing. Further in, on the table, stood three bottles of wine. They'd really hit the sauce. Probably to block out their consciences. But no. They didn't have those. They were not human. I almost touched the bottles but pulled back my hand. Two Cabernet Shiraz. One Merlot. Plonk and Indian curry. And was that a joint I could smell in the air? A boozy, spicy, romantic supper for two. Valentina's voice came into my head:

Which rig do you work on?

Mikey's:

Oh, come on. Don't even pretend to be interested.

Focus.

One of my oil lamps stood next to the bottles. Its oil reserve was low but the tiniest flame still waved from the end of the blackened wick. The sight should have stabbed me through the heart but, like the endless, jumbled replays that ran constantly through my mind, it was a distraction, nothing more. My heart could not be penetrated, not now. It was no more than a fossil, the petrified evidence of where life, or love, had once lived.

A creak from upstairs. I froze. Someone was coming down. I had no time to get out. I backed up, dipped under the laundry and hid behind the pulley, knowing my legs were completely visible. One hand clamped over my mouth, I closed my eyes and channelled all my energy into keeping my breathing silent. In the hallway a child's toy skittered across the tiles, a voice.

"Ouch."

Her.

Her naked feet. Her painted toenails. Mikey's robe wrapped around her body. Her long red hair flowing down her back like molten lava. Water flushing into a glass. She was a metre away, maybe a little more. She was standing drinking water at the sink. Her back was to me now, yes, but she could turn around at any point.

Silently, slowly, I reached out. My hand found the hard edge of the shelf. The hammer, where was it? The gulp, gulp of water down her white throat. There was a fish gutting knife somewhere here too. I ran my hand along the shelf. Tough rubber – the hammer handle under my fingertips. Valentina coughed, sniffed. My hand closed around the rubber handle. The flush of water again, a second glass. She was less than a metre away. She was taking another drink.

I breathed in deeply and picked up the hammer.

I took a step forward, felt the laundry caress the top of my head.

327

I raised the hammer up.

Glass in hand, she walked away, back towards the hallway, coughing. I did not move. A moment later, I heard her footsteps on the stairs, the creak of the top stair, the bedroom door open and shut.

I collapsed forward, almost dropped the hammer on the stone tiles. I was weeping without tears, gasping without a sound.

After five minutes, timed on my watch, I placed my clumsy, enlarged feet one after the other on the stone tiles. I felt like I was walking on the moon but I made it through the kitchen and into the lounge. The cot was collapsed and stored against the wall. I picked it up and carried it out, taking care not to bump the doorframes or walls. I retraced my slow space steps, to the stable. Once inside, I switched on the head torch and put up the travel cot. My hands were shaking – I couldn't get it to click into an open position. I had never had trouble with it before.

"Click," I hissed. "Fucking click."

Finally the sides locked, the base fell snug into the bottom. I wriggled the rucksack from my back, pulled out the fleece blankets and laid them over the base. I left the stable, turned off the torch and moved as quickly as I could back towards the cottage, checking the rucksack was on my back. Nothing could be left behind, no trace.

The moon drifted out, a moment of light, enough to move freely by. Another five minutes had passed. Ten since I had almost plunged a hammer into her soft head. I scooped up the tray and carried it, waitress style.

I found my way back along the cottage wall, to the back door and laid the tray on the mat outside. The kitchen was a mess, I saw now in the moonlight – containers everywhere, packets. I took the stairs two at a time. Took care not to step on the last, the creaky one. Our bedroom door was shut, thank God. Their. Their bedroom door. I leant towards it, listened as long as I dared but heard nothing. Mikey would normally snore like a pig after a curry and so much red wine. A flashing image came: her getting back into bed, sipping her water, rolling him onto his side to get him to shut up. The intimacy of that. The normality. I closed my eyes a moment, held onto the top of the bannister.

Focus.

Isla's bedroom door was open. In her cot, Zac slept, splayed and massive as a toad. I heaved him up, tried to take the weight of him on my legs, tried not to groan with the effort. He half-woke, gave me a dozy smile, said "Do-dah." I clapped my hand over his mouth and smiled back. I raised my eyebrows, widened my eyes playfully. He mirrored me like an idiot. Aunty Do-dah's no threat. Aunty Do-dah looks after you all the time. This night-time caper is no more than a game.

I stroked his hair and whispered with my mouth to his ear. "Hi Zacky." I kissed his head, put my hand back over his mouth, carried him down, one stair at a time. By the time I got to the bottom, the sweat was prickling on my back.

There was enough light to light my way back to the stable but, as I stepped inside, the moon returned to hiding. I had to edge towards the cot, feeling ahead with my foot before sliding the other one forwards. The sweat cooled, covered my back with an icy second skin. Shivering, I laid Zac in the cot on one of the blankets, covered him up with the rest and gave him the bottle. I could hear the warm boozy milk straining through the plastic teat before I'd even stood up. He hadn't noticed the brandy. He'd be flat out in no time, dead to the world.

It was getting on for half past two. But more haste, less speed. Outside was still black. Arms out in front of me, feet big and slow, I made it out of the stable. It was even darker than it had been two minutes ago. I could not see the hand in front of my face. That's the countryside for you. Dark as all hell. My jaw would not stop juddering. My whole head shook, my whole body. From cold or fear I couldn't tell.

The moon teased, a burlesque feather dance amongst the clouds – hidden, revealed, hidden once again. I made out the white rendering of the side wall, the miniature silhouette of the oil lamps on the tray outside the back door. I picked up both lamps, elbowed the door open and stepped inside once again.

The police would find other lamps – in the kitchen cupboards, one on our bedside table, plus the ones they'd actually used tonight. The chief detective would conclude that we – sorry, they, used these lamps a lot. It was a quirk, a romance. This evening, the bobbies would think, had been one of soft light, of rich food and red wine, of love gone awry. That's the trouble with passion – the scant regard it has for health and safety.

The smell of kerosene was strong but I was on the home straight. I struck the match and tipped it. The flame held. I lit both wicks, put one lamp on the kitchen table, under the picture of Mikey and me and Isla taken just after she was born. I slid the other one across the counter, over to the curtain's edge. Tut-tut, Shona, did you forget to vent those lamps? That is highly dangerous, young lady.

In the half-light, I stood back and watched. The walls flickered. The flames began to elongate, a slow belly dance. It would take maybe half an hour for them to grow long enough. The flame reached up and up, millimetre by millimetre, pawing ever nearer at the curtain's edge. It would get there sooner or later. I opened the kitchen window, threw down the arm of the latch and brought the window shut with the latch dangling outside. That's another danger – the pesky breeze that blows the catch – terrible for wafting a perfectly innocent flame. Before you know it, your house goes up in smoke.

And that's where we come full circle. Once upon a time. That woman, here in the deep dark wood, frozen in the February night, staring at a home that was never hers in a fairy tale that never was. That woman is me, Shona

330

McGilvery from Govan, a woman beside herself. There she is, someone I no longer recognise. She is a mistress, a stalker, an outcast. She is an impostor. She is humiliated, homeless, a lone horse left to graze in a field. Inside, the legitimate family sleep in their warm home. It is all she ever wanted: that family, that warmth, that home. She stands outside, fingers pressed up against the invisible screen that separates her from her own life. She is no longer the daughter her parents raised, she will return to them a changeling. She is vengeful, bitter. She has been emptied of trust, filled with hate. From now on, everyone she has loved or will ever love will know her only by the lies she herself will tell. They will not know her at all.

She is no longer Shona. Burnt out and nameless, I can only watch her as she walks over to the stable door, takes Valentina's phone from her pocket and opens up Facebook. Once that's loaded, she dials 999. A woman's voice asks which service she requires.

Shona takes a breath.

"The fire service," she says in her best English accent, her best panicking voice. Because, you see, Valentina, Wendy, Georgia or whoever the fuck you are, Michael, Mikey, Captain fucking Hook, Shona can put on a voice too, if the circumstances demand it. She's a great mimic.

"I can't get back in," she cries when her moment comes. "There's too much smoke!" She sounds so damn afraid, she almost laughs. She sounds so exactly like her former friend she could be her.

The lady on the phone is very sympathetic, very soothing. In her tight Aberdeen brogue she stresses the need to stay calm.

"Can you tell me your name, darlin'?"

"Georgia," she sobs. "Georgia Smyth-Banks."

"That's wonderful, darlin'. Now, Georgia, my love, if you can tell me where you are, we can send help as quickly as possible. Can you do that for me, dear?" How skilfully the nice lady coaxes the address out of the poor shaking woman.

"Burns Cottage, Burns like the poet," Shona stutters, gives the postcode through gasps and sobs. She doesn't joke about the irony of the name. In the circumstances, she knows, that wouldn't be authentic.

"That's wonderful, dear ..."

"Oh God!" Shona cries. She is sobbing.

"Georgia, my love," says the nice lady. "Listen to me, darlin'. The fire response unit is on its way. Did you hear me? They'll be with you very soon. Stay calm, Georgia. Can you do that for me?"

"My baby!" She breaks down. Check her out – she is good.

"Is the baby in danger? Georgia? Is the baby in danger?"

"He wouldn't sleep! Oh God, I put brandy in his milk. I only wanted him to sleep."

"Georgia, can you tell me where the baby is?"

"We're in the stable. I had to get him out of the house. I was in the kitchen ... I only lit the lamps to ... oh God ... I was on Facebook, I wasn't concentrating. There must've been a draft from the window. I think the curtain ... I didn't think it would catch, you know? I wasn't thinking ... oh God, my husband's still inside ... I've got to go back for him ..."

Too much? Shona doesn't think so.

She hears the woman radio this nugget of info: *baby in the stables, repeat, check the stables, spouse inside ...*

The next thing she will tell Georgia, who is of course Shona, is not to go back in the house – but Shona rings off before she says that. She wipes the phone down and throws it so it skitters under the cot. She doesn't need the nice lady's advice and she doesn't need to be told the baby's going to be all right. She knows he'll be all right. Funny, when the real Georgia actually tries to call for help, she won't be able to use the landline because she'll never get downstairs. When she looks then for her phone, she'll shout and swear because she'll remember that she thinks Shona took it. *No need to worry, Georgie!* Shona wants to shout up to her. *You've already called the fire brigade!*

It's out of her hands now, to be honest. In a minute or two she'll be away back to Govan to pick up the shattered pieces of her life. In the morning, Davie will take the van back to wherever he got it. He'll come back with a paper, maybe some extra milk for Isla. He likes an early morning walk. A little before eight, her mum will bring her a cup of tea in bed and ask if she's had a good sleep. She'll tell her she slept like a log.

The firemen will smash the bedroom window and pull them to safety. Husband and wife will live, of course. Shona's not a murderer. But they will be frightened and they may be scarred. Like her.

But you, you've stuck with her all this time and what she, what I, Shona McGilvery, really want say to you is this:

They will know, the people who stole my life from me. They will sit in their separate interview rooms and they will hear Georgia's desperate voice crying for help in the night, sobbing down the line to the nice lady from the emergency services. And they will know that voice is not Georgia at all. They will know that the voice is me, Shona. But how can they pin the crime on me without telling the police all about the whole Valentina deception? *I pretended I was Australian*, Georgia will say. *I told her my name was Valentina.*

And if they squawk, which they surely will, the police will beat a path to my door right enough. The police officer will sit me down and ask me *do you know a Ms. Valentina D'Angelo?*

Valentina? I will say, confusion all over my face. *Valentina who?*

They will try another name. *What about Georgia Smyth-Banks?* And there my face will clear and I will say

Georgie? Of course I know Georgie! She's my best friend. Why? Nothing bad's happened to her, has it?

So you see, all the evidence will contradict everything they say, back up what I say. *Shona drove off in a fury in the dead of night, officer.*

Nah. I drove calmly down to Glasgow to see my folks. See me, waving at the CCTV at The Horn? There I am, calm and happy with my wee girl.

She burnt us to the ground!

Er – I don't think so. I was in my bed in Govan and three people can testify to that.

Fingerprints in the Fittie house? Did you no' hear me, pal? We were best friends, me and Georgie. We practically lived in each other's houses. But I had no idea, no idea whatsoever she was sleeping with my partner, let alone married to him. Give me a minute – I think I'm in shock.

And so, the truth they found so flexible, that they twisted and manipulated for so long, has become brittle. One more manipulation and it will snap in their faces. It will take their damn eyes out. They will look like lunatics. They will have no home.

Like me, then, mad, homeless, lost to the flames.

I'm half a mile away, maybe more, when I hear the sirens coming up the lane.

MAN KILLED IN COTTAGE FIRE

Police and fire fighters were called to a cottage in the Banchory area of Aberdeenshire at around 03.05 GMT yesterday morning.

A man, confirmed as in his late twenties and named as Mr. Michael Quinn, was found dead in an upstairs bedroom. The survivors, his wife, Ms. Georgia Smyth-Banks, also in her late twenties, and their one-year-old boy, lived with the man at the property, which was extensively damaged by the fire. The child was found safe in an outbuilding.

The property is situated in a remote area of Aberdeenshire. No neighbours witnessed the blaze.

Ms. Smyth-Banks is being treated in hospital for extensive injuries. Police confirmed that she sustained two broken legs after jumping from an upstairs window and has suffered serious burns.

The fire appears to have been started by oil lamps found at the scene, however police said officers are unable to rule out the possibility that the man died before the fire began. Ms. Banks will be taken into custody pending post-mortem examination and will face questioning. No more information is available at this time.

Colleagues of Mr. Quinn and his wife, who worked together, say they had no idea the couple were married but that they were often seen chatting at work.

"They were very private," said a colleague. "They only joined the company recently. We thought they might be together but you don't like to ask, do you? It's no one's business, is it, other people's romantic arrangements?"

BOOK CLUB QUESTIONS
These Questions Contain Spoilers

What were your first impressions of Mikey? Of Valentina?

The reader knows something is wrong before Shona. How accurate were you in predicting what was amiss?

How often are we truly ourselves?

Is early friendship a little like the early stages of romance?

What does the novel say about trust? How important is it to trust people?

Have you ever felt like a friend is taking advantage of you? How have you reacted, if at all?

Shona believes the role of a friend is not to judge. In fact she says a best friend should help bury the body. How far do you agree with this?

How often are we willing to stand up and be honest about situations or do we buy into realities presented to us even when we know they are fake?

When Shona and Valentina first meet, how does their high-energy interaction compare to your own experiences of making a new friend?

How does Shona change from the feisty woman who takes on a bunch of thugs to the woman she is after weeks alone with a baby in the cottage?

Shona's whole life is revealed to be a lie. To what extent is this a metaphor for how it feels when trust is shattered in one's primary relationship?

How do things like loneliness, extreme tiredness and change in status affect our social choices?

Do Michael and Georgia have a point when they imagine a life lived beyond convention?

Have you ever found yourself at a low ebb? How did that affect you?

Is Shona honest with herself or does she close her eyes to the things that don't square up?

Georgia is placed in a no-win situation by Mikey. To what extent does she wrest back control?

Do you think there is ill feeling or judgement between women who work full time and stay-at-home mothers? Have you ever judged or heard anyone judge another woman for their life choices?

How does having a baby affect a woman's confidence?

What did Shona's parents teach her about love and life? Valentina's? Mikey's?

How did Valentina's father's cold treatment and abandonment of the mother affect her feelings about men?

How did her mother's suffering affect Valentina's attitude towards control?

Structurally, how effective was it to hear from Georgia only in part two?

Georgia talks of the advantages of a part-time relationship. Can you identify with what she says or see the attraction? Do we all need freedom and is that lacking in most relationships?

How limited is Shona in her worldview?

How effective was the women's direct address to the reader? How did the narrator/reader relationship change in both instances?

ACKNOWLEDGEMENTS

Like ageing, writing a novel is not for wimps and any writer needs all the support they can get. So the thank yous are many and they are all big ones. Thanks to Sara Bailey, my first tutor, for getting me into this whole writing malarkey and telling me to stop fretting and carry on. To the woman who read *Valentina* and said not no, finally, but yes: Blackbird Commissioning Editor, Rosalie Love, you were that mythical person I'd heard about, you exist! To mother Blackbird, Stephanie Zia, who agreed with Rosalie – you have both dedicated to this project your expertise, generosity and patience but most of all your unwavering faith, and have returned to me the confidence I had lost somewhere between the sofa cushions many years ago. To my Richmond Writing Group, aka the Turbots: Zoe Antoniades, Callie James, John Rogers and Sam Hanson, for sharing their own excellent work and for giving feedback on mine, not to mention many pints of beer and laughs along the way. To my Kingston MA Writing Group led by most excellent alpha dog, Hope Caton, with Robin Bell, Catherine Morris, Colette Lewis, Andrew Baird, and Sam Hanson (again) for giving all that time and energy, again with much laughter, cheap plonk and plenty of cheese. To the Creative Writing tutors on the MA programme at Kingston University – this course fostered new ways of thinking about writing and process and gave me a group of writers who became trusted friends. To David Rogers, who keeps us loosely tethered through Kingston Alumni and who lent me much needed support in the early days when I could easily have given up. Thank you to all my students at Richmond Adult Community

College for their support, enthusiasm and for forcing me to think about what works and what doesn't, then figure out how the hell to explain it – inspiration works both ways and you have all inspired me. To strange fruits Jayne Farnworth, Richard Kipping and Melanie Mortiboys, who for years have been reading my stuff and cheering me along. To my pals who don't see me from one month to the next when I am hibernating like a badger with a laptop but who make me laugh, lift me up and help me persuade the pub landlord to do a lock-in. To chief listener and devil's advocate on many a long dog walk, Fi Kelly, who has suffered much droning on, plot wrangling, existentialist doubt and muddy boots. To my dad, Stephen, who isn't a reader but who supports me in many other ways and always shares his lettuce plugs. To my readers who read excerpts or early drafts, I add apologies to the thanks: my sister, Jackie Ball, who saves the world, raises three kids and still makes time to read my early drafts, to Sally Franklin, Hope Caton, Susie Donaldson, Barbara Wheatley, Lucy Aliband, Sue O'Dea, Elizabeth Bazalgette, Jackie West, Bridget McCann and Jean McLeish. This book is dedicated to Jean, who read the manuscript just before she was taken from us far too soon. To Susy Smith, I owe you a favour. To my beta readers and gremlin spotters, Susie Kelly and Diana Morgan-Hill, thank you. To my brother, Robert M Ball, for the iconic cover design – you are a genius – it runs in the family, ha. To my kids Ali, Maddie and Franci, who must bear the fact of me being in the room but away with the makey-uppy folk. And most of all to two very important people: my mum, Catherine Ball, who has read every embarrassing first draft, every lame story, every cringe-worthy metaphor, every toe-curling piece of dialogue, and without whose unfailing belief and support I would never have continued beyond that first monologue. And finally, to my husband, Paul, who encouraged me from the very beginning to take writing seriously, who rushed home from work so that I could do the MA or get to writing group,

341

who didn't complain when I wanted to teach in the evenings and at weekends because I thought it was important, who has given me the time and space to try and make a go of my dream: you are beyond brill, but I can't say more just now because someone might read this.

This book belongs to all of you. Thank you, thank you.

S.

ABOUT THE AUTHOR

After graduating from Leeds University, S. E. Lynes lived in London for a couple of years before moving to Aberdeen to be with her husband. In Aberdeen, she worked as a Radio Producer at the BBC before moving with her husband and two young children to Rome. There, she began to write while her children attended nursery. After the birth of her third child and upon her return to the UK, she gained an MA in Creative Writing from Kingston University. She now combines writing with teaching creative writing at Richmond Adult Community College and bringing up her three children. She lives in Teddington, SW London. Connect with S. E. Lynes on Twitter @SELynesAuthor and Facebook S_E_LynesAuthor.

Keep up to date with all S. E. Lynes news and new titles, join the S. E. Lynes Mailing List at:
http://eepurl.com/9QUyn
(All email details securely managed at Mailchimp.com and never shared with third parties.)

READER AMBASSADORS

You are one of the very first readers of this debut novel. If you enjoyed it, please would you consider leaving a review? Word of mouth is so important in the early stages of an author's career. *Valentina* is listed on most major retailers' websites including Amazon, iBooks, Barnes & Noble, Waterstones and at www.goodreads.com. Thank you!

If you would like to know more about becoming a Reader Ambassador for *Valentina*, please email us at **editor@blackbird-books.com** and we'll let you know how you can become a valuable, visible part of this book's journey to a wider audience.

More Original Quality Titles at
Blackbird Digital Books

Fiction
That Special Someone by Tanya Bullock
The Modigliani Girl by Jacqui Lofthouse
Moondance by Diane Chandler
The Dream Theatre by Sarah Ball

Nightingale Editions
Dark Water by Sara Bailey

Non-Fiction
I Wish I Could Say I Was Sorry by Susie Kelly
Love & Justice by Diana Morgan-Hill
Schizophrenia – Who Cares? A Father's Story by Tim
Salmon
Tripping With Jim Morrison & Other Friends by
Michael Lawrence
Cats Through History by Christina Hamilton
*A London Steal: The Fabulous On-A-Budget Guide to
London's Hidden Chic* by Elle Ford

Blackbird Digital Books

The #authorpower publishing company

Discovering outstanding authors

www.blackbird-books.com

2/25 Earls Terrace, London W8 6LP
@Blackbird_Bks

blackbird